Annie Nelles Dumond

The life of a book agent

Fifth Edition

Annie Nelles Dumond

The life of a book agent
Fifth Edition

ISBN/EAN: 9783337057459

Printed in Europe, USA, Canada, Australia, Japan

Cover: Foto ©Andreas Hilbeck / pixelio.de

More available books at **www.hansebooks.com**

Annie Nelles

THE

LIFE OF A BOOK AGENT

BY

ANNIE NELLES (DUMOND,)

Author of

"Scraps; or Sabbath-School Influence;" "Ravenia; or, The Outcast Redeemed;" "National Reform; or, Liquor and its Consequence;"
"Happy at Last; a Sequel to The Life of a Book Agent,"
etc., etc., etc.

(FIFTH EDITION, REVISED.)

PUBLISHED BY THE AUTHOR,

1522 LUCAS PLACE, ST. LOUIS,

PREFACE.

There are several motives which, have actuated me in the preparation of the following sketch: among the first is to assist the book agents in their work, by giving them the experience of a successful book agent, one that has been successful in the business.

To enable the young and inexperienced to avoid, as far as possible, the rocks and shoals upon which her bark made shipwreck, is one of the objects of this publication.

The world is full enough of misery and sorrow caused by man's treachery and wrong; and if I can in any degree, however small, check this torrent, I shall feel myself abundantly repaid for all time and labor the effort may cost me. May this little volume lead some stray lamb back to the fold.

That the present work contains many errors and inaccuracies of language, is undoubtedly true; but, of one thing the reader may be assured: the main incidents therein described are actually and literally true, and are freely given to the public for the reasons and motives above indicated.

With all its faults and errors, and in the humble hope that it will be kindly received and tenderly judged, the work is submitted to a generous and discriminating public, by

THE AUTHOR.

CONTENTS.

(7)

CHAPTER VII.

CHAPTER VIII.

CHAPTER IX.

CHAPTER X.

CHAPTER XI.

CHAPTER XII.

CHAPTER XX.

CHAPTER XXI.

CHAPTER XXII.

CHAPTER XXIII.

CHAPTER XXIV.

CHAPTER XXV.

CHAPTER XXVI.

CHAPTER XXVII.

THE LIFE OF A BOOK AGENT.

CHAPTER I.

ANOTHER wretched, dreary, rainy day. It really seems as though the god of the weather had a spite against me. For the last week it has rained almost constantly, and I have consequently been unable to prosecute my business with anything like success. Last evening I thought the rain was over, and that we were going to have pleasant weather, but the first sound which caught my ears upon awakening this morning, was the rain beating and dashing against my window. And still the dreary, monotonous patter, patter, of the falling torrents goes on, without the least prospect of cessation. And then the mud in the streets! It is almost unfathomable, and is getting worse every moment. Ugh! it makes me shudder to think of going out to canvass for subscribers to-day. I can not do it.

And yet, what is to become of me if I do not? I can not live unless I work, or unless I do better than I have thus far. I have sold but one book this week, and only made one dollar profit on that. I have to pay six dollars a week for my board, and have nothing to pay with. Ah! poor Book Agents! They have a hard time of it. Certain am I that they earn every cent they get. Here am I without a cent to pay my board, or even post a letter, and no prospect of being able to do anything for—the Lord only knows how long. Were it not for my two precious babes, I should almost give up in despair of ever accomplishing anything.

My weekly board bill is due to-day, and how to meet it I do not know. I pawned my furs for money to pay my last board bill, and now I have nothing I can spare—Oh! yes, there is my watch, brother's watch—but how can I part with that? Dear brother! Little did I think when, in happy days long since past, you gave me this precious keepsake, that I should ever be driven to part with it. But I must. Stern necessity knows no law, and there is no help for it. One by one all my little treasures—bright mementos of happier days—have gone to enable me to keep life in my wretched frame, and appease the demands of hunger; and now this last token of affection—this priceless gift, which I thought to keep till my dying day—must go as all the others have done. But it is useless to spend time in vain repining—so, away through rain and mud and storm, for the pawn-broker's.

It is a dismal, gloomy-looking den. Its rough exterior, innocent of paint, and narrow, low en-

trance, seem to frown ominously at one, and warn
me not to seek an entrance. But my wretched
fortune drives me to it, and after a moment's
hesitation I enter the forbidding portal, while a
shudder of agony, at the thought of what I am
about to do, involuntarily runs through my frame.
Once inside, I am compelled to wait until my eyes
become accustomed to the dim light which enters
the dingy apartment through windows covered
with cobwebs, and begrimed with the dirt of
years, before I can venture to transact any business. As my eyes become able to penetrate more
distinctly the gloom which pervades the place, I
discover a gloomy, heartless-looking old man, in
whose soul the last spark of humanity seems to have
been long since crushed out by the hard and spirit-
blighting avocation he is pursuing. Hesitatingly
and timidly I approached the old man, and laid
my priceless treasure on the counter before him.

"Sir, what will you loan me on this watch and
chain?" I said in a choking voice. "I will
redeem it in a month. It is a precious keepsake—the gift of a very dear friend—and I would
not lose it for ten times its value."

"Madam, I yoost gives you ten dollars. I no
like to take him; he not much vort—him not much
sale," said the old man, turning over in his hands
and carefully examining my treasure.

"Oh! sir, the watch alone is worth fifty dollars,
and the chain cost twenty-five but a year ago."

"Vell, madam, such t'ings be not much sale—

him be not much vort; me no got much monish
to spare, but I gives you twelf dollar. Dat ish
more as him ish vort, but I gives you dat."

"Oh! sir, I can not take it. Twelve dollars for
a watch and chain worth at least seventy-five!—
a treasure with which I would not part for five
times that amount. You can certainly give me
more than that."

"Vell, madam, I gives you feefsain dollar. Dat
ish too much—dat ish much more as him ish vort—
but I gives you dat, and not one cent more."

"Sir, I accept your offer. Give me the fifteen
dollars and make out my ticket. I will redeem
it in a month from this time."

"Was ish de name?"

"Mrs. Minnie Ford."

The old man gave me my ticket, handed me
fifteen dollars in bank-notes, and thus was the
sacrifice completed. Turning from this den of
darkness, almost choked with the violence of my
emotions at parting with the treasure which was
so highly prized on account of the precious
memories clustering around it, I again sought my
boarding-house. My mind was so much preoccu-
pied with the contemplation of my wretched
condition that I scarcely noticed that my feet
were soaking wet, until my eyes, falling upon the
well-filled show-window of a large shoe store,
reminded me that my shoes were full of holes,
and utterly unfit to wear in the prosecution of
my canvassing during such weather. I hesitated

a short time, and then, entering the store, asked for, some stout shoes. The accommodating salesman showed me some, and I selected a good pair, for which I paid three dollars, and again set out. Reaching my boarding-house I went at once to my room, and sat down to muse over my situation and prospects.

I was now in possession of twelve dollars—enough to pay my board in my present quarters for two weeks; when that was gone, unless my business improved very much, what would become of me? How could I live on one dollar a week—all that my utmost efforts had been able to earn during the last week? And still the rain continues to pour down; still I sit in forced idleness in my lonely room; and still my mind is dreamily contemplating my present and past, and speculating of the future. The past! ah! the sorrowful past! It is full of grief and bitterness; all marred and scarred over with the baleful effects of passion, and wrong, and treachery, and deceit; and, as I contemplate the fearful picture, my brain almost becomes wild with the dreadful retrospection. Suddenly I start up with convulsive energy. "I can not sit still in idleness." I must go to work again with my books. My friend, Mrs. A. N. D., heard me say this and asked me for a history of my life, which we will tell in the following pages.

CHAPTER II.

I was born on the 7th day of September, in the
year 1837, six miles from Atlanta, in the State of
Georgia. My father, whose name was George F.
Hamilton, was an Englishman by birth, and was
a grandson of George Hamilton, of London, a
celebrated Freemason, who, in the year 1737, as
Provincial Grand Master, established the first
lodge of that ancient and honorable fraternity at
Geneva, Switzerland. My father was made a
Mason in early life, and in due time attained to
thee degre of Royal Arch. I do not know that he
ever attained any position of very great trust or
dignity in the fraternity, but there is abundant
proof that he was a faithful and zealous member,
and was very warmly attached to the principles
of the Order. I mention his connection with
Masonry only to more fully explain some events
of my life which would otherwise, perhaps, be
partially in the dark.

My mother was a Frenchwoman. She was a
daughter of Louis Lacorne, Count of Clermont,
celebrated in the annals of Freemasonry, and
Grand Master of the Grand Lodge of France.

My parents were married in the city of London,

England, in the year 1822, and resided there for
three years. I have not been able to learn that
their lives were marked by any events of special
importance during this time. They appear to
have lived very quietly and happily together for
the entire period. About the beginning of the
year 1825, my father, having been impressed with
the growing greatness of the new world, determined
to emigrate thither, and accordingly, in the summer of that year, he and my mother came to the
United States. Upon their arrival here they
settled in Virginia, where they continued to reside
until the year 1831. During their residence
there, my oldest brother and sister were born.

In 1830 father purchased the plantation where
I was born, near Atlanta, as before stated, and
in 1831 removed there. The country was comparatively new at the time, and Atlanta then
presented but little appearance of the flourishing
city it has since grown to be. My father and
mother continued to live contentedly and happily
in their new home until 1840, during which time
two children were born to them—my brother next
older than myself, and the subject of this sketch.
Our family then consisted of six persons—father,
mother and four children, Franklin, Kate, Henry,
and myself. We had a valuable plantation, well
stocked with slaves, horses, cattle, etc.; a beautiful home in the midst of a lovely grove of cedars,
magnolias, and other magnificent shade-trees;
while the air was laden with the perfume of flowers

2

and filled with the music of the feathered songsters who inhabited the wood. A bubbling spring, but a short distance from the house, lent an air of delicious coolness to the landscape. What was there left to desire? But, alas! even in the garden of Eden pain and sorrow found an entrance and a a resting-place, and so it was with our little paradise.

But, before treating of the events which finally led to the entire separation of our family, I must beg the indulgence of my readers while I speak more particularly of myself. My childhood was far from being a happy one. Even in my earliest years it was easy for me to perceive that I was no favorite with my mother, though I would not willingly utter a word against her memory. She was kind to me, and always strove to do her duty toward me, but it was plainly to be seen that her kindness toward me was the result of a sense of duty, and was not prompted by the powerful over-flow of maternal love and affection which influenced and controlled her conduct toward the elder children of the family, and especially toward my sister. I do not know whether there was anything particular in my appearance or deportment which caused this distinction to be made, but certain it is that the difference existed, and that its effect was finally to produce an entire change in my disposition, and doubtless exerted a marked influence upon my entire life. As a result of this coolness, it may be mentioned that at the early age of four or five years, I abstained almost entirely from taking any part in the sports of my brothers and sisters. Even at that early age, I was fond of solitude—used to steal away by myself to brood over my loneliness, and to wonder why it was that the love which I daily saw lavished upon others, and for which my heart so piteously yearned, was withheld from me. People were accustomed to say of me, " What a strange child she is !" and to express surprise at my serious, old womanish ways. Ah ! parents, beware how you blight the sunny days of childhood by any seeming indifference toward any of your offspring. See to it that you chill not the spirit of one by a more kindly or affectionate demeanor toward another. You may think that the neglected one has not sufficient discrimination to perceive the difference, but be assured that no one is as well able to discern the absence of affection as an infant child. It may not be apparent to those of more mature years, or even hardly perceptible to yourself, but in infancy there is a kind of spirit-communion which infallibly detects the want of love, and the knowledge of that want may exercise a most baleful influence upon the entire future of your child. But to return to myself.

With my father the case was quite different. I always appeared to be a favorite of his, and when he was at home, and I could enjoy his society, I was as happy as heart could wish. But this was only a small portion of the time. Business frequently and constantly called him away, and engrossed the greater portion of his attention, and thus my life went on—a dark, gloomy sky, o'ercast with clouds, with only here and there a ray of sunshine breaking through the rift.

In the latter part of 1840 my father's health began to fail, and it soon became apparent that without some relief he would ere long

"Sleep the sleep that knows no waking"

His physician having advised a change of air and scenery, it was decided to go to Philadelphia, where he had a half-brother living, in the hope that the bracing air of the North would restore somewhat of vigor to his shattered frame. Accordingly the whole family went thither and took up their abode in a pleasant mansion in the City of Brotherly Love.

Month after month passed away, but brought no relief to the weary and enfeebled frame of the sufferer. Slowly, but surely and steadily, he approached the confines of that land "from whose bourne no traveler returns," and when we had been in Philadelphia about two years, my father one day called me to his bedside, and, laying his hand upon my head, said:

"What will my poor little daughter do when she has lost her papa? who will then love her as papa does now?"

I asked him what he meant by saying I would lose him, and he told me he was going to live with Jesus, and that if I was a good child and prayed

to God, he would let me live with Jesus too.
Never while I live can I forget the effect of this
simple conversation upon my mind. I had but
little idea of what he meant, but his solemn
manner produced the most saddening effect upon
my childish heart. I had a sort of dim impression
that his language imported some great calamity
to me, but just what it was, was quite beyond my
comprehension. Poor child that I was. I have
since learned in the bitterness of unmitigated
sorrow the awful portent to me of the journey
which my dear father was about undertaking, but
then I only regarded it as some earthly journey,
and cried to accompany him, saying I wanted to
go when papa did.

The next morning father sent for his friend,
Captain Charles Lake. When he came I was
sitting on the bed with my father. Father put me
in his arms, saying, "Be kind to my little pet
when I am gone." Captain Lake promised to be
a father to me, and soon afterward the doctor came
in with two attorneys, and I was carried from the
room. I did not know what was going on, but
thought they were going to do something to my
papa—was terrified and wanted to get back into
the room. I did not see him again that day, and
when night came, and my old nurse, aunt Silvia,
put me to bed, saying he was sleeping and must not
be disturbed to give me my usual good-night kiss,
I felt as though my heart was broken, but finally
sobbed myself to sleep. My father was already

sleeping the sleep of death, but I knew it not.

The next morning I wanted to see papa, and old nurse took me in her arms and carried me into the room. Father lay on a board, covered with a white sheet, and I thought him asleep, and asked old nurse to let me kiss him. She put me down on the floor, and I kissed him, oh, so gently, for fear of waking him, and then went into mother's room. I found her in tears, and said:

"Mother, what is the matter? What are you crying about?"

"My child," said she, "did you. know your father was dead?"

"What do you mean by saying papa is dead? He is asleep. I just saw him and kissed him very easy, because I did not want to waken him."

"My poor child! your papa will never waken; he will never come back to you any more."

Just then sister Kate came into the room. She was crying bitterly, and I too began to cry. I did not realize or fully understand that my father was gone, never to return; but they were all crying, and my childish heart being filled with terror, I cried in sympathy with them. This morning was the last time I saw my father's remains until the day of the funeral.

How vividly did the incidents of that first funeral I ever witnessed imprint themselves upon my memory! Even the most trifling events of that sad day are as distinctly photographed on my brain as though they occurred but yesterday.

Captain Lake took me into the parlor—the room was filled with strange people—and there in a coffin, the lid of which was raised, lay all that was left of my dear, dear father. Obedient to the direction of Captain Lake, I pressed the last kiss upon the cold and marble lips of the inanimate form before us, and then the funeral services began. The man of God read, from the eleventh chapter of the Gospel according to St. John, that beautiful story of the raising of Lazarus from the grave by our Saviour, and told us that even so would Christ in the latter day raise our father from the tomb; and then they sung,

> Hark, from the tombs a doleful sound,
>   Mine ears attend the cry;
> Ye living men, come view the ground
>   Where you must shortly lie.

I have never heard that beautiful, yet mournful, hymn sung since that time without a strong inclination to shed tears. Never do I hear its melody swelling and floating on the air but memory carries me back through the checkered scenes of my life to that sad, sad day when my sorrows really commenced. Oh! could I have then foreseen what the next twenty-five years of my life would bring forth—could I that day have had even the most transient, fleeting, uncertain glance at what was in store for me in the future, how gladly would I have been laid to rest beside the still form in its last, narrow house! But let us not anticipate.

When we reached the grave, and preparations
were made for depositing in the ground the coffin
in which I had just seen the remains of my father
inclosed, then, for the first time, I began to realize
that I was forever separated from him whom I had
so loved, · Oh! how my little heart then throbbed
in its agony. Frantically I begged Captain Lake
not to let them put papa in that dark, deep hole,
and implored him to take the loved body away
with us. The services were finally concluded by
the congregation singing,

> Why do we mourn departing friends,
> Or shake at death's alarms?
> 'Tis but the voice that Jesus sends
> To call them to his arms.   ·

The grave was filled up, the congregation slowly
dispersed, and I returned with my mother, brothers
and sister, and Captain Lake, to our now lonely
home.

· Lonely, indeed, was this home to me. All that
made it dear to my childish heart was gone. My
father, the only one who had ever seemed to love
me; the only one who had ever taken any interest in
my childish joys or sorrows; the only one to whom I
could go with my little griefs or cares, and feel
assured of sympathy; the only one toward whom
my heart had ever gone out in love; in short, my
all, was lying cold and motionless in the graveyard we had just left; never more to listen to my
childish tales of grief and sorrow; never more to
whisper sweet words of comfort and paternal love,

or to gladden and cheer my desolate heart with his presence. He was sleeping the last, long sleep —that sleep which can know no waking until the last great day when the trump of the angel Gabriel shall summon all nations, and the Great King shall come to judge the quick and the dead. Yes, I am alone, and with a heart strangely saddened for one so young—with a spirit crushed, broken and blighted, by the sad scenes through which I had passed, I sought my couch and sobbed myself to sleep.

CHAPTER III.

Six months have passed away since the close of the last chapter—six months have rolled into eternity since my father's death, and we are again at our old home near Atlanta. Oh! how vividly does everything recall to my mind the dear friend I have lost. Every room in the large, old-fashioned, two-story house recalls to my mind some scene of joy and happiness in which he had participated; the porches which surrounded it on all sides were those in which he used to sit, on summer evenings, while he amused and instructed me with many a quaint, and, to my childish nature, interesting story—even the grove, the flowers and birds seemed vocal with memories of my lost parent. What wonder that I wept as I reflected that I should never see him more? For to my young fancy it seemed that the entombing of the remaims which I had witnessed, was neither more nor less than an eternal separation. I left the house and went to the negro quarters—a row of small, neat white cabins, which gave the place the appearance of a little village— but even these reminded me of my poor, dear, dead papa, and I turned away and wept in the bitterness of my grief. If it be thought strange that a child of six years of age should feel sorrow so

acutely, and retain such a vivid recollection of it,
it must be borne in mind that the peculiar circumstances of my childhood had given me habits of
reflection far beyond my years, and that such
reflection had taught me that with the death of
my father the sunlight of my young life had
gone out.

When my father's will was published, it was
found that he had appointed Captain Lake as his
executor, and had also nominated him as guardian
for the children. He was to have the general
superintendence of every thing; was to care for
the property and to see that the children were
properly raised and educated. How well he fulfilled his trust let the sequel show. My father's
plantation, the slaves and other property on it,
were valued at thirty thousand dollars or there-
abouts, and there was, besides, twelve thousand
dollars in cash. By the terms of the will, this
money was to be put at interest, and the interest
applied to the education of the children—the
balance of the property was bequeathed to our
mother for her natural life, and after her death was
to go in equal proportions to the children.

The weeks and months passed away, and
nothing was done toward the education of the
children, so carefully provided for by my dear
father's will. Nineteen months passed away thus,
and it began to be whispered about that our
guardian would soon take our father's place
in the family and be invested with the entire

control of everything.   The children were all very
much opposed to mother's marrying him, and I, in
particular, was very bitter upon the subject.   I
had early learned to dislike the man, and I had a
sort of intuition that evil would come of this marriage if it was finally consummated.   We knew
that father had placed the utmost confidence in
Captain Lake as an intimate friend and a brother
Mason (how unworthy he was of that high and
holy name let this truthful history tell), but still
his strange neglect of our interests had led us to
distrust him, and it was believed that his only
object in marrying our mother was to get more
completely the control of the property, the more
effectually to carry out his deliberately formed
plan of robbing the orphan children of the man
and brother who had trusted him with all.   The
elder children remonstrated with mother on her
contemplated marriage, and I declared that I
would never call him my father or acknowledge
him as such.

But all our remonstrances and our opposition
were of no avail.   On the 7th day of March in the
year 1845, Captain Charles Lake and my mother
were married, and he was acknowledged master of
the house and invested with the powers which he
had so long coveted.   The wedding took place on
that blackest of all days in the calendar—Friday—
and was a very quiet affair.   But few guests were
present, and thus was accomplished the second
great sorrow of my life, Oh! tongue can never

tell the vast amount of sorrow, and wretchedness, and suffering, which would have been saved to us all, had mother but heeded the remonstrances of her children, and foregone this marriage. She doubtless thought, in uniting herself with Captain Lake, she was promoting her own welfare and happiness and that of her children; but in after years, when it was too late for repentance, she found, alas! that she had been most sadly deceived. Were one disposed to be superstitious about "black Friday," they could find in this marriage a very strong argument in support of their faith, and could well exclaim: "How appropriate that they should have been married on a Friday."

After the marriage of my mother, matters, so far as the children were concerned, were even worse than before, for whereas, Captain Lake had before given some little attention to them in order to deceive my mother and induce her consent to the marriage, he now totally neglected them, and she very soon found that she had injured, instead of improving, their prospects by marrying again. Studied neglect, then cool indifference, and finally positive dislike, took the place of the slight interest which the Captain had before manifested in us, and but a very short time elapsed ere mother became aware that, in marrying the second time, she had committed the greatest mistake of her life.

Brother Henry's health, meantime, was failing rapidly. His was a delicate frame, a finely organized nervous system; one of those organizations on which pain and sorrow produce their most blighting effects, and which are always selected by disease as their special victims. He had almost worshipped our father in his lifetime, and the intense anguish caused by his death had sensibly affected brother's health, and half produced effects from which he never recovered. Some time before mother's marriage it was feared he was going into a decline, and about the time of the wedding it became apparent from the hectic flush upon my poor brother's cheek, the hollow, hacking cough, the bent form and listless step, that the fell destroyer, consumption, had fastened its fangs upon his delicate frame. This was the disease with which my poor father had died, and Henry had inherited it from him. The seeds had lain undeveloped in his system until the present time, and perhaps, but for the weight of sorrow which pressed upon us all, he might have been spared even for years. But it is one of the characteristics of this fatal disease that its effects are hastened, and its early development promoted, by great emotions of joy or sorrow; and brother Henry was no exception to the general rule. The cloud of sadness and grief which o'ershadowed us all, had, in the most fearful degree, hastened the crisis of the disorder; and now, when summer was filling all the earth with beauty and gladness, he was a confirmed and hopeless invalid. All that care and skill could do to stay the onward march of the

destroyer was done, but without avail. He
lingered some time; like our dear father, he clung
with sorrowful tenacity to life, but at last the time
had come when the fell monster and grim tyrant
could no longer be resisted.

Since mother's marriage the summer had waxed
and waned; autumn, with its gorgeous dyes and
gaudy colors, had passed away; another and
another round of seasons had rolled away into
eternity; and when autumn leaves were again
falling, my brother was at rest. Sadly we laid his
mortal remains in the silent tomb, there to rest
until the omnipotent voice of Him who has said,
"I am the Resurrection and the Life," shall summon him from the dust of the earth to everlasting
happiness at the right hand of God.

Upon my already tortured heart this blow fell
with crushing force. After the death of our father,
Henry had essayed, so far as was in his power, to
supply his place to me. He had seemed to take
much more interest in me than he ever did before.
He had petted and caressed me; called me his
dear, his pet; strove by all means in his power to
cheer and comfort me, and had succeeded in
awakening in my little heart a feeling of love,
second only to that which had warmed it toward
my poor papa. Judge then, dear reader, of the
bitter anguish as I stood beside his grave, and
beheld the clods of the valley piled upon his
breast, hiding forever from my earthly vision his
much loved form. What wonder that in the utter

desolation of that moment I even dared to murmur
against the justice of the decrees of Providence.
It seemed to me that a blighting, withering curse
was upon me. Every object upon which I gazed
with the eyes of affection was doomed to fade and
die before me.

> " 'Twas ever thus from childhood's hour—
>   I've seen my fondest hopes decay;
> I never loved a tree or flower,
>   But 'twas the first to fade away."

> "I never nursed a dear gazelle,
>   To glad me with its soft black eye,
> But when it learned to love me well,
>   And know me, it was sure to die."

But though my beloved brother was gone, I was
not yet entirely desolate. I had a darling little
half-sister—one of those cherubs which are said to
more nearly approximate the angels of heaven
than any other created thing upon the face
of the earth. At the time of Henry's death she
was nearly a year and a half old, having been
born about a year after mother's marriage with
Captain Lake. She was, I think, the sweetest
child of that age I ever saw; so bright, so smart
and intelligent, as it were—far beyond her tender
age. Oh! how I loved that darling babe. I was
never so happy as when I had her in my arms, or
was romping with her upon the nursery floor.
And the little thing seemed to fully reciprocate all
the love and affection which I so warmly and
freely lavished upon her. I had named her May,

and she, in her childish, lisping voice, always called me Nin. "Many a time and oft" would she come to me, and, putting her little white, soft arms about my neck, would lisp out, " Me 'ove oo, Nin," and then put up her little mouth for the kiss she was sure to receive.

Besides her, there were still little brother Frank and sister Kate. They were, both of them, much older than I, and there was but little in common between us; but still they were my brother and sister—the offspring of a dearly-loved father—and that of itself was a bond of sympathy between us. The affectionate reverence in which we held the memory of that dear, departed parent, would have bound us together even if there had been no other ties existing between us, and we were further united in a most cordial dislike of our step-father. Besides my step-father was cross and abusive to Frank, and sympathy with him, under the injustice of which he was often the victim, had drawn me yet closer to my only remaining brother.

But I was soon to be separated from them—from my brother and sister, baby May and all. Father had a half-brother, by the name of Adam Mason, living in New Orleans, whom I had never seen, though I knew his wife, aunt Kittie. He and father had never been on good terms with each other, though between our family and aunt Kittie the most kindly feelings had always existed. She had visited us on several occasions, and had taken a great fancy to me—called me *her* girl, said she

3

was going to take me to live with her—and did all in her power to win my childish love and affection, in which efforts I must say she was rather successful. I loved her more than any one else outside my own family; but when, some two and a half years after mother's second marriage, she wrote to us, asking that I might come and live with her, keep her company, and do errands for her, I felt my heart sink within me at the prospect of leaving the home and friends to which I was so warmly attached. But my mother thought it best for me to go; my step-father was unkind and often cruel, not only to me, but to all the family, and mother thought that, the pang of separation once passed, I would be happier with my uncle and aunt—removed from the tyrannical treatment of my step-father, and beyond his blighting influence—than I would be at home. Accordingly, it was decided that my step-father should accompany me to New Orleans, place me in the care of my uncle and aunt, and then return to his home. The arrangements were all made, and at last the day arrived upon which I was to bid farewell to home and friends, as it seemed to me, forever.

Ah! how shall I describe that parting? I was to go forth from home and friends; to exchange the society of those from whose companionship I had never been separated, for association with comparative strangers; to leave mother, brother and sisters, and to accept in lieu of the kind and fraternal attention I had received from them, the friendship of relatives of whom I knew next to nothing, and above all, I was to be deprived of that which had been my principal solace and comfort since the death of my brother Henry—the society of my constant playmate, baby May. And to add to the bitterness of my sorrow, in that hour of parting from my little cherub, something whispered me that I should never see her again in this world. Was it a presentiment? What wonder, then, that when this, to me, sad day came, I wept as though my heart would break, or that, long after the journey commenced, I refused to be comforted, and sat in the corner of my seat, sobbing in all the violence of unalloyed and unrestrained grief?

But all things earthly must have an end, and so it was with my journey and my grief. We at length reached the Crescent City, and were received by my uncle and aunt with a degree of kindness which went far toward reconciling me to my lot. After seeing me safely installed in my new home, and transacting some business which he had in the city, my step-father prepared to return home. Although I did not love him, still I hated to see him go, for it seemed like severing the last link that bound me to home and friends. I did not shed any tears at his departure, and yet it must be confessed that my heart swelled a little as I saw him walk away from the house and disappear around the next corner. My uncle and aunt after his departure treated me, if possible, with more kindness than before, and apparently did all in their power to make me happy, and induce me to forget, or at least to remember without regret, the home I had left behind.

In this they were to a very great extent successful. I was then but about ten years old, and at that age old forms and old impressions are easily effaced from the mind. The bustle and stir of city life, the new faces and new scenes presented to my vision each day of my life; the constant change going on around me, all conspired to wean me from thoughts of home and friends, while the kindness of my uncle and aunt went far toward supplying the place of the protectors I had lost. They were quite aged, and had no children of their own, and upon me they lavished all the affection which would have gone out toward their own offspring had they ever been blest with any. Thus time passed, and I would have been happy could I have had baby May with me. But I longed for her society, and there were times when, even in my happiest moments, thoughts would rush across my mind and so stir up the fountains of my heart as to cause my feelings to well up in tears which I could not repress.

The autunm leaves were falling when I went to live with aunt Kittie, and when the stern winter months had come and gone, and spring with all her beauties was upon us, my aunt one day received a letter conveying the sad intelligence that both sister Kate and baby May were very ill, the

latter with scarlet fever. Upon hearing this news
I wanted to go home at once, but aunt Kittie would
not consent, saying I would take the fever if I
went. I urged and entreated; almost implored,
but it was of no avail. I felt sure May wanted to
see her old playmate "Nin," but aunt was resolute
in her refusal, and of course my will had to yield to
hers, and I staid. I have now no doubt that what
aunt did was for the best, but at that time it did
not seem so to me, and my spirit was strongly inclined to raise up in rebellion against hers. And
had it been possible for me to have foreseen what
I now know, there is but little doubt that I should
have gone, despite aunt's commands to the
contrary, or, at least made an attempt to have
done so.

But a few days had passed when another letter
was received, and this time it bore the sable seal
which tells, even before it is broken, the sad tale
of death, and sorrow, and mourning. My darling
pet, my poor, dear, little May was no more. How
I regretted that it had not been in my power to see
her before she died—how bitterly I wept and refused to be comforted, I leave to the imagination
of the reader. But this was not the only sad intelligence which this ill-starred letter contained.
Sister Kate was not expected to survive—was,
indeed, at the point of death, and there was an
urgent request that I should be sent home at once.

Of course, there was no delay in obeying this
sad summons. Uncle Adam accompanied me, and

we hastened to Atlanta by the most expeditious
mode of conveyance ; but, alas ! our speed was too
slow for that of the grim monster who was claim-
ing my loved sister. When we reached the old
plantation her voice was not raised in kindly
greeting to her returned sister; she stretched forth
no hand to grasp mine in sisterly welcome; her
eyes darted forth no beaming ray of love for the
long absent one; her heart-throbs had ended, and
she was cold and motionless in the embrace of
death. She had drawn her last breath but ten
minutes before our arrival. She had died with my
name upon her lips—almost her last words being
an eager inquiry for my arrival. This intelligence
almost stunned me with grief. Why should I be
thus tried? It almost seemed to me that Fate
was about to empty her entire quiver of arrows
upon my devoted head.

Reader, bear in mind that I was at this time
less than twelve years of age—recall the sorrows
amid which my young life had thus far been passed,
and then say was human life ever so chastened
before? First, I had followed my loved father to
the grave—then came the inexorable summons for
him who endeavored to supply the place made
vacant in my heart by that first death, my brother
Henry; next, the pitiless monster called for my
darling little May, and lastly sister Kate was
taken away. And to add sting to the poignancy
of my anguish, the last two had died in my
absence. It was not permitted me to be near

them in their dying moments; to receive their last kisses of affection; to receive their latest sighs and final adieus; but, far removed from me they had died, and I could never hope again to listen to the music of their voices until the great day. I was then young, and had not learned to bow in mild submission to the will of "Our Father who art in Heaven;" nor had I learned that great lesson, under all trials to meekly say, "Thy will be done." What wonder then that I murmured at the dispensations of his providence, or that, in the abandonment of utter despair, I cast myself prostrate upon little May's grave, and prayed that I, too, might die? God forgive me the wickedness of that prayer. I have since learned to bear trials with more fortitude, and have, I trust, learned to bow with something of submission to whatever chastenings His hand may lay upon me, and in so doing have secured "that peace which passeth all understanding."

The next day a sad procession wended its way to the graveyard, and there, under the spreading foliage of a mighty oak, beside the low mounds which marked the last resting-places of brother Henry and sister May, a third grave was fashioned, to which, with appropriate ceremonies, we committed the mortal remains of sister Kate; and brother Frank and I were alone—the only survivors of a family of five children. 'Tis true, our mother was still spared to us, but she was so much under the influence of our step-father that she seemed

more like a stranger than like a blood relation—
much less a mother. And to make our position
still more unpleasant, it was evident that our step-
father—our guardian—the possessor of all the
property which father had left for our benefit, but
from which we were destined never to reap any
advantage—he who had solemnly pledged to our
dying father his honor as a man and a Mason that
he would befriend and protect his orphan children,
and who was now only seeking to deprive us of
our patrimony—evidently hated us, and desired
our absence, no doubt the more effectually to carry
out his base purposes toward us.

It is one of the immutable laws of human nature
that when we have done or meditate a wrong
toward another, the presence of the one wronged,
either in thought or deed, becomes hateful to us.
The presence of the person to whom we have done
wrong is a sort of standing reproach to the wrong-
doer—an ever-present, active and powerful monitor
to the conscience which, however calloused and
seared with the crime of years, can never be wholly
stifled—ever condemning the crime which has been
perpetrated, and sleeplessly demanding restitution.
Our step-father was no exception to this general
law of our nature. Our father had left in his
hands a sacred trust to be exercised for the benefit
of the orphans; years had passed away and not a
single step had been taken toward the execution
of that trust, but instead he had by his course
deprived us entirely of the benefits which our

father's legacy was intended to secure—he had wronged, robbed and defrauded us, and as a matter of course our presence was hateful to him. Our sister's funeral was therefore hardly over until he instituted a system of persecution against us with the evident intent to drive us from our home.

It were a useless, unpleasant, and unprofitable task to recount in detail the various means resorted to by him to · drive us from that home which of right belonged to us; suffice it to say that he was successful—that our mother was unable, or unwilling, to stem the tide which was setting against us, and that but a short time elapsed after I had seen my sister Kate buried beneath the sod until I was again on my way to the home of my uncle and aunt in the city of New Orleans. But this time I went not alone. My brother Frank—the last survivor beside myself of our once happy circle of brothers and sisters—unable to endure the annoyance and cruelties which were daily meted out to him, accompanied me, and in due time we reached the city, where we were kindly welcomed and tenderly cared for by our uncle and aunt. But we will reserve for another chapter the incidents which attended our sojourn there.

CHAPTER IV.

I MUST ask the reader to imagine that a period of three years has elapsed since the close of the last chapter. Brother Frank and myself are still living at uncle Adam's, and have become so thoroughly domiciled there as to regard it as our home. During all this time our lives had been one constant scene of peace—scarcely a ripple had occurred upon the surface of the stream of time as we quietly glided down its surface toward eternity, and the only strange circumstance I have to record of those three years is the fact that, in all that time we had not once heard from home. I do not know whether uncle Adam or aunt Kittie had heard from there or not; I suppose they must have done so at some time or other, but if so, they never said anything about it to us. For some time we thought very strange that mother did not write to us, but we finally came to attribute it to indifference toward ourselves, and thus comparatively dismissed the subject from our thoughts. I have since learned to believe that this long silence was brought about by the machinations of Captain Lake, and was part of a deliberately formed plan to harass mother to an untimely grave, and thus get more complete control of the property of which he was steadily and systematically robbing us. God forgive me if I judge him wrongfully; he has grievously wronged me and mine,. and yet I would not willingly or knowingly charge him with a single crime of which he is innocent.

About three years from the time of our last arrival in New Orleans, uncle Adam one day brought home with him a gentleman from the neighborhood of our old home ; one who intimately knew all our family. Of course, the most eager inquiries relative to the family were at once made. Judge of my horror and surprise upon being informed by him that my mother was dead—had been dead then about a year. Great God! could it be possible that my monster step-father had allowed my mother to pine away and die without informing her only relatives in theUnited States—her own children—of the sad fact?

"Yes," said my informant, "it is all true. It is now just about one year since we followed your mother's remains to the tomb."

"And where is my step-father?" I asked.

"He is still upon the plantation, and is about to give it a new mistress. The last time I was there he was refitting and refurnishing the place for his bride, and by this time next week they will be married."

"What! did mother make no disposition of the plantation or other property? Did she leave all our patrimony, so carefully provided for us by our father, to that wretched man whose whole efforts since he took charge of us beside our father's dying bed, have been directed toward robbing us?"

"As to that I can not say. I never heard of
any will after the death of your mother, and only
know that matters, so far as the property is concerned, appear to go on just as they did in her
lifetime. He still lives upon and manages the
plantation as before."

"Then God help me," I cried; "I am indeed
desolate and alone in the world. No father or
mother—not a single one in whose veins runs a
drop of my blood, except brother Frank—no
home—no means of support—what will become
of me?"

"My child," said he gently, "do not give way
to such paroxysms of grief. Remember that God
helps those who help themselves, and that He
has promised to be the God of the orphan and the
Father of the fatherless. Doubtless some means
of support will yet be found for you and your
brother."

But, despite his kindly efforts to cheer me, I
refused to be comforted. She who had gone,
though never treating me with such affection as
parents generally evince for their offspring, was
still my mother, and I sincerely mourned her loss.
And then the future looked very dark to me, for,
comparative child that I was, I was still able to
realize to some extent our situation. Uncle Adam
and aunt Kittie were very old and were poor; we
had neither of us ever been taught to work for our
living; our education had been so badly and
criminally neglected by our guardian and step-

father that we could scarcely ever hope to derive
anything from that source ; the course of that man
assured us plainly that we had nothing to hope
from him ; and what were we to do? As long as
uncle and aunt lived, we could have a home with
them, but they were both very feeble, and could
not be expected to live for a great length of time,
and after their death what was to become of us?

It must be borne in mind that we were but
children, and ignorant of law and our own rights,
and were without any one to advise or assist us.
Uncle Adam did, I think, make some effort to get
at the right in regard to our matters, but my step-
father had laid his plans skillfully, and had
so hedged himself about with technicalities and
the forms of law that it was impossible to reach
him except by a long and expensive litigation.
This we could not undertake. We were without
means, and uncle Adam was too poor to furnish
it to us; and thus villainy was for the time
triumphant, and the orphans robbed of their just
dues. But, thank God! it will not always be so.
There is a time coming when all that to us has
seemed strange and unnatural in this life will be
set right—when ample justice will be done—when
the secret of every heart will be made manifest,
and when no amount of ingenuity will enable the
robber of the orphan and the fatherless to escape
the just punishment of his deeds.

After this we continued to live on with uncle
and aunt as before. They had a fine, large garden,

and our principal employment was to cultivate
this and dispose of the vegetables. From this
source, and the milk of our one cow, we managed
to obtain a very comfortable support for the entire
family. It must be understood that my uncle had
no business, and that he was too old and feeble to
do much gardening or anything else, and hence
the principal support of the family devolved upon
my brother and myself. He was now about sixteen, and I was about thirteen; our work was not
hard, and we managed to get along very well.

But the seasons passed away—spring had gone
—summer had followed in train, and the gorgeous
Southern autumn had made its appearance, when
we found that our uncle's lamp of life was speedily
dying out. The oil which had so long and steadily
fed the flame was exhausted, and but a short time
had elapsed when we laid him to rest in "the
narrow house appointed for all the living." Our
venerable aunt sincerely mourned for him by
whose side she had so long trod the rough paths
of life, and grief at his loss preyed heavily upon
her enfeebled frame. She became a helpless
invalid, and an object of our constant care. It
was a terrible burthen for two comparative children as we were; but, thank God! we never faltered
in the discharge of this painful duty. Looking
back throught the vista of years to that period, I
cannot find a single instance in which my conscience reproaches me with any dereliction of duty
in the care of my aunt.

But this could not last long. The scene was evidently drawing to a close, and but a few months had passed since the death of uncle Adam before it became painfully evident that she would soon follow him to the silent tomb. At length, one bright spring morning, when all nature was putting on her gayest robes, and the whole earth was brightening with smiles, and joy, and sunshine, we stood by the bedside of our aunt and beheld the Angel of Death slowly o'ershadow her with his dark wing, while her freed spirit took its flight to realms of immortal bliss, there to rejoin his by whose side she had lived and moved so long. With the assistance of kind neighbors we laid her to rest by the side of him who had gone so short a time before, and leaving them to that repose which shall never be broken until the day of the last resurrection, we returned, with bowed heads and stricken hearts, to the lonely cottage which had so long been our home.

We were now alone, and without means, and consequently helpless. We were old enough to know that the future would not take care of itself —that something must be done, but just what that something was to be we could not tell. To increase our distress, we now learned that the place we occupied did not belong to our uncle. He only had a lease of it during his lifetime, and we were now really without a shelter for our heads, although the owner of the cottage kindly consented that we should remain where we were

for a short time until we could perfect our plans
for the future. Many a long and anxious conversation did we have upon the subject before we
were able to arrive at any definite conclusion.
Various expedients were suggested, but each was
in time found to possess some fatal defect, and
one after another they were rejected. Meantime
the days were passing away, and something must
be done; we could not stay where we were, and
our means were about.exhausted.

At length, one day my brother came to me with
a beaming countenance.

"Now," said he, "I will tell you what we must
do. I can get a situation in St. Mary's Parish as
a gardener, at fair wages. This will furnish me
a living and enable me to help you some, and
your must go to Mrs. Armstrong's and assist in
her housework."

"But suppose Mrs. Armstrong should not want
me?"

"Oh! but she does. This is no new plan of
mine, and I have been to see her, and talked
matters all over with her. Her ladyship wants
you—I am sure she will be kind to you, and I see
nothing else for us to do."

"But consider, Frank, I have scarcely had any
experience in doing housework, and I am afraid
she will not be satisfied with me. If she should
not, and should turn me away, what then is to be
done?"

"She will be satisfied with you. I have talked

with her about your experience ; know just what she expects and requires, and feel sure you will just suit her."

"But why can we not go to Georgia and compel Captain Lake to take care of us."

"Sister, I would rather beg, or starve among strangers, than to go to that man who has robbed us of our all, and ask charity at his hands. Never will I ask any thing of him. I will die first."

"It would be only justice."

"Yes, but until we can demand it as an act of justice I am not willing to go and ask alms of him. This plan of mine, though unpleasant in some respects, will enable us to earn an honest living, and I really see no other course for us at present. Perhaps in the future something better may turn up."

So it was finally settled. He went with me to Mrs. Armstrong's house and introduced me to my new mistress. The house was a fine, large mansion, situated in a pleasant locality, and surrounded with trees; the furniture was handsome, rich and costly, and everything reminded me of the home in which my earlier years had been passed. But, ah! how different was my situation from what it was there. I thought I was unhappy at home, but there I was a child, and an heiress of the wealth which surrounded me ; here I was a servant, laboring and toiling for my daily bread. Mrs. Armstrong was always kind to me, but her kindness could not comfort me, or cause

4

me to forget that I was a mere servant in a house
similar to that which should have been my own,
had justice been done me.   Wherever I went, or
whatever I did, this reflection was ever present to
me, burning and branding itself into my brain
until the thought at last sort of dazed me.   I would
stand for an hour at a time, motionless as a statue,
and when spoken to by any one, would not hear or
heed a word that was said.   I seemed in a sort of
waking dream.

This intense mental excitement at last did its
work, and I was prostrated with a brain fever.
I knew nothing at the time, and only learned what
followed when, eleven weeks after, I awoke as
from a long trance, and found brother Frank
sitting by my bedside.   I felt weak, and when I
attempted to address him, it was with difficulty
that I could hear the sound of my own voice.

"Brother, what has happened?   Why am I so
weak?   Why are you here, and how long have
you been here?"

"Sister," said he, "it has been eleven weeks
since you were taken down with the fever, and I
have been with you all the time.   You first lost
your reason, and the doctor said you would never
recover it.   Then you became speechless, and have
never uttered a sound since, and everybody said
you would never speak again.   I thought, Nin, I
was going to lose you, but, thank God! you are
better now."

"Eleven weeks! It can not be possible that I have been sick so long."

"Oh! yes, it is true. They all thought you were dead at one time, and you would have been buried long ago if I had consented to give you up. You were as cold as ice, but your cheeks were somewhat flushed, and I could not believe you were dead. But it was only when I held a looking-glass to your lips, and the moisture gathered upon it, that I succeeded in convincing them that you were still living. This is all that saved you from being buried alive. But you are too weak to talk at present. You must lie still and gain strength, and when you are better I will tell you more."

He spoke the truth. Even this conversation had been almost too much for me in my enfeebled state, and, with a sense of inexpressible weariness, I closed my eyes and again slept. When I again awoke it was mid-day, and brother was not there, but in his place sat one of Mrs. Armstrong's servants. I lay and tried to think, but the effort was too much for me, in the enfeebled and confused state of my brain, and I gave it up.

I have often since shuddered at the thought of how near I came to being buried alive, and each time that memory presents this horrible picture, does my mind and heart go out with more of love to that brother whose constancy and fortitude saved me from such a terrible fate. And often, in the silent hours of the night, does my heart well up with gratitude to the Giver of all good, for bestowing upon me such a faithful and trusty friend. But, at that time, I felt that I would almost as soon have died as not. I felt that I was almost alone in the world—a useless, helpless thing, a mere waif upon the stream of time—and had it not been for the love I bore the brother who had so tenderly and constantly watched over me ever since poor Kate's death, I should have wished to join her in that other world to which we are all hastening. But I knew how it would wring his heart if his only sister were to die; I knew he would then have no one to love or care for; and, for his sake, I prayed to God that I might get well.

And God heard my prayer. Slowly, oh! how slowly, but surely and steadily, strength returned to my emaciated frame, and I was at length pronounced out of danger. It was long and weary weeks before I was able to leave my bed, and the weeks had grown into months before they would permit me to go out of doors; but at length it was pronounced safe by the physician, and I was allowed to go into the yard attended by a servant. From this time I gained strength more rapidly; my excursions about the grounds were longer and longer each day, and at last I was pronounced, by the kind old physician who had attended me during the whole of my sickness, to be convalescent.

With the return of my health came an almost irresistible longing to revisit my old home in Georgia. I wanted a change of air and scenery;

I wished to see the dear old place which my father had improved; I wanted to visit and water with my tears the graves of the dear ones in that far-off burying ground. Brother Frank had gone back to his employer in St. Mary's Parish, and I matured my plans and made my arrangements for going before consulting him, for I felt certain he would oppose me. But my mind was fully made up, and I was resolved to go at all hazards. I did not suppose they wanted to see me there, but they could do no more than turn me out of doors, and I could go to some of the neighbors. Go I would, and go I did.

When my plans were fully matured and my arrangements made, I then communicated my intentions to my brother. As I had foreseen, he was very much opposed to my going, and vainly used every argument in his power to dissuade me from the undertaking. He spoke of my yet feeble constitution, of the perils and difficulties of the journey, and of every other consideration which his love and solicitude for my farewell could suggest, to induce me to abandon the adventure. To all that he could urge, however, I was deaf, and, in my turn, plied him with arguments to induce him to accompany me, but with equal want of success. Finding all my efforts vain, I at last bid adieu to Frank and the kind friends who had done so much for me during my illness, and set out on my journey alone. In due time, and without any incidents worthy of note, I finally reached

Atlanta. In my enfeebled state, however, the journey had been almost too much for me, and when I arrived there I looked like one risen from the dead. I was myself startled at the haggard appearance presented by my own face as I gazed in a mirror, and was weary and worn out to the last degree, but after resting a short time in the city I thought I was strong enough to undertake the journey out to the plantation, and accordingly procured a conveyance and went thither.

When I arrived near the place I decided that I would not go at once to the house—not being certain of my reception—but thought it best to go to the negro quarters and learn what I could of the situation of affairs. Accordingly I left the conveyance a short distance from the house, clambered over a fence, passed through the orchard, and thus finally, by stealth, gained the cabins of the negroes. How strange it seemed thus to steal my way into that place which should be my own! I felt like a guilty thing, seeking to avoid the gaze of man as I stole into that inclosure and trod upon those broad acres which of right belonged to me, but which I now visited with fear and trembling.

The first one I met was my old nurse, aunt Silvie—the very one of all others I would have chosen should first welcome me to my old home. When she caught sight of me she threw up both hands.

"De Lor' bress you, chile! If dare aint little Missus Minnie, or am it her ghost?"

"No aunt Silvie, I am no ghost, but really and truly your own little mistress Minnie."

"Bress you, chile, but you really looks like a ghost, and I most beliebes you is one. De Lor' bress us! here I'se done been talkin' to a ghost, sho."

"No, aunt Silvie, I am not a ghost, but am really flesh and blood: come and feel me."

"Den what is de matter? You looks like you had just risen out ob de grabe. Hab you been dead and just come back to life? I 'clar', if I don't beliebe yer am a ghost. Come here, old man, and see if dis am Miss Minnie, shure enough, or am it just her ghost? Bress us! See dem holler eyes."

"I tell you, aunt Silvie, I am no more nor less than your own child, little Miss Minnie. I have been very sick, and have but just recovered."

"Recobered! I don't see de recober. You is sick as you can be. Jess look at dem thin han's, and dem bony cheeks, and den say you is recobered. I like to know what yer is recobered."

By this time uncle Tom had come up to where we were sitting,

"Why, de good Lord-a-massy, Miss Minnie, dis aint you? Why, is ye done been dead and berried, and come ter life again, or wa't de Lord-a-massy does ail yer?"

"Why, uncle Tom, I have been sick, and have just got well enough to come here and visit the graves of my dear ones. Do you think I will be welcome at the mansion? I think I will get entirely well if I can be at the old house awhile."

"Bress ye, honey, yer is come her' to be berried wid der rest ob der family, dat is what yer is."

"No, uncle Tom, I have come to have aunt Silvie nurse me well again."

"Well, de old Capt'in done heard ye's been berry sick, and he t'inks ye is dead. Yer can scare him to death if yer likes, for we don't any of us like him—not an inch of him. But de missus, she am a good 'oman, and we all likes her. She'll take good care ob yer, if yer gets into her good graces."

"Well, Tom, you go and see Mrs. Lake; tell her I am here, and if she will give me a welcome, come and let me know."

"Dat dis chile will do. Come, old 'oman, make Miss Minnie somet'ing for to eat. Has yer done forgot yourself"

While he was gone I had a long talk with aunt Silvie about my mother, and the cause and circumstances of her death. After Frank and I went to New Orleans, matters had gone from bad to worse. Captain Lake had treated her with cold cruelty and indifference, until at last her spirit sunk under her trials, and she had gone down to her grave in sorrow. She had never seemed quite herself after the death of May and Kate, and this rendered her less able to endure the ill treatment of her husband. She had finally died—the doctors said of fever, but, the negroes thought, of a broken heart. For more than a week before her death she had been entirely deprived of her speech, and had therefore said nothing about her children in her last moments. About a year after her death, Captain Lake married a Miss Blackburn, and they now had a son about three months old. She also told me the Captain was now away from home, and that he seemed very much attached to his wife and child.

I was acquainted with the Blackburns before I left the place, and I knew Mary (his wife) to be a good, kind-hearted girl. Though much older than I, she had always been very friendly toward me—had always treated me with the utmost kindness, and I felt sure she would not turn me away from the house, especially as she knew that if I had my rights, that house and plantation, those broad acres with their growing crops, those negroes, cattle, horses and other stock—in fine, all that was there, would be mine. She knew that it had all belonged to my father; that Captain Lake was his executor, and my guardian, and she must have known that he had betrayed his trust and wronged me. I felt that she knew all this, and yet she was my step-father's wife. Still, I could not believe that that relation would obliterate all her sense of justice and morality, and I resolved in my own mind to appeal to her for justice against her husband. The appeal could only be rejected, and could not make my case much worse, and I would risk it.

These reflections passed through my mind very rapidly, and by the time I had arrived at this conclusion I saw Tom returning from his interview with Mrs. Lake. Although I would not really allow myself to doubt the result of that interview, still I could not repress a feeling of anxiety as my messenger drew near. What if he had been unsuccessful, and if, instead of the welcome I had persuaded myself to hope for, he bore an order for my departure from the place? It must be borne in mind that I was yet but partially recovered from my severe fit of sickness, and that both mind and body were reduced to a state of almost childish weakness, and hence my views of everything were sadly distorted and awry. The reader must also remember that I was fasting, for when I was in the city my anxiety to see my home kept me from eating anything, and since I came here, though aunt Silvie had prepared a very nice meal for me, my agitation had been such as to prevent me from partaking of it. My system was, therefore, in a very poor condition to endure the intense anxiety which oppressed me, and my agitation was so great that when I saw Tom coming, and knew that the crisis of my fate was at hand, my feelings overcame me and I sunk to the floor. I only heard aunt Silvie say, "Dere, I tole her she came here to be buried wid de rest ob de family, and now she is done gone a'ready widout seein' de grabes ob her friends." This I heard, and then I sunk into utter oblivion and unconsciousness.

When I again opened my eyes, I was lying in a comfortable bed, in a well-furnished room. A beautiful, sweet face, with goodness beaming from every lineament, was bending over me, and a soft, low voice, which thrilled me with its kindly tones, asked me if I knew her. Yes, indeed, I did know her. It was Mary Blackburn, or Mrs. Charles Lake, as I should rather say. I looked around the room. With what a thrill of satisfaction did I realize the fact that I was in the same room I had occupied when I lived in that house with my mother, now dead and gone. Everything in the room was the same as when I had last seen it. There was the same old-fashioned, high-post bedstead, with its rich crimson canopy; the same wardrobe and bureau stood in the corner of the room; the same chairs were arranged along the wall; the same carpet was on the floor, and all was just the same as memory so faithfully reproduced it to my imagination. Everything, did I say? No, one thing was gone, and I sought in vain for it—it was baby May's crib, with the lovely face of its occupant; and as I looked in vain for them, sad memory reminded me in thunder tones of the many changes which had taken place since I last occupied that room, and it was with the utmost difficulty that my tears could be repressed.

Mrs. Lake waited until I had completed my survey of the room and its furniture, and then, in her sweet, musical voice, replete in every tone with kindness, she said :

"I have had this room arranged for you, as nearly as I could remember, just as you used to have it. Are you pleased with it, or would you prefer to lie in some other room?"

"I thank you most heartily and sincerely for your kindness to me," said I. "I would rather be in my own room than any other"—then recollecting myself, I hastened to add, "or rather, what was once my own room."

"It is yours still, Minnie," said she, "it shall be yours just as long as you choose to occupy it. We will do all in our power to make you happy just as long as you see proper to stay with us. And then I have a little playfellow for you—a baby whom you can pet as you used to little May. I know you are passionately fond of children, but now you must not talk any more; you must go to sleep now, and when you are rested I will bring my little pet to you."

"Yes, I will try to be calm, but I must ask one or two questions. Where is Captain Lake? Does he know I am here? And how long have I been here?"

"My dear child, you ask too many questions in one breath. You have been here just two days. The Captain is away from home, was away when you came, and will not be at home for a month to come. But if he were here he would welcome you kindly, and would be glad to see you, I am sure. So be quiet now, and take your rest, and I will go and prepare something for you to eat."

With that she stooped down, and, kissing my pale, hollow cheek, left the room. After she went out, I lay still and tried to compose myself to sleep, but the effort was in vain. Busy memory was at work with the past, and would not allow my worn out body to rest. I thought over all the incidents which had transpired since I last occupied that room; the trials and sorrows through which I had passed; the scenes of death I had witnessed; the troop of friends whom I had seen fade and die from around me like autumn leaves: my uncle and aunt, sister Kate and baby May—all, all passed in mental review before me, and I could not but wonder why it was that they were all taken away and I was spared. Doubtless, in the inscrutable mysteries of the providence of God there was good reason for this; but why I should have been selected from among them all, to endure this great weight of bereavement and sorrow, was far beyond my feeble comprehension. Another subject of contemplation with me, and one from which I experienced a most bitter sense of anguish, was the awful contrast between what my situation was at the present time, and what it was then, and would be now, had not the foulest injustice lent its aid to increase the evils which Providence had seen fit to visit upon me. Then I was in the midst of comparative affluence, ease and comfort—unhappy in some respects, it is true, but still far from miserable; now I was a wretched outcast, without a home, without friends, without means of support, and actually dependent upon the charities of others for a place in which to lay my miserable head, and for the little sustenance necessary to keep life within my enfeebled frame. Then occurred the thought, most horrid of all: what if I should again be sick, as I was at Mrs. Armstrong's? I was in high fever, and, of course, my mind was to some extent disordered, and took but a distorted view of all subjects, and I could not divest myself of the impression that my illness was about to assume the same terrible phase it then did—in which event, without my brother's fraternal care, I should surely die—nay, perchance, be buried alive, as was so near being the case before. The idea of death would not have been, of itself, so very terrible; but with it was connected the thought that my brother would never know of it. It did not occur to me that in case of serious illness those around me would, of course, notify him of the fact; but the dread of being forever lost to him was most insupportable. Then my cogitations assumed another form, and filled me with unspeakable physical terror. What if I should be ill when Captain Lake returned, and he should be angry with me for coming there, to be a burden to him? His anger would most certainly kill me. Or what if, in his wrath, he should, despite my enfeebled condition, turn me from his house, to live or die as best I might! What would become of me then?

Thus these vagaries chased each other through my brain until it almost went wild, and I am sure

I should have become utterly distracted but for the return of Mrs. Lake to the room. She came in with a sweet smile on her lip, and a lovely little babe in her arms, upon which she gazed with all the pride and affection which fills the heart of a young mother for her first-born.

"Here, Minnie," said she, "is my baby, my own darling little pet; don't you think he is a perfect little cherub?"

"He is certainly very beautiful," I said, gazing with delight upon the sweet, innocent face, yet free from the corroding marks of care and sorrow. "You must love him dearly."

"Oh! indeed I do. And you will love him too," she continued, laying the laughing babe upon my arm. "Why, Minnie, you look like a young mother with the babe in your arms."

I looked in its angel face. It was almost the exact picture of my darling, lost, little May, at its age. It had the same large, deep-blue eyes, and dimpled chin; the contour of the forehead was the same as hers; the same fat, dimpled chin was hers; the features were all identical with hers, and as my eyes, at a glance, took in all these details, I for a moment half thought my darling had come back to me. But in another instant came the recollection that I had seen her grave and watered it with my tears, and nothing short of the power of Omnipotence itself could ever restore her to my loving embrace again, and I turned away my head and wept bitterly. I could not help it. The recollec-

tion of the happiness I had once enjoyed with her
whom it so nearly resembled, and who was forever gone from my grasp, was too much for me, and
I sobbed as though my heart would break.   Mrs.
Lake respected my grief, because she divined its
cause, and her heart was one to appreciate such
emotions.   She waited until the violence of my
emotion was passed, and then quietly removing the
babe, she gently smoothed my hair and said :

"You must now take your rest, Minnie, and
when you get stronger you shall have baby again,
and I know you will learn to love him almost
as much as I do."

And she was right.   Day after day my affection
for the child and its mother grew in strength, and
at length I learned to look and long for nothing
so much as the coming of Mary Lake with her
sweet, innocent babe.   I was always very fond of
children, and especially loved a pretty babe during
the days of infancy—this was almost the exact
picture of her whom I had once loved more than
any other human being—what wonder, then, that
my heart should have gone out towards this
precious one almost, or quite, as it did toward my
own dear sister, sweet little May.   Yes, I could
love him, though I knew he was destined to come
between me and my rights.   Though fully aware
that he would inherit the Hamilton estates—that
property which should have been mine—there was
no envy in my heart toward him.   I did not blame
him for the crimes of his ancestor, and I loved him

with all the fervor of my nature. Yes, he was the sunlight of my life, during the long and weary days, weeks and months of the confinement which followed that relapse. He was my only solace and comfort then.

Wearily the lazy hours dragged themselves away, confined, as I was, a close prisoner to my room. The hours grew into days, days into weeks, and weeks into months, and still languid, helpless, I lay, longing once more to behold the outer world, and fretting at the close confinement I was enduring, but utterly unable to leave my room. Would I ever be able to go out again? It seemed doubtful, and, even now, I feel that to the kind and affectionate care of Mary Lake, and the cheering companionship of her lovely babe, I am indebted, under the Giver of all, for my restoration to health and strength.

But I must not lose sight of brother Frank during this long and gloomy illness. I received several letters from him during the period of my confinement to my room, for which my heart was full of gratitude to him, and which were a source of great comfort to me, for he was now my all. He was still at work in St. Mary's parish, and was doing very well. He often spoke of coming to see me, but the urgency of his duty to his employer prevented it. Ah! how I would have prized a visit from him, but if this could not be, it was still no little consolation to know that he thought of me.

The winter had passed away, and it was a bright

5

morning in spring when I was able to leave the
house for the first time for weeks. With what a
sense of exhilaration I gazed upon all nature, clad
in ' her gayest robes, and inhaled the soft, balmy
air, and listened to the music .of the feathered
songsters, as they made the air vocal with their
melody, I leave the reader to imagine. Ask the
wretched prisoner who, after months of weary confinement in his solitary cell, to which the feeblest
rays of the sunlight of God but seldom penetrate ;
where the walls reek with filth and dampness, and
the atmosphere is tainted with foul and noisome
smells ; where the only living creatures beside
himself are the moles, and rats, and vermin, with
which his gloomy abode is thronged ; who has almost felt hope die out within his breast, as day after
day passed into eternity, and brought with it no
hope of release, is suddenly restored to the blessed
sunlight of liberty and freedom, what his feelings
are—receive his answer, and you can form some
idea of my feelings at my release from the gloomy
bondage of pain and weakness which I had endured. I felt that God had bestowed upon me a
new lease of life, and my heart was full of thankfulness to Him who had thus far watched over and
protected me all along the journey of life. There
had been times when, in my heart of hearts, I had
wished that my life might end—that the voyage
so full of bitterness and woe as mine had been,
might be brought to a close ; but with the sense of
returning health and strength, after my prolonged

illness, came new thoughts, new hopes, and new aspirations. Yes, I would live, and would try to render my life a source of happiness to others, and thereby to myself—would endeavor so to live that when He should see fit to call me I would neither fear death as a monster, nor welcome him as a friend, but would receive him with the calm resignation of the Christian who obeys without reluctance the invitation of his Master to cease from his labors on earth and enter the paradise of eternal rest on high. Who of my readers, upon arising from a long and painful confinement to a sick bed, have not had the same feelings and formed the same resolutions—to be perhaps kept, and perhaps broken.

CHAPTER V.

How grateful to the sense of the patient who has
been for weeks, or it may be for months, confined
to the bed of sickness, consumed with fever, and
racked with pain, is the balmy air of spring,
especially in the latitude of central Georgia. It
seems to me almost impossible to conceive of anything more delicious, more invigorating, or more
health-giving, than the breezes which, during the
months of the season aptly termed the youth of
the year, come sweeping up from the Atlantic
Ocean, retaining in their journey of an hundred
miles, that peculiar freshness imparted to them by
the salt water, and ladened with the perfume of
the magnolia, the lilac and the thousand other
fragrant flowers for which central Georgia is so
justly celebrated. The system must be, indeed,
sadly shattered, which does not attain somewhat of strength and vigor under their kind
ministrations.

Thus it was with me. The days wore on, and
with each returning sun came additional feelings
of vigor and healthfulness. It must be borne in
mind, however, that, for the greater part of a year,
with but one brief interval, I had been a helpless
invalid, my system the seat and prey of disease,
my vitals almost consumed by the burning fever

which had been my constant attendant, and of
course it was to be expected that some time would
elapse before a system so reduced and disordered
would be restored to its normal condition as
regards strength and vigor. My improvement,
therefore, though sure and constant, was so slow
as at times to excite considerable impatience
in my mind. With renewed health had come the
desire, ten times intensified, to visit the grave
which I had traveled so far to water with my tears,
and it may be that my anxiety on this subject, to
some extent, retarded my convalescence.

It had been but short time from the day on
which I had been first permitted to visit the world
out doors and inhale the fresh air, after my long
confinement, when I received a shock which, for a
time, threatened to reduce me to the condition of an
invalid again. It will be remembered that in the
first interview between Mrs. Lake and myself, she
told me that her husband would not be at home for
a month. That month grew into two, before the
business which called him from home could be adjusted to his satisfaction: two months lengthened
themselves into three, and the business still proving
refractory, the whole winter was consumed before
it could finally be closed up. Mrs. Lake and I had,
therefore, been alone all the winter, and in the enjoyment of unrestrained intercourse with her, I had
almost insensibly forgotten my dependent and
lonely situation, but it was suddenly recalled most
vividly to my recollection.

A letter arrived from Captain Lake, written from a town but a short distance from us, in which he informed his wife he should follow the letter, and would be at home on the next day. My agitation, on being informed of this, by Mrs. Lake, was extreme and very painful, and, for a time threatened to prostrate me again. I could not divest my mind of the reflection that I was but a trespasser on his bounty, and in all probability a most unwelcome guest, though, in justice and equity, my right there was superior to his. Still the power was with him, and my old pet horror returned most vividly to my mind. "What if he should drive me from the house?" In my present state of health it would be fatal to me. Nay, even an unkind or harsh word, an angry look from him, would, in my enfeebled condition of both mind and body, be attended with the most serious consequences. In vain Mrs. Lake tried to cheer me with the assurance that my fears and apprehensions were utterly groundless—in vain she assured me that the Captain would make me welcome, and treat me with kindness. It was impossible for me to dismiss from my mind the recollections of the dislike, nay, almost hatred, which formerly existed between us, and now that he had the power to still further gratify that hatred, would he not be likely to exercise it? Besides the memory of the foul wrong he had already done me was ever present to my mind. There we were upon the very scene where that wrong had been perpetrated, and my presence would be a standing reproach and rebuke to him. What so natural as that he should ask to remove this living reproof of his infamy by sending me from the plantation?

These thoughts and apprehensions so worked upon me that I retired to my room and went to bed, feeling almost certain in my own mind that the morrow would again see me a homeless outcast, dependent upon the cold charities of the world, and of comparative strangers, for the poor boon of a shelter, and the food necessary to sustain life. My head ached violently, and, for a time, it seemed to me that I was again about to be attacked with the dreaded fever, so high was my state of mental excitement; but, as night came on my mind became somewhat more composed, and at length I sunk into a dreamy, uneasy slumber.

The next morning I awoke feeling very wretchedly. The excitement of the day before had prostrated my entire nervous system to a very great extent. I had a dull, nervous headache, and a sense of weariness and lassitude oppressed my entire frame to the last degree. I felt so badly that I did not rise from my bed at all, and, to tell the truth, I was not sorry that there was a sufficient excuse for me to retain my own room. I dreaded meeting Captain Lake, and was desirous of avoiding what I was certain would be a sad calamity to me as long as possible, never once reflecting that we must meet sooner or later, and that delay would only injure, instead of improving, my chances. I therefore kept my bed, only engaging aunt Silvie (who had been my constant nurse all through my illness) to tell me when the Captain came, and what he said in relation to me.

But the morning hours dragged slowly by, and no aunt Silvie came. I was feverish with anxiety, and speculated all the forenoon upon the probable result of the coming interview. Fancy still presented to me the most terrible consequences as likely to result from that interview, but having become somewhat accustomed to their contemplation, I no longer dreaded them as I did in the shock caused by the first announcement of the Captain's speedy return. Still I could not divest myself of a considerable degree of uneasiness; and my intense anxiety to have it over with, and know my fate, became almost insupportable as hour after hour passed away, and my faithful messenger came not.

It was almost noon when aunt Silvie came to my room with the intelligence that the Captain had made his appearance. How my heart beat as I listened to the few words in which she imparted this simple information. How I longed, yet dreaded, to inquire what the Captain had said about me, or whether he had been informed of my presence in his house. For some time I hesitated in painful indecision as to whether I should ask her anything, or wait until my fate chose to reveal itself, but at length my anxiety overmastered every other feeling, and I addressed my sable nurse thus:

" Well, aunt Silvie, does the Captain know I am
here, and what does he say about me ? "

" Yes, Miss Minnie, he knows ye is here. Missus
done told him when he most first in de house."

" What did he say when she told him ?   Did he
appear to be angry or displeased at my coming ?
What did he say ? "

" He did n't say much ob any t'ing.   He only
say, ' I t'ought she was dead long ago ;' and den
missus tell him you was berry sick, and came berry near dyin'. "

" But what else did he say, Silvie ?   Tell me all
he said."

" Why, Miss Minnie, he only said what I'se done
tole you, and nuthin' more."

" Did Mrs. Lake tell him how long I had been
here ? "

" Yes, missus she done tole him when you came
here, and how you was most dead when you comed,
and how she done tuck care ob you, and she did n't
tell him I tuck most ob de care of ye ; and den he
say, ' My dear, you done ebery t'ing just right ;'
and den missus she look kinder pleased, and den
dey talk about sumfin' else."

" Did he appear to be angry when she told him
how long I had been here? "

" No, Miss Minnie, he just say what I'se done
tole you."

" Did he say any thing about brother Frank ?"

" Yes, he ax where he was, and what he was
doing ; and missus done tole him all about him,

den he say he was glad he was doing so well."

" What else did he say, aunt Silvie?"

" He didn't say nothin' else." ·

" Aunt Silvie, do you think he will send me away, or will he 'let me stay here, where I have really more right than he has?"

" No, Miss Minnie, I do not t'ink he will send you away. Missis wouldn't let him do so if he done wanted to. I guess he will not say much to you if you don't say much to him."

At this moment Mrs. Lake came into the room and directed aunt Silvie to go and bring my dinner. As soon as the negress had fairly got out of the room she came close to me and kissing me, said:

" Well, Minnie, you have not been up to-day. The Captain has come and wishes to see you. Can you get up and come into the drawing-room for a short time? He will make you welcome, just as I told you he would."

" Please, Mrs. Lake, excuse me to-day. My head aches very badly, and I do not feel well and strong enough to meet the Captain to-day. Indeed I am not able to get up."

' " Perhaps your headache is caused in part by lying in bed so long, and it may relieve you to get up. Come, Minnie, you must come down stairs. The Captain wishes to see you, and besides he has brought home with him a handsome young widower, with whom he says you must get acquainted. Who knows but you may get him for a husband?" said she playfully

I was but just turned of sixteen, had never been in company any, or seen much of the world, and her remark about the handsome young widower brought the blood to my face. However, I insisted upon being excused, assuring her that my headache was too severe to admit of my rising. My real reason for declining to get up, however, was because I did not feel well enough, or strong enough, to encounter the agitation of meeting the Captain, and besides I knew that I looked like a ghost. Was it a tinge of ordinary female vanity that led me to avoid, if possible, meeting this handsome widower in my present wretched-looking condition? At any rate, I said to myself I could keep my bed, under pretense of illness, until he went away; but to my dismay, Mrs. Lake told me, the next moment, that he was going to stay for several days, and it might be for weeks. Of course, all thought of avoiding him had to be given up, but still I adhered to my resolution not to meet him, or the Captain that day. Mrs. Lake finally, seeing that it was useless to urge the matter, gave it up, and I was left alone; and right glad was I to be in company of my own thoughts once more.

Though still somewhat in doubt as to the manner in which Captain Lake would treat me, I anticipated much from the kindly feeling which I knew Mrs. Lake had for me, and from her intercession in my behalf, and I felt much more hopeful of my future than had been the case for a long time.

Could it be that Providence had meted out to me the full measure of my afflictions, and that the residue of my life was to be passed in comparative comfort? Time alone can tell; but at any rate, after the interview with Mrs. Lake, just referred to, my heart was more at peace than it had been for years. That night I slept soundly, and awoke next morning very much refreshed, and feeling much stronger than on the day previous.

It was a lovely day, and I dressed myself and went down stairs. I did not see Captain Lake or the widower till tea time, however. I did not get up in time for breakfast, and immediately after the morning meal they went to the city to transact some business, whence they did not return until long after the dinner hour was past. I was in my own room when the bell rang for tea, and upon going down was greeted by the Captain with a kindness which was as unexpected as it was pleasant and grateful to my feelings. His welcome was not merely cordial, it was really kind and affectionate, and in the grateful surprise of the moment, I for a short time forgot the great wrong he had done me, and my heart warmed toward him in spite of myself. How much of his kindness was produced by my spiritual, almost unearthly appearance, how much by some motive he had in view, and how much by genuine sympathy and affection, I leave each reader to judge for himself in the light of the most truthful history.

I was next presented to Mr. Giles, " the hand-

some young widower," as Mary Lake had called
him; but, it being almost my first introduction to
any one, I was so much embarrassed that I hardly
dared look at him, or even raise my eyes from the
floor. Immediately after this ceremony we took
our seats at the tea table, and I then had an
opportunity to observe him more closely. I did
not think him very handsome, nor was he bad
looking; perhaps better looking than the average
of mankind. He was of medium height and well
proportioned, neither too stout or too slender, his
form was erect and manly; he had auburn hair,
blue eyes, light complexion, and his countenance
expressed more than ordinary intelligence. Altogether he was one to attract a second glance from
any one who was as susceptible to the effect of
good looks as I was. He was an excellent conver-
sationalist, capable of pleasing almost any society
into which he might be thrown, and his elegant
manners, and the delicate little attentions he paid
me during the meal, made a very favorable impression upon me.

Before we left the table, Caroline, the nurse,
came in with Mrs. Lake's baby. She had taken
more than usual pains in attiring him, and the
care with which he was dressed, added to his
natural loveliness, made him as sweet an appearing child as I ever saw in my life. When baby
had been sufficiently admired, caressed, and com-
mented upon to satisfy even as fond and proud a
mother as Mary Lake, Mr. Giles went on to speak

of his own babe and his other children. He had been married when very young, and had three children, all boys. The youngest was only about six months old, and had been deprived of a mother's care almost from the time of his birth, his mother having died when he was only about a week old. The others were aged, respectively, about two and a half and four years, and all were sadly in need of that care and attention which only a mother could give them.

Thus the evening wore away in pleasant and interesting conversation, interspersed from time to time with music, and when, at its close, I retired to my room, my heart was lighter, and I felt happier than I had for many a long day. It was late, however, before my eyes were closed in sleep. Mr. Giles had been quite attentive to me during the entire evening, and, as these were the first attentions I had ever received from one of the opposite sex, my mind was in a perfect whirl of pleasant excitement. Already, in imagination, I saw myself the wife of Eugene Giles, the mistress of his establishment, and the mother of his boys. He was in comfortable circumstances, so far as worldly property was concerned. I was passionately fond of children, and knew I could love him best; and, altogether, fancy might have presented a much more unpleasant fate to my mental vision. I did not love or dislike him, nor had I any reason to suppose that the vision presented to me would ever be fulfilled, but it must be remembered that

I was then ignorant of the world and its ways, and to my simple ideas the attentions which every gentleman naturally pays to a lady were indicative of love and speedy marriage. Let not the reader blame my simplicity or laugh at my ignorance. I have since learned to appreciate such attentions at their true value.

From this time I date a new era in my life. I had long been accustomed to regard myself as a bark drifting helplessly on the ocean of life, with no one to care for me, or to interest themselves in my fate; no one who cared in the slightest what became of me, without hope, or end, or aim, or inducement to live, and had become careless as to what became of myself. Now all was changed. I felt that I was no longer the helpless child of destiny, but was a woman, with something to live for, some end to accomplish; and though it was not entirely clear to me what my future was to be, still I was not alone in the world, a mere useless atom of creation. That first evening spent with Mr. Giles, in Mrs. Lake's parlor, was to me the birth of a new life. I went to the tea-table that evening a careless, aimless, and helpless child; I went to my room a woman in spirit, thought, and action, with all a woman's hopes, fears and aspirations developed within my heart.

Time passed on, and Captain Lake and his wife continued to treat me with the utmost kindness. No allusion was made to my leaving there, and in a few weeks I came to be regarded, and to regard

myself, as a member of the family, and never allowed myself to reflect what would be the end of
this season of comfort and contentment, if, indeed,
it should ever end but with life. During all this
time my health was constantly improving; and restored vigor of body, as well as contentment of
mind, with plenty of air and exercise, were fast removing all traces of my late fearful and prolonged
illness. The wasted form and haggard countenance, the hallow, lusterless eye and colorless
cheek, and the halting, uncertain step of convalescence were rapidly being replaced by the rounded
form, the bounding step, and the bloom and freshness of youth.

Mr. Giles, meantime, had been very constant in
his attentions to me. For several days after that
first evening he had remained an inmate of the
Lake mansion, during which time he constantly
sought my society, and as constantly bestowed upon me the most tender and delicate attentions—
attentions which I was only too willing to receive.
Did I wish to walk about the grounds? His arm
was ever at my service. If I wished to ride out, it
was he who ordered the carriage and drove the
spirited horses; he was my constant attendant in
every scheme of exercise and pleasure, and never
wearied in caring for my comfort and happiness.
Such attentions won upon my feelings, and I soon
learned to look upon him as something more than
a friend, and to anticipate the fulfillment of the

vision which fancy had presented to me as I lay upon my couch after that first evening.

At length he had concluded certain negotiations, in which he was engaged, for the purchase of a livery stable in Atlanta, and the time had arrived when he must cease to be an inmate of the Lake mansion, and go to the city and take charge of his property, and superintend the business in person. I hated to see him go, for I had become very much attached to him, and though no word had been spoken between us, I felt assured in my heart that he loved me. But there was no help for it, and he went away, and for some time I saw but little of him. He came out occasionally, however, to see us; then his visits grew more and more frequent, until at last I learned to look for him almost every day, and he very seldom disappointed me. He became a constant visitor, and never appeared (as I really never was) so happy as when he was by my side, engaged in animated conversation, or reading to me from some interesting book. He frequently spent nearly the whole day at the plantation, and a marriage between us at an early day came to be a subject of general conversation among the servants, but still he had not spoken.

One beautiful evening, we were, as usual, seated beside each other, on a low bench, in the garden, admiring the beauty of the setting sun. For some time we sat in silence. "The fiery orb" had disappeared from view, twilight was deepening around us, and still neither spoke or moved. With me,

6

memory was busy with the gloomy past, and I could not help contrasting that fact with my present happy condition. Suddenly he caught my hand, and poured forth into my ear the oft-told tale of love, and asked me to be his wife. He told me how lonely he had been since the death of his wife— how his children needed a mother's care—how desolate the world seemed to him, and begged me to cheer his loneliness and brighten all his future by giving him the right to call me his. As for his ability to take care of me, he was in good circumstances, could give me a good home, and had an abundance to maintain me in comfort, and even luxury—would I consent? I was startled, and told him I was too young to marry; that we knew but little of each other, and ought to wait until we were better acquainted; that Captain Lake was my guardian, and I did not know what he would say to our marriage. To this he replied that he had already spoken to the Captain, and had his permission to make me his wife. My other reasons he met with a lover's argument, and a lover's impetuosity, and still implored me to accede to his wishes. During this scene, I was trying, as well as I could under the circumstances, and amid the excitement which I naturally felt, to analyze my feelings toward him. I thought I did not love him as I ought before becoming his wife, yet he was dearer to me than any one else of my acquaintance; his earnestness sort of terrified me, and when he said, "Say, Minnie, will you be a mother to my children?" I tried to answer him, but could not—the words choked me, and I remained silent, but did not withdraw my hand from his grasp. He waited a short time for an answer, but I could not speak—and when he said, "Shall I take silence for consent?" I only looked up into his eyes. He was answered; and, clasping me in his arms, he kissed me with all a lover's fire and ardor—the first kiss I had ever received from him.

And thus it was settled that I was to become his wife—to give up my freedom, my individuality, my all, into his keeping. Oh! could some kind angel have lifted, for one moment, the vail which shrouded the dim future, and have shown me the misery, shame, and wretchedness, which were to be the results of that first kiss, methinks I would sooner have leaped into an abyss of living fire than have suffered his lips to come in contact with mine. But in the inscrutable mysteries of God's providence the future is wisely hidden from our view, and fortunate it is for us it is so. At the time, my only thought was that I had at last found rest; that the troubles and sorrows which had thus far beset my life were now at an end; that in the future I was to know nothing but peace and quiet, and recur to the past only as some horrid dream or nightmare. How far my imagination was from the reality, let future pages disclose.

From this time I saw more of my lover than ever before. He was with me almost constantly, and was unwearied in his efforts to please me and

gratify my every wish. He was exceedingly
solicitous to anticipate. and supply every desire of
my heart, and never seemed so happy as when he
was doing something for me, or in some way con-
tributing to my comfort and happiness. Such
earnest and unwearied devotion could not fail to
produce its effect, and, in time, I learned to love
Eugene Giles with all the force of my nature. My
disposition was naturally very affectionate and
tender. It is a necessity with me to have something to love, and hence, as is the case with all
similiar natures, when love is once aroused, it
absorbs and overwhelms every other feeling of my
soul. Thus it was with my feelings toward my
betrothed. I soon grew to be lonely and unhappy
in his absence, and to sigh constantly for his
return; but when by his side, all thoughts of
sorrow were forgotten, and no one, it seemed to me,
could be happier than I was.

I also found great pleasure in the society of his
children, whom he often brought to see me,
frequently leaving them with me the entire day.
As has already been stated, I am passionately
fond of children, and these were, I think, the
sweetest little boys I ever saw in my life. Besides,
they were the children of him to whom I had
pledged my hand, and whom I loved with all the
fervor and intensity of which my soul was capable.
What wonder that I should have dearly loved, and
should have been so happy in their society ?

But time passed, and my lover began to grow

impatient to have the day set for our marriage.
With the timidity natural to a young girl, I still
insisted upon a postponement, and, whenever he
broached the subject, managed to put him off in
some way, until at length he became too importu-
nate to be resisted, and with the sanction of
Captain Lake, the 7th of September ensuing, being
my seventeenth birthday, was fixed for our union.
We were to be married at the Episcopal church in
Atlanta, and it was arranged that after the wedding
we were to go to the city of New York, and other
places in the North, and to return in about three
months. Meantime our house was to be fitted
up for our occupancy, and immediately upon
our return we were to commence housekeeping
in Atlanta.

It would no doubt be very interesting to my
lady readers—at any rate, men say we have unbounded curiosity in such matters—if I were to
describe the bustle and confusion which pervaded
the Lake mansion during the few weeks which
intervened before my wedding day—the laces, the
satin, berages, and other goods which were brought
into the house to be made up into wedding-dresses,
traveling-dresses, and all other kinds of dresses—
the small army of dress-makers and seamstresses
who were employed in the house to work up all
this finery; but the task would be a hopeless one,
and I forbear. Brother Frank, too, was to be
sent for, for I could not think of being married in
his absence, and without his blessing. Captain

Lake kindly took charge of this part of the programme, and, accordingly, informed Frank of the entire contemplated arrangement, and in due time received a reply from him, saying he would be present at the wedding, and would then accompany us to New York on his way to California, whither he had determined to emigrate, the California fever being then at its height.

At length the eventful day arrived, and a lovelier day never dawned upon this earth than that upon which I became Mrs. Eugene Giles. There was not a cloud to be seen in the skies; the air was mild and balmy, and came to us in a gentle breeze ladened with the perfume of the gayest flowers of a Southern autumn; the orchards were laden with a bounteous crop of fruit, now ripening in the mellow sunlight; the earth was groaning under the burden of a bounteous crop of corn, cotton, and other products of the sunny fields of the South; and all nature seemed swelling with thankfulness to the Great Giver of all good. Need I say that my heart partook of the general emotion, shared the great voice of nature, and that I was that day the happiest of all the happy throng I saw around me?

I trembled a little when we stood before the holy man of God to promise the words which were to bind us together for a lifetime, but it was not with fear or dread. A deep sense of the solemnity of the act we were performing, a vivid appreciation of the immense responsibilities I was assum-

ing, rested upon me, and caused a sort of shuddering agitation lest I should be unable to fully discharge those responsibilities; and when, in answer
to the question of the minister, I promised to be
a good and faithful wife to him who stood by my
side, to love and honor him so long as we both
should live, in my heart of hearts I ratified the
solemn promise, and uttered a secret vow to my
Maker that it should be kept in spirit as well as
in letter, and that I would be to my husband all
that my obligation implied. If every girl who
becomes a wife had as full an appreciation of the
solemnity of the step they take in so doing as I
had; if they as fully realized, and as religiously
observed the obligations imposed by the marriage
contract as I did, we should have fewer divorce
cases, less unhappy homes and domestic quarrels,
and fewer instances of husbands abandoning
their wives and children for the false and fleeting
charms of licentious dissipation. I by no means
excuse men for their derelictions in this respect,
but I most firmly believe that, in many instances,
they are driven to this course of conduct through
the fatal mistakes of those who should be their
guardian angels in the hour of temptation, but
who, not understanding, or not regarding the
obligations of the marriage contract, drive them
from the homes where they should find happiness to the haunts of dissipation, in search of
those enjoyments which are elsewhere denied to
them. To do this it is not necessary that the

wife should be cross or quarrelsome or peevish,
though these are, doubtless, very potent agencies
for evil. But if she ceases to render home attractive, and pleasant, and cheerful; if she ceases to
practice on the husband the thousand little arts
by which she won the attention of the lover,
my word for it, that wife will, when it is too late,
and when her husband has been irreclaimably
driven from her side, realize the full force of the
mistake she has made. It is true there are men
so debased by nature and early education as to be
incapable of reformation, but in a majority of
instances the wife has the remedy in her own hands,
and if she fails to apply it, she will, in time, awake
from her lethargy to find herself the most miserable of human beings—a despised, neglected and
forsaken wife.

But to return from this digression. The ceremony was performed, and we returned to the Lake
mansion for dinner, after which we were to go to
Atlanta, for the purpose of starting on our wedding
tour. It was a gay party which sat down to
dinner that day in Mrs. Lake's dining room.
The dinner was excellent; every one was in the
very best of humor, and mirth, wit and merriment
were the order of the day, and each one vied with
the others in doing honor to the happy groom and
his bride, and to our hospitable entertainers.
Wine, too, lent its aid to increase the hilarity, and
for a time the demon Care was entirely banished
from our midst. But the dinner at last ended, the

old family carriage was at the door, trunks were
packed and loaded upon the clumsy-looking
vehicle, adieus were hastily spoken, kisses and
promises to write were exchanged, and we entered
the carriage and were rolled away in the direction
of Atlanta.

CHAPTER VI.

Our journey to New York, though devoid of any incidents worthy of note, was to me very tedious and tiresome. My husband was unremitting in his attention to my comfort, and did all he possibly could to relieve the tediousness of travel. But I was unaccustomed to journeying, and it was a very great relief to me when we at last found ourselves in the city of New York. We took rooms at the St. Nicholas Hotel, and retired very early, but I was too weary to sleep, and for a long time after my husband had yielded to the influence of the drowsy god, I lay awake and contrasted my present situation with what it was a year and a half ago. Then I was a kitchen servant in the family of a Southern aristocrat; now I was the honored wife of a man of sufficient wealth to maintain me in ease and luxury, and who had already shown that his disposition was entirely commensurate with his ability to provide everything necessary for my comfort. Was I not a happy woman? Loved, petted and caressed, as I was, by one whom I thought the perfection of earthly nobility; loving him with all the affection of which my soul was capable; possessed of the means to gratify every rational wish; what more had I to desire?

But there was one thing for which I would will-

ingly have bartered all I possessed. It will be
remembered that my father had provided, by his
will, for the proper education of all his children;
but, through the fraud and dishonesty of our guardian, the benefit of this provision had been withheld from us. It must be observed that at the
South we had not the benefit of the Northern system of free schools, by which every one, however
poor, is enabled to obtain a sufficient education for
all the ordinary purposes of life; and the kind old
uncle with whom my youthful days had been spent
was too poor to afford me any advantages in this
respect. Hence I had grown up with scarcely any
education at all, and now I felt the deprivation
more keenly than I ever had before. I had never
ventured to tell Mr. Giles of my deplorable ignorance; though frequently intending to do so, a
sense of shame had always kept me quiet, and I
had waited for "a more convenient season," ever
dreading the loss of respect, and consequently of
his affection, when he should learn how ignorant I
was. But I knew, of course, he must find it out
some time; and to have been able to avoid this
discovery I would have given anything save only
his love. But the discovery was even nearer than
I thought.

To such an extent had my education been neglected that, though I could read a little, I could
not write a single word, not even my own name.
Frank could write a little, so that it could be read
by any one accustomed to reading writing; but I

did not know the form of the first letter.   Judge,
then, of my dismay when, the next morning after
our arrival in New York, my husband came to me
with pen, ink, and paper, and said:

"Come, little wife ; let me see what a sweet, pretty letter you can write to Captain and Mrs. Lake,
just to inform them of our safe arrival here, and
how we feel."

"My dear husband," said I, "I do not feel able
to write to-day. I have a very severe headache
and wish you would write for me."

Heaven forgive my duplicity. I was still afraid
to tell him I could not write ; but my brother, who
happened to be in the room, came to my assistance.
Said he :

"Allow me to speak for my sister. Eugene, do
you know anything of Minnie's past life, or of our
history ? "

"Nothing, except what I have learned from Captain Lake. I have never asked Minnie, or any one
else any questions."

"And what has Captain Lake told you ? "

"He has told me that he was your step-father;
that you have both lived with an aged uncle and
aunt since infancy; and that, since their death,
Minnie had been living in his family."

"Was that all he told you ? "

"That was about all."

"Well," said he, rising, and speaking excitedly ;
"he forgot to tell you the most important part. He
forgot to tell you that every dollar he calls his ;

every dollar he is worth; the plantation that he
lives upon; the servants who till his lands; even
the carriage which bore us to Atlanta : all were
our father's. That, by the terms of our father's
will, he was appointed our guardian; that he married our mother; that he cheated us out of our
property, and drove us from home. Even the
money which our father's will provided for our education was, by this man, appropriated to his own
use, and we were left to grow up in ignorance.
Your wife, my sister, to-day can not write her own
name; but it is not her fault that such is the case."

"But it seems almost incredible to me. I have
regarded the Captain as an honorable man. Is
this all true that you have been telling me?"

"It is gospel truth, every word of it. For that I
pledge my sacred word and honor."

"How was it about you living with your uncle?"

"That is true. When our guardian, by his cruelty and abuse, drove us from home, having no
other place to go, we went to live with an aged uncle in New Orleans, who was too poor to send us
to school, and Captain Lake did nothing for us;
and thus we grew up without any education."

"Frank," said my husband, "I thank you for
telling me all this. It has opened my eyes to some
things I could never before fully comprehend; but
now I see it all."

Judge of my feelings while this conversation was
going on. I reclined upon a lounge, my face covered with my hands, and trembled for the result

of this exposition. I had, to a certain extent, deceived my husband, and I wondered if he would love me less on account of that deception. But I had not long to wait. He came over to the lounge where I lay, gently drew my hands from my face, and, stooping down, kissed my cheek—

"My dear wife," said he; "how you have been wronged. Why did you not tell me before?"

"Oh! Genie, I was afraid to tell you. I was afraid of losing your love if you knew how ignorant I was."

" You should have had more confidence in your husband. Of course, I could not love you less for that which was your misfortune, and not in any sense your fault."

"I should have told you some time, but I did not want you to know it now."

"Well, my Minnie, never mind it now. I will educate you myself, will teach you to read, and will set you copies and teach you to write; and the world will never know of your situation at this time. And, Frank," said he, turning to my brother, "if you will give up going to the gold regions I will send you to school, and you shall have a good education, after which you shall study a profession. What say you?"

" You are very kind, indeed, but I do not feel willing to alter my plans. I have been all my life dependent upon some one else, and now there is a chance of making myself independent, and I do not feel like neglecting it."

"But, consider, Frank, how much better it will be for you to stay at home, and, after obtaining a good education, you will then have an opportunity of rising to distinction in some honorable profession; while, if you go to California, your education will probably never be any better than it now is. Besides, think of the dangers and hardships you must encounter in that wild region—all of which will be avoided by the plan I propose. Think well of what I say, before you decide to reject my offer."

"I thank you most heartily for your kind offer, but my mind is made up. I should like to have a good edudation, but can not give up the chance of becoming independent. As for the dangers and hardships of which you speak, they do not dishearten me in the least, but rather confirm me in my determination. I am firmly resolved to go."

Argument and entreaty were utterly unavailing to move him, or to shake the resolution he had formed; and, although Eugene used all the art he was master of to induce him to stay, and although I seconded the efforts of my husband with all the eloquence of affection, we found it impossible to change his determination. Go he would, and go he did.

When we finally gave up all hopes of inducing him to forego the journey he had planned, we set ourselves earnestly to enjoying the few days we could yet spend in his society. We visited every place of note in the city, and saw and admired all the works of art which abound in such profusion there. But while we were thus enjoying ourselves, we did not neglect the very important duty of furnishing brother with everything which could conduce to his comfort or safety on his journey. I superintended in person the preparation of his outfit, and, by the aid of some valuable hints received from an old hunter of the far West, who was to be his companion on the perilous trip, my brother was at length provided with everything which care, ingenuity and affection could suggest to render his journey pleasant.

From New York we went to Boston, and visited the numerous historic sites with which that region abounds. We went to Lexington, and stood upon the green which was moistened by the life-blood of the first martyrs of the Revolution; we visited the classic grounds of Bunker Hill, and gazed with admiration upon the majestic shaft which commemorates the sturdy resistance made by the untrained militia of the colonies to the veterans of England; we climbed the frowning heights of Dorchester, and stood upon the place occupied by the artillery of Washington, and which finally compelled General Howe to evacuate the city; and paid our respects to every spot which the incidents of those times have made dear to the American heart; after which we began to talk about returning to our home in Georgia.

But before returning, I had a duty to perform. My dear father was lying in the graveyard at Philadelphia, far removed from all his friends, and I had

reason to suppose his grave was in a sadly neglected condition. To visit that sacred tomb, and see
that it was properly cared for, was my duty ; and,
accordingly, we proceeded by steamer from Boston
to Philadelphia, and once more I stood beside that
sacred shrine of a daughter's affections. I found
my worst anticipations fully realized. The resting-
place of my father's remains was overgrown with
grass and weeds, and the slab of wood which was
his only monument was so defaced by time that it
was with difficulty we could determine by the in-
scription thereon that we really stood beside his
grave. I was shocked to find it in such a condition,
and at once went to work to remove these traces of
neglect. Before we left the city the ground was
cleared of weeds, and beautifully planted with evergreens and roses, while a tall and stately column
of marble appropriately commemorated the virtues
of my father and the undying affection of his children.

And there I parted with my only brother. The
time had come when he must proceed to New York
to join the party with which he was going to California, while my destiny lay in the opposite direction. Beside the grave of our departed father we
held our parting interview, exchanged our kindly
wishes for each other's future welfare, and renewed
our pledge of never-ending affection, after which he
wended his way to the steamer in which he had
taken passage for New York, while I returned to
our rooms at the hotel. This parting with the last

member of my family was painful in the last degree, for I felt that I should never see him again. A journey to California was then something more than the mere pleasure trip it has since become, and it seemed to me that the parting was forever. Still, it was not like former times when I had parted with him. I was no longer alone in the world, but was blessed with a kind and indulgent husband, who would spare no pains to render my lot a happy one.

The next day we bid adieu to the city of Brotherly Love, and turned our course toward the city of Atlanta, which was to be our future home. Our journey thither was unattended with any incidents worthy of note, and we finally reached the Lake mansion on the fourteenth day of February, after an absence of five months, which had been, to me, productive of more real happiness than had ever fallen to my lot in the same space of time. Each day of our absence had been productive of some new scene of pleasure, while the kind and delicate attentions of my husband had left me nothing to desire. I really thought that I, who had so long been the plaything of fortune, had at last reached the haven of rest, and that my future life was to be as pleasant as the past had been miserable. Poor, blind mortal that I was. I could not discern in the horizon the gathering storm which was to make my future life a desert indeed, and by the side of which the past was to be as calm as a May morning. But let us not anticipate.

Our reception at the Lake mansion was more than cordial—it was kindness itself. Captain Lake and his lovely wife met us at the gate, and greeted us in the most affectionate manner, the children shouted their welcome at the tops of their little voices, while the negroes, clad in their holiday attire, and displaying broad rows of ivory, stood at a respectful distance and indulged in the heartiest expressions of delight at the return of the wanderers. Aunt Silvie, however, was not satisfied with this formal display of welcome. Scarcely had Mrs. Lake imprinted her kiss of welcome on my lips, when my old nurse rushed from the group of servants, clasped me in her arms, and covered me with kisses, calling me her child, her darling, and invoking an endless torrent of blessing on my head. I was not a little moved at this evidence of affection on the part of my old nurse. But it was not at all surprising. My acquaintance with these simple children of nature has taught me that they are more devoted in their attachments, and more intense in their affections, than the more refined, but more cold-blooded white race. And this demonstration of aunt Silvie's was but the natural outburst of her affection for one whom she had reared through the tender years of infancy as her own child.

We passed a very pleasant evening in the society of our friends, during which it was arranged that we should remain with them as their guests for a few weeks, until our house in the city could be prepared for our reception, when we would go to housekeeping by ourselves. And thus passed the evening of our return from our wedding tour.

CHAPTER VII.

THERE are times in all our lives when the hours seem to pass on leaden wings; when our impatience to reach some ardently-desired event so far outstrips even the marvelous speed of Time as to cause us to wonder that it should move so slowly, and to seek, but in vain, for expedients to hasten its flight. Witness the lover, as he watches the sun declining in the heavens, and giving place to the "queenly orb of night" which is to light him to the presence of his mistress; or that mistress, as she awaits, in the accustomed trysting place, the coming of him who is dearer to her than life itself, and in whose absence the hours seem heavy indeed. Who has not experienced this feeling of impatience at some time or other, and not once only, but on numerous occasions?

Such were my feelings during the four or five weeks which followed our return from the North. It had been settled that we should remain at the Lake mansion while our house in the city was undergoing some necessary repairs, and being refitted and refurnished, when we were to go to housekeeping. My impatience to become the mistress of my own establishment was so great that it seemed to me the necessary preparations

would never be completed. Almost daily I was
in the city, watching the workmen with childish
impatience, fretting at what seemed to me their
frightfully slow progress, and foolishly but vainly
wishing that I could do something to hasten the
work. My anxiety was so intense as to reach
almost fever heat, and each night I retired to rest
almost worn out with impatience and excitement.
I really believe that if this state of mental emotion
had continued much longer I should have suc-
cumbed to it, and been really sick; but all things
earthly must have an end, and so it was with the
preparation of our house. At length it was decided
that everything was ready, and we were to take
possession of the house on the following day; and
that night I was perfectly wild with childish excitement and eager anticipation, and the next
morning I could scarcely wait for breakfast before
starting for our new home.

In the fitting up and furnishing of our house I
found fresh proofs of the kindness of my husband's
disposition and of the depth and sincerity of his
love for me. He had superintended everything—I
was so much of a child, and so much excited, that
I was incapable of rendering much assistance—
and everything was arranged in the most convenient, comfortable, and even luxurious manner.
Besides the magnificent and luxurious style in
which the house was finished, Eugene had purchased from Captain Lake, my old servants—Tom,
Silvie, and Caroline—solely because he knew that

it would afford me satisfaction to have them around me. Could any one have done more to gratify my every wish than he had done?

I shall never forget the first meal I got in our own house. The Empress of the Russias could not be prouder than I was as I sat at the head of the table, opposite my husband, poured his tea for him, and duly assumed the throne as mistress of my own household. I strongly suspect that my houskeeping, at that time, was not of the very first order—it would be strange if it were, considering the circumstances of my past history; but, nevertheless, I was the mistress of our own elegant mansion; and, as busy memory compared and contrasted the present with the past, my heart filled with gratitude toward him who called me by the name of wife, and who had wrought so great a change in my apparent destiny. Need it be added that my love for him was, if possible, intensified by these reflections, and that I felt as though the devotion of an entire life would be but a small return for his kindness?

Our children, too (for I now called them ours), were a constant source of delight to me. Willie was now five years old; Frankie was past three, and Eddie was about fourteen months; and I do not think I ever saw more quiet or better dispositioned children than they were. But my especial pet and favorite was Eddie. He was then just in, what is to me, the most interesting period of childhood—was just beginning to lisp "papa" and "mamma," and learning to walk. Many an hour did I spend in training and guiding his timid, halting, staggering footsteps, and the exercise endeared him to me almost beyond description. He was a most lovely child; he had large, blue eyes, light curly hair, and as fair and clear a complexion as I ever saw. In training and developing his infantile mind and person, I found ample employment of the most pleasing and interesting character. Ah! how happy I was during these days.

One year and four months passed away after our marriage, and I had another object to which my affection was directed. On the first day of January, I presented my husband with a most precious New Year's gift; a fine, lovely, healthy daughter. She was the very image of her father, and, it seemed to me, was the handsomest child I ever beheld. Doubtless all young mothers think the same of their first-born, but be that as it may, my cup of happiness was now full, and I could think of nothing more to desire or wish for in this world. My husband was all kindness, and was, in my eyes, perfection itself. My home was one of the most comfortable and luxurious that the imagination could conceive, and I was the proud mother of the loveliest child upon which the sun ever shone. Was not my lot a happy one?

But, alas! how true it is that earth's highest pleasures are but ephemeral in their existence, and that the sweetest joys are shortest in their stay.

It is the common lot of mankind that at the moment when we are elevated to the highest pinnacle of happiness, we are nearest the brink of the awful abyss of misery and black despair; and my experience has been no exception to this general rule of our fallen humanity. In a few short months I was to be prostrated from my throne of happiness into a gulf of misery more terrible than any that in my checkered life I had been called to endure.

The first terrible blow was the loss of my precious little wild flower. The angel, whose company I had fondly hoped to keep during the residue of my pilgrimage below, was too bright for earth, and was summoned by the Father to her home in the skies, leaving my heart desolate. Upon the breezes of April the angel of Death spread his wing, and summoned my cherub to join the bright throng above, and the showers of May brought their wealth of flowers and strewed them upon the grave of our darling. Her life was brief, but it was not bitter; she was spared the sufferings and trials which must inevitably have attended her more mature years; and though my heart was wrung with anguish as I listened to the dull sound of the clods falling upon her little coffin, I can now look up to heaven and say, "Thy will be done." My subsequent misfortunes and sorrows have taught my heart a lesson of resignation which I did not then feel.

Upon my husband the loss of our child seemed

to fall, if possible, with more crushing weight than it did upon myself. It is not usual for the father to experience the same degree of love and affection for the offspring as the mother—it does not seem so much a part of him as of the mother, who has given a portion of her very life to bring it into existence, and his heart does not, therefore, go out toward the child with the same intense yearning as that of the mother. A father may give to his children all the love of which he is capable, but as compared with the intense, selfish devotion of a mother toward her young, it is, in general, but feeble. But in the case of our Mary, who was so early taken away from us, I was surprised to find that my husband felt her loss even more keenly than I did. It hardly seemed possible that my grief could have been excelled; but while my sorrow was as a tempest to my soul, his was a perfect tornado; and I think it was partially owing to the intensity of his grief that my husband was led into the commission of acts, soon to be recorded, which gave fresh poignancy to the anguish we already endured.

What a grievous mistake it is—what a sin against God and humanity—what worse than folly, when he whose soul is borne down by the weight of sorrow turns for consolation to the ephemeral and blighting excitement of dissipation; to the forgetfulness of intoxication, the enchantment of the gaming table, and the forced and senseless mirth of bacchanalian revelries. No man

ever did, or ever will, secure immunity from sorrow
by resorting to such agencies as these. The poor
wretch who resorts to these means to get rid of
his burden of sorrow, may succeed for the moment
in diverting his mind from its contemplation, but
the relief is only temporary, and when reason is
restored, and the mind returns to the contemplation of its grief, its pangs are but intensified by
the very means used to arrest them; for to the
former sorrow is superadded the recollection of
grievous wrong committed to get rid of it. Nor is
the effort to obtain even temporary relief at all
times successful. Numerous instances are recorded of parties who have resorted to dissipation
to drown sorrow, and who, in the height of a
debauch—perhaps in the midst of some bacchanalian song or obscene jest—have suddenly been
arrrested, and the words frozen upon their lips by
the vivid recollection of their great sorrow. Better,
a thousand times better, endure with submissive
meekness the most painfully afflictive dispensations of our Father's providence, and thus rob
them, in great part, of their sting, than to endeav-
or to drive away their memory by means which,
in the end will only increase their power in a ten-
fold degree. But to this philosophy and this
reasoning my husband, like thousands of others,
was a stranger, and he fell into the, alas! too
frequent, but ever delusive and unsuccessful attempt, to drive away his sorrow by dissipation.

It was but a short time after the funeral of our

little girl until I began to perceive he was becoming irregular in his habits. Before that sad event
he never staid from home later than until about
ten o'clock at night; now I often sat and watched
and waited for him until midnight, one o'clock,
two, and even as late as three o'clock. Many and
many a time have I thus watched for him for long
hours after the children were asleep, almost vainly
striving to crush back the tears which would well
up from my burdened heart to my eyes, but which I
sternly repressed in order to prevent him, when he
should come, from knowing how I had been weeping.
Vain were all my efforts to divine, satisfactorily
to my own mind, the reason for this change in him;
but still I forebore to complain, and always greeted
him with a smile, a kiss, and all the demonstrations of affection which had marked our happiest
days. And still matters went on from bad to
worse; he still became more and more irregular in
his hours, and I began to detect, in his breath, the
scent of the noxious fumes of alcoholic drinks.

Oh! the misery of those nights of watching no
human tongue can tell. Night after night, when
the children were in bed and fast asleep, and the
servants had all retired to rest, have I, the only
waking being about the house, sat, and alone
watched for my wayward husband, frequently pro-
longing my vigils until the coming day would gild
the eastern skies, and still no Eugene would come.
Often, after passing the entire night in watching,
have I gone down alone to my cheerless breakfast,

my eyes red and swollen with weeping and wake-
fulness, while my heart throbbed with an anguish
which none can know, save those who have endured
the same fearful trials. Have you, my lady reader,
ever endured such trials as these? If not, may
God in his mercy spare you this great agony.

Never shall I forget the first time he came home
in a state of intoxication. It was long past the
midnight; the moon, which was at its full, was
shining brightly, and made it almost as light as
day, and the stillness and serenity of the air seemed enough to hush every display of human passion.
I was sitting by the window, gazing out upon the
brilliancy of the landscape, which shone like silver
in the radiant light of the moon, when suddenly,
borne to my ears upon the breeze of the night, came
a succession of sounds which almost caused my
blood to curdle, and my hair to stand erect with
horror. I do not think that ever in my life have I
heard such frightful oaths and such shocking, blas-
phemous obscenity as disturbed the quiet of that
lovely night. As soon as I recovered a little from
the first shock of horror, I opened the window, and,
bending eagerly out, endeavored to ascertain the
source from whence proceeded the frightful sounds.

A gang of half a dozen drunken men were approaching the house, and in their midst, almost
utterly helpless from the extent of his intoxication,
and supported by two of his companions, who were
not quite so far gone as himself, was the well-
known form of my husband. From him and his

boon companions had proceeded the sounds which had so thrilled my soul with terror. As I took in, at a glance, the situation, and the fell import of the scene before me forced itself upon my comprehension, I uttered a cry as though a dagger had pierced my heart, and rushing to the door, opened it just in time to receive the helpless form of my husband from his supporters. Once inside the door, and missing their support, he fell at full length upon the hall floor, where he lay, utterly helpless and unable to rise. It was a task requiring all my strength to get him into the room, undress him and put him to bed, but it was at length accomplished, and I seated myself at the window to pass the remainder of the night, for sleep I could not. My heart was too full of sadness and sorrow to take any rest. Had any one told me, a short year before, that my husband would become a common drunkard, I should have scouted the idea as an absurdity, but now there was no avoiding it. The proof was there before me, and how I shuddered as I contemplated what the future might have in store for me. Already, in fancy, I saw myself pointed and sneered at as the wife of a drunkard, while the children, who were as dear to me as though they had been my own, were devoted to a life of wretchedness and shame. The agony that I endured, as these thoughts passed through my mind, during the remaining hours of that night, can never be told.

Similar scenes to these were of frequent occurrence from this time forward, until at last they became so common as to be rather the rule than the exception. A majority of the nights my husband came home more or less intoxicated, while not unfrequently he was so far gone as to require assistance in getting home. During all this time he was not unkind or abusive to me—never spoke angrily or harshly to me, but was practising upon me a species of cruelty far more dreadful than any personal violence could be.

I soon discovered that he was burdened with some terrible secret which constantly weighed down his spirits, but which he refused to share with me. When sober, there was an air of sadness about him which I at first attributed to remorse for the debaucheries in which he was constantly participating; but though that doubtless contributed somewhat to his moroseness, it was not long till I made úp my mind, from some words which he carelessly let fall, that there was even something more than this pressing upon his spirits. No sooner did I arrive at this conclusion than, with fear and trembling, I set to work to find out what it was. True, I dreaded the discovery, but still I felt that it was necessary to know the worst, and anything was better than the suspense I was enduring. Accordingly, one evening when, at my earnest solicitation, he consented to stay at home with me, I broached the subject.

"My dear husband," said I, "I am certain you have some great trouble on your mind, and that it is that which leads to all our recent sorrows. Is it not so?"

"Why, Minnie, why do you ask such questions? What if my business does vex and annoy me a little, is that any reason why you should borrow any trouble about it?"

"But I am certain it is not your business. There is something besides business weighing upon your mind. I have seen it in your eye, averted whenever I tried to look you in the face; in your moody, restless air; in your half-suppressed sighs, and in a thousand other little circumstances which none but a wife would observe. Eugene, I am your wife, and have sworn to love and honor you, to share your joys and sorrows—why should you conceal anything from me? If your are in trouble, tell me, and let me share it with you. Will you not, dear Genie?"

"Oh! Minnie, do not urge me. If I have troubles I must bear them alone. They are not for you to share."

"Not for me to share! Who should share your troubles if not your own true and loving wife? Tell me, my husband, what is it that so oppreses you, and my woman's wit shall find some way to relieve you of your distress."

"Minnie, it would kill you to know it, and beside it is entirely beyond your power to afford any relief. Why then should I trouble you with it? No, the troubles which oppress me I have brought upon myself, and I will bear them alone. No one, much less you, my precious wife, must suffer for my own faults."

"But this suspense is worse, and far more pain-ful to me, than any knowledge could be. If you have erred, tell me all about it—be assured of my forgiveness beforehand, but do not conceal any-thing from me. Come, my husband, tell me all, and not only relieve my suspense, but let us devise means to get rid of the trouble which has destroyed and is destroying all our happiness. Tell me, my husband, tell me all."

But all my efforts and entreaties were vain. To all I could say he would only answer that it would kill me, and that he must suffer alone, and I retired to rest that night with a heavier heart than I had known for a long time. It was impos-sible for me to divest myself of the impression that some terrible calamity was impending over us, and what it was I could not divine. I mused over it for a long time after my husband was asleep, but could arrive at no conclusion satisfactory to myself, and was finally forced to give it up en-tirely. How much better it would have been for all parties, had my husband then yielded to my entreaties, and imparted his trouble to me, let the sequel show. Oh! husbands, think not to save your wives from sorrow by endeavoring to conceal from them the troubles which oppress you. In many instances their quick wit, sharpened by affection, will devise means of avoiding the evil where to you there seems no chance of escape,

8

while concealment only leads them to imagine the
worst, and thus produces far more pain to them
than knowledge of all the facts would. Beside,
it is their duty and their right to know and share
all your sorrows and all your troubles; and, my
word for it, to the true wife the path of duty is
always the path of pleasure. What though that
path be rough and thorny, still she treads it
not only with satisfaction, but with joy, and finds
her reward in promoting the happiness of him to
whom she has given her purest love. As you
value that love, pain not her gentle spirit by striving to conceal from her that which it is her right
and her duty, as well as desire, to know.

Some weeks passed away after this conversation,
and my husband grew no better. His evenings
were nearly all spent away from home, and not
unfrequently he would be gone the entire night,
and when he came home, instead of being the
strong man of vigorous intellect that he was when I
first knew him, he would be a mere infant in
strength, and but little more than a driveling idiot.
Such are the effects of alcoholic drinks, and such
they are known to be by every one. Why is it
that men, made in the image and likeness of their
Creator, will persist in the use of that terrible
poison, which reduces them below the level of the
brute, and only fits them for the companionship of
the lost spirits of the bottomless pit, and qualifies
them for the commission of any crime?

One night my husband was, as usual, away from

home, and I was sitting alone in my room, waiting and watching for his coming; for, during all this time, I never once failed to sit up and wait for him to come. I felt it my duty to do so; and, beside, I thought if there was any hope of reclaiming him, it would be accomplished in that way and no other. As I sat there, worn and weary with my constant vigils, suddenly the door-bell was rung with a violence which caused me to start from my chair, with the impression that something terrible had happened. I was sure it was not my husband, for he had a latch-key, and could come in at his pleasure, and my first thought was that he was dead, or had met with some terrible accident; and while I stood trembling with alarm and undecided what to do, again the terrible summons pealed through the house, if possible with more violence than before. I did not dare to go to the door, but called Tom and Silvie and directed them to see who was there, and what they wanted at this time of the night. Aunt Silvie got up and opened the door and found a basket sitting on the step, but no person was to be seen, nor was there any clue as to how it came there. Tom went out into the grounds and made the most diligent search about the yard and buildings, but could find no traces of any one.

The basket was brought into the house, and when opened we found it to contain a little girl, apparently aged three or four weeks. The child was well dressed, and, at the bottom of the basket

was a note well written, but in a hand entirely unknown to me. It ran thus :

MRS. GILES—Take this little one and take care
of her. Whatever of wrong her mother may
have committed, she at least is innocent, and
should not suffer for the wrong of others. Some
day you will know all about her parentage, but
not now. Her name is Carrie, and she will take
the place of the little one you have lost. As
you value your happiness and peace of mind, take
good care of her.

It was without signature, and I could not imagine
who was its author, or why it should have been
sent to me. I knew not what to think or what to
do. How I wished for the presence of my husband
that he might advise me in this emergency. How
could I take care for it? I already had three
children; my health was becoming delicate on
account of the conduct of my husband; and it
seemed impossible for me to add this foundling
and its care to my already heavy burdens. And
yet, the thought of sending it away was in the
last degree abhorrent to me. What should be
done?

I was recalled from these musings by the child
beginning to cry. It was evidently hungry, and
I told aunt Silvie, who had been standing silently
by all this time, to get some milk and feed it.
She started as if from a trance, and turned to obey
me, muttering as she went something, of which
I only heard, "a pretty kittle of fish," "bet it's
massa's young 'un," and something else which I

could not catch. This gave a new direction to my thoughts, by disclosing to me the suspicions which were floating through her mind. Could it be that my husband was false to me, and that this child was the fruit of his guilty intrigues? Oh! no; it could not be. He had always been so kind and affectionate to me that it was not possible he was deceiving me in this manner. With these reflections I tried to dismiss the subject from my thoughts; but still my suspicions had been aroused, and I could not cease to think of old Silvie's muttered words. After the child's hunger had been appeased, I took it in my arms, and, for the first time, went to bed without my husband; but though the infant sunk into a sound slumber, and did not wake during the entire night, my thoughts, fears and suspicions would not allow me to sleep. With the first faint streak of dawn I arose and assumed my watching.

About six o'clock Eugene came home, and, to my surprise, he was entirely sober. I at once showed him the little foundling, handed him the note, and stood by to watch him while he read it. I thought if he was guilty, as aunt Silvie thought, it would be impossible for him to conceal it; but the closest scrutiny of his features failed to reveal anything to confirm those suspicions. He was evidently as much surprised at the circumstance as I had been, and, in my own mind, I was convinced he knew nothing of the paternity of the child, and

at once acquitted him of the wrong of which he
had been suspected.

We then discussed the disposition to be made of
the child. He proposed sending it away some
where; but now that I was convinced of his innocence I would not consent to this, and insisted
upon adopting her as our own. To this he finally
consented, and it was so decided—he saying, that
since we had concluded to keep it, he was glad it
was a girl, as we already had three boys, and
none of the other sex. We therefore bestowed
upon her the same care and attention which we
gave our own, and in time she grew to be sufficiently sweet and interesting to more than repay us
for all our trouble. But still the secret of her
birth was wrapped in profound mystery, and
caused me many an hour of anxious thought.
It is true my husband was no longer suspected
of any wrong in connection with it; but my
inability to fathom the mystery was a source of
constant uneasiness to me. It did not then occur
to me that he might be guilty after all, and that
his surprise was but simulated to convince me of
his innocence. I did not then know him as well as
I have since learned to do.

I tried by all means in my power to stimulate the
interest of my husband in the new accession to our
household, hoping that it would have some influence to wean him from the evil ways into which
he had fallen, and, for a few days, flattered myself
with the hope that my efforts were going to prove

successful. For some days after the advent of the little foundling, he spent his evenings at home ; but just as I began to flatter myself that he was reclaimed, he suddenly relapsed, and was, in a very short time, just as bad as ever. Again were repeated the scenes of lonely nights, of weary watching, of helpless intoxication, and beastly debauchery, amid which my time had been passed almost constantly since the death of our little girl ; and again I drank to its dregs the cup of bitterness ever presented to the lips of a neglected wife. But this could not last always, and finally the end came.

One evening, a few weeks after the events I have just related, my husband came home very early— about seven o'clock, I think it was—and was evidently very much depressed in spirit. He came in without a word, and, taking his seat, sat for some time without speaking. At length the silence grew irksome to me, and I went up to him, and, putting my arm around his neck, said :

"Eugene, you must tell me what is the matter with you. For a long time you have not been yourself, nor have you confided to me any part of your troubles. I have borne it until my heart is well nigh breaking, and now I feel that I can not stand it any longer. Do tell me, I implore you, what it is that troubles you."

He made no reply, but laid his head upon my breast and wept like a child. I said nothing, but let his head rest upon my bosom until his grief had somewhat subsided. Indeed, I was too much alarmed and astounded to say anything. I had never seen any man, and much less him, moved as he was by my simple question, and knew not what to say or do. When his sobs had somewhat subsided, I kissed his brow, and again urged him, by all the endearing words at my command, to impart his grief to me. Without looking up, he said:

"Minnie, I can not tell you all. I am ashamed to confess it all to myself, much less to you. Oh! if you knew all that I have done, the depths to which I have descended, you would fly from me and never see me again."

"Eugene, you wrong me. I can forgive anything for your sake—can endure anything except this concealment; so tell me the worst, and see how bravely I can bear it."

"Oh! Minnie, you are so kind, so affectionate, and so dear to me, that I would gladly spare you this trial if I could. But I can not conceal it any longer. Minnie, I have been gambling for a long time, and am a ruined man. At first I was successful, and became infatuated with the love of play, and, when fortune turned against me, I kept on in the hope of retrieving my position; and so it has gone on, until I have lost all, and my wife and children will soon be homeless. This house, furniture, servants, my livery-stable and all, will not pay my debts, and I may even have to go to jail. What will become of you and the babies?"

I was struck speechless by this revelation. In

all my imaginings as to the cause of his irregular-
ities, it had never occurred to me that this might
be the case. The worst that had suggested itself
to my mind was, that he had been unfortunate in
business, and was compelled to sacrifice his property; and had this been so, had he lost every dollar he was worth, but lost it honorably, I could
have borne it all without a murmur. Oh! yes, I
could have endured the very lowest depths of poverty with him, without complaint, had he been reduced to those depths without dishonor on his part,
and simply by the frowns of fortune; but to know
that he had brought it all upon himself and us by
the contemptible, soul-blighting, and God-dishon-
oring vice of gambling so completely overwhelmed
me with astonishment and horror that, for a time,
I was incapable of uttering a single word, or, indeed, scarcely comprehending it.

How any man gifted with sense and reason can
so far debase himself as to engage in the pernicious
vice of gambling—that pursuit in which all the
better and finer feelings of human nature are swal-
lowed up in the fierce and unholy excitement of the
gaming-table, and in which the demon Avarice
takes entire possession of a man, to the exclusion
of everything noble and praiseworthy; that pursuit
which is the fruitful parent of intemperance, licen-
tiousness, and every other vice to which frail humanity is subject; that pursuit which almost
inevitably accompanies and leads to theft, highway
robbery, and even murder; which, in short, trans-

forms men into demons—is beyond my power to
comprehend. Had I a son, I would a thousand
times rather see him inclosed in his coffin than to
see him seated at the gaming-table : the first would
only be the death of the mortal body, while the
last would be neither more nor less than the eternal death of an immortal soul. Oh! young man,
just starting upon the troublous voyage of life,
shun the soul-killing excitement of the gaming-
table as you would the bite of an adder. The moment in which you yield to its seductive influences,
that moment you may abandon all hope for the
future, and "Lost" will be the epitaph you write
upon your own tombstone. But to return to my
story.

As I have said, I was incapable of uttering a
word, but sat stunned and speechless by the terrible revelation just made. After the silence had
continued some time, my husband raised his head
and looked timidly in my face. He started at the
expression he saw there.

"Why, Minnie," said he, "how pale you look,
and so dreadful. Do not look with that fixed and
stony stare. Reproach me ; curse me, if you will—
I deserve it all—but do not look so terribly upon
me."

"Oh! Eugene," I said, bursting into tears, "why
have you done this? Tell me all about it."

"Minnie, I have nothing to tell, nothing to say
in excuse for myself. You know that, in my business, I am constantly thrown in company with

what are called 'fast men;' and that it is my disposition to be gay and lively. Well, at first— they began on me a long time ago—they used to say: 'Come, Eugene; go with us to——'s;' but I would refuse, telling them I must go home to my wife and babies; 'my wife will sit up until I come.' ' 'Well, Eugene,' they would say, 'go and get a drink with us first.' Thus urged, I would yield. One drink would be taken; then another and another, until I would forget all about wife and children. But it was a long time before they could get me to take a card. At last, one night, after I had been drinking pretty freely, it was proposed that we should have a quiet game of cards for fun. To this I consented, and we began to play. Finally, my partner proposed a bet of five dollars on a hand he then held. I refused to have any part in it; but he and another man bet, and my partner won. They then laughed at me for being so fearful of a paltry bet; and thus, by ridicule and entreaty, and by plying me with liquor, they at last got me to betting. For some time I won almost constantly, and then I began to lose. Maddened by my losses, and by the liquid poison in my system and muddling my brain, I kept on until at last I awoke to find myself a ruined man. That, Minnie, is the whole story."

It was the old, old story. It was but a repetition of the arts by which those fiends insatiate—those sharks, who prey upon the follies and weaknesses of their fellow-men, only to rob them of wealth,

honor, and all that makes life desirable—always
ensnare their victims. If there is one being upon
the face of the earth who is more to be despised
than another, surely that being is the professional
gambler; if one sinner deserves a higher meed of
punishment than any other, it is that creature who,
wearing the form but lacking the soul of a man,
makes the weak points of those with whom he is
thrown in contact his special study, only that he
may the more certainly rob them of all the jewels
which a kind and beneficent Creator has bestowed
upon them ; and, if it were possible that one portion of the eternal burning should be hotter than
another, surely those demons would, by the justice
of the Almighty, be consigned to that hotter portion.

I could not reproach my husband; I loved him
too well for that; and, beside, I felt that he was
more to be pitied than blamed. Possessed of a
gay and lively disposition, generous to a fault, and
fond of society, he was just the man to be selected by these sharpers as the victim of their dev-
ilish arts; and he must have been possessed of
more than human virtue had he been able to resist
the many wiles and temptations with which they
studiously surrounded him : and yet, I could not
repress the reflection, that had he confided in me,
at the time I first appealed to him, I might have
saved him. But that was now all past. He had
tried to conceal it from me as long as he was able ;
had retained the secret in his own breast until

concealment was no longer possible ; until he must give up his stables, his horses, carriages; his fine residence and furniture and servants ; and now, the only question was, "What was to be done?" An examination of his affairs showed that, after giving up everything he had in the world, he would still fall short nearly a thousand dollars of paying his indebtedness, and, womanlike, I began to cast about to see what I could do to help him.

I had some fine jewelry and a valuable watch— presents from Eugene in our brighter and happier days. I could raise two or three thousand dollars on them, but what would that amount to in the payment of the enormous debt hanging over my husband? It would be but a drop in the bucket ; but, still, every dollar would help, and though it ground my heart into the very dust to think of parting with these precious mementoes of his love, stern necessity knows no law, and I decided that they must go. But what could be done to save us a home from the general wreck? I could ask Captain Lake to aid us in this emergency; but though he had money enough, which of right belonged to me, to pay off all Eugene's debts, I very much doubted if he would do anything, for he was a close, miserly man, who never gave a cent for charity on any other noble and generous purpose. But what else could be done? Our home would be sold the next day, and we would be without even a shelter for our heads, and I must try what I could do.

Accordingly I went to Captain Lake and told him all about Eugene's temptation and fall, and my plans and hopes for the future, and besought him to aid me to save my servants and furniture and to my agreeable surprise he agreed to do so. I blessed him from the bottom of my heart, hastened home and told my husband we could save our furniture, and keep our home; for if the house was sold I would sell my diamonds and raise money enough to pay the rent of it for a year, and this would give him a chance to turn around and begin business anew. I told him of my interview with Captain Lake, and what he had promised, and informed him of my plans for the future. He wept tears of joy and gratitude, not unmingled with sorrow, at the sacrifices I was making on his account, and solemnly promised me, upon bended knees, that he would reform, and would apply himself once more to business, and try to redeem our property. He implored my forgiveness for the sorrow he had given me, and faithfully promised that he would never practice such concealment from me again.

Of course I gave him my entire forgiveness, but could not refrain from telling him how much better I thought it would have been for both of us, had he placed in me the confidence which every husband should feel toward a true and loving wife. He assented to all I said upon this point, and over and over again called me his guardian angel, and promised never to have any secrets from me again. But even at the time of registering this solemn promise he bore within his breast a fearful secret which was one day to destroy all my confidence in him, and more completely blight my happiness than anything else could have done.

The day of sale came, and with it an immense crowd; some attracted by a desire to speculate out of our misfortunes, and others by that insatiable and inexplicable feeling of curiosity which always prompts envious mortals to gaze upon the fallen grandeur of others. I could not stay at home and see all those articles which were so dear to me hawked about by an unfeeling mob, who knew not their sacredness, and accordingly went to Captain Lake's. On my way out I passed Captain Lake going into the city. He merely smiled, and said, "All is well," in response to my eager salutation. My heart was heavy with grief, but it is impossible to portray the feeling of comfort and consolation which those simple words imparted to me. I felt that it was indeed well, and went on my way with a lighter heart than before. The bidding upon some articles was quite spirited, but Captain Lake bought all the furniture, and the three servants, had the bill of sale made out in my name, and handed it over to me saying, "Here, Minnie, is a father's gift to his daughter." I felt as if I could have fallen down and kissed his feet for very joy, and my heart was full of gratitude for his kindness in this my hour of trouble. I concluded Captain Lake was not, after all, so bad a man as I had always thought him, and my heart smote me, as I remembered the bitterness which had once filled my heart toward him.

In the evening, after the sale was over and the crowd had gone away, I went home and soon after reaching there a gentleman called who gave his name as Mortimore. I at once recognized the name as that of a man notorious throughout the city for being a great gambler, and scrutinized his countenance closely. It was cold, impassive, hard and brutal, just what the countenance of a gambler should be, and, though his manners were elegant, his voice and speech exactly tallied with his countenance. My husband was not in when he came, and without any preliminaries he told me the house belonged to him; that he had bought it that day at the sale, and he would like us to move out immediately, as he had use for it. This information was imparted in a hard, measured tone, which was plainly intended to intimate that the matter would admit of no debate.

" But, sir, what use do you intend to make of it? Do you intend to occupy it yourself?"

"No; I shall rent it."

"But we cannot move to-night, and, beside, this furniture and the servants are all here, and must be taken care of."

"The gentleman who bought the niggers and furniture will no doubt take them away immediately; and as I can get eleven hundred dollars a year for the house, I want to rent it at once, and

you must move.   Of course, you have no money to
pay rent with."

"Is eleven hundred dollars a year your price for
the house?"

"It is."

"I will take it for a year."

"You, madam!"

"Yes, sir I will take it.   You can call day after
to-morrow morning and get your money for a year's
rent."

"You will pay me eleven hundred dollars day
after to-morrow?"

"I have said so."

"But what will you do for furniture?"

"Know, sir, that this furniture and these servants are mine.   The gentleman who bought them
is my father, and he bought them for me."

"Madam, I beg your pardon.   Did I understand
you to say that this furniture was yours, and that
you would pay me eleven hundred dollars, day
after to-morrow, for the house?"

"I said so, sir.   Can we have the house?"

"Certainly, madam—certainly."

"Will you now do me the favor to go?"

He at once complied with my request, and bowed
himself out, quite crestfallen, and much more
respectful in his manner than when he came to
order us to vacate at once.   Soon after his departure my husband came in, and when I told him
what had taken place, his indignation knew no
bounds.   He was for following the brute, and in-

flicting summary chastisement, upon him for his impudence. He had no kindly feeling toward the author of all our misfortunes, and this last insult caused the cup of his wrath to boil over. But I restrained him, and finally soothed him into a promise to take no notice whatever of his brutality.

The next day I sold my jewelry, my watch and chain, and all my silverware, and we found that, after paying the year's rent, we could raise about two thousand dollars for my husband to begin anew with. He thought that, by going into the business of buying and selling horses, he could do well, and, in time, regain something like our old position. This would necessarily take him from home a great deal, and I dreaded his removal from my influence, fearing he would relapse into his old habits again; but there seemed no other chance to do anything, and I yielded a reluctant consent.

Mortimore came the next morning for his rent, but his manner was altogether different from what it had been when he was there before. Eugene would not see him at all, fearing he would be so much exasperated at the sight of him as to be unable to restrain himself; but I paid him his money, and took from him a receipt in full for one year's rent of the house that had been ours alone before the baneful shadow of his presence fell across my poor Eugene's pathway. My heart was full almost to bursting as these reflections rushed across my mind; but, in the midst of all, I rejoiced that I had been able to save even so much from the general wreck.

After making the necessary arrangements, my husband set out on a trading trip, intending to be gone about six weeks; and he solemnly renewed to me, at parting, his promise that he would not touch either cards or liquor. And I have every reason to believe that, during that trip at least, he faithfully kept his promise.

CHAPTER VIII.

IT had been about six weeks since my husband started away, and the time of his expected return was at hand. My anxiety to see him was intense; for, despite my confidence in his promises, I could not repress a feeling of uneasiness lest he should be met by temptation too strong for him to overcome. I knew that he was not fully weaned from the excitement of his former evil associations, and dreaded the effect of his meeting once more the society into which I supposed he would be thrown.

As for myself, I had got along finely during his absence. I had hired Tom and Caroline out, retaining only aunt Silvie at home, and, with the wages which they earned, and the little money I had when Eugene went away, had lived very comfortably, and had managed to save a little something. Caroline was the nurse, and, as I had never been accustomed to having the care of the children myself, it went rather awkwardly at first to do without her, but I could do it, and would do that or anything else, to economize our slender resources, and enable my husband to get another start in the world.

At length Eugene came. And as soon as I saw him I was satisfied he had been true to his promise.

His eyes and countenance were clear, and bore no trace of dissipation, and he met my gaze without flinching. He seemed to read my anxiety in my countenance, and laughing a little, quiet, good-natured sort of laugh, he said:

"Minnie, dismiss your fears and doubts. I have most faithfully kept my promise, and have broken company forever with those vile habits which caused our ruin."

What words of joy to me! Although I had never really doubted him, still it was, before that time, impossible to rid myself of some slight traces of fear, not for the uprightness of his intentions—oh! no, I never even suspected that—but I trembled for his strength. I knew he had once been tempted and had fallen, and I trembled at the bare thought of his being thus fearfully tried again. But now I felt that temptation was powerless against him. He was clad in impenetrable armor, and could laugh to scorn the fiercest shafts of the enemy.

He had met with the most extraordinary good fortune during this trip, and had, during the short space of less than two months, almost doubled the money with which he started out. He had purchased one drove of horses, upon which alone he had cleared nearly one thousand dollars, and every adventure in which he had engaged had been in the highest degree successful. Of course he could not always expect to meet with such success; doubtless he would sometimes lose on some of his bargains, but the happy results of this trip elated

us in the highest degree, and we at once set about
forming our plans for obtaining another home.
Our rent was paid for a year where we were, and,
of course, we would remain there until that ex-
pired. He would continue his trading speculations
during that time, and, if attended with any degree
of success, he would be able, at the end of the
year to purchase a home of our own, and thus save
the enormous rent we were now compelled to pay.
Thus we looked at the future; thus in roseate
colors it presented itself to us, and we were as
happy that night as two human beings could well
be—happier, I doubt not, than if we had never
known the chastening fires of adversity.

And our fine laid plans were carried into effect.
During the entire year my husband spent but
little time at home, applying himself with the
utmost assiduity to the calling he had marked
out for himself, and though never again, during
the entire year, did he have such extraordinary
good fortune as upon that first trip—though he
even lost money on some of his investments—still
he was slowly but steadily increasing the sum at
his banker's which was finally to buy us a home.
I, too, did what I could to aid him, continued to
practice every species of economy of which I was
mistress, and the result was, that at the end of the
year we found ourselves in possession of sufficient
means to buy a very comfortable house, though by
no means equal to the one we were quitting. But
we left it without regret. If our new home was

less stately and magnificent than the old one—if I
had not as fine jewelry and costly plate as before—
still the home was our own, and, best of all, my
husband was saved.   Was I not once more a happy
women!

But fate was not done persecuting us, nor were
our misfortunes yet ended.   Scarcely had we got
settled in our new home, when our little Carrie was
prostrated by a most violent attack of fever, and
for three weeks she lay at death's door.   Eugene
was from home when she was taken ill, and it was
a long time before I could get any message to him,
not knowing his whereabouts, and I really feared
she would die before he came home.   We had
learned to love her as one of our own, and the idea
of her dying in his absence was inexpressibly
painful to me.   The thought of losing her under
any circumstances was the most acute torture ; but,
when to this was added the dread of her dying
without her adopted father seeing her, the agony
was almost insupportable.

But, thank God, I was spared this trial.   I succeeded in learning where my husband was, and at
once sent a special messenger for him.   Of course
he dropped all business at once, and hastened
home by the most expeditious conveyance, and but
a few days elapsed after his arrival until the old
physician, who had given her the most unremitting
care and attention, announced to us that the crisis
of her disease was passed, and that her life would
be saved.   Never was a sentence uttered which

conveyed more joy to a human heart than that did to mine. During her long illness I either sat by her little crib or held her in my arms almost the whole time, and to know that my watching and care had not been in vain, and that she would be saved to us, filled my heart with thankfulness. Of course she was not out of danger yet, and it was a long time before she was well again; but the worst was now over, and together we lifted up our voices in thanksgiving to Him who had kindly given us the life of our little one, even after almost all hope seemed lost.

But another of our little family was to pass through the same ordeal. Scarcely had the crisis of Carrie's illness passed when Frankie was smitten down by the same disease. The attack, though less protracted than Carrie's case, was more violent; and for ten days his moans of anguish and cries of pain thrilled in my ears, and transfixed every nerve of my frame with the most acute agony. But he, too, through the mercy of God, and the skill of our venerable physician, was saved to us; and again we wept tears of joy and thankfulness as we bent over our little lamb, snatched, as it were, from the very jaws of death.

But these afflictions had sadly deranged our affairs. We not only had heavy medical bills to pay, but the constant watching had so worn me out that we were compelled to summon Caroline home, and we thus lost the aid of the wages she was earning, while our expenses at home were perceptibly increased. Besides, Eugene had entirely neglected his business in the care of the children, and through the incapacity, or rascality, of an agent whom he had left in charge of his stock when he came home, he not only entirely lost several horses, but the others, for want of care and attention, so much depreciated in value that he lost nearly a thousand dollars upon the stock he had on hand. This amount which would once have appeared so trifling to us, at this time made a very serious hole in our limited finances, and rendered still further economy and care necessary in the management of our affairs.

About this time, also, I received a letter from the far away land of California, which caused my heart to beat with the most anxious fears, for though it bore the Sacramento post-mark it was written in a strange hand, and my first thought was that my brother, the only member of my father's family under the broad canopy of heaven, was dead. I felt sick at heart, and for a time hesitated to open it, dreading the confirmation of my worst fears, but when I finally mustered courage enough to open the seal, it was not quite so bad as I had thought, though still bad enough. Frank was not dead, though very sick, and among entire strangers, his only acquaintance there being the friend and comrade who had written the letter to me at his request. The writer stated that Frank was very much disheartened, and was under the impression that he would never be any better, but that his bones would be laid to rest in that far-off land.

The reader may imagine, but words will hardly express the pain with which this intelligence thrilled my heart. My brother Frank—my last surviving blood relation, the brother to whom I had been wont to look for direction and assistance in every trouble—was lying dangerously ill in a distant country, among strangers—doubtless deprived of every comfort, and even of the nursing and attention which his condition demanded, and I was powerless to do anything to aid him. I would have given anything to be with him, but many thousand miles of wild and sterile land separated us; and even had it been possible for me to get to him, the situation of my own family would have precluded me from making the attempt. I looked at the date of the letter—it was nearly three months since it had been written—and who could tell whether my poor brother's gloomy anticipations had been realized during that time? Yes; I felt that it must be so. His depression of spirits, it seemed to me, must have exercised a serious influence upon his disease; and I felt assured that his career must have ended, far from home and friends, and that his last resting-place was in some wild, gloomy dell, unmarked by any memento which would aid me in any way to identify it, should I ever wish to visit and water it with my tears. Ah! how sad was this reflection to my already sorely-tried spirit.

For the next three weeks I was infinitely miser-

able. Fancy was constantly presenting to my
mental vision the most vivid pictures of the imag-
inary death-scene of my brother; and even in my
dreams I heard his voice calling upon me for that
assistance and comfort which I was utterly powerless to render. But, at the end of that time came
a letter which turned all my mourning into joy,
and my weepings into songs of praise and thanksgiving. My brother, instead of dying as he anticipated, and as his friend thought he certainly
would, had finally recovered, and would start home
as soon as he could close up his business, which
would be in about three or four weeks from the
date of the letter.

According to this, he must be on his way home,
and would no doubt soon be here. Oh! with what
joy I received this intelligence, and how earnestly
did I look forward to the time of our anticipated
meeting. Time seemed to me to move all too slow,
and it was with the utmost impatience that I
watched for his arrival. When it is remembered
by the reader that it was almost five years since
I had parted with him, beside the grave of our
father, in the city of Philadelphia, it will not be
thought strange that my anxiety for his coming was
almost insupportable. My husband used to rally
me, good-naturedly, of course, upon my impatience,
and to say that he should be jealous if I persisted
in such demonstration of evident affection for " this
foreigner," as he styled him; and I would retort

that, if he became at all disagreeable, I should forsake him entirely for the " foreigner."

At last he came, and the reader need not be told that his greeting was the warmest that it was in my power to bestow, for words will hardly express my joy at again meeting him. But how he was changed in the five years since our adieus were spoken beside our father's tomb! Then his appearance was that of a smooth-faced and rather delicate-appearing youth : now he was a man—tall, robust and stalwart, his face bronzed, and his muscles hardened by toil and exposure, while a heavy, dark beard and mustache entirely concealed the lower part of his face, and gave him a sort of brigandish look, so different from his former gentle and almost effeminate appearance that, had I not been expecting his arrival, I should certainly never have recognized him. But how he had improved! His robust, manly frame, and fine muscular development, now challenged my admiration, as his kindness to me in former days had won my affection; and I was now as proud of my brother as it was possible for a sister to be; while, upon his part, his affection for me seemed to be stronger and more enduring than ever. But we were not permitted long to enjoy the happiness of our reunion. Events were already at work which were to sever forever the ties that had bound us so closely to each other during the whole of our lives.

My brother returned from California in the month of December, 1860. The election of

Abraham Lincoln as President of the United States had just taken place, and the events of that fall and winter are fresh in the minds of my readers. The entire South was full of feverish excitement. State after State was adopting the ordinance of secession; the air was vocal with the sounds of military preparation; and the universal topic of conversation was, independence and war to the knife against the so-called Abolition encroachments.

I am about to enter into no apology for the rebellion which so long convulsed our land and drenched it in fraternal gore; which has clothed every house in mourning, and inflicted wounds which cannot be healed until this generation shall have passed away. On the contrary, impartial history will record our late civil war as the most egregious folly, if not the most gigantic crime, of the world's annals. Abjuring at once all obligation to that Government which had so long fostered them, and under which they had become opulent and powerful, the Southern States plunged into a ferocious and bloody warfare, for the purpose of protecting certain species of property against the fancied designs of men who were supposed to be hostile to its further continuance: and the result has been just what might have been anticipated by any one not maddened by the excitement which ruled the entire South at this time. The property in defense of which they took up arms has been swept away entirely and forever; their land has been impoverished to the extent of millions of dollars; and every Southern heart is compelled to bear the burden of mourning for relatives slain and maimed in the cause upon which the blessing of heaven never rested.

That there were many good men whose hearts disapproved of the part they were acting, and who saw no just cause of rebellion in the then existing condition of affairs; but who were forced into the revolt against their will, by the force of popular opinion, by the wily arts of unscrupulous demagogues, and by the mischievous doctrines of "States' rights" which had been so long inculcated by leading Southern politicians, is no doubt true; and for such men I have no words of condemnation. While their folly is to be most bitterly deplored—not only for the sake of general humanity, but, also, in view of the fearful consequences which have followed their delusion—still must they be acquitted of the terrible criminality which attends their leaders. But for these last, for those who imposed upon them that delusion—those who molded and formed that public opinion by which they were precipitated into the rebellion—the blood of a million of slaughtered victims, and the tears of countless widows and orphans cry aloud for vengeance. And so sure as there is a just God who shall hereafter reward every man according to his works, so sure will these men have a fearful account to render hereafter.

My brother was one of those men who, by the arts of those leaders, was duped into giving his support to this movement. Born and bred in the South, thoroughly imbued with the pernicious doctrine of State sovereignty, ignorant of the arts of wily and scheming politicians, reading only those publications which depicted in the most glowing terms the dangerous doctrines and designs of the abolitionists, generous and manly to a fault, and glowing with a hatred of oppression and resentment for real or fancied injury, what wonder that, viewing the matter from a standpoint to which he had been educated, he earnestly espoused the cause of his native section, threatened, as he supposed her to be, with almost entire destruction by the fanatics of the North? In vain I reasoned with and entreated him not to engage in the struggle at all—to at least remain neutral. His reply was that his honor was at at stake, and that his conscience would not suffer him to remain an idle spectator of the contest in which it might be the life of his country was the stake. In vain my husband seconded my arguments and entreaties with the means at his command—we were powerless to move him, and each day saw him a more and more ardent advocate of the independence of the South. Captain Lake, who had embraced with the utmost ardor the cause of the South, used all his influence with Frank against us, and his doctrines harmonizing entirely with

Frank's inclinations, made him a most powerful antagonist.

At length came the actual commencement of hostilities, the attack upon Fort Sumter, and the entire nation, both North and South, was convulsed as by a mighty electric shock. As the news flashed from place to place along the wires, business of every kind was suspended, and everything gave way to the work of raising troops for the struggle then inaugurated. The city of Atlanta was no exception to the general rule. The stores were generally closed, eager and excited crowds thronged the streets ; the stirring notes of fife and drum were heard at all hours of the day and night ; at every street corner excited and eloquent speakers harangued equally excited crowds, urging them to rush to arms in support of their threatened and endangered liberties ; the listeners testified their approbation by consent and wild cheering, and the enlistment of men proceeded with almost marvelous rapidity. Young and old, rich and poor, all classes vied in their efforts to secure a place in the ranks of the army, and none who applied were turned away. Could they, at that time, have foreseen the results of the mad excitement of that hour, could they have had the slighest glimpse of the horrid events of the coming four years, how many would have recoiled, shuddering, from the act they were now so eager to do.

Among the earliest to enroll himself was Captain Lake, though already over fifty years of age. He was lustily cheered by the unthinking mob, who saw him sign his name to what eventually proved his death-warrant, and was rewarded for his "patriotism" by being elected commander of the company of which he was a member. He at once proceeded to organize his command, was duly commissioned a captain, and entered the service of the Confederacy in that capacity.

The next day my brother, whom I had not seen since the beginning of the fierce excitement, came home and told me that he, too, had enlisted and had been chosen First Lieutenant of his company. I wept bitter tears at this intelligence, but the deed was done, and it was too late to undo the evil, nor would I then urge him to forsake his plighted faith. Although my heart disapproved the cause, still I could not but admire the manhood which led him to this step, and having once taken it, I felt that he would be dishonored were he to retract, but the contemplation of the future had no charms for me. He tried to comfort me by telling me that there would be no war, that the North would not fight, and that all they had to do was to make a display of force, and in six weeks their ends would be obtained, and they would all be at home again. But all he could say to me did not divest my mind of the impression that I should never see him again. Was this a presentiment? He then tried to induce my husband to go into the army with him, using all the arguments his imagination could suggest in favor of this course,

10

and making the most extravagant promises of
future good if he would consent to do so.   But his
arguments and entreaties were alike unavailing,
and Eugene continued firm in his refusal.

But a few days were allowed the newly raised
troops in which to prepare for leaving their homes,
many of them, alas! never to return.   Captain
Lake, before his departure, perhaps realizing how
foully he had wronged me, and willing to make
what amends he could, made a sort of will, devising fifty thousand dollars to me in the event of
his death.   My brother, too, having been eminently
successful in California, made the most generous
provision for me in case of his death.   He had
brought home some eighty thousand dollars, and
he gave the strongest proof of his fraternal affection
by devising the whole of this vast sum for my benefit.   Had I been able, gentle reader, to secure the
benefit of this munificent provision for my future,
this story had most likely never been written, for
many of the vicissitudes of my life had then never
taken place.

Within a day or two after these dispositions were
made my brother came to bid me good-bye.   He
was clad in the uniform of his command, and though
at sight of it my tears flowed afresh, still I could
not but feel a natural pride in the erect and manly
carriage which distinguished him, and the grace
with which he bore himself in his new position.
But the adieus were soon spoken, and in a few
minutes I had again parted with my only living

relative, and this time it really was, what I had often before imagined, a parting forever on this side of eternity.

CHAPTER IX.

Time in its ever-ceaseless flight passed away— the days lengthened into weeks, and the weeks grew into months, and instead of the war being ended in six weeks, as its advocates prophesied, it was evident to the most casual observer that it was but just begun. The North had displayed a spirit entirely unexpected by the leaders of the secession movement. The unanimity of the people of that section in springing to arms was most astonishing, and, if possible, excelled the ardor of the Southerners. Bloodshed there had been, too, notwithstanding the predictions of the champions of rebellion to the contrary. The bloody battle of Bull Run had been fought, and, though resulting in a victory over the National forces, had carried grief and mourning to many a Southern home, and had clothed in the habiliments of woe many a fair daughter of that sunny clime. My brother participated in that battle, and for a long time after tidings of the conflict came, how earnestly did I look for some intelligence from him, for I trembled lest his name, too, should be found among the long list of the slain.

But at last I received intelligence from him. His regiment had been engaged and had suffered severely; his captain had been killed, and the com-

mand of the company having in consequence devolved upon him, he had discharged the duties of
his trust in such a manner as to win the favorable
notice of his colonel. He had been recommended
for promotion, and had no doubt he would be commissioned captain in the place of him who had
fallen. How proud I was to have this intelligence
of him ; for though I regarded him as the victim of
a dreadful delusion, still was he not my brother,
and should I not glory in his bravery and manhood, even though displayed in a bad cause ? Accompanying this letter was a list of the killed and
wounded of our acquaintances, which I waded
through, shuddering as I came to each familiar
name, until, when the end was at last reached, I
felt sick at heart. Uninformed and ignorant as I
was of all that pertains to war, I could see that
this was but a beginning, and I trembled as the
question forced itself upon me, what would be the
end, and how long it would be before the name of
my brother would be included in some such horrid
list as the one before me ! I felt an almost assured
conviction that he would fall sooner or later, and
this thought was ever present, poisoning all my
joys, and investing my solitary hours with a bitterness almost insupportable.

Meantime the war went on. The North was
making the most strenuous exertions to raise and
equip an army sufficient to bear down all opposition, and corresponding exertions had to be made
by the Southern States to bring into the field an

army sufficient to cope with the National force. The Southern people found that the war was not the mere play-spell they had anticipated, and the force of popular opinion was no longer sufficient to raise such armies as the exigency demanded. In order, therefore, to give new force to that popular opinion, the President of the Confederacy, about this time, issued his famous proclamation, warning all persons who were not willing to take up arms in defense of their country to seek a more congenial home in the North.

This despotic order struck my husband, as it did thousands of others, with the utmost consternation. Up to this time, we had endeavored, by keeping perfectly quiet and attending strictly to our own affairs, to avoid offending the sense of the community in which we lived. But now the time had · come when this would no longer suffice. He must either go into the army and fight for a cause in which he had no heart, or we must dispose of what little property we had, at such sacrifice as we might, and make the best of our way north of Mason and Dixon's line. The first was not to be thought of, and the second was, therefore, the only alternative left us. And thus it was that the Southern people began to reap the sad fruits of the rebellion into which they had so madly and unnecessarily plunged.

We were, at this time, in comfortable circumstances, though far from being rich, and we could ill afford to make the sacrifice requisite to comply

with this cruel order. But neither time nor opportunity was afforded for remonstrance or hesitation.
The order was imperative, and close upon its heels
followed a most rigorous and merciless conscrip-
tion, which was to sweep into the military service
of the Confederacy every man who had not complied with the other dread alternative by banish-
ment. How wretchedly were these poor people
deluded and imposed upon by their designing leaders! Taking up arms to escape from the pretend-
ed tyranny of the Government of the United States,
they now found themselves subjects of a despotism
as much more terrific and intolerable than that
from which they were fleeing, as is the Government of Turkey more absolute than the constitu-
tional monarchy of England. But these reflections
did not help our situation in the least.

Accordingly, my husband set to work to dispose
of what property we had on hand, preparatory to
our emigration from the land of our nativity. In
this matter he met with no little difficulty. The
very fact that he was selling off his property to go
North, at once stamped him as a "disloyal aboli-
tionist;" and, in the opinion of those with whom
he attempted to trade, at once absolved them from
all obligations of honor or honesty toward him.
More than this, he was met with gibes and covert
sneers from those who regarded him as less patriotic than themselves, and was, on several occasions, met with positive insult by parties to whom
he applied to make sales of property. He soon

found that it was impossible to sell except at
enormous sacrifices; but the emergency admitted
of no discussion, and, accordingly, he disposed of
all our property for about two-thirds of its real
value, and we set out for Memphis, Tennessee, as
the most convenient point of egress from the now
hated Confederacy.

During this time I had received several letters
from my brother. He was enthusiastic over the
cause in which he was engaged, and at all times
expressed the utmost confidence in its complete
and speedy triumph. Although I could not believe that such would be the case, nor wish well to
an enterprise which, in my heart of hearts, I con-
demned, still these letters were a source of constant gratification to me. They assured me, from
time to time, of the welfare of a dearly beloved
brother, and my heart overflowed with gratitude
to that God who had thus far mercifully and kindly protected and preserved him amid the perils of
camp-life and the dangers of the battle-field. He
had been promoted two or three times, and at the
time we left Atlanta for Memphis, he occupied the
position of lieutenant-colonel in the same regiment
in which he had gone out as a mere subaltern.
How my heart throbbed with a sister's pride as I
contemplated those evidences of appreciation of
his merit, let those who have thus watched the
upward and onward course of a loved brother
judge. But to return to ourselves and our journey
northward.

My husband had, of course, taken the precaution to procure passes for us from the military authorities at Atlanta; but, notwithstanding this, we were frequently stopped by conscript officers, ourselves and our passes closely scrutinized, our baggage searched, time and again, for articles contraband of war; and, not content with annoying us by all legal means in their power, these petty tyrants, in more instances than one, added insult to injury, by stigmatizing my husband as a traitor and a coward "for leaving his country in her hour of danger." Poor fools! They could not realize that we were fleeing to our country for protection from the persecutions, annoyances and dangers of an illegal and unholy despotism, backed and supported by as fierce and brutal a mob as ever thronged the streets of Paris.

In one instance I thought our journey was to be summarily arrested. Justly incensed at the overbearing and insolent manner of a petty official, who had stopped us to overhaul our baggage, and losing his accustomed control of himself, my husband expressed his opinion of the contemptible little tyrant before us in language more forcible than polite. This he chose to construe into disloyalty to the "great government" of which he was the representative, and Eugene was at once seized by a file of soldiers and thrown into prison. They allowed me no communication with him, and, for a short time, I was utterly at a loss what to do; but after hesitating a time, decided to go to General Jackson, who was in command there, and endeavor to procure his release. The general listened kindly and courteously to my story, and after asking me a few questions, gave me an order for his immediate release. Armed with this missive I flew to the prison, and in a short time we were again on our journey. I shall always retain a most grateful remembrance of General Jackson, for his kindness to me under these trying circumstances.

In due time we arrived at Memphis, which was then in possession of the Confederate forces, but which was invested by the land and naval forces of the Union within a day or two after our arrival. And there I first witnessed the actual horrors of war. It was in Memphis that I first heard the sound of hostile guns, the screaming of shot and shell, the bursting of bombs, and all the horrid sounds which accompany the destruction of human life on the field of battle. Here, too, I first saw wounded men, and my brain turned with horror as I beheld the mangled and bleeding forms of those who had once been stout, healthy, and vigorous men; and as their piteous moans smote upon my ears I shuddered in every fiber of my frame, and hastened to convey myself beyond sight and hear-of these sickening objects.

Of course, under the present state of affairs, it was impossible for us to get any further North, and we remained in Memphis until the surrender of that place to the National forces, when we procured passes and transportation for Cincinnati, where we arrived without further incident. And now, for the first time since the promulgation of the order before referred to, we could feel that we were free. Once more I could lie down to rest at night and feel assured that my husband would not, before morning, be torn from my arms by merciless conscript officers, and hurried into the army which was using all its energies for the destruction of the Government which now sheltered us beneath its protecting wings.

Our stay in Cincinnati was of short duration. We were among strangers, and Eugene did not readily find any avenue of business open to him, and we could not live without doing something. Having heard there was a good opening at London, Canada West, Eugene decided that the best thing we could do was to go there; and, accordingly, we went there, after having staid in Cincinnati but about three weeks. Our journey to that place was unattended with any incidents worthy of record, or in any degree interesting to my readers. I may remark, however, that on our journey through Ohio I was forcibly struck with the vast superiority of the country over anything I had ever seen in the South, in point of improvement and advancement of every kind. Large, well cultivated farms bounded the prospect on every hand; while the comfortable, and often elegant, residences of their owners gave the very highest evidence of thrift and prosperity. Every little town, too, boasted its manu-

facturing establishments; all of which were now
stimulated to the highest degree of activity by the
demand for supplies of all kinds for the use of the
army. I was immeasurably astonished at the little derangement produced here by the war, as
compared with the Southern States. Here business
of all kinds was flowing in its accustomed chan-
nels, with, perhaps, greater' briskness than before
the war; while there, everything was almost at a
stand-still, and a sense of uneasiness and distrust
seemed to pervade the entire community. I wondered, then, at this difference, but have since
ceased to feel any surprise at it.

Upon reaching our destination my husband went
at once into business, and, for a time, prospered
finely. Money was plenty, and as Eugene was a
good financier, we were soon on the fair road to
comfort, if not to wealth. But the climate was so
much colder than we had been accustomed to, that
we were far from being contented. Born and reared beneath the sunny skies of the South, we were
illy prepared to endure the rigors of a Canada
winter, and decided to return to the United States ;
and we were strengthened in our determination by
the fact that Willie, who had always been rather
delicate, was attacked with a severe cough, which
we—whether justly or otherwise, I know not—attributed to the cold and damp climate of that locality. Accordingly my husband, in the fall of
1862, disposed of what property we had there, and
we returned to Cincinnati.

I ought to remark here that, while in Canada, I received letters from my brother—the first intelligence I had had from him directly since we left Atlanta, and the last I was ever destined to receive. Henceforth the fate of war separated us as completely from each other, and as entirely destroyed our communication with each other, as was after-ward done by his death, which occurred in front of Atlanta during the campaign of 1864. At this time, however, he was well, and was still on the high road to preferment. He had been several times promoted since I had heard from him, and was now gracing the position of a brigadier-general. He was as ardent in the cause of Southern independence as ever, and was still just as confident of ultimate success as when he marched from Atlanta in the comparatively humble position of a first lieutenant; at least so he stated in his letters. But I fancied that I detected in his language a sort of undercurrent of despondency which induced me to think that, perhaps, after all, he was not as hopeful as he tried to induce me to believe.

But, be that as it might, I could not but feel proud of the record of gallantry he was making for himself. How much better pleased I should have been had this record been made in behalf of the Government, instead of against it, may easily be imagined; but still we are constrained to admire bravery wherever we see it, even though it be in a bad cause. How natural, then, was it that I should be proud of the evidences of merit displayed

by my only brother, and should rejoice with all
my heart to hear of these successive promotions.
But, alas! how short-lived are the honors and
pleasures of this life! Two years later my poor
brother was buried by strange hands, in an unknown grave, while no friend or sister near him,
in his last hour, listened to his dying words, or
wiped the death-damps from his pale brow as he
breathed forth his parting sigh.

CHAPTER X.

I HAVE said that we returned to Cincinnati in the fall of 1862. This time my husband was more fortunate in getting into business than when we were here before; an opening was soon found, and we took rooms at the Spencer House. My health was so poor, by reason of the excitement that we had undergone for some time, and I was so much worn out by the constant changes and journeyings of the last year, that I did not feel equal to the task of undertaking the management of a house; and hence our determination to board for a time, until I should become somewhat improved in vigor.

For the next few weeks we were very happy. My husband had entirely quit drinking, and spent all his evenings at home with me; my children were in good health, and were four of the sweetest little cherubs to be found anywhere; they gave me very little care or trouble. Save some anxiety on my brother's account, my mind knew not a single burden. The children had forgotten all about their mother, and did not seem to know that I was not their maternal parent, and, on my own part, I loved them as if they had been my own. My husband was as kind and considerate to me as it was possible for any one to be; my every want was supplied, and I almost forgot that I had ever been unhappy.

(159)

But, alas! my happiness was not to last long. A blow from a new and unexpected quarter was impending over me, and was destined soon to shatter into atoms forever the frail fabric of bliss which now surrounded me; to cast me down from the pinnacle of happiness upon which I then rested into the very lowest depths of an abyss of misery and wretchedness so profound that I shudder when I think of it. The time for the revelation of that fatal secret of my husband's, to which allusion has already been made, was fast approaching, and yet I suspected it not. Like Damocles at the festival, when the sword was suspended by a single hair over his head, I reveled in the enjoyment of the bliss presented to me, all unsuspicious of danger, and never dreaming that my happiness could be brought to an end. Then, how terrible the shock when it did come, and with what crushing force the blow fell upon my suddenly-blighted spirit, let the reader imagine; for any words of mine are utterly incapable of describing.

Early one evening I was alone in our sitting-room. The children were all in bed, and my husband had not yet come in, though I was momentarily expecting him. There came a gentle tap at the door, and one of the boys employed about the house came in with a card, which he handed me with a polite bow. I looked at the card—the name was a strange one to me—it was Mrs. Martha H. Mason, a name I had never heard before, nor could I imagine whom she could be, or what should induce her to call upon me. To my look of surprised inquiry, the boy answered that the lady who gave him the card wished to see me in the parlor. In an instant I was struck with an undefinable dread of some approaching evil, but what it was I could not for a moment imagine. Who could she be, and why had she come to seek me? Her summons certainly boded me no good, and I felt sure some deep calamity was in store for me, but what it was I could not divine. I grew weak and felt myself turn pale as these thoughts, in an instant, flashed through my mind; but I retained sufficient strength and control of myself to tell the boy I would be down in a few moments, when he bowed and withdrew.

After he was gone I sunk back into my seat and tried to collect my somewhat scattered thoughts. I ran over, in my mind, all the names with which I was acquainted and could call to mind, and all I remembered to have heard my husband mention, but could not think who Martha H. Mason was. What would I not have given at that moment for my husband's presence and counsel, and at first I thought of waiting until he came in, before according the desired interview. But no; that would not do. Perhaps it was something which affected his honor, in which case it were better for both that I should know the whole truth before seeing him. I did not for a moment imagine that it was anything which would prove him to be guilty of actual crime against the laws

11

of God and man ; and the conclusion at which my
mind finally arrived was, that it was Carrie's
mother, and that she had come to reclaim her
child.   But let the cause of her coming be what it
might, or whoever she might be, I must see her
and know the worst.

Accordingly, after making some slight changes
in my dress, I went down into the parlor.   There
sat a lady dressed in deep mourning ; and the
first glance at her pale, sweet face told me that I
had never seen her before.   Her age was not far
from thirty, as near as I could judge ; and, despite
the evident marks of care and suffering which
her countenance displayed, she was surpassingly
beautiful.   She rose as I entered the parlor and
timidly approached me.   In a low, and finely-
modulated voice, she asked :

" Are you Mrs. Eugene Giles ? "

" I am," I answered.   " What do you wish with
me ? "

" Are you Mr. Giles' first wife ; or was he married before ? "

" I am his second wife.   His first wife died
some eight years or more since.   We were married in about seven months from the time of her
death."

" Had he any children by his first wife ? "

" He had three ; all boys.   But may I inquire
why you ask all these questions ? "

" I will tell you soon.   May I ask the names of
these boys ? "

"The eldest one's name is Willie—he is fourteen years old. The second is Frankie, aged eleven years; and the youngest is Eddie, aged about nine. Do you know Mr. Giles, or why are you so particular in your inquiries about him and his family?"

At this question her entire manner changed, and she answered almost fiercely:

"Do I know him? Yes; far better than you do. Look at this! and she handed me an ambrotype-case. I opened it and found it to contain two likenesses—a young man and young woman. In an instant I recognized them: the young man was my husband, and the young woman was the lady before me. Who was she, and what could it all mean? As I asked her these questions she handed me a written paper and bade me read it. My husband had not kept up the lessons he began with me, and it was with some difficulty that I could read it; but I made out that it was a certificate of the marriage of Eugene Giles Mason and Martha Hart. As the fearful import of this document thrilled through my brain, I was nearly wild with anguish. Could it be that this woman was his lawful wife, the mother of his children? Oh! no! Eugene could not be such a villain. Perhaps she was his wife's sister; and there was so much resemblance between them that I had mistaken the likeness for hers. I turned to her to ask an explanation. She was weeping silently but bitterly.

"Who are you?" said I, "and what is all this to me? What have I, the wife of Eugene Giles, to do with the marriage of Eugene Mason and Martha Hart?"

"The man who now calls himself Eugene Giles," said she, speaking slowly and bitterly, "is no other than Eugene Giles Mason, and I am Martha Mason, his lawful wife, the mother of the three boys whose names you have just given me. Is this nothing to you?"

Had a two-edged sword at that moment pierced my heart, I could not have suffered half the agony I endured as she pronounced these fatal words.

"This can not, can not be!" I cried in my anguish. "Eugene would never be so base. Beside, he told me his wife was dead. Oh! take back those cruel words!"

"It is all true that I have told you," said she. "I have other proofs of the truth of my statements. Will you look at them?"

Alas! there was no need. I felt that her words were true, and that Eugene was not my husband; and the thuoght of my situation, in an instant, flashed upon me.

"If all you have been telling me is true—if Eugene is not my husband—if you are his wife, my God, what am I?" I cried out, and sunk to the floor.

I had not fainted, for I could hear and see every-thing that was said or done in the room, and my mind seemed imbued with unnatural activity, but

the suddenness and violence of the shock had deprived me of all physical vitality, and I was
powerless to rise from the floor. I could not move
or speak. The last words I had uttered were ringing in my brain. If she was his wife, what was I?
I was only his mistress, and had been such for
these many long years. Could it be so? Was it
possible that my husband's real name was Mason,
and that he was the base and unprincipled villain
that her words would indicate? Oh! no; it could
not be. Eugene would never, never, never have
wronged me thus. There must be some terrible
mistake here. His first wife was surely dead, and
our marriage was lawful. This woman was some
base adventuress who had, by some means,
possessed herself of his marriage certificate, and
was now using it for some purpose of her own. Or,
more likely, it was some one else's marriage certificate, which she was trying to fasten upon my
husband. But, then, those likenesses—what could
they mean? But I could not, would not believe
Eugene was so base. Were he here, he could explain all.

While these thoughts ran riot through my brain,
I lay helpless and motionless on the floor, and the
woman who had been the cause of all this misery,
sat staring at me with her great, black eyes, until
they seemed to burn and sear into my brain. I
could not remove my eyes from her face, nor could
I speak. I had never been so completely prostrated and unnerved as I was by this terrible

revelation, and did not care whether I ever moved or spoke again. At length she arose and came to my side. She knelt down by me and spoke substantially as follows, while she rested her hand upon my head:

"Poor child; I do not blame you in the least for this terrible affair. No; you are innocent, and have been the victim of the most grievous wrong, as well as myself. My husband left me when I was confined with my fifth child, little Eddie. He stole my babe, only a week old, and my two little boys, and left me with two little girls. He has now been gone for more than eight years, and, during all that long and weary time, I have been traveling in search of him. I have roamed from place to place, throughout the whole of the United States, with no other object but to find my darling babes. No doubt the heartless monster thought I was dead when he married you. He naturally thought that the loss of my children, in my enfeebled condition, would be too much for me, and that the shock would kill me. But, thank God, I have disappointed him. I have been wonderfully spared and preserved, and high heaven has kindly answered my prayer and guided me to him—and once more I shall possess my darling children, once more I press them to the lonely heart which for years has mourned and sighed for them. But I pity rather than blame you. You have been most grievously wronged as well as myself, and I would not harm

a hair of you head : all I ask is the possession of
my babes, and vengeance upon the heartless
wretch who has deceived and betrayed us both.
Where are my precious darlings? I long to see
them and clasp them to my heart once more."

She pronounced these last words with a vehe-
mence and energy which indicated the depth of
her feeling upon this subject. I strove to reply
to her eager question, but my tongue refused to
obey the mandates of my will, and I remained
silent. She gazed at me a moment, then sprung to
her feet and rung the bell with the utmost violence,
and then turned to raise me and place me on the
sofa. She had barely accomplished her task when
the proprietor of the house made his appearance,
and, in an eager and excited manner, she demanded to be shown to Mr. Giles' room. Probably
he did not observe me lying on the sofa, or he
would have known there was something wrong ;
but he proceeded at once to comply with her demand, and they left the room.

I strove to rise and follow them, but I was completely paralyzed by the horrid events of the last
hour, and my limbs totally refused to obey my vo-
lition. I then tried to speak, to call out and attract
their attention, but was powerless to even move
my tongue. I would have given anything to have
witnessed the meeting between her and Giles, and
to have heard him defend himself against her accusation, for I still half believed there was some
terrible misunderstanding, and that he could ex-

plain it all satisfactorily. Although I was satisfied
she had once been his wife, my faith in him was so
strong that I believed he would be able to explain
away the horrible tale she had unfolded to me.
And now, for the first time, occurred to me the
thought that they might have been divorced, and
Engene might still be innocent of any wrong. But,
then, why should he have told me she was dead?

These thoughts passed through my brain, and
then came the reflection that it mattered very little
to me whether her story was true or false. I felt
that I should never recover from the horrible paralysis into which these astounding revelations had
thrown me. I knew that, in the sight of God, I
was innocent of any wrong; and if I was to die,
what matter whether my association with Giles
was legal or not? Immorality, on my part, I knew
there was none; and as long as my soul was pure
and uncontaminated, what mattered it that I h id
sustained toward him a station not sanctioned by
the laws of God or man? I knew that I was innocent in the sight of high heaven, and I could well
afford that the scorn of those who thought themselves better than I should be visited upon my
memory after my spirit had taken its everlasting
flight to the bosom of my Heavenly Maker.

For a long time I lay alone in the room. No
one came, and I was utterly unable to help myself
in any way, or to give any alarm or make my
wants known. It seemed to me an age—I suppose
it was about half an hour, but it seemed much

longer—before any one made their appearance, and
then Giles came into the room. He came and knelt
by my side, clasped me in his arms, and called me
all the pet names which had been so dear to me in
our happier days, and implored me to forgive him;
told me that he loved me better than his own life,
and could not give me up, and begged me to speak
to him again. I tried to speak, but the terrible
paralysis still held my tongue, and I was unable
to utter a word. Meanwhile he continued his
demonstrations of affection, and the most passion-
ate entreaties for just one word to assure him of
forgiveness. He did not deny that he had wronged
me beyond redress, or that the woman was his lawful wife; he did not dispute the truth of her horrible revelation; but he urged his unbounded and
uncontrollable love for me in extenuation of his
folly and his guilt. And all this time I lay unable
to move or speak.

Eugene finally observed my situation, and starting suddenly to his feet, he hastily left the room.
He was gone but a few moments when he came in
as hastily as he had gone out, accompanied by a
physician, whose name was Wood. He brought
the doctor to my side, and, in the most frantic manner, implored him to save me if within his power.

The doctor took hold of my arm, felt my pulse,
placed his hand upon my forehead for a moment,
then put his ear down to my heartbeat, and, without speaking a word, took a lancet from his
pocket and stuck it into my arm. The blood did

not start readily, and he held hartshorn to my nos-
trils for a short time, which had the effect of starting the crimson current in a steady, vigorous stream.
The flow of blood loosened my paralyzed tongue,
and, in a low voice (for my strength was all gone),
I asked the doctor to leave the room. I wanted to
talk with Eugene, and hear from his own lips the
confirmation or denial of the awful revelation which
had had such a terrible effect on me. But the man
of physic replied that my situation was extremely
critical, that my life was in serious danger, and
that he could not leave until I was better. . However, he asked no questions as to the cause of my
sudden and violent illness. Doubtless his science
revealed to him the cause; but he said nothing in
relation to his suspicions, whatever they may have
been, but steadily and carefully attended to his
business until my arm was bandaged, when he
took his leave—having first left some remedies to
calm my terrible nervous excitement and reinvig-
orate my feeble frame.

As soon as we were once more alone, Eugene, at
my request, came and sat down by my side.

"Eugene," said I, "as you value your soul and
your eternal happiness, tell me the whole truth
relative to this sad, sad affair. Is this woman your
wife?"

"Yes, Minnie," he replied, "she is my wife—the
mother of my three boys."

How the light of hope went out of my bosom as
I listened to this confession, uttered in a low tone

of voice, and with half-averted head. Up to this time I had hoped, notwithstanding the solemn asseverations of the woman, that he would deny it, and that I would be spared the shame and mortification which were now my lot. My faith in him had whispered that either her tale was a fabrication, or she was the victim of some dreadful hallucination. But when he answered me as he did, this last lingering ray of hope faded out, and, with a deep groan, I sunk back upon my pillow, from which, in my excitement, I had half risen to propound my eager inquiry.

"Minnie, I love you enough to give up everything for you. I never knew happiness until I met you, and if you leave me I can never know happiness again. I can be happy with you, but with that woman, never."

"Where is she?" I asked.

"She is up in our room with the children. They were afraid of her, and she was trying to conciliate them by telling them she was their mother, and endeavoring to persuade them to go and live with her. But they would not believe her. They told her their 'ma was down in the parlor—that she had gone there to see a lady who called for her. But she will succeed in convincing them— they will go with her, and she may have them if she will only go away and let us alone."

"Eugene, you must not talk so," I replied as firmly as I could, although it cost me a terrible effort, "we were happy in each other's society be-

cause we supposed we were innocent, and without
innocence there can be no real happiness.   Let us
not, then, forever destroy our happiness and stain
our souls with the guilt of doing wrong with our
eyes open."

But all I could say was of no avail. He still
insisted that he could not and would not part with
me; and, at length, worn out with conflicting
emotions, and with the terrible excitement of the
scenes through which I had passed, I ceased to
contend any longer. He continued to talk for some
time after I had become silent, when thinking, perhaps, that I needed rest, he, too, subsided into
silence and allowed me to indulge my own sad
thoughts.

And sad and gloomy indeed they were. Notwithstanding the awful strain which had just been
imposed upon my mental faculties, my mind was
comparatively clear, and my first thought was for
Carrie. What would become of her? For the
reader will readily conceive that, though I had
ceased to contend with Eugene about the matter,
I had no idea of remaining with him after the
dreadful expose that had taken place. I only
ceased to contend with him because it was useless
to do so, and because he refused to be convinced
of the sin that lay in the course he advocated.
What, then, would become of Carrie? Should I
take her with me, or leave her to the tender mercies
of that dreadful woman? This, it seemed to me, I
could not do. It is true she was no relation to

me, but she was a lovely child, and I loved her
almost as my own. Ah! yes, my own. How I
thanked the God of high Heaven, then, that he had
seen fit to take my own little girl to himself in
the bright days of infancy, before her pure spirit
had been blighted and sullied by contact with this
sinful world. Let not the reader shudder, or think
me inhuman, that this thought found a lodgment
in my breast. Nothing but my overwhelming love
for my offspring gave birth to the idea. What
would have been her fate had she lived to adult
age?

Of illegitimate birth—born to an heritage of
shame and disgrace—a mark for the finger of scorn
and contumely—who can ever guess to what depths
of sin, and degradation, and shame, the dark cloud
which would have rested upon her during the
whole of her life might have driven her! Yes, it
was far better for her as it was; and in pure sin-
gleness of heart, and actuated by naught but the
most exalted love for her, I blessed God that she
had died upon the very threshold of life.

Then my thoughts turned to my own future,
and, look which way I would, nothing was presented but black misery, shame and despair.
Who and what was I? The mistress of a married
man; and for long years I had been living in a
state of adultery with him. True, I was innocent
of any intentional wrong, but, nevertheless, the
black and damning fact stared me in the face, and
would not down at my bidding. And what had I

to hope or anticipate? Alone, aye, doubly alone
in the wide world—my brother Frank, my only
living relative, far away and, perhaps, wounded
or dying on some battle-field, perhaps already
dead—no one to care or provide for me, and utterly unfitted by my education to earn a livelihood—
with the dark stain of the past resting upon me
and clouding my fair name—what wonder that I
groaned in spirit, and even questioned the goodness of the Almighty in his dispensations toward
me? What wonder that my bowed and crushed
heart cried out in bitterest anguish, "My burden
is greater than I can bear? Oh! Thou Eternal
God, what have I done that I should be so much
afflicted above all the children of men? Why is
my pathway strewn only with thorns, and why
dost Thou utterly withdraw thy face from me?"
And then, anon, my spirit became more calm,
and I fervently prayed for strength and grace to
conquer and overcome all ills that beset me. Ah!
how I shudder even to this day as memory recalls
the events of that terrible night.

At length I became more calm, and with returning strength came the desire to go to some other
room, where I would be less exposed to observation than in the public parlor of the hotel. Accordingly Eugene called for another room, and
obtained the key of one adjoining the parlor, and
with his assistance I got into it and lay down on
the bed. He urged me to undress, but I would
not, for I had formed the resolution to leave the

house that very night, and in my feeble condition
I did not want the trouble of dressing. I had also
determined to take Carrie with me, and, accordingly, as soon as I was comfortably disposed on
the bed, I asked him to bring her to me. He went
to our room and brought her, and informed me
that the other children were all asleep, and their
mother lying down with them. They had evidently become reconciled to her, and the fact of their
making up with her so quickly caused me a secret
pang, though I knew it was really nothing to me,
and that their happiness would be promoted thereby. I then asked Eugene to go and bring my
trunks, and all mine and Carrie's things, into this
room. I think this request aroused some suspicion
in his bosom, for he hesitated a little, and asked
me what I meant, and what I was going to do;
but if so, I quieted his apprehensions by telling
him, in an indifferent manner that I did not want
them in the room with that woman, and that I
only wanted them where I could get at them conveniently without meeting her.

Accordingly he ordered the trunks brought
down, and closely following them came "that
woman." Doubtless she thought we were intending
to slip away from her, and this idea aroused the
virago in her bosom.

"What are you about?" said she. "You need
not think to give me the slip now. I have spent
too much time hunting you, and now that I have

got hold of you, I intend to keep you. I am not done with you yet."

"I have no idea of slipping away from you," replied Eugene. "But this lady is very sick, and wants her things in her own room. And, beside, she is not in a condition to be agitated by such violence just now."

"You are very careful of her just now; would it not be just as well for you to have some care of me?"

"But I assure you she is indeed very ill. You can see for yourself."

"If she is so very ill, you can get some one to stay with her. But, as for yourself, you had better come up stairs with your wife."

How that last word grated on my ear, emphasized as she emphasized it. And yet it was true. She was his wife, and I was only his mistress. His place was with her and not with me, and I wanted him to go. And, aside from the question of right and wrong, I had other reasons for wishing him to leave me alone and go to her room with her. In the first place, his absence was necessary in order that I might carry out the plan I had formed of taking my departure from the house that very night. Beside, I knew that a prolongation of this interview would only result in exciting me to such a degree as to wholly prostrate me again, and the little strength I had was barely sufficient for my contemplated flight. Accordingly I seconded her demand with my entreaties, and urged him for the

sake of peace, and for the sake of my health, if not
for the sake of my life, to go with her. After
some urging he went and brought me some
matches, and under pretense of placing them within my reach, came to the bedside, snatched a kiss
before I knew what he intended, and whispering
me that he would be back as soon as she went to
sleep, left the room. She was waiting for him
just outside the door, and I heard them ascend the
stairs together.

Then I knew it was time for me to act, for I was
certain he would be back before long, and any
delay might be fatal to my plans. As soon as the
echo of their footsteps, therefore, had died away at
the head of the stairs I rung the bell, and when
the messenger came, ordered him to send the proprietor of the hotel to me. The landlord came in
a few minutes, and I briefly told him the whole
shameful story—how I married Giles (or Mason)
long years ago, and had lived with him ever since,
believing him to be my lawful husband; how this
woman had come and claimed to be his lawful
wife; and how he had admitted the justice and
correctness of her claim, and that she was really
and truly his wife; and of my resolution to leave
at once, and then begged his assistance in my endeavor. I told him I could not stay to see them
again, and asked him to get a carriage and send
me away at once. He used all his persuasive
powers to induce me to stay where I was until I
was better—told me over and over again that it

12

would kill me if I went out that night—but it was all in vain. Indeed, the suggestion of death was the very poorest argument he could have used, for so intensely bitter had been my lot in life thus far that I would as soon have died as not.

When he found I was unalterably resolved to go that night, he professed his readiness to help me, and asked me where I intended to go. I had not selected any place, and, hesitating a moment, replied that it did not matter where I went—anywhere in the country—until I was better, and could seek a home in some other part of the country. He then informed me that he had a sister living on a farm but six miles from the city, who he was sure would make me welcome and treat me kindly, and would give me such care as my situation demanded. He assured me that I would be comfortably situated, and offered to get a carriage and take me there himself. I thanked him from the bottom of my heart, for his kind and generous offer, and he went out to call a carriage.

But a few minutes elapsed since his departure, and there was a gentle tap at my door. A moment more and it was opened, and the landlord's wife came in. She was about forty years of age, of gentle and ladylike manners and disposition, while goodness and kindness beamed from every lineament of her face, and furnished an unerring index to the noble qualities of her heart. She approached my bedside, laid her hand gently and caressingly upon my forehead, and, with a world of kindness in her tone, said:

"My husband tells me you are going away to-night. Is there anything I can do to assist you?"

"Oh! Mrs. ——," replied I, quite overcome with kindness, "God will reward you for your kindness to a poor, unfortunate stranger—I never can."

"There, my dear child," said she gently, "don't say anything about that, but just tell me what I can do for you. I know all about it, and I were less than human to withhold offers of assistance under such circumstances."

"You may dress Carrie, if you please; and should any reverse ever befall you, or you be in need of assistance, may God deal mercifully with you, even as you and your husband do with me at this time."

She made no reply; but as she dressed the little girl, I could see, by the quivering lip and moistened eye, that I had a friend indeed in her— one upon whom I might rely with the most implicit confidence under all circumstances.

By the time Carrie was dressed, and I had, with the assistance of my kind friend, put on my wrappings, her husband came in to tell me that the carriage was ready; and as he saw the evident indications of emotion, he began to rally us on our tenderheartedness; but, while he did so, there was a tremor in his voice and a moistness in his eye, which told me that he, too, had a heart to feel for the sorrows of others, and that contact with the world had not deadened all the finer sensibilities of his nature.

His wife took Carrie in her arms, I leaned upon Mr. ——'s arm, and we proceeded to the carriage. When I had been assisted in, she kissed Carrie and placed her by my side, and then holding my hand in hers, said, in a tremulous voice :

"If you want any assistance, at any time, do not hesitate to come to me, and be assured that your petition will never be in vain."

I tried to reply, but could not. My emotions, at such unexpected kindness, quite overcame me ; and, after trying in vain to give utterance to the deep thankfulness of my heart, I leaned back in the carriage and burst into tears. Her husband without a word, sprang into the carriage beside me and we rolled away toward the house of his sister, where we arrived about two o'clock in the morning. Of course the family were all asleep at the time, but he called his sister up, introduced me, and briefly explained the cause of our untimely visit.

She welcomed me with a degree of warmth and kindness which showed that my painful fortune had touched a tender chord in her heart, and that nature had bestowed upon her the same noble soul which animated the breast of her brother and his wife, and at once set about making arrangements for my comfort.

Upon seeing me comfortably installed in my new home, Mr. —— took his departure and returned to the city. I have never seen him or his angel wife since, but should these lines come under their observation, let them be assured that my heart still cherishes a lively sense of gratitude to them for their kindness in that dark hour of my life, and that daily and nightly my prayers are offered up to heaven for its choicest blessings to rest in rich profusion upon them. And, though their reward may not be of this earth, at the great day, when all shall stand before the bar of God, then shall the righteous Judge say unto them: "Inasmuch as ye did it unto one of the least of these," and "Come ye blessed of my Father."

CHAPTER XI.

Mrs. King, the lady at whose house I was now staying, was a middle-aged woman, in whose countenance a genial, sunny disposition, and an abundant stock of all the better and nobler feelings of human nature were plainly revealed. Utterly devoid of all affectation or absurd display, calm and self-possessed, and having an unusual amount of strong, practical common sense, she was just the right guardian for me in my present lonely and bewildering situation. For, to tell the truth, the terrible incidents of the last few hours had so shattered my nerves that, for the time being, I was almost incapable of thinking intelligibly upon any subject, or of devising anything for the future.

As soon as her brother had taken his departure she led me into a room adjoining the one in which she had received us, and told me that was to be my room so long as I chose to occupy it. I looked around the room, and everything bore the most ample testimony to her character, as the neat, orderly, and unpretentious housekeeper she was. The furniture was all plain—much of it was old-fashioned—but everything was scrupulously clean and in the best of order. There was a rag-carpet on the floor; in one corner of the room stood a comfortable-looking bed, covered with a clean and

(182)

marvelously white counterpane; an old-fashioned
but neat and comfortable-looking sofa occupied one
side of the room; there were two or three chairs, a
small table, and a washstand; while on another
side of the room was a small fire-place, in which a
bright and cheerful-looking fire had already been
started by my kind hostess. She drew the sofa in
front of the fire, brought a pillow, and told me to
lie down. She then left me, saying she would return in a few minutes with something to refresh me
after my ride. In vain I assured her I did not need
anything—that I did not wish her to take any
trouble: she replied that I must take something,
and went away.

She was gone but a short time, and came back
with a tray, upon which was a pot of strong tea,
cups, sugar and cream, nice white bread and fresh
butter. These she placed upon the table, and
laughingly told me to eat my supper and go to bed
like a good child. I thanked her kindly, and replied that I had had my supper, but would drink
some tea before retiring. She then told me to lie
and take my rest in the morning—that she did not
have breakfast early, and would rap on my door
when it was time for me to get up; then she bid
me good-night, and left the room.

After she had gone I drank a cup of tea, undressed Carrie and put her to bed, and then sat
down before the fire to try to think and devise
some plan for the future. Oh! how dark and dismal my lot, both present and future, seemed, as I

sat there and mused upon it during the still hours
of that night. Here I was, an entire stranger; eight
dollars, which I had in my purse, constituted my
entire fortune; I had myself and Carrie to care for,
and I could think of nothing at which I could make
a comfortable support, and raise and educate her
as I wished to. It was true I was under no legal
obligation to provide for her : she was no relation
to me ; but I loved her as if she were my own; she
did not know but that I was her mother; and
the thought of casting her upon the cold charities
of the world was not to be endured for a moment.
But what could I do?

Once the tempter whispered me to apply to Mason for her support. Nothwithstanding his resolute denial, I felt confident she was his child ; and
surely it would be but justice that he should be
charged with the burden of her maintenance, rather
than myself. But the suggestion was no sooner
made than it was rejected. No ; I had deliberately
fled from him, and had taken measures to conceal
my whereabouts; and not for worlds would I now
let him know where I was, because this would defeat the very object of my concealment from him.
But why not send Carrie back to him? Because I
could not make up my mind to part with her in
my desolation. She was the only living being
around whom the tendrils of my affection could
entwine themselves for support; and, were she
taken away, then, indeed, " my house were left unto me desolate." No; keep her with me I would;

and she should never know but she whom she called "mother" was of her own flesh and blood. Yes, she should stay with me; and my trust in God was strong that he would find some way of escape from my present embarrassing situation.

Thus I sat by the fire and mused the remainder of that eventful night, and it was not until daylight was dawning in the east that the chilliness of the atmosphere (my fire had long since burned low in the grate, though I noticed it not) admonished me that I should retire to bed to keep myself from suffering. I undressed and got into bed beside my little darling, and, worn out by feebleness and the exciting events of the night, I sunk at last into a sound and refreshing slumber.

When I awoke it was late, for the sun was high in the heavens, and was brightly shining into my room through a slight opening in the curtains. Everything around me looked strange, and for a moment I could not realize where I was. But soon the recollection of the horrid events of the past night rushed across my mind, and, with a groan of anguish, I sunk back upon my pillow and closed my eyes as if to shut out the hated vision. But vain, vain were my efforts. The dread past was branded and burnt into my brain in characters of living fire, and there was no escape from the horrid torture of its contemplation, and again I groaned aloud in my agony. Poor Carrie was awake and was frightened at the violence of my emotion, and, in piteous tones, asked me what was the matter.

The sound of her gentle, bird-like voice recalled me to myself; I turned over toward her, and, after caressing her for a few moments, looked at my watch. Judge of my surprise to find that it was a few minutes after ten o'clock!

I immediately arose and proceeded to dress myself and Carrie, when we went into the next room. Mrs. King was sitting there alone, engaged in knitting. She looked up, with a pleasant smile, as we came in, and said kindly:

"Good morning. I hope you have rested well."

"If late hours are any evidence, I certainly have. But why did you not call me as you said you would?"

"I did tap once on your door about eight o'clock, but you seemed to be sleeping so soundly that I thought it a pity to disturb you. I knew it was late when you went to bed, and thought the rest would do you more good than anything else. So I kept your breakfast warm, and just left you alone. Will you have it now?"

"Yes, I thank you. It was, indeed, late when I went to bed, for I did not lie down until daylight was appearing in the east. But I am sorry to put you to so much trouble."

"Say nothing about that. Poor child! what is my trouble compared with yours?"

"But I brought my trouble upon myself, innocently, it is true, and it is not right for me to cause you trouble."

"My Master tells us to bear each others' bur-

dens, and, although I fall far short of obeying His
commands, at all times, I can not avoid so plain a
requirement of duty as this."

This little conversation, during which she had
been engaged in placing our breakfast on the
table, gave me a new insight into the character of
my kind hostess. I now understood the secret of
the calm contentment which ever rested upon her
features, and the genial sunshine which ever pervaded her presence. She was an humble, consistent follower of the meek and lowly Jesus, and her
simple, Christian faith imparted to her character
a calm and elevated refinement which I have never
seen excelled. Surely there is a crown of glory
laid up for her at the right hand of her heavenly
Master, which Christ, the righteous Judge, shall
give to her in that day.

My heart was too full for reply, and, without a
word, we took our seats at the table, but my emotions choked me, and I could scarcely eat the
food she placed before me. But Carrie, poor child,
had nothing to pre-occupy her mind; she did not
realize or know the situation in which we were
placed, and she eat heartily, prattling away meanwhile in all the merry light-heartedness of childhood. How I envied her freedom from care and
sorrow, and almost wished that I, too, were a child
again.

Surely, childhood is the happiest portion of life;
it can not be otherwise. In infancy we know
nothing of the deceit and sinfulness of the world;

the spirit has not been blighted by contact with
the rough scenes of adversity which invariably
accompany more mature years ; the world seems
but a vast storehouse of pleasure, instead of the
scene of strife and conflict which later experience
demonstrates it to be ; and life seems one long day
of sunshine, instead of a succession of tempests,
which too often break and blight the spirit of man
as he reels before the unequal conflict.   It is true
that childhood has its griefs, and its little sorrows,
but their memory is soon swept away by the
torrent of happiness which speedily follows, and
all is bright again.   Happy, thrice happy, days of
childhood !   Would that ye were mine again.   But
vain is the wish.   Ye are gone never to return,
and I, a lone wanderer amid the children of men,
am left to breast the storms of maturer life as best
I may.   God give' me his grace to sustain me in
the dreadful conflict, lest I succumb in the unequal strife !

After breakfast was over I took Carrie on my
lap and talked to her.   I felt certain that Mason
would do all in his power to regain possession of
us, and proceeded to give her such instruction as
it seemed to me would prevent her childish prattle
from betraying the place of our concealment.   I
told her she must never ask for her papa or her
little brothers ; that they were all dead, and she
would never see them again, and that if any one
asked her about them, she must say they were
dead.   The poor child did not understand the im-

port of my language—she knew not what I meant
when I told her "they were dead"—she knew,
however, there was something wrong, and my
solemn looks, and impressive tone and manner,
awed her into submission to all my requirements.
She promised compliance with my wishes, and I
have every reason to believe she kept her promise,
notwithstanding her tender years at the time of
making it.

As I had anticipated, Mason made great efforts
to discover our whereabouts. I had been at Mrs.
King's but two or three days, when there appeared
in the columns of the "Commercial," and other
papers of the city, a notice, calling for information
of a lady and child, giving a perfect description of
Carrie and myself. This was inserted for three or
four days in succession, when, it having evidently
failed to elicit any information, it was discontinued, and another, offering a "liberal reward," for
tidings of the fugitives, appeared in its place.
Mrs. King called my attention to this notice, and
said, laughingly, that she thought she had better
answer it and get the "liberal reward." But I felt
no uneasiness, notwithstanding Mason's evidently
earnest attempts to ascertain my whereabouts.
We very seldom saw any company, and I had too
much confidence in the only persons who were in
possession of my secret, to have any fears of their
betraying me. These advertisements, therefore,
gave me no alarm whatever, and I remained quiet,
fully believing that Mr. ——— would let me know

when it was safe for me to leave my place of concealment.

And my confidence was not misplaced in the
least. For some time, advertisements of various
kinds continued to appear in the journals of the
city, all pointing to me, and directed to the object
of my discovery, but after a time they ceased, and
the pursuit appeared to be abandoned. Doubtless
Mason would have found me had I sought a hiding-
place in some distant part of the country, but the
fact that I had taken refuge so close to him—under
his very nose, as it were—seems never to have occurred to him, and his efforts were all directed too
far away. A day or two after the advertisements
ceased to be in the papers, my kind friend, Mr.
——, sent word to me that Mason had gone to
New York with his wife, and that all fear of de-
tection was over, for the present at least. Now I
felt free again, for though I had never had any
fears that either Mr. —— or Mrs. King would
betray me, still I thought that I was not perfectly
safe so long as he continued the search for me.
I knew that he had money, and I was well aware
of the wonderful power of gold in stimulating the
efforts of detectives. And I had every reason to
believe that he would spare neither time nor money
in his efforts to find me. And there is ample evidence that he did employ a large number of
special agents, not only in Cincinnati, but in other
cities, to discover my hiding-place.

Now, however, the search was ended, and the

question arose, what was I to do? It was very evident that I could not stay in my present quarters—
something must be done to support myself and my
child—and what could it be? I knew something
about painting in water-colors, and could paint on
glass, but it would take time and means to get up
a class of pupils, and, beside, I had no great confidence in my ability to earn a living in this way.
And, even if successful, how was I to support Carrie and myself while I was getting a class and
obtaining the practice necessary to enable me to
teach properly, for I had paid no attention to painting for a long time, and was sadly out of practice.
I had no money, having paid Mrs. King what little
I had when I came there, and my way seemed beset
with difficulties on every hand. But something I
must do.

I mentioned my difficulties to Mrs. King, and she
proposed that I should stay with her, while her
brother would get me a class, and that, in the
meantime, I could get material from the city, and
attend to my practice until I was able to take
charge of the class. To this kind proposition, I
objected that I had already burdened her brother
and herself sufficiently, and that I was unwilling
to tax their kindness any further. It was finally
settled that I should leave Carrie with her while I
went to the city and found some employment at
which I could earn my own support while making
the necessary preparations to take my class. I
dreaded parting from my child, even for the short

time which it was supposed would elapse before I
could reclaim her; but there seemed no alternative, and I bade her good-bye and went to the city.
The result of my efforts to get employment will be
found in the next chapter.

CHAPTER XII.

Upon leaving Mrs. King's house I went to the city, and at once made my way to the Spencer House, but what a disappointment awaited me there. The kind friends who had formerly kept the place, and from whose countenance I had anticipated so much, were no longer there. Mrs. ——'s health had been getting delicate for some time, and they had finally rented the house and gone on a journey for her benefit, having left the city that very morning. It will be borne in mind that nearly a week had elapsed since Mr. —— had sent me the intelligence of Mason's departure, and in that time their arrangements had been completed, and they had gone away. What was I to do? I was alone in a great city, without money, and without a single friend to whom I could apply for even the miserable boon of a crust of bread and a night's lodging.

I rested for a short time, and then set out in search of something I could do. By dint of persistent inquiry I at last found a stopping-place, in the family of a Mr. Jennings, on Main Street, near Seventh. They gave me no regular employment, but consented that I should remain there, and work for my board, until something better should turn up. Poor as this arrangement was, it

13   (193)

still furnished me with food and shelter until I could do better. For this I was duly thankful, and entered upon my new avocation with zest and gratitude, while, in the meantime, I spared no pains to find some more lucrative employment. But days passed, and no opening presented itself —every avenue of honorable support seemed closed to me, and despair was fast settling down upon my mind. But temporary relief was at hand, and that, too, from a quarter of which I had not dreamed.

One day, as I was returning from market, whither I had been for Mrs. Jennings, I met a gentleman who was about passing me without notice, but who suddenly stopped, and exclaimed:

"My God! Mrs. Giles, is that you?"

I recognized him in a moment. He was an old neighbor of mine in my happier days, and I returned his greeting as warmly as it was given.

"Where do you live, and where is Giles?" he asked, when our first greeting was over.

I told him where I lived and how I lived; that I knew nothing of Giles; and that, if he would call on me that evening, I would explain everything to him. He promised to do so, and we shook hands and parted, he going down the street and I returning to what was my home.

In the evening he came, and I told him all that had happened since we had seen each other, and with which the reader is already acquainted. He seemed much moved at the story of my misfortunes, and, when I told him of my projects for the future, and that if I could only get to Captain Lake I was sure he would let me have the means to carry my plan into execution, he at once offered to loan me the money to go to Atlanta. He had left there before the war broke out (it was now ended), and he had not been back since, and did not know whether Captain Lake was there or not, but he would let me have the money to go and see. I accepted his offer with thankfulness, and the next day saw me on my way to my once pleasant home.

But I was doomed to the bitterest disappointment I had experienced since discovering the perfidy of Mason. I do not refer to the horrible devastation which had been wrought by the cruel hand of war in and around Atlanta; this is matter of history, and I was, in some measure, prepared for it—but Captain Lake was not there, nor were my efforts to obtain any intelligence of him successful. It was a long time before I could even find any of my former acquaintances. All had gone, and their places had been filled by others, and at the home of my childhood I was in a land of strangers. At length I succeeded in finding an old man who had known me in better days, and from him I learned that Captain Lake was somewhere in the North, but he could not tell me where. The Captain had been so severely wounded that his life had been despaired of, and he had been compelled to leave the army; and, at the close of the war, finding his property destroyed, in a great measure, and himself nearly a bankrupt, he had made his way North in hopes of repairing his shattered fortunes to some extent.

This was all he could tell me; and sad intelligence it was to me. What was I to do next? My hopes of getting assistance from that quarter had failed, and there I was without any means of supporting myself, or even of scarcely paying my way back to Cincinnati, whither I must go. My child was there, and I must go to her at all hazards. Beside, in the disordered state of things at Atlanta, it was preposterous for me to think of trying to earn a living there.

The difficulties which stared me in the face might well have appalled a stouter heart than mine, but I met them bravely and, thank God! have been to a considerable extent able to overcome them.

Through the kindness and with the aid of the old man above mentioned, I succeeded in obtaining from a merchant in Atlanta the loan of some money to pay my fare back to Cincinnati, where I proposed to start anew in my search for fortune. Upon arriving in the city, my first duty was to pay a visit to Carrie, and the reader may rest assured that I never performed a duty more willingly in my life. I had not seen her for more than a month, and when it is remembered that this was the first time I had ever been separated from her, the reader will have no difficulty in believing that it was with emotions of no little joy that I clasped her to my heart once more.

I found both her and her kind guardian in the best of health, and was greeted by both with a kindness which told the esteem in which I was held. After spending a day there, I went back to the city, took up my quarters at a boarding-house at No. 208 Fifth Street, and at once set about refreshing my knowledge of painting and seeking for pupils. I also took the necessary steps to secure proper rooms in which to receive my class, if I should be so fortunate as to get one.

My success equaled my most sanguine expectations. In about ten days I had a class of some twelve pupils, and had so assiduously practiced my art, that I felt competent to take charge of them. I had also secured very comfortable rooms at No. 115 Elm Street, and had decided to keep house there, thinking it would cost me less than to board, while my duties to my pupils would leave me plenty of time to do my own housework.

For a time I got on swimmingly. The interest of my pupils in their lessons seemed to increase from day to day, and as they progressed under my instructions they took pains to speak of my school to their acquaintances. Others applied for admission to my school, and in a short time I had all the scholars which my rooms would accommodate. I even began to think of taking my little girl from Mrs. King, and taking charge of her myself—something I had not yet done for the reason that my finances were not in such condition as to enable me to pay her board in the city, as it would cost much more than to keep her at her present location.

But I had lived in my present quarters only about three weeks, had only got fairly started with my school, when the owner of the house came to me and told me that he was about selling it, and that I must look for rooms elsewhere. Of course there was no help for it, and so dismissing my school for a time, I set out on the weary quest of another stopping place. My search was long and tedious; but why inflict the annoyances of "house-hunting" upon my readers? Suffice it to say that I finally succeeded in getting rooms for barely two months—nothing would induce the owner to rent them longer—at No. 10 Harrison street. And to tell the truth, I did not wish to stay there very long, for I had to pay a most exorbitant rent, and my finances were not sufficient to stand the heavy drain for very long.

When my time was up, I again found temporary quarters in four rooms—I had to take all or none—on the third floor of a house on Sixth street. But financial considerations induced me to make my stay there as brief as possible, and in a short time I removed from this location to a small cottage at No. 38 Barr street, where I remained as long as I staid in Cincinnati. During all this time I had had a good class in painting, and my receipts had been considerably in advance of my expeditures. I was in fact doing very well.

But from some cause which I have never been able to explain to my own satisfaction, my business began to decline. The pupils who composed my first classes had obtained all the knowledge I was capable of imparting to them, and no others appeared to take their places. Becoming convinced that my day of usefulness and pecuniary success in Cincinnati was past, I made up my mind to sell off my furniture, remove to Detroit, and try my luck there; and at once proceeded to carry my determination into effect. Accordingly I converted what few household goods I had into money, and with this in my pocket went to Mrs. King's to get Carrie, preparatory to my journey to the city of Detroit.

I found Mrs. King almost unwilling to let Carrie go away. She had no children of her own, and she had become so attached to "the little darling" that she hardly knew how to part with her. She conceded my right to take her, but, at the same time made the most liberal offers if I would only consent to, let her keep my child. She had an abundance of property, and if I would only let Carrie stay with her, it should be hers at Mrs. King's death. Perhaps it would have been better for Carrie if I had consented to let her stay, but she was all I had to love in the wide, wide world, and I felt that it would be the next thing to taking my life to part with her. Accordingly I declined her munificent offers, and took Carrie away, loaded with presents, and, I am convinced, sincerely mourned by her who had so long acted a mother's part toward her. Before we left, she exacted from me a promise that if at any time Carrie became a burden to me, and I found it necessary to part with her, she should have her. This promise I gave the more readily because I felt sure that the condition upon which it was based would never arise. And, thank God! it never has arisen. I have been steeped almost to the lips in poverty's depths—I have seen the time that I hardly knew where my next meal was to come from—I have been driven to pawn my wearing apparel, my jewelry, and even (as has been seen) the keepsakes of dear and valued friends, in order to purchase the means of appeasing my hunger, but amid it all, the time has never come when I was willing to part with that child. And though she is no relation to me, though no ties of consanguinity bind us together, though there is no bond between us save that arising from the care I had bestowed upon her in the helpless days of infancy, the time will never come, so long as I am able to earn the merest pittance of food for myself or her, in which I shall be willing to have her care and training transferred to other hands than my own. I may, of course, consent that temporarily she shall be placed in the care of another, as a school-teacher or the like, but further than this I never will while I have life and reason left.

My journey to Detroit was attended with no incidents worthy of notice in these pages. There

was the usual amount of annoyance and weariness
attending railroad travel, and with which all my
readers are familiar; there was the usual amount
of uproar and confusion at the various stations;
there was the usual annoyance from porters,
hackmen, omnibus drivers, etc., which is to be
met with in all the principal cities of the United
States, to the disgrace of human nature in general,
and of municipal officers in particular. But we
managed to live through it all, and, in due time,
found ourselves in the city of Detroit.

I had no very well defined plans in coming to
this place. So far from designing to pursue the
avocation which had afforded me such a comfortable subsistence in Cincinnati, I had become disgusted with it as a means of livelihood, and was
firmly resolved to resort to it only in case all other
means failed to produce the desired results. I
was therefore totally at sea as to the future, and
could do nothing but stop at a hotel until something should turn up, or, until I could decide upon
my future course of action.

The prospect looked cheerless enough. There
I was, in the midst of a large city, amid the moving
myriads of whose population I was not aware that
I knew a single soul, with but little means in my
possession, and entirely at a loss which way to
turn for succor and relief. But my confidence in
Providence, or my lucky star, was unabated; I
felt sure that some means of relief would be presented to me; and I retired to my room at the

hotel, and slept as soundly as though the future had been to me a cheerful day of summer sunshine instead of the dark and gloomy cloud which it really was.

CHAPTER XIII.

THE next morning after my arrival in Detroit I took an inventory of my means, with a view of determining upon some mode of support for Carrie and myself. Upon one thing I was decided—that I would not resort to teaching if I could find anything else to do. Not that teaching was in itself so disagreeable to me—many things are more unpleasant; but it was very confining, and the confinement was telling upon my health. Indeed, this was one reason why I was so willing to give it up and leave Cincinnati.

I found myself in possession of something over five hundred dollars—enough, I thought, to enable me to furnish a house, and open a small boarding establishment, at which I was confident I could make my own and Carrie's living. The next thing was to secure a house, and I at once set out in quest of one, leaving Carrie in charge of one of the girls at the hotel. My search was long and tiresome, but was at last successful. I found a very neat cottage of six rooms, which was vacant, and which I secured, paying three months' rent in advance, and then at once set about furnishing it. My furniture was comfortable, though plain, but everything was high, and when my house was furnished, and a supply of provision bought, my five hundred dollars had been reduced to an alarmingly small amount. Still I had had several applications for board, and I felt confident of success in my, to me, new enterprise.

A day or two after opening my house I met on the street with one whom I little expected to see there, and who on his part was equally surprised at the meeting. It was none other than Captain Lake. He had been living in the city for some time, but had no idea I was so near him, though he had made considerable effort to find me. The last trace he had of me, he had obtained from Giles (or Mason), who had been to him in search of me, and had told him all the circumstances of our parting, avowing, at the same time his determination to find me and live with me again. The Captain had been very uneasy about this, and was very much relieved when I assured him that under no circumstances would I consent to any such arrangement—that I was not his wife, and nothing should induce me to become his mistress.

I then inquired about himself and family. His family were well, but he was suffering severely from a wound he had received while in the army, and which it was thought would cause his death. I may remark here that this wound did finally end his life. He had lost a great share of his property during the war, but had saved enough to afford himself and family a rather moderate support. And it was from him at this time that I learned what I have before stated; that my

brother had fallen during the campaign against
Atlanta. Although I had not heard anything of
him for a long time, I had hoped until this moment
that he had come out of the terrible conflict un-
harmed, but this hope was now suddenly dashed
to earth, and with what terrible force the blow fell
upon my heart can only be imagined by those,
who like me, have been called to mourn the loss of
a dear and only brother. And poignancy was
added to my sorrow by the reflection that he had
fallen in what I could not but consider an unjust
and unholy cause. But it was vain to mourn.
He was gone, and I was alone in the wide world.

Captain Lake told me where they were living,
invited me to come there, and offered me a home
in his family, saying I should want for nothing so
long as I refused to hold any communication with
Giles. I thanked him for his kind offer, but told
him what arrangements I had made for obtaining
my support, and that I preferred not to depend
upon anyone—assured him that I had every prospect of succeeding in my undertaking, and said
that in case of failure it would be time enough to
tax his generosity for my support. He seemed
very much pleased at the energy I had displayed,
and assured me that if at any time I found it
necessary to call upon him for assistance it would
be cheerfully rendered. He, however, advised me
to drop the name of Giles and take my maiden
name, which I told him I had already done, and
now called myself Mrs. Hamilton. He then bid

me good evening, and left me, saying that Mrs.
Lake would come and see me the next day, and I
must return her visit.

In accordance with his promise, Mrs. Lake came
to see me on the morrow. She seemed pleased to
see me, as I certainly was her; but she was, oh!
so changed. In the few years since I had seen her
she seemed to have lived half a lifetime—her once
smooth and lovely brow was now deformed with
incipient wrinkles; her blooming complexion had
faded; and her hair in various places was streaked
with gray. It could not be that age had wrought
so much of change in her, and I could not avoid
the conviction that her married life had not been
very happy. Nevertheless, she possessed the
same degree of humor and gayety as of old—it
might be subdued a trifle by the years which had
passed over her head—and we passed a very
pleasant day together. When she went home,
I accompanied her, and spent the night at their
house, returning early the next morning; for I
had advertised in the Free Press for boarders, and
I anticipated applications for my unoccupied rooms
during the day.

And my anticipations were not disappointed.
Before nightfall my rooms were all engaged, and
I had been compelled to refuse two or three applicants. My success had more than equaled my expectations. In less than a week from the time
of opening my house I had filled it with as agreeable a family of boarders as I ever met in my life.

Two of them, a Mr. and Mrs. Hopkins, were especial favorites of mine, particularly the lady. I do not think I ever knew a more charming woman than she was, while her husband was just my ideal of a gentleman. My situation was very pleasant, and, for a time, things went on to my entire satisfaction. As I have said, I called myself Mrs. Hamilton, and I gave my boarders to understand that I was a widow, and that Carrie was my daughter. I had considerable trouble to school her into this little deception; and my heart smote me not a little as I trained her to utter the falsehood which was to shield my own reputation and hers. She would insist that her father's name was Giles, and would persist in asking for him and for her little brothers. It was a long time before I could educate her to the point at which I felt it safe to allow her to talk alone with others; but at length I succeeded, and the lie was fastened upon her pure, young spirit. Was it a sin to teach her thus to deceive? Answer me, ye casuists, who shudder with horror at the thought of the least concealment of the truth in others, how many of you, under the same circumstances, would have done otherwise than I did?

But, though everything was going so pleasantly upon the surface, there was one matter which gave me no little secret uneasiness. I dreaded lest Mason might succeed in the determination he had expressed to Captain Lake—might succeed in discovering my whereabouts, which, it was very ap-

parent to me, would be immediately and everlast-
ingly fatal to all my prospects of success; and my
anxiety was not in the least dissipated when Captain Lake told me he had reason to suspect that
Mason was in the city, and was still engaged in
the prosecution of his search. I did not know
what to do. I hardly dared to go out for fear of
meeting him; and the probable consequences of
such a meeting were the burden of my dreams by
night. One thing which caused this secret dread
to weigh heavier upon my spirits, was the fact that
I had no one to whom I could confide my burden.
I had but one living friend to whom I could have
unfolded the tale, and he was in San Francisco,
California. Sometimes I thought of writing to
him about the matter, but I could not broach the
subject without giving him the whole history of
my past life, and I dreaded to see it in writing:
so I kept my burden to myself, and struggled on.

But the burden, together with my constant confinement, was fast wearing me out. I grew pale
and thin; I was flushed and feverish at night, and
my whole system was enervated and unstrung to a
most alarming degree. At length I yielded to the
solicitations of my friends, and applied to a physician of eminence and standing for relief. He
pronounced my case consumption, and gravely assured me that there was no relief for me; that I
must die ere long, and that all that could be done
was to smooth my passage to the tomb.

Although I was satisfied he was in error as to

what ailed me, still I thought it quite likely he was right about my early decease, and this reflection but increased my uneasiness. For, when I was dead, what would become of Carrie? Who would care for the little bud which was just developing into the perfect flower? As this inquiry, in all its dreadful vividness, presented itself to my mind, I again thought of writing to my friend in California, and asking him to take care of my child when I was gone; but how could I tell him of her without telling him all my history? And again I shrunk from the dreadful exposition. My courage was not then equal to the task I am now pursuing. Wronged as I felt that I had already been by fate and the world, I had not yet sustained enough of injury at their hands to rouse me to the pitch of desperate courage which would enable me to lay bare for the inspection of mankind all the miseries and sorrows which had been my lot since my advent upon the stage of existence—to relate, as guides and warnings to the young, the many and fatal mistakes of my career. And, above all, I shrunk from acquainting him with my condition, feeling assured (so devoid was I of confidence in any of the human family) that if the truth, with which the reader is already familiar, were unfolded to him, he would at once and forever blot my name from the list of his friends, and he—almost the last tie which bound me to the mass of humanity—be lost to me; and from this fate I shrunk with the most painful apprehension.

14

I am now well assured that in this I judged him wrongfully, and that the revelation, so far from alienating him from me, would but have bound his spirit more closely to mine; but it is the province of misery to render us suspicious of all around us, and at this time I was intensely miserable.

And now was about to occur an event which was destined to work an entire change in my life—an event whose consequences were to endure as long as my life shall last, and which was destined to sink me to still lower depths of misery and wretchedness than any I had yet tasted, although, even at that time, it seemed to me I had already drained the bitter cup of sorrow to its very dregs.

I was going to market one evening with my basket on my arm, and, as I walked along, was musing upon the wretchedness which had attended my every step in life, and wondering why I had thus been made the target at which fate delighted to launch her sharpest and bitterest arrows, when, accidently raising my eyes, I beheld a sight which for a moment caused my heart to stand still, and almost froze the blood in my veins. Crossing the street just in front of me was Eugene Giles Mason—he from whose face I had been so carefully hiding for the last two or three years, and than whose presence I could conceive of nothing more dreadful. Fortunate for me it was that his eyes were bent upon the ground, and that he was looking neither to the right nor the left: had his eyes been cast in my direction he could not have failed to see and recognize me, and I shudder even to this day when I reflect upon what might have been the consequences of such a discovery. I stood still, hardly daring to draw my breath until he had passed out of sight, when I turned and flew homeward as rapidly as my trembling limbs could carry me.

Arriving at my own house, I sat down and tried to devise a plan to meet the emergency, but for some time my mind was incapable of anything like clear or connected action. The one great and terrible fact that the destroyer of my peace and happiness was in the city, doubtless in search of me, loomed up before my mental vision in fearful proportions, and for a time obscured everything else. It is true, I had heard of him from time to time, still engaged in the prosecution of his search for me; but I had escaped so long that I had come to regard his discovery of me as of so little probability as to give me little or no uneasiness. But he was here in the city—I had seen him with my own eyes—and now the chase seemed so near up as to fill me with the most fearful apprehensions, and to deprive me for the time of all power of rational reflection.

At length, however, the fever of excitement having passed away, I set myself to calmly consider what was best for me to do. One thing was evident—I could not remain where I was, nor did I deem it safe even to stay in the city where he was stopping. Of course, he had photographs of me, and, by the aid of these and the assistance of the police, he would doubtless soon be able to find me, no matter how much care I might use in concealing the place of my abode, or how obscure the station I might assume. I at once, therefore, determined to sell out what property I had, in the most secret manner possible, no matter at what sacrifice, and leave Detroit. But whither should I go? This was a question of no little difficulty with me; but, after debating it some time in my own mind, I decided upon Chicago, believing he would be less likely to seek me in that direction than in any other.

It may seem strange that I did not consult Captain Lake and his wife before deciding a matter of so much importance as an entire change in my mode of life, as well as location; but I must confess that my hasty and capricious temper, which has been the bane of my life, had put it out of my power to do so. I will explain. The reader is familiar with the means by which Captain Lake had succeeded in possessing himself of the property which should have been of right mine. One day when his wife was visiting me, smarting under a sense of my wrongs, I had unjustly and ungratefully (for had she not nursed me back to life from the very door of death's gloomy pavilion?) accused her of being a party to her husband's wrong—an accusation which she resented with proper spirit; and the result had been an entire cessation of intercourse between us. Oh! how often and bitterly have I repented my injustice and ingratitude ; but what availed 'my repentance ? I never saw her again—she died when I was far away, without my ears being gladdened by the sound of her whisper- ed pardon; and yet I know that her pure spirit has long since forgiven the great wrong I then heaped upon her.

No sooner had I determined upon my course of action than I hastened to carry it into effect. I sold out my furniture, gave up the lease of my house, found a good place for Carrie (for I did not wish to take her with me until I became settled), wrote a note to Captain Lake, telling him my reasons for leaving, but not where I had gone ; and with the little means realized from the sacrifice of my property, set out to commence life anew in the Garden City of the great West, with- out a single plan of my future course in earning a livelihood.

CHAPTER XIV.

In due time I arrived at Chicago, and stopped at the Massasoit House, at the corner of Dearborn and Randolph streets, where, however, I remained but one night. My means were by far too limited to allow me to remain there, or anywhere else, in idleness, and my first care was to find some cheap but respectable boarding-house, conveniently located for carrying on the occupation I had determined to adopt, for a time at least—that of a plain seamstress.

I succeeded in finding a very comfortable room, and reasonably good fare, at the house of a Mr. ——, near the corner of Lake and Halstead streets, for which I paid, in advance, the sum of seven dollars per week. I view of the fact that I had less than three hundred dollars in my possession, a part of which it was absolutely necessary for me to lay out in clothing, the price seemed to me very high; but, nevertheless, it was the best I could do, and I comforted myself with the reflection that I could earn at least this amount each week with my needle. Poor fool that I was? I did not then know that sewing-women do not *live* by their work—that they sew and *starve*, while wealthy manufacturers reap the reward of their toil. Nor did I know that, before I could get any work, the most fearful inroads would be made upon the little pittance I had brought from Detroit.

As soon as I had secured my room and adjusted my furniture (and scanty enough it was, let me assure you,) to my satisfaction, I set out in search of employment, for I realized the fact that I could not live in idleness and pay seven dollars a week for my board. And, even if I had been able, I could never have ventured to sit down without employment of some sort to divert my mind from the contemplation of the gloomy past, and the fearful apprehension of the future. The dread of discovery by Mason had received a new impetus from the momentary view I had had of him in the streets of Detroit, and this fear, together with the contemplation of the past, would have driven me wild had I remained idle. So, with as stout and brave a heart as I conld conjure up, but feeling, nevertheless, a little like " a cat in a strange garret," I went forth. And the history of my adventures in search of the employment I sought—the rebuffs and refusals with which I met on every hand— the covert sneers and almost 'open insults with which my applications were frequently answered— the heart-sickness with which, as refusal after refusal were meted out to me, I pursued my self-imposed task—all these, if written out in full, would make a volume much larger than the one, dear reader, now before you. But my heart would fail me were I to undertake to write them out, and yours would weary in reading them, and for both

our sakes I for bear. A few instances must suffice
to illustrate the treatment I encountered.

One of the first places at which I called was a
large retail clothing store, but a short distance
from my boarding place. I omit the name and
location of the house for the reason that I have
not enough good-will toward them to care about
advertising for them free of charge.

As I entered the door, a spruce, dapper-looking
little clerk came forward, bowing and scraping;
but when he came near enough to see, from my
dress, that I was not one of the *ton*, but simply a
working girl, his excessive politeness vanished in
a moment, his back stiffened, and his manners became almost freezing in their cold formality.

"Good morning, ma'am, anything wanting?"

"Yes, sir," said I, a little haughtily, for I felt
somewhat piqued at his manner; "is the proprietor
in?"

"I don't know whether he is or not. Did you
want anything in particular?" said my dapper
friend.

"Yes, sir; I wish to see him."

"Jem," calling out to a boy who was lounging
in the back part of the store, "won't you see if
Mr. —— is in? Here's a person wants to see
him."

"Jem" departed on his errand, while the
gentlemanly (?) clerk stood watching me as though
he suspected I intended to steal something. After
a time he came leisurely forward, and, in a drawl-

ing tone, informed me that Mr. —— would see me.
Following him into the counting-room, I found
myself in the presence of a fat, pompous old
gentleman, of about fifty years of age, somewhat bald-headed, and wearing enormous gold
spectacles.

"Good morning, madam," said he, very pomp-
ously; "did you wish to see me?"

"Yes, sir. I am in search of employment. Have
you any plain sewing that you wish done?"

"Well, yes," he replied slowly, scanning me
closely through his spectacles; we have a good
deal of sewing to do; have you ever sewed
much?"

"Considerably," I replied.

"Of course you have references; let me look at
them."

This was a poser. I had, as the reader is aware,
but just arrived in Chicago, and knew not a single
soul there, and where was I to look for references?
For a short time I stood silent and undecided
what to say or do. At last I managed to falter
out that I had but just come to Chicago, was a
stranger, etc., but was suddenly interrupted by
my pompous friend with—

"Well, madam, if you can not give us good references, we can not give you work. We never employ any whom we do not know, without the best
of references. "Jem," calling the boy who had
conducted me thither, "show this lady to the

door," and, waving his hand with a lordly air, he dismissed me without further ceremony.

This was the result of my first effort, and it was far from reassuring to the shrinking spirit with which I had set out. For a time my heart was full, and I was almost tempted to return to my lodgings and make no further attempts that day at obtaining employment. But, remembering that my financial status would admit of no sickly sentimentality, or shrinking, because of a single rebuff, I once more set out. After visiting several places without meeting with any success, I at last found myself face to face with a little bullet-headed, hard-featured wretch, who, when I made my errand known, replied briskly:

"Oh! yes. We have lots of work to do. What do you prefer, pants or plain shirts?"

"What prices do you pay for each?"

"One shilling and sixpence for pants, such as we would want you to make, and two shillings for shirts. How many will you have?"

"What prices did you say, sir?" said I chokingly, for the idea of trying to earn seven dollars at such rates as these filled me with dismay.

"Eighteen pence for pants and two shillings for shirts."

"But how do you expect me to make a living at at those prices?"

"That is not our look-out, madam," he replied heartlessly; "those are our prices, and if you do not wish to work for them you can go elsewhere.

We can get plenty of hands to sew for that. What say you? Time is precious," said he, pulling out and glancing at a large and showy-looking gold watch, filched, no doubt, from the toil of sewing girls to whom he had paid the magnificent prices he had just offered me.

"Say?" I replied indignantly, "I say that I will sooner starve without work than starve at such prices as you offer."

"Just as you please, ma'am; it is none of our business, you know," replied he, coolly, and I went out from his presence, feeling that the only difference between him and the Southern slave-driver was, that this man, born and reared in the North, was much the worse of the two. They both believed that capital should own labor, but while the Southerner would make slaves of his inferiors, and would furnish them enough to eat and wear, such as it was, this Northerner would subject to the most galling bondage his kinsmen and equals, and would deny them the miserable pittance sufficient to keep them from starvation and nakedness.

But why weary my readers with detailed accounts of my efforts to procure employment, at prices which would enable me to keep the gaunt wolf of starvation from my door; the wearisome search, day after day, until my heart was almost ready to sink with the weight of despair; the cold, heartless, sneering rebuffs and repulses which everywhere met me, until it seemed to me that my brain must go wild, and I sink into the abyss of

shame and degradation which I saw around me on
every hand, engulphing thousands of those whose
lots were cast in the same mold with mine? Suffice it to say that I still struggled on, vainly hoping
against hope, working at such employment as I
could get, even at starvation prices, until at last
my strength failed in the unequal strife, and I was
prostrated upon a bed of sickness, from which, but
for the sake of my helpless Carrie, I should have
prayed that I might never rise.

How I lived through that long night of sickness,
among strangers, and with no loving friend near
me to bathe my fevered brow or cool my parched
lips, or even to administer the remedies which the
physician prescribed for me from time to time, I
hardly know. It is true, my landlady was kind to
me, and gave me all the attention which her own
household and other duties would permit; but she
had her own family and boarders to care for, and
she could spare but little of her time for me. Long
time I lingered at death's door, but at last my
constitution triumphed, and I began slowly to
mend, and at length was able to rise and walk
about my room. I even tried to do some work,
but when I bent my eyes upon my sewing, my
brain whirled and I almost fainted from sheer
weakness, and when my physician called to pay
me his customary visit, he found me with a very
considerable increase of fever.

He at once forbade, most peremptorily, any
further attempts at work, and, instead, ordered me

to take exercise in walking, extending, however, my promenades no farther than I could do without incurring too much fatigue. At first my strolls were very short—not more than half a block—but my strength gradually increased under this treatment, and in a short time I was able to walk half an hour without any great weariness. Oh! how I longed to get strong and able to renew my struggle with the world. And, indeed, stern necessity demanded it; for during my long illness my little treasury had entirely dwindled away, and I had even been compelled to part with some portions of my scanty wardrobe to supply the necessities occasioned by sickness. My board, too, was considerably in arrears, and though my landlady was very kind, and never alluded to the matter, this gave me no little uneasiness, and doubtless contributed materially to retard my restoration to strength. But relief was at hand, and that, too, from a source of which I did not dream.

One day, as I was taking my accustomed walk, I turned a corner and found myself face to face with my step-father, Captain Charles Lake. I was so filled with hysterical joy at seeing him that, for the moment, I was incapable of speech or action. Nor was his surprise at the meeting less than my own, although less visible effect was produced upon him. Coming close up to me he extended his hand, and said:

"Minnie, my child, is this indeed you?"

"Yes," I replied, bursting into tears of joy, for

I saw at once exemption from the miseries which
had so sorely weighed me down; "I am, indeed,
your wretched, unhappy daughter."

"Where are you living?" he continued kindly.
"You look as though you had been sick."

"Indeed I have. I have been sick both in body
and mind. But, come home with me, and I will
tell you all that has happened since I left Detroit."

Drawing my arm within his own, the Captain
accompanied me home, where I acquainted him
with all that had transpired, and with which the
reader is already familiar. He seemed much
moved at the recital of my sufferings, and at its
close, said:

"Poor child! you have had a hard time, but it
is now all·past. You must go home with me, and
Mary shall nurse you back to health and happiness again. I shall be ready to leave the city to-
morrow, and in the meantime you must get ready
to go with me."

But at this, the recollection of the injustice I
had done her flashed across my mind and suffused
my face with a crimson glow, and I at once replied
that I could not think of going there.

"Why not?" he asked, in some astonishment.

And then I told him that I had done Mary a
great wrong, and in no event could I go there to be
a dependent upon her bounty. In vain he urged
me to go, or at least to reveal to him fully the
reasons which so powerfully deterred me. I was
well aware that I had done her a gross injustice,

and no amount of persuasion could ever have induced me to open to him the subject of that injustice. When he found that I was not to be
shaken, he said:

"Well, I will not insist further. You will at
least allow me to make provision to avoid in the
future such suffering as you have been subjected
to since coming here."

To this I consented, of course; and, seating himself at the table, he drew up an agreement binding
himself to pay me seventy-five dollars per month,
and a letter of credit authorizing me to draw upon
his bankers at Detroit for the same, which he
delivered to me, then called my landlady and
discharged my indebtedness to her in full, after
which he bid me an affectionate farewell, and I
never saw him more. He, like the rest of my
friends, has passed away, but the memory of this
deed of kindness will never be effaced from my
recollection. It has almost entirely obliterated
from my mind the memory of the great wrong
which he undeniably did to me in my childhood,
and I fully forgive him all.

When my step-father had gone, I sat down and
began to consider what was best for me to do.
I did not intend to leave Chicago, for I must live
somewhere, and I was just as effectually concealed
from the pursuit of Mason there as any where,
and that concealment was now the prime consideration. I finally decided to try keeping house,
believing that it would be less expensive than

boarding, and I would feel much more independent than I now did.

Accordingly I set out in search of rooms to rent, but for some time I was as unsuccessful as in pursuit of employment. But, after some days spent in search, I was fortunâte enought to find some rooms to let on the second floor of a house' at No. 51 West Lake street. There were four rooms—more than I wanted, and the rent consequently higher than I wished to pay; but it was the only opportunity presented, and I decided to take them, thinking perhaps that I could rent one or two of them, or, failing in that, could take one or two boarders, and so reduce my expenses within something like reasonable limits. I drew my first draft on Detroit, paid my rent for a month in advance, and on the eighteenth day of November, 1865, took possession of my rooms, and advertised for boarders.

I had become acquainted with a young lady by the name of Rosa ——, a seamstress, and a very lively, intelligent girl, of good principles, and a very agreeable companion. As soon as she knew I was taking boarders, she came to apply for a place with me, and was my first boarder. Two young gentlemen, who were employed in a store immediately below us, applied, and were received as day boarders; others also made application, and, in a short time, I had all the boarders that my rooms would enable me to accommodate, and, for a time, I got along very well indeed. But my

unlucky star was still in the ascendant, and it was
in this boarding-house that I found some acquaintances who were doomed to exert a most baneful
influence upon my future life.

The first was a man by the name of Alvord.
He was a constable, and was doing some business
for a boarder who had some difficulty with a
former employer about a balance of wages due
him. He called several times to see him on this
business, much to my disgust, for I believed he
was a bad man, and took no pains to conceal my
dislike of him. This aroused his ill-feeling toward
me, and when, at a future period, an opportunity
was presented him of wiping out the old score, he
did not hesitate to repay me with interest.

It was here, too, that I formed the acquaintance
of him whose name I now bear—a man who, with
the exception, perhaps, of Mason, has caused me
more suffering than any other one with whom my
checkered life has brought me in contact. But I
reserve for another chapter an account of the incidents attending our introduction and subsequent
acquaintance and marriage.

15

CHAPTER XV.

One evening, a few moments before tea-time, a gentleman called in answer to an advertisement which I had sent to one of the Chicago papers for boarders and roomers. He was very polite in his manners, and of genteel appearance, and introduced himself as Mr. Frank C. Ford. I was favorably impressed with him at first sight, though, of course, not the slightest thought of love at that time entered my mind. I only looked upon him as a very pleasant, good-natured and sensible fellow, though he appeared very quiet, and rather inclined to be reserved, as he really was. Little did I then foresee, or even anticipate in the least degree, the sorrow and misery to me, of which that man was to be the author.

He staid and spent the evening with us, and a very pleasant evening we had. There were Miss Rose and another lady boarder, three young gentlemen, Mr. Ford and myself. All were in good spirits, and the hours flew by unheeded until eleven o'clock struck, when the party separated. I invited Mr. Ford to call again, and he accepted the invitation with thanks. I had all my rooms rented.

From this time he was a frequent visitor at my house, and was always gladly welcomed. I had

(226)

made inquiries about him, and learned that he
bore a good character, and was considered very
respectable in the community in which he lived—
that he occupied a responsible position in the employ of the street railway company, and was supposed by his steadiness and prompt attention to
duty to be accumulating some property, while he
was constantly rising in the estimation and confidence of his employers. The evidence as to his
character was certainly satisfactory in the highest
degree, and he was soon established on the footing
of a warm and valued friend at the house. For a
long time his visits, though frequent, were general,
and excited no remark—that is, no one of the
ladies seemed to be the special object of his visit,
or to receive more attention from him than another, nor did he ever inquire for one more than
another.

He had always been inclined to reticence con-
cerning himself and his circumstances, but I had
learned from him that he was a widower, and was
still keeping house in the same place where he had
lived with his former wife. When he told me this,
I asked him jestingly if he kept bachelor's hall,
and told him Rosa and I were coming around to
see where and how he lived. He replied, in the
same light, trifling style, that nothing would afford
him more pleasure ; that he did not live alone, but
had a housekeeper, but that she did very poorly,
and we would not find the house a very attractive
one. But while we thus jested, I had no idea of

ever carrying out my senseless proposition—it was only made in a spirit of playful badinage, and with no idea of its ever being thought of again.

I was therefore not a little surprised when, some days after the conversation, Rosa proposed that we should carry out our promise, and visit Mr. Ford at his home. I asked her if she supposed I was in earnest when the proposition was made, to which she replied that she did not know whether I was in earnest or not; that she was, and that she had determined to go that very afternoon, and that she would have no excuse, but I must go with her. I asked her if she thought it was exactly proper for us to visit a gentleman at his lodgings, to which she answered that it was altogether differ-ent from that; that we were not going to visit a gentleman at his lodgings, but at his house, pre-sided over, as he had informed us, by a lady who was his housekeeper, and that there would be no impropriety in our doing so; that go she would, and go with her I must. I advanced numerous other objections but without avail; she overruled them all, and insisted so strongly that I was finally silenced, if not convinced, and against my better judgment consented to accompany her. Beside, if the truth must be confessed, I felt a little anxiety to follow the matter out to the end, and see what was to be seen; and, accordingly, after dinner we equipped ourselves for walking and set out. It must be admitted to the reader, though we did not at the time mention it to each other, that we both had some secret misgivings as to the course we were pursuing, but we were both animated by the spirit of fun and adventure, and were resolved to follow it out to the end. I omitted to mention in the proper place, that Ford had told us he had three children by his first wife, only one of whom, however, lived with him.

Well, we went to the house where he had informed us he lived. We found a store in the front part of the house, went to the rear, which appeared to be finished as a dwelling-house, and knocked at the door, but received no answer. The only sign of life was a little dog inside, barking most furiously at what he evidently deemed an attempted intrusion upon the premises which he had been left to guard. We then went to the place where Mr. Ford worked, and were there told that he had just gone to the house. Again we returned to the house, and still finding nobody there, we went to the store in front, and inquired if there was a man by the name of Ford living in that neighborhood, and were informed that he lived in the rear of that building. We then inquired how many there were in his family. They replied they did not know, but that, when he rented the house, he mentioned, incidentally, that he was going to occupy it with his wife.

By the time we had finished our inquiries, Mr. Ford came up, and we at once accosted him, asking about his own health and that of his wife, telling him we heard she had just gone down in town, etc. There was a lady just crossing the street in front of the store, and he called our attention to her, telling us there she came; and, as soon as she unlocked the house, he would go in with us and give us an introduction to her. We accordingly went in with him, and were introduced to the lady, but not as Mrs. Ford; he called her Miss Carney, and informed us she was his housekeeper.

We staid some time, and had a very pleasant visit, for Miss Carney could be very interesting and pleasant when she chose; and that afternoon she seemed to take special pains to make herself agreeable. She was then in good humor, and did all in her power to entertain us in the most lady-like manner. I afterwards knew, to my sorrow, how differently she could act toward one whom she regarded as an enemy, as will more fully appear in the sequel of my story.

At length I decided it was time for us to go, and said as much to Rosa, to which she assented, and we rose to take our departure. Miss Carney protested against our going, and urged us, very earnestly, to stay to tea; but we refused, and were soon on our way home. Mr. Ford accompanied us; and, when we reached home, he went in, took tea, and afterward spent the evening with us. This was, to me, a fatal evening, for it was the one upon which I gave up to Frank C. Ford my freedom, my individuality, and upon which I once more agreed to take upon myself the fearful duties and responsibilities of married life. It was upon this evening that I entered into a contract of marriage which was to fill to overflowing my cup of misery.

I had now been acquainted with Frank C. Ford for several months, and had seen nothing to indicate that he was the monster he afterward turned out to be—nay, now, I will confess that his kind and genial disposition, his (as I supposed) steady character and correct habits, had awakened feelings in my bosom which I supposed would never exist there again, and I already regarded him with more of favor than I usually bestowed upon my friends. I will not admit that I really loved him at this time, but I thought very kindly of him; and though he never said anything, or indicated any marked preference for me, yet I knew, by some sort of intuition—by that instinctive feeling that pervades a woman's bosom—that he thought more of me than he did of either of the other ladies at the house. He had never called to see me more than any one else; he had never inquired particularly for me; he had never specially sought my society at the house, and yet I knew, in some indefinable way, that I was dearer to him than either of the others.

I was not, therefore, very much surprised when, seizing a favorable opportunity, he asked me to be his wife. He recalled the circumstances of our acquaintance; told how lonely he had felt since the death of his first wife; how his home needed the watchful care of one whose interests were identified with his; how he had watched and studied my character; how he thought we could be happy together, and begged me to take pity on his loneliness and make him blessed by becoming his wife.

I said I was not suprised, but, to some extent, I was; for, though I felt very confident such a proposition would some time be made, still it was unexpected at this time, and my answer was not ready. I therefore pleaded surprise, and begged time to consider of the matter before giving him a decided answer to a question of such tremendous importance. He acceded to this, and we parted for the night. I did not tell Rosa, with whom I slept, of the proposition which had been made to me, but chose to keep it within my own breast until I had finally decided upon it, although there remained in my own mind but little doubt that it would be finally accepted. But I had once accepted such a proposition in haste, and the result had been the most unmitigated woe, and I was now determined to deliberate well before acting; and yet all my deliberation was in vain, as subsequent events will show.

Ford was to come at the end of the week for his final answer. I was alone in the world; for Captain Lake had taken Carrie and sent her to a sister of his in New Orleans who was rich and would raise her like a lady, and I had nothing to care for except two little canary birds. Why not marry him and end all my troubles for this life at once? Besides, it was not my nature to be alone

in the world; I was so constituted that I must
have somebody to love ; some one toward whom
the love of my heart would go out like a mighty,
rushing torrent, and why not him ? I was sure I
loved him more than I loved Giles (or Mason) when
I married him, and surely I had seen some happy
days in my married life (for so I persisted in calling it) with him before my peace was all destroyed
by the evidence of his unworthiness; and I
thought it was reasonably certain that the same
cause for unhappiness did not exist in the case of
Mr. Ford.

But then, on the other hand, I thought I would
never marry again; my past experience had not
favorably impressed me with the joys of married
life, and I hesitated before entering into that state
again.   Besides, if I married Ford or any one else
the seventy-five dollars which Captain Lake had
kindly settled upon me, monthly, would end, and
would the sacrifice pay me?

But why recount all my cogitations upon this
point.   Such reflections ever have but one end, and
hence the reader will not be surprised to learn
that when Mr. Ford came for his final answer, I
laid my hand in his and promised him that, God
being my helper, I would be to him a true and
faithful wife so long as we both should live.   And
to this day, I call high heaven to witness that I
kept faithfully the vow until his tyranny and
brutality drove me from home and placed it out of
my power to keep it any longer.

There was one thing in connection with our engagement in which my conscience does not acquit me of all blame, and that was in relation to the dark and gloomy scenes in my past life and history. I did not impart them to him. It may be possible that, had I done so, it would have spared us both some trouble in the future, but I could not bring myself to speak of it. I knew I had married Giles in good faith and I was not to blame if he had a wife living when he married me. And I left him as soon as I knew it. I did not think it necessary to tell Ford this. And here was committed one of the worst errors of my life. Far better for me had the revelation been made before our engagement was consummated, and trusted to his affection for me to overcome the effects of such a sad recital as mine, than to leave him to learn it in an exaggerated and distorted form from another source, while to the intrinsic evil of the story, would be added, in his mind, the reflection that I had deceived him. The fullest and freest confidence should be maintained between affianced lovers at all times; just as full and complete as that which should exist between husband and wife. Nay, I insist that wedded love will tolerate even more concealment than will simply plighted faith; because, while the first is prone to create the most unbounded confidence, the last is proverbial for its suspicion and its jealousy. How important, then, is it that in no case any concealments be suffered to exist during the engagement,

if we would avoid misery and woe during the
wedded life which is to insue. But I did not then
practice upon this principle, and to this cause may
be attributed no small portion of my subsequent
sorrow.

I have not told the reader anything about the
family of my betrothed, and will now turn for a
short time to them. His father had been dead
some time, but he had a mother and several brothers
living at Waukegan, of whom he had frequently
spoken, but none of whom I had ever seen. He
also had two married sisters living in Chicago,
one of whom I had seen at the time we plighted our
faith to each other, but the other I had not. The
first one lived on Milwaukee avenue, and Frank
and I had spent one evening there; the other I
had not met. I liked this one very well. Frank
had three children, the youngest of whom he told
me, much to my surprise, was thirteen years old,
while the others were old enough to care for themselves. He was older than I had supposed, being
at this time more than forty years of age, though
he did not really appear to be more than thirty-
five at the most.

Soon after our betrothal, Frank invited me to go
with him to spend the evening at the house of Mrs.
Spalding, the other sister of whom I have before
spoken, saying:

"You know she will soon be your sister, and
it is not becoming to have a sister whom you do
not know."

I accordingly went with him to visit her. We passed rather a pleasant evening, though it must be confessed I did not like her as well as I did her sister. There was something in her manners, impossible to be described, but which was very displeasing to me. It was not pride, or ill-nature, nor could I say what it was ; "but there was that sort of distinctive dislike which we sometimes feel toward a person, and for which we are unable to account, even to ourselves.

> " I do not like you, Dr. Fell;
> The reason why I can not tell;
> But this I know full well,
> I do not like you, Dr. Fell."

And yet she was a good, kind-hearted woman, and when I afterward had occasion to test her goodness of heart and disposition, I found that I could rely upon her with the confident assurance that she would not disappoint me.

When the evening. was ended, and we started away, Mrs. Spalding urged me very earnestly to come and see her again, saying, in a voice and manner which convinced me that she knew of the relationship between Frank and myself, that " we must get to be very good friends indeed." This was the only allusion that was, at any time during the evening, made to our engagement. Frank accompanied me to the foot of the stairs leading to my own home, and there bid me good night, promising to call and see me the next evening. The next evening came, but he did not. I was

sadly disappointed at even this trifling affair, and
really felt as if he had slighted me, merely because he for once failed to keep his promise to meet
me, and, could I have seen him then, don't know
what I might have said to him. He had already
become dearer to me than I thought, and I was
jealous of even any appearance of neglect.

The next evening he came, and, ah! how swiftly
the hours flew by in his society. We were both
so happy that we took no note of passing time,
and when he looked at his watch and declared
that it was almost twelve o'clock, words could
hardly express our mutual surprise. It did not
really seem to me that it could be more than nine,
and it was only when I consulted my own watch,
and found that the small hours were indeed approaching, that I could be convinced that his time
was not too fast.

"Well," said he, "the last car is gone, and I
shall have to walk home. But never mind, the
time will soon come when we will not part at all."

After this he spent nearly all his evenings with
me, and the scene just detailed was often repeated.
How happy we were. But during all this time I
could not help feeling a sort of vague uneasiness,
a dim, indefinable dread of the future, and I trembled inwardly lest our happiness should pass away
forever. It may be that it was because I had seen
so much of sorrow, and so little genuine, unalloyed
happiness in my past life, that I felt so insecure in
this. And of a truth, my past experience had been

such as to render me suspicious and distrustful to
a degree. How often had I seen myself raised to
the highest pitch of happiness, only to be in the
next moment, as it were, precipitated from my
pinnacle of joy to the very lowest depths of the
abyss of misery and pain. And is it strange that
I should have trembled in view of the possibility
of a repetition of my past sad experience? And
hence it was that my jealous love was ever sug-
gesting doubts as to the future. Would he always
love me as now? Would he ever enjoy, as now,
the evenings spent in my society? or would that
love of his, which now seemed so ardent, in time
wither and fade away, and I be left alone, a miserable and neglected wife? And then my own deep
love, and my confidence in him, would whisper
that it could not be; that his affection was true,
even as my own; that our devotion to each other
could never know any change, and that, hand in
hand, we would travel adown the vale of life
together, and our destinies be separated only by
the dark rolling stream of death. Could I have
imagined what less than a twelvemonth would
bring forth, how gladly would I have laid down
and died ere linking my fate with him whom I
now so fondly loved.

As our wedding-day approached I began to
make preparations for its celebration. I advertised my rooms "to let," and my furniture "for
sale," and in a short time had an application from
a newly-married couple, and sold out to them.

They desired to take immediate possession, and I agreed to allow them to do so, they boarding me until the wedding-day. When married, Frank and I were going to Waukegan, to visit his mother and brothers there, after which we were to return to Chicago and go to keeping house, living for the present at least, in the same house he now occupied. This was our programme, but, like all other programmes of merely human beings, it was liable to fail in some particulars. And in this particular case it was not to be fulfilled, at least until after intense sorrow and trouble to one of the parties concerned.

But I will close this chapter here, and in my next, give come account of the events preceding my marriage, and immediately following it—events which gave me a new insight into the character of Frank C. Ford, and led me, even at that early day, to almost regret the step which had bound me to him, and placed me in his power.

CHAPTER XVI.

TIME had rolled away until but a few days intervened between us and the day which was to witness our marriage, when suddenly Mr. Ford discontinued his visits. Up to this time he had been in the habit of calling on me almost every day, and I could imagine no reason for the sudden change. At first I thought nothing of it, but when three or four days passed away and he came not, I began to feel uneasy, for it was something which had never occurred since our engagement. Accordingly, I sent him a note asking him to call and see me at a particular time therein mentioned.

He came, but oh! how changed he was. He was no longer the same man, but briefly and coldly he saluted me, and, without noticing the chair I offered him, he remained standing, and apparently waited for me to address him, which I did in a quivering voice, for my heart was full.

"Frank," said I, "for heaven's sake, what is the matter?"

"Do you know Charles Alvord?" he asked.

"Yes," said I; "what of him?" for I knew him to be a man who was capable of anything, and my heart misgave me as soon as he pronounced that name.

Ford then went on to tell me that Alvord had

been to him and told him that he understood he
was going to marry me, and he felt it his duty to
warn him against me ; that if he married me he
would be sorry for it, and that he had better break
off with me while there was yet time.

As I heard these cruel words, I sunk upon the
sofa utterly overcome by the violence of my emotions.   What had I ever done to this man, that he
should attempt to destroy me in this manner ? I
had never harmed him or said aught against him
in any way, and why he should seek to injure me
was past my comprehension.

These reflections passed through my mind as I
lay upon the sofa, but I could not answer him a
word, and it was only when he asked me, after a
long period of silence, what I had to say, that I
found language to answer him.   I then told him
the truth with regard to the past, with which the
reader is already acquainted, gave him my reasons
for not telling him before, and wound up by saying that we had better not marry, and that I did
not wish to marry him unless we could live happily together.   As I said this, he turned on his heel,
and saying, " Good night, if that is your answer,"
he started to leave the room.

I had never done anything to disgrace my character.   But I could not let him go thus.   To part
in this way would kill me, for I loved him more
than my own life, and I could not have felt worse
had he plunged a knife in my bosom.   I told him
that I was not to blame for the past, if he would
16

trust me, he would find me a true wife; that I would endure suffering, starvation, and even death in the midst of poverty, before I would prove false to him; that I would not marry him to make him miserable, but if he would only give me his love, I could and would endure anything in the world. To this appeal he only responded "Good night," left the room, and closed the door behind him.

Once outside the door, however, he seemed to relent, and I listened in vain for the sound of his footsteps descending the stairs. It would, perhaps, have been better for both if he had gone, but he did not. I sat and listened some time, and then arose, went to the door and opened it. He was standing on the threshold, and as I opened the door he stepped inside, took my hand in his, and led me to the sofa, where, seating me, he placed himself by my side.

"Forgive me," said he. "I was wrong and hasty just now. But forgive and forget; and let us be married as though nothing unpleasant had ever occurred between us."

"I forgive you freely," said I; "but answer me one thing. If we are married, now that you know all the sad past, will you ever throw it up to me, or taunt me with my errors of by-gone days? Promise me that you will not do this, let what may arise."

His answer to this request I can never forget. It is engraved on my heart in characters of living fire. It was:

"Minnie, I do not blame you, for you did think you was his wife, and if I married you, I would never cast up anything to you. Nay, more, if I married you under such circumstances, I would live with you, and treat you kindly, so long as you were a true and faithful wife to me after our marriage."

This allusion was to my marriage with Giles. We were married in a few days after this conversation. God is my witness, that in word, thought and deed, I was a true and faithful wife to him; and how he redeemed the solemn promise just recorded, let the future tell. May God forgive him, as I do, for the black and soul-killing perjury of which he has been guilty in this respect.

Our wedding was set for the sixth day of February, 1866. We were to be married at two o'clock in the afternoon, at the Baptist church, corner of Morgan and Monroe Streets, by Rev. Edgar J. Goodspead, pastor of that church. I was just trying on my wedding-dress, before breakfast, in the morning, when there was a rap at the door at the head of the stairs. Mrs. Singer, the lady with whom I boarded, opened the door. There stood a girl, who inquired for Mrs. Mason. Supposing it to be one whom my dress-maker had sent on an errand, I stepped forward, when she handed me a letter, and immediately turned and disappeared down stairs. I called after her, but she went on without paying any heed to me.

I hardly knew what to make of this; but, without wasting any time in vain conjectures, at once opened the letter. It was a sheet of foolscap paper; all four of the pages were written full, in a strange hand, and I could not imagine who should be writing to me, or why. But I had not read far until I understood what the writer was driving at; for it was filled with such vile and disgusting language as is seldom used by a woman. I can not give any portion of its contents; they were unsuitable for publication. Suffice it to say it was written by Angeline Carney, Mr. Ford's housekeeper, and, if true, revealed a state of depravity, on his part, almost too shocking to be believed.

I knew not what to do or think. If the charges contained in this letter were true, he was not the man to whom I could entrust my honor and happiness; if they were not true, he ought to have a chance to explain them away. True, I did not believe them; but still every word might possibly be true: and, if so, I ought to know it before it was too late. I had no one to whom I could confide the matter, and, hence, no one to advise me how to act. But it was near nine o'clock of our wedding-day, and something must be done, and that quickly. I hastily put on my bonnet and shawl, took a street car, and was soon at Mr. Ford's place of business. Arrived there, I was told he had gone to the house, and at once sent a man there to tell him to meet me on the next corner, where I would wait until he came up; for I was resolved I would not marry him until that matter was explained to my satisfaction.

I had not long to wait. My messenger had barely reached the house, when I saw him and Ford coming out of the yard. Frank came up to where I was standing, and, in a voice of some concern, asked what was the matter. I replied by placing the scurrilous letter in his hand, and asking him to explain what it all meant. He read it through, without a word; and, then, handing it back to me, said Angeline was angry because he was going to get married, and thus throw her out of a place; that she had a violent temper, and would do anything she could to accomplish her ends. As for the scandalous letter: he said, most emphatically, that there was not a word of truth in it; that it was only a part of her programme to break up the marriage, and urged me to pay no attention to it whatever. He further told me, that she would be sent away that very day, and that he had employed a German girl to clean up the house and take charge of it till our return from our trip to Waukegan; after which, he observed, it would be in my care.

His explanation did not fully satisfy me, and I said as much to him and expressed my determination to go to the house to see her, and learn from her own lips what they were to each other. I told him we could never be married until this matter was cleared up to my entire satisfaction.

He thereupon called a young man from the

house, introduced him to me as his son Wallace, and referred me to him for the truth of what he had said. I showed him the letter and asked him if he knew anything of it. He replied, after look-it over, that Angeline Carney, his father's house-keeper, had written it and had told him about it after she had sent it, and gave the same explana-tion of the motives which had prompted it as his father had already given. He also added that Angeline was very angry, and would be sorry for what she had done as soon as she had time to reflect a little. But all this was not satisfac-tory to me, and I expressed my determination to go to the house and see her about it, and hear what she had to say, and accordingly started in that direction. Mr. Ford went with me, and Wallace went on before to tell her we were coming.

When we reached the house I went at once into the bed room. Miss Carney sat there crying as if her heart would break. I asked her at once why she had written me such a letter as that, and she replied that she had done it because she was angry, and wanted to break up the match. She did not say it was not true, but only left that to be inferred by saying she had written it because she wanted to make trouble, and break up the marriage if possible.

I decided in my own mind that, dearly as I loved Ford, I would not dare to trust my happiness in his keeping, and walked out of the house intend-

ing to go home and have nothing more to do with
him. A street car was just passing. I signaled it
to stop, and at once got on board. I was not
aware that Ford had followed me, until I turned
around to take my seat, when I found he was with
me. He begged me to get off and go with him
where he could talk it all over with me, which he
could not of course do on the car.' For some time
I refused, and only yielded when I became afraid
that his earnestness would attract the attention of
the other passengers to our quarrel, or whatever it
might be called.

Accordingly we got off the car and went to an
oyster restaurant where we had a long talk. He
protested his entire innocence of all the charges
contained in the letter, and strove to induce me to
say that they would make no difference in my
mind, and that I would marry him. But this I
would not do, for though I almost believed his protestations I wanted time and opportunity to think
the matter over alone. I did not want to act
hastily, and hence evaded giving him a direct
answer. He finally ceased his persuasions, we
left the restaurant and walked down the street until
a car came along, when I took that, and was soon
at my home.

I had been there but a few minutes when a half-
brother of Ford, by the name of Emsley Sunderlin,
and his son, Gussie Ford came to see me. They
had been informed by Frank and Wallace of the
rupture, and came to induce me to change my de-

termination and go on with the marriage. They asseverated his entire innocence of the charges, and urged me to pay no attention to them, assuring me I should have no further trouble on her account, and begged me not to allow that bad woman to break up the marriage by her mean and spiteful jealousy. They told me that Frank was taking it very hard, and had sent them to talk to me about it in the hope of persuading me to accede to his wishes.

I replied that I was fearful we should never be happy in each other's society, and that I believed it would be as well for both of us if we never married. But even while I uttered these words my heart was wrung with anguish, for I really loved Frank, and the idea of giving him up was very painful to me. But they still pleaded with me, urged and entreated me to reconsider my determination, and at length I yielded, almost against my better judgment, and told them they might inform Frank that I would be ready at the time appointed. I asked no further pledges or protestations from him, for I thought that if the promises he had already made, together with those he would make before the man of God, would not restrain him, no others would, and it was worse than useless to demand them at his hands. I did not feel entirely justified in the step I was about to take, but I loved him, and thought he loved me, and I trusted to that love to avoid any difficulties in the future. I have since learned that, however powerful a motive love may be, it will not avail to procure peace and happiness unless sanctioned and controlled by high moral principle.

Two o'clock was near at hand, and still I was not fully decided in my own mind as to my duty in the premises. I fancied that duty said, " remain single," while inclination quite as strongly demanded that I should go on with the wedding. And thus I remained in the most painful suspense, and even delayed my dressing on this account until the clock was close upon the stroke of two, when I suddenly made up my mind to go through with it at all hazards, hastened to complete my remaining preparations, and, just as the clock struck two, gave Frank Ford my hand to be led to the carriage in which we were going to the church. He handed me in, sprang in after me, and we rolled away to the church, where, in the presence of a very few friends, whom we had invited to witness the ceremony, the man of God pronounced the words which bound us together forever. Forever, did I say? This was a mistake. It was said to be forever, but we shall soon see how, in a few short weeks, I was, by the tyranny and brutality of the man who, this day, promised to love, honor, and cherish me until death, driven from my nome to become a wanderer among strangers, and seek a precarious existence by my own exertions.

After our marriage we went to Mrs. Marshall's for dinner, had a very pleasant time, and then at four o'clock took the cars for Waukegan, where we were to remain over night at the house of his mother, then visit two days among his other relations there, and return to the city the next day. Emsley Sunderlin accompanied us, and just before we reached Waukegan, he proposed to play a joke upon his mother and the guests whom we knew she had invited to greet us. Accordingly, when we reached our destination, he offered me his arm to conduct me to the house. I accepted it, and when we got in he introduced me to the assembled guests as his wife, Frank in the meantime remaining in the background. Everybody was taken by surprise. The old lady had invited them to meet her son and his bride, and they had understood that it was Frank who was coming with a newly-made wife; judge then of their astonishment when one so much younger than Frank, but still a son of the old lady, claimed the honors which they supposed were due to Mr. Ford. Nevertheless we were greeted with the same warmth which they were prepared to extend to Mr. Ford and his bride, and many were the congratulations and kindly wishes showered upon us, all of which Mr. Sunderlin received with as much gravity and unction as though he were really entitled to them.

When supper was announced, Emsley, who had never quitted my side for a moment, in order to keep up the deception, offered me his arm and conducted me to the table. We sat side by side at the head of the well-filled board, and "many a time and oft" the health of the bride and groom was pledged by the joyous guests, Sunderlin very coolly appropriating these honors to himself, while Frank sat near the foot of the table, coolly and quietly enjoying the joke which was being perpetrated.

The company were not undeceived until the close of the festivities, late at night, when they were immeasurably astonished at seeing Frank and myself retire to a room together. They at once appreciated the fact that they had been the victims of a huge "sell," and proceeded to inflict summary vengeance upon the offenders. I will not detail all the means resorted to to punish us for the joke we had played upon them; let the reader draw upon his imagination, or his recollection, for the wildest pranks which usually attend weddings in the rural districts, and then double everything he can imagine, and he will have some idea of the events attending our first night's stay in Waukegan. In vain Frank's mother tried to control them, and induce them to let us alone; with protestations of vengeance for the deception we had practiced upon them, they continued to invade the privacy of our chamber all night long, and we never closed our eyes for a moment during the entire night.

We were to have returned to Chicago on Friday, but, the evening before, Mr. Ford received a telegram from that place, which, he informed me, was from his son, Daniel, and made it necessary for him to return at once to the city. I tried to induce him to tell me the nature of the dispatch, or let me see it, but he declined to do either, saying it only pertained to some business matters of no special importance, and that I would know all about it in time. I asked him when he would go to the city, and he replied he should go that night, but I must stay in Waukegan, at his mother's, until he sent for me, which he said would be very soon. I could not understand the reason for this secrecy, and did not like it; but felt sure some trouble was brewing. I could form no idea what it was, but my fears led me to imagine something very horrible; and, after my husband left, I walked the floor, constantly, until Daniel Ford came in. His train arrived about eleven o'clock, and he, at once, came to his grandmother's, where I was.

I was glad to see him, for I knew his father had arrived in Chicago before he started out, and I felt in hopes he had brought a message to me to return to Chicago with him the next morning. But in this I was disappointed—he told me his father wished me to stay in Waukegan a few days longer, and would send for me soon. I tried to induce him to tell me something about the difficulty which took him away so suddenly; but he protested that he could not explain anything; that he had been advised to send the dispatch, but that he really knew nothing about the trouble, save that it was something about the possession of the house.

Finding that I could learn nothing from him, I gave it up, and retired to rest, with my mother-in-law. She was a dear old lady, one whom I esteemed from the first moment I ever saw her; and, as I came to know her better, I loved her as though she had been my own mother. When she found that my nervous excitement would not allow me to sleep, she began to talk to me; and, as she was a sincere and pious Christian woman, her conversation, naturally enough, flowed into that channel. She asked me if I was a member of any church, and expressed her satisfaction when she was informed that I was a member of the Christian Church.

She spoke of Frank's being a member of the Baptist Church, but said she thought he had almost ceased to comply with the outward and visible forms of religion; expressed much sorrow thereat, and thanked me, kindly and heartily, when I told her that, though not a Baptist, I was a Christian and would use all my influence to induce Frank to attend church and resume family worship. In such soothing conversation as this, the night passed away, until, my nervousness being somewhat relieved, I at last sunk into slumber.

When I awoke in the morning, however, I was as anxious as ever; and, as the day wore on, I could think of nothing but the strange air of mystery which attended Frank's departure. I was continually wondering what could be the matter which so imperatively called him home; but which I, his lawful wife, must not know, and I finally determined to be put off no longer.   Accordingly, I sent a letter down by Daniel, to his father, telling him I was coming home the next day; that I could not stay away any longer, and asking him to meet me at the depot in Chicago.   This letter brought no answer, but still I thought, of course, he would meet me as requested.

The next day I went down to Chicago, and as we rolled slowly into the depot, I looked around on every side for my husband, but he was nowhere to be seen.   How bitter was my disappointment! Although I knew he did not approve of my coming, still no thought of his refusing to meet me had ever crossed my mind, and now, to be treated with such apparent neglect, seemed the very height of cruelty to me, and the tears gushed into my eyes at the thought.   I hesitated for some time what I should do.   I had never been installed mistress of his house, and did not feel like going there.   Beside, who could tell what difficulty might be caused if I went there, not only unexpected and unannounced, but in direct opposition to what I knew and understood to be his wish; and finally I decided that I would go to my old home, and stay there till he came for me.   Accordingly I walked over there, it being but a short distance from the depot.

I had been there but a short time when he came for me, and asked me to go home with him.   And then, for the first time, I knew what had summoned him home so unexpectedly, and also why he had not met me at the depot, according to my request of the day before.

It seems that Mr. Ford's housekeeper, who had been sent away from her position on the day of our marriage, being highly incensed at the loss of her place, had gone to Mr. Alvord, and under his advice, she had returned to the house, expelled the German girl who was left in charge, and, taking possession of the place again, had avowed her determination to remain there, at least until the arrival of Mr. Ford. The faithful girl, whose rights were thus invaded, had gone to Daniel for redress, and he at once telegraphed his father to come down and settle the dispute. Mr. Ford came down at once, and found her in absolute possession of the house. She avowed her determination to maintain her possession against all comers whomsoever. He first tried to make a treaty of peace with her, but without effect—all his overtures were scornfully rejected. He then resorted to expostulation, then to entreaty, and finally to threats, telling her he would give her in charge of the police if she persisted in her extraordinary and outrageous conduct; but to this she was equally indifferent. In this way had passed the entire day, and finally he had gone, that very morning (the day of my arrival), to carry his threat into execution. In this way he had succeeded in getting possession of the house; but in what a condition! While he was gone for a policeman, she seemed to have tried to dismantle the fortress which she could no longer hold; or, in other words, she appeared to have used all the means in her power to render the house as nearly uninhabitable as possible. The carpets were torn up, the window-curtains taken down, and over the floor were scattered fragments of broken dishes and furniture. These matters had delayed him until too late to meet me at the train, according to my request.

By the time he had finished this recital we had arrived at the house, and such a sight as it was I never saw before, and hope never too see again. Scattered over the floor were fragments of crockery, glassware, mirrors, and every thing that would break; while strips of carpet, fragments of broken furniture, shreds of curtains, and everthing one could think of, lay in profusion all around. I was heart-sick, but it was no time to mourn, and, with the assistance of our faithful German girl, we set vigorously to work to repair damages as far as possible, and in course of time rendered the place quite habitable.

CHAPTER XVII.

BEHOLD me once more, dear reader, installed as mistress of a home which I could call my own, and the wife of a man whom I loved and was willing to do anything in my power to render happy. I would endure any cross, privation, or trial without a murmur for his sake, and would only ask in return the inestimable boon of his love and confidence. The light of his countenance, and the kindly affection which I knew my conduct merited, was all that was needed to render me perfectly happy; but, alas! there were causes at work which were destined to undermine the castle of peace which my hopes had erected, reduce it to a wreck, and my life to a barren waste of wretchedness and black despair. Let me, in the present chapter, unfold some of the causes to the reader.

As I now look back to those days of misery, and scan my conduct with the most scrutinizing care, I am unable to recall a single instance in which I failed in my duty toward my husband, or, in word, thought or deed, violated the promise made at the altar before God and man, to "love, honor, and obey." I did not, during all this time, give him an unkind word, or even a look; it mattered not though my very heart-strings were quivering with

17 (257)

pain, I always met him with a kiss and smile when he returned from his labor, and at parting the same seal of affection was always exchanged between us. Again, I felt that, as my husband was by no means wealthy, it was my duty to do all I could to help him along in the world, and hence, when he proposed that we should take some of the hands employed in the railroad shops to board, I at once assented to it, although really not able to do the work for our own family, to say nothing of adding the cookery of four or five men to my already heavy burdens. And thus day by day I toiled on, though often almost fainting with weariness from over-exertion, vainly hoping against hope, that by patience, kindness, and the most unselfish devotion, I would be able to reclaim the love and affection which I saw gradually slipping away from me, as I feared, forever.

Other means, also, I resorted to to accomplish the one great object of my life. The reader will remember that my husband was a member of the Baptist church, and that I had promised his mother that I would try to recall him to a discharge of his duties as a follower of the meek and lowly Jesus. Accordingly, the first night that we passed in our new home, I brought the Bible, and, laying it on his knee, asked him to read a chapter, and have prayers before we retired. He looked at me in some surprise, and inquired if I was a member of the church, adding that he had understood that I was not. To this I replied that I was a Christian, and by the blessing of God, and his assistance, hoped we would both be true Christians. I belonged to the Christian church, he was a Baptist; he did not like the Christian church, he said. "Well, I will go to church with you," I said. He made no further remark, but opening the Word of God, read a chapter and then we knelt together and offered up our petitions to the throne of Divine grace. And each evening before our retirement for the night, this scene was repeated for some time, and each evening I induced him to go on in the path of duty, hoping, by the power of God's grace, to attract his heart more closely to mine. At times I would, at his request, read the Word of God while he listened, after which we would unite in prayer.

I also endeavored to induce him to attend church with me, believing that by so doing I could win him more closely to my side and away from the associations which were poisoning his mind, and for a time I was successful in this. For several Lord's days he accompanied me to church, and on such occasions he invariably treated me with more kindness and consideration after our return than he did before going. But the effect was only temporary. And there was a time coming in which I was to be deprived of even this partial influence over him, and when my efforts in this direction were to become of no avail.

While I was thus trying to discharge every duty toward my husband, my bitterest enemies were as assiduously working to destroy him forever.

There is something incomprehensible in the determined, relentless hostility of these miserable beings to one who had never done them any wrong whatever. It is easy to conceive why one who deems himself injured by another, should, at the moment and in the heat of passion, strive to avenge his real or supposed injuries, but how one can thus through a long period of time continue a course of unfounded and unmerited persecution, is utterly unaccountable to me. It must be remembered that theirs was not the work of an hour or a day; for weeks, and even months, they labored unremittingly in the pursuit of their unholy scheme, until their diabolical perseverance was at last crowned with the most complete success—they got him to drinking liquor.

Such effect had the persistent attacks of my enemies upon my husband, that, in time, he came to apparently avoid my society as much as possible. He no longer spent his evenings at home with me—no longer we knelt in prayer before the throne of grace—no longer we wended our way together to the house of God to listen to the teachings of his Word; we no longer visited in company any place of amusement, or went out together at all. Solitary and alone, with the light of my husband's love withdrawn from me, with my path hedged about with bitterest thorns, I groped my way alone in darkness, only wondering what the end would be, and how soon it would come.

But it was not upon my husband alone that

these attacks had their effect to my injury, though
the loss of his love was the severest blow which
could befall me. The friends and acquaintances
I had made, one after another, turned aside their
heads and refused to recognize me, or to speak
to me when we met ; no one visited me or returned
my calls, and in a short time I was as completely
ostracised from society as if banished to a desolate
island in the midst of the Pacific Ocean.	,

God pity and help the unfortunate wretch upon
whom, whether guilty or innocent, society once sets
the seal of its condemnation, for there is no help
for him or her short of the wisdom and power of
Omniscience itself. There is no more unjust,
arbitrary or tyrannical ruler upon the face of the
earth than this same society. It has no toleration
for errors, and admits no repentance in its wretched
victims. Let any one, and especially a woman,
commit a single error, and attempt afterwards to
repent of that error, and retrieve their standing and
position—will society aid them in the slightest
degree ? Will the friendly hand be stretched
forth to aid´them, and lead them into brighter
paths of peace and happiness ; or will the kindly
glance of sympathy, and the genial smile of en-
couragement, cheer them on in the reformation
they have attempted ? Will society whisper to
the penitent, sin-sick soul, " Come, I will lead, and
assist you, by pathways strewn with thornless
flowers, into a purer, brighter and holier atmosphere, where strength and vigor shall be restored

to you; where you shall breathe airs which are never deadly, and gather fruit which holds no lurking poison; where innocence and joy abound forever more, and where the sins of the past shall be remembered no more forever?" No; it rises with a whip of scorpions, drives the poor victim from the door, and, with contumely, scorn and reproach, pursues him to the very brink of the grave; and, not content even with having hunted the poor wretch to the tomb, it pursues him beyond, and loads his memory with execration and reproach.

And thus it is that society renders almost impossible the reform of one who has once gone astray. Our Savior was not ashamed, when on earth, to take by the hand the penitent sinner, and, with kindly words and approving smiles, lift him up once more to the position he occupied before his fall; but society, composed of men and women who profess to be His disciples and followers, gathers its robes around it with a sort of Pharisaic pride, and saying, "I am more holy than thou," shuts the door in his face, and drives him back to the darkness from whence he would fain emerge. Out upon such foul hypocrisy and hollow pretense as this! Is it any wonder that there are so many outcasts in the world when their reform is thus made impossible? And will not that thing called society have a fearful account of wrong and outrage to settle in the day of the final adjustment of all things? How many souls that might otherwise have been saved, have been driven to eternal perdition by the course to which I have alluded? Who can contemplate the fearful record without shuddering? But to return to the story of my trials.

During all this time I had no suspicion that my husband was not true to me. I knew he had many sins to answer for, but this one I never laid to his charge, and I could endure almost anything so long as I believed him true to me, as I was to him. But I was soon to be undeceived, and to find myself that most miserable of all beings, a neglected and forsaken wife.

I was one day mending a coat which he usually wore about his work, and which he had this day left home for this purpose. As I turned it over, a letter fell from one of the pockets to the floor. I picked it up, and something in the superscription attracted my attention at once, and I immediately opened it, and there found my worst suspicions more than confirmed. The letter was from a woman whom I already knew for one of my worst enemies. She spoke very disrespectfully of me—called me that "thing" he had married—assured him of her undying love—told him she could not give him up, and appointed a meeting with him, that very night, in the ladies' sitting-room at the railroad office.

How my blood boiled within me as I read these damning proofs of his treachery and deceit! What should I do? As I sat thus, with the evidence of his falsehood in my hands, I was for a time almost incapable of thinking rationally upon any subject. My first idea was to retain the letter until he came home, then show it to him and charge him with his guilt; but upon reflection, my charity for him suggested that perhaps this letter was written only for the purpose of being seen by me, as a part of her system of persecution, and that he might, after all, be innocent. But, then, why should it be in his pocket? Why should he have preserved it so carefully? Nevertheless I decided to wait until I had more complete proof of his guilt, and accordingly returned the letter to his pocket, and when he came home made no allusion to the matter.

But when he went out that night, I hastily threw on a bonnet and shawl and followed him at a distance sufficient to avoid his observation. He went directly to the place of meeting. The woman was in waiting for him, and they went away together, I following them at a safe distance, until they finally disappeared within the door of a low saloon, of the very worst class in the city.

From this time forward I watched his movements with the closest and most careful scrutiny. Many a time have I searched his pockets and found letters from this abandoned woman, in which she would speak of prior meetings with him, and make appointments for the future; and I invariably observed that he went out whenever the time came to fulfill these appointments. During this time, too, I was making inquiries among those who might be supposed to know something about these matters, and was told that Frank C. Ford, my husband, was a constant visitor of this woman. And yet, when I had accumulated proofs to satisfy myself a thousand times of his guilt, and charged him with it, he had the effrontery and the hardihood to deny it all. And when I told him what I had seen with my own eyes, he flew in a rage, repeated his asseverations of innocence, swore that I had never seen anything of the kind, and actually had the temerity to call upon his Maker to witness that the whole thing was a fabrication, or the offspring of a disordered brain!

Great God! is there no punishment for such terrible falsehood and blasphemy? Here was this man whom I knew—not suspected, but *knew*—to be guilty of the worst crimes which a husband can commit against a wife, and yet he dared to call high Heaven to witness, what? That what I had seen with my own eyes was not so; that my sense of sight had deceived me; that I was in the wrong, instead of being the victim of the most outrageous and grievous indignity which could ever be offered to a true, faithful and confiding woman. And was there no remedy for all this? What could I do? I was helpless, powerless in his hands. The crimes which had already been perpetrated against me, and to which I was now satisfied he was a party, had put it out of my power to do anything to support myself in Chicago, and what to do I did not know. I had no means to go elsewhere, and I could see no way of escape from the horrors of my position. The only thing I could see was to stay and suffer on until death should kindly relieve me from my sufferings. To such a state of despair had I been reduced by the course of persecution and suffering to which I had been subjected.

But there is a point at which we pluck courage and energy, even from black despair, and that point was fast approaching in my case. I had endured, it seemed to me, almost everything that a woman could endure, and yet there was one more indignity and insult to be offered to me—one that was beyond even my capacity for endurance, and which, at last, resulted in our final separation.

One day my husband came home, and appeared to be in a great rage; though it was very usual for him to be abusive, angry, and violent toward me. On this occasion he seemed much more so than usual, and led me to think at once something terrible was going to happen. But I was wholly unprepared for the terrible accusation he was about to bring against me. What it was need not be told; suffice it to say, it exceeded in horror and studied insult anything which I had before been called upon to endure at his hands. I was thunder-struck! Not only did I know that the accusation was wholly false and unfounded, but that he, too, must know it to be so, and yet I was fully aware that denial would avail me nothing. The accusation had evidently been made for a purpose, and to deny it would serve nothing toward defeat-

ing that purpose, and yet how could I rest under-
such a terrible charge, and take no steps to dis-
prove it? He accused me of seeing Mason.

We were then expecting his mother to visit us
the next day. She was in the city, at the house of
Mrs. Spalding, and had sent us word that she
would most likely come to our house on the day
following, and stay several days with us. I decided to tell her all my troubles, including this
last insult, and ask her advice; for though she
was his mother, I had sufficient confidence in her
to believe that she would judge impartially between us. But disappointment awaited me. The
morrow came; but, though I waited and watched
anxiously for her coming, she did not make her
appearance, but remained at Mrs. Spalding's.

When Frank had gone I threw myself upon a
lounge, and calmly and deliberately reviewed my
situation. In the name of Heaven, what was I to
do? My husband evidently wished to be rid of
me; the falsehoods which had been put in circula-
tion about me had blasted my reputation and
ruined all my hopes; I could see no way of supporting myself, and could not stay where I was—
what was then left for me but death? Yes; death
would end the struggle forever, and would be a
welcome relief from miseries which, it seemed to
me, there was no other way of avoiding. And then
the tempter whispered me, "There is that vial of
laudanum in the cupboard; it will afford speedy,

sure and painless relief from the miseries you are now enduring."

There is a certain class of philosophers who maintain that the life of a human being belongs to himself, and that whenever, for any cause, it becomes a burden to him, he is fully justified— nay, that it is a praiseworthy act, and commenda-, ble in the sight of God and man—in ending it by his own hands. I thank Heaven that I am not, and never have been a subscriber to any such doctrine. Life is the immediate gift of God to man, bestowed upon us for wise and beneficent purposes, and not to be ended until the same will which bestowed the gift sees proper to recall it, and we have no more right to endeavor to thwart His will in this particular than in any other. It was just as apparent to my mind then, as it is now, that I was committing a most heinous sin in thus conspiring against my own life; but, yet the misery I endured was such as to render me willing to take any consequences which might follow this last desperate effort to end it, and I went about my preparations for suicide as coolly and deliberately as I ever did anything in my life.

I first sat down and wrote a letter to my husband, telling him that my life, by his persecution and neglect, had been rendered a burden to me; that anything was preferable to the life I was leading, and that I had determined to end my existence and my sorrows together. I also informed him of my former marriage, and how my husband had proved to be a married man; and begged his forgiveness for any wrong or injury I might have unintentionally done him. I told him I had loved him with all my heart, and had been a true and faithful wife to him; that he had not appreciated me and my devotion to him; that I was satisfied he hated me and wanted to be rid of me, and that I would die to free him. This letter I sealed and directed to him, and placed it on the table, where he would be most likely to find it; then I took the vial of laudanum in my hand, and raised it to my lips. Then the thought of what I was about to do caused me to hesitate, and, for a moment, my heart failed me, but it was only for a moment. Gathering new courage, I once more raised the vial to my mouth and drank of its deadly contents; then calmly undressed myself and went to bed, waiting for the poison to accomplish its destined work. But the end was not yet.

It was about eight o'clock when I took the poison. There was an over-dose of it, and it was not until I had been very sick, and had thrown up a portion, that it seemed likely to produce the effect I desired. Ah! the horror of that deathly sickness, when death stared me in the face, and when his coming was eagerly and earnestly desired, no one can ever know. Not for a single moment did I repent the course I had taken, and my greatest anxiety was lest not enough of the drug would be retained in my system to accomplish the object for which it had been taken. But at last my sickness partially ceased; I felt a delicious languor stealing over my body and pervading every fiber of my frame, and I sunk into dreamless unconsciousness. The last thing I remembered, before the period of unconsciousness which followed, was the clock striking ten. Frank had not come at that time; I was alone, and the world with all its sorrows, its cares and griefs, as well as its joys and brightness, was fast fading from my vision.

I have no means of knowing what time Frank came home that night. When consciousness was restored to me, which was not until almost morning, he was sitting by my bedside, with the doctor through whose instrumentality my restoration had been effected and my scheme for the present·defeated. I had, then, no thanks for the kindness which had prompted them to save my miserable life, but wished they had allowed me to die, and inwardly vowed to renew the attempt at another time and under more favorable circumstances. Since then, dear reader, I have learned to value life; and I thank God, that He, in his mercy, interposed that night to save the life which was then deemed so worthless; and under Him, most heartily do I thank the doctors (for there were two of them), by whose exertions my mad attempt upon my own life was defeated.

As soon as I was restored to consciousness one of the physicians left. The other remained until some time after daylight, administering to me such remedies as my situation demanded; when, having seen that my condition was no longer dangerous, he, too, took his leave, promising to come back during the course of the day.

He came again in the afternoon, and found me much better, but still very weak and sick from the effects of the terrible dose I had taken. From this time Ford seemed to actually hate me, whereas he had before only slighted and neglected me. Now his whole feeling seemed turned into hatred toward me, and language would scarcely suffice to recount the various means of which he made use to display that hate. He did not resort to actual violence, from very shame perhaps, but treated me as a hired servant, and not as his equal, and the woman he had sworn to love, honor and cherish 'in sickness as well as in health, until we should be parted by death. There was a cool, calculating, cruel coldness in his manner toward me, an effort to degrade me in my own estimation, and to make me feel that I was his inferior, which was really demoniac.

And as soon as my health was somewhat restored, he proceeded deliberately to make arrangements for our complete and final separation. He first gave up all our rooms on the ground floor, and moved up stairs into three small rooms which could only be reached by a stairway passing through a hall belonging to the lower floor of the house. I protested against this arrangement as inconvenient and unnecessary, but it mattered not to him. He deigned to hold no consultation with me, or to make any explanation of his designs or intentions—it was sufficient that he wished it. At this time no idea of immediate separation had occurred to me. I felt sure it would come ere long. If he had not demanded it I should, for to live with him after what had passed was simply impossible, but my health was still too feeble for me to think of leaving him. But when the new arrangements were completed to his satisfaction, he coolly told me he was not going to keep me any longer ; that he had been discharged from the employment of the railroad company, and that I must now look out for myself, and asked where I intended to go ! I made no remonstrance and offered no protest; first, because the programme was not at all objectionable to me, and secondly, because I was convinced of its utter uselessness. I merely asked him for some money, which he refused to give me, saying he had none for me, then put on my bonnet and shawl, went to an employment office, and on applying for a situation, succeeded in getting one to do general housework for a family in Niles, Michigan. I was to go that very afternoon to enter upon my new sphere of duty.

When I had completed my agreement and settled all the terms, I went back to the house and told my husband of my arrangements for my future support. I was to do kitchen-work, in a large family, for two dollars per week. He made not the slightest objection to my going out to work as a kitchen girl, nor do I suppose he would have objected to anything else which took me out of his way. No, he was entirely willing that his bride of a few weeks standing should go out to the most menial servitude to subsist herself, so he was only left free to follow the baser passions of his nature, relieved from even the trifling restraint which my presence imposed.

And this was the man who had vowed to protect me from the cold and chilling blasts of fate in this world! This was the man who had once professed to love me, and whom I had promised to love, honor and obey—the man with whom I had expected to walk, hand in hand, all adown the vale of life, our pathway all strewn with the flowers of love, and our lives crowned with peace and happiness. How bright had been my anticipations of happiness before marriage! How sad and gloomy the reality to which I had been subjected! Then I supposed that I had found a haven of rest from all the ills and cares of life—I found in reality that so far from being a haven of rest, it was the most troubled and tempestuous sea of sorrow upon which my frail bark had as yet been set afloat. How gladly then I hailed any arrangement, however unpleasant or disagreeable it might be, so it only involved my release from the horrid bondage under which I was suffering! But my arrangements were not yet complete. The train which it was necessary for me to take to reach my destination would go at five o'clock, and I had not a cent

18

of money to pay my fare. I spoke to Ford about this, and asked him for some money. He replied that he would bring me some in time for me to leave, turned on his heel and left the house.

I felt confident he would keep this promise, despite the habitual falsehoods in which he was accustomed to deal with me, because I felt sure his desire to be rid of me would prompt him to truthfulness, knowing that it was impossible for me to go without money. But the day gradually wore away, and he came not. The time for my departure was drawing near, and still he had not made his appearance. My trunk was packed, and all my arrangrments were complete for starting; but still no money to pay my fare had been received, and now the conviction forced itself upon my mind that he intended to do nothing for me. As this opinion gained strength in my mind I began to cast about me to see how I could raise the means necessary to accomplish my object. It would cost me something to go to the scene of my new engagement, and I did not wish to land there, among entire strangers, with no money; for, in case anything was to happen—myself and my employer should not agree, or sickness should intervene— what would become of me?

I was always fond of pets, and had a large cage of very fine canary birds; but they were the only objects upon which I could now lavish my affection, and I did not like the idea of parting with them. I looked around. The house was well supplied with furniture, bedding, dishes and the like, toward procuring which my labor had contributed as much, at least, as his; and I greatly feared that, as soon as I was out of the way, they would be taken possession of by others whose claim was not so good as mine. Why should not I take some of the most valuable of the articles, and make them conduce to my support? Surely, morally, there could be no wrong in my taking them. Before proceeding, however, to pack them up, I saw Wallace Ford and sent him in search of his father, to tell him I must have money to start upon the trip which was to take me out of his way forever.

Wallace went away, and was gone a long time. I waited as long as I dared, and then went to work to packing up, in a box, the articles upon which I designed to raise the means for the prosecution of my journey. I took two comforts, all the sheets and pillows in the house, all the best dishes, and some other articles, and packed them in a box; and my only regret, when I looked around me, was that so much had to be left. About the time my packing was finished, Wallace came back, and said he could not find my husband, and immediately went away again.

Meantime, however, an express wagon had come for my baggage; the driver was already grumbling, and saying we would be too late for the train, and no more time could be spared to wait for my truant husband. My trunk and box were therefore loaded into the wagon, I clambered up to a seat

beside the driver, and before Wallace got out of
sight he saw us trundling away to the Central
Depot. Arrived there, we found the prediction of
the expressman true; the train was just moving
out as we entered the inclosure, and there was
nothing for me to do but to wait for the next train.

Before it was time for the next train to leave,
Ford came, gave me fifteen dollars, accompanied
me on board the cars and found me a seat, bade
me a cold adieu, left me alone, and, in a short
time, I was on my way to push my fortune among
entire strangers as best I might.

> " BE it so; we part forever;
>   Let the past as nothing be—
> If I had not loved thee, never
>   Hadst thou been thus dear to me.

> " Had I not loved thee and been slighted,
>   That I better could have borne—
> Love is quelled when unrequited,
>   By the rising pulse of scorn.

> " Pride may cool what passion heated,
>   Time may tame the wayward will,
> But the heart in friendship cheated,
>   Throbs with woe's most mad'ning thrill.

> " Oh! there is a silent sorrow
>   Which can find no vent in speech—
> Which disdains relief to borrow
>   From the heights that song can reach.

> " Like the clankless chain enthralling—
>   Like the sleepless dreams that mock—
> Like the frigid ice-drops falling
>   From the surf-surrounded rock;

" Such the cold and sickening feeling,
    Thou hast caused this heart to know—
Stabbed the deeper by concealing
    From the world its bitter woe.

" Once it fondly, proudly deemed thee
    All that fancy's self could paint—
Once it honored and esteemed thee
    As its idol and its saint.

" More thou wert to me than mortal,
    Not as man I looked on thee—
Then, why, like all the rest deceive me;
    Why heap man's worst curse on me?

" Wert thou but a friend assuming
    Friendship's smile and husband's art,
And, in borrowed beauty blooming,
    Trifling with a trusting heart?

" By that eye which once could glisten
    With appealing glance to me—
By that ear which once could listen
    To each tale I told to thee;

" By that lip its smile bestowing,
    Which could soften sorrow's gush—
By that cheek, once brightly glowing
    With pure friendship's well-feigned blush—

" By all those charms united,
    Thou hast wrought thy wanton will,
And, without compunction, blighted
    What thou would'st not kindly kill.

" Yet I curse thee not in sadness—
    Still, I feel how dear thou wert—
Oh! I could not, e'en in madness,
    Doom thee to thy just desert.

" Live, and when my life is over,
    Should thine be lengthened long,

Thou may'st then, too late, discover
  By thy feelings, all my wrong.

" Ere that hour, false one—hear me--
  Thou shalt feel what I do now,
While my spirit, hovering near thee,
  Still recalls thy broken vow.

" But 't is useless to upbraid thee
  With thy past or present state—
What thou wert, my fancy made thee—
  What thou art, I know too late."

CHAPTER XVIII.

As the train slowly moved out from the depot into the darkness of the night (for it was nearly eight o'clock of a dreary, stormy night on which I left Chicago), I felt that I was really alone and desolate in the wide world; and my heart sunk within me as I thought of my prospects for the future. I was going to a place of which I knew nothing, and where there was not a single soul whom I knew, to enter upon the duties of a life of which I had had no experience, and my purse contained just fifteen dollars—all my fortune—and even a part of that I must pay for my ride to my destination. And then, what if my experiment at Niles should prove a failure?—what would become of me in that event? Heaven only knew.

These thoughts occupied my mind during the whole of my ride from Chicago to Niles, and most effectually prevented me from sleeping any of the time; and, when we reached my stopping place, I knew not what to do or where to go. I had never stopped there before, did not know a single soul in the place, and had no idea of where my employer lived or where to make inquiries for him. I inquired of several persons, and was finally directed to an aristocratic looking (for that place) mansion, where I found what was expected to be my future home, and first met with the woman whom, for the first time since my childhood, I was to call mistress. That first interview satisfied me that my stay at her house would be short. There was an air of haughty disdain about her, a sort of reckless contempt for the feelings of others, which, though regarded by some of the shoddy aristocracy of the present day as evidence of good breeding, is, in my judgment, the very reverse, and stamps its possessor as at once devoid of all the finer feelings, which mark the true gentleman or lady.

What though the necessities of society demand that there should be gradation and distinct classifications among its members! what though some are born to wealth and fortune and others to poverty and toil? is that any reason why the first is any better, or has any finer feelings, than the last? If one is born to an heritage of poverty, and compelled to labor from day to day in order to obtain the bread which sustains their existence, and another is born to wealth, and thus enabled to employ the paid labor of the less fortunate class: does that, by any means, demonstrate that the latter class is possessed of *all* the finer feelings and sensibilities of our common humanity? or does it give them a right to trample upon and disregard all the feelings of their less fortunate employes? Or, suppose one to be born to wealth and station, and by some reverse of fortune be swept from their high estate to mingle in the walks of poverty and want; and suppose another born in

the circle of indigence, and, by some stroke of
fortune, be suddenly placed in the possession of
the most boundless wealth : can any advocate of
the privilege of aristocracy tell me by what sort of
alchemy the first is at once debased into an animal
destitute of all feeling and sensibility, while the
last is at once invested with all those delicate
nerves which, in the opinion of some, make up the
delicate lady of fashion ? No, indeed. Well has
the poet said—

> "Honor and fame from no condition rise;
> Act well your part—there all the honor lies."

Before I had been with my new mistress two
days I had made up my mind to leave her, and
resort to some other means of earning my livelihood. The haughtiness and contempt for the
feelings of her employes, which I had marked
during our first interview, were displayed in the
most offensive manner upon every possible occasion, and soon rendered my position there not only
unpleasant but unendurable. I accordingly left
there, and, having determined to try some other
mode of earning a livelihood, left Niles for Detroit.

Arrived there, I rented a small house already
furnished, took two or three boarders, and also
took some washing to do. Getting to Detroit had
consumed my fifteen dollars, and I hardly knew
what I should do to get along until my boarders
began to pay up, which, of course, I did not expect them to do until the end of a week at any

rate. My washing, however, brought me a little
money, and I managed to get along, though compelled to go in debt at my grocer's and my
butcher's. I wrote to Ford, telling him of my
situation and asking some assistance from him,
but without eliciting any reply. Doubtless he
was too much engaged to take any notice of
letters from one who was no more to him than
his wife. He had gotten me out of his way and
did not intend to be troubled with me any more.

Still I struggled on, and tried to make a comfortable living, but the work was too hard for me,
and I soon found that something else must be
done. I could either have managed my boarding-
house, or done what washing was on hand, but
both together I could not do, and neither one
alone would support me. I have already informed the reader that Captain Lake was dead—
his wife had returned to her family in the South,
and there was no one to whom I could apply for
advice or assistance; but one thing was manifest—
it was impossible for me to stay there and live in
this way. Accordingly I gave up my house, and,
going to an employment office, applied for a situation. They sent me to the house of a Mr. Cones,
an Express agent, and a most thorough and
perfect gentleman.

Upon my arrival at his house, I found the family
to consist only of himself, his wife and her sister,
and his father-in-law, one of the kindest and most
agreeable old gentlemen I ever knew. They were

all very kind to me, but this good old man was
more than kind—he could not have treated me
more affectionately had I been his daughter. I
hired to them to do general house-work, at two
dollars per week, and for a time everything
passed off in the most pleasant and agreeable
manner. The work was not beyond my strength
and the family could not have treated me better
than they did. I passed for a young widow, and
for some time no one of the many visitors at
Mrs. Cones, or even the family, knew any better.

But, although my lot was outwardly as happy
as could have been expected under the circumstances, inwardly my mind was borne down by
a weight of sorrow almost too heavy to be borne.
Nor is it strange that such should have been the
case; for what was there in my past life to excite any but the most sorrowful feelings? My
life had been one constant scene of clouds and
darkness, with only here and there a ray of sunshine, which served but to make darkness, both
preceding and following it, more dense, impenetrable and frightful. And in my present employment I had abundance of time and opportunity
to think of these things. As I daily witnessed
the happiness of the family around me, and compared it with my own wretched lot, it made my
own fortune appear so dark by the contrast, that
it well-nigh made me murmur against the justice
of God who had meted out such different fortunes to us. Do not think I envied them their

happiness. I did not, nor would I have detracted one single atom from their felicity to have purchased for myself a lifetime of unalloyed happiness. But I could not help making the contrast between their lot and mine.

Constant brooding over these things was not without its sad effects, not only upon my mind, but also upon my physical health. I became first moody and morose, and then, finally, really ill, and unable to perform my daily tasks. I was compelled to abstain altogether from work, and took to my bed, from which it was thought for some days I would never rise. But the kind care and attention of Mrs. Cones and her sister, aided by my naturally strong constitution, triumphed over the disease, and in time I was restored to comparative health once more.

During my sickness I had been deranged a great part of the time, and had raved almost constantly about my family troubles, thus most effectually revealing the fact that I was other than I seemed. And when, as my convalescence approached, Mrs. Cones came to me one day and seating herself by my bedside, asked me to tell her all about my past life, and who Eugene Mason and Frank Ford were, I expected to be severely blamed for having deceived her as to my being a widow. But not so. As I explained my situation to her, the tears of sympathy welled up from her warm, full heart, and gathering me to her bosom, she said:

"My poor child! how you have suffered. Why did you not tell me of this before?"

"Because, I was ashamed to reveal the story of my troubles. I preferred to suffer them in silence rather than inflict so uninteresting and unlovely a tale upon any one else."

"And this silent suffering is what has made you sick. If you had confided your secret to me, had shared it with me, it would have been safe, and you most likely spared this fit of sickness."

"I know I ought to have trusted you, but I was afraid to. One is so uncertain of meeting any sympathy in this world."

"That is true, but no one ever appealed to me in vain. I must tell my husband, and we will then see what can be done for you."

"Mr. Cones asked me some questions, after hearing my story from his wife, and then wrote a letter to Ford in which he told him I was there sick, out of money, and in debt, and that he ought to do something for me. No answer was ever received to this letter, and, as the weary days grew into a week, the anxiety which I constantly endured about my situation caused me to relapse, and again Mr. Cones communicated my condition to Mr. Ford. He informed him by telegraph of my severe illness, and told him if he wanted to see me alive to come on without delay; but to this dispatch no answer was ever vouchsafed. I was at that time inclined to be charitable, and to think that Ford had never received this letter and telegram, but he has since acknowledged to me that he did receive both! So much for the love he once professed for me. Had our situations been reversed, and had he sent for me, I would have gone to him, had I gone barefooted and begged my way from house to house. But I can not believe that all men are thus inconstant.

But it was not the will of Providence that I should die at this time. Gradually I recovered—little by little health and strength came back to my wasted and enfeebled frame, until at last I was able to leave my bed, then my room, and finally, the house. As soon as my health was sufficiently restored to enable me to go about, I began making arrangements to leave my kind friends; for I felt that more active life was what I needed—something in which there would be less of monotony, and in which the excitement of change would prevent my mind from brooding so constantly over the dark past. It was this which had caused my sickness, and I feared to encounter the same dread monster again. They urged me to remain with them; but, when I gave them my reasons for going, they acquiesced in their justice and propriety, and ceased to offer any further opposition. They asked me what I intended to do; but this was something I had not decided upon. Mr. Cones then suggested that I should engage in canvassing for some publishing house—in short, should become a "Book Agent." I did not like this much at first, fearing I should fail; but, at any rate, it would possess the merit of constant change—would keep my thoughts employed—and I finally decided to adopt it.

This matter settled, the next question was, where, and from what house, I would endeavor to obtain employment. After debating the pros and cons of various places, for some time, I at last made up my mind that I would return to Chicago and seek employment there. The reader may think strange that I decided to go to a place where I had endured so much of sorrow, and where so many of my bitterest enemies were living; but I had an object in so doing, which will more fully appear in the sequel.

But, before going to Chicago, I wished to go to Indiana and locate my residence there. I had several objects in doing this: the first of which was this—I had determined to obtain a divorce from my unworthy husband, in case certain matters turned out as I thought they would, upon my visit to Chicago; and I had been informed that the laws of that State were such as to render the attainment of that object comparatively easy and inexpensive to a resident of the State; and, as I had no particular ties to bind me to one place more than another, I might as well live where I could easily accomplish this object as any place else. And, I may remark here, that I have never seen any occasion to regret having chosen that State for my residence. Some of my warmest friends are inhabitants of the noble State of Indiana; and, in all parts of the

State, I have met with a kindliness of feeling, and a genuine heart-welcome, which convinces me that the Hoosiers are as generous in sentiment as their soldiers, in the late civil war, proved themselves to be brave and fearless in battle. But to return to my story.

As my funds had long since been exhausted, I had but one way of raising the means necessary to prosecute my plans, and that was by selling some of my clothing. Mr. Cones offered to loan me the money; but his kindness had already been severely taxed, and I was unwilling to test it any further, preferring to be independent, if it was in my power. I accordingly went out and sold my wedding-dress and some other clothing, from which I realized a very handsome sum of money, and started for Indianapolis. Upon arriving there I selected lodgings, left the greater part of my clothing there, taking with me only enough for a change or two, and started for Chicago, to see what could be done in the way of pushing my fortune. Another object, which I wished to accomplish, was to learn if Ford was still living, what he was doing, whether he had received Mr. Cones' letter and dispatch, and why he had not answered them.

Upon reaching Chicago, I went at once to the railroad office, on State Street, and called for Mr. Webb, the Superintendent. He and Ford were well acquainted, and I felt confident he could tell me of his whereabouts if he was in the city, and my confidence was not, in this instance at least, at all misplaced. He told me at once that Ford was in the city, was alive and well, and was working for a man by the name of Lake, on Randolph Street, near Union. I knew the place very well— went there, and almost the first person I met was my step-son, Wallace. He seemed very much surprised to see me, they having considered me dead some time since, but he seemed pleased at the meeting, and when I asked if his father was there, promptly replied in the affirmative, and at once went to call him.

He came, but oh! how cold and constrained the meeting. He did not ask me where I was living, nor about my health, or manifest the least interest in my welfare, nor would he even take me to his boarding-house, or tell me where it was. I then asked him for some money to pay my expenses, but he refused, saying that he had none that he could spare. He, however, promised to come to the Rock Island House, in the evening, to see me, and said he would then give me some money. But he only said this for the purpose of getting rid of me, for he never came near me. I must not omit to state that, in this interview, he admitted that he had received Mr. Cones' letter and telegram during my illness, but offered no excuse for not answering them in any way.

After this interview, I went back to the Rock Island House, fully resolved in my own mind, if he did not come (and I had not much idea he would) that evening, according to his promise, never to

19

call upon him for assistance again, or in any way
to recognize him as my husband, save by going on
with my proceeding for divorce just as early as
the laws of the State where my residence now was
would permit of my doing. Evening came, but,
according to my anticipations, he did not, and
from that day to this I have never seen or communicated with him.

At the Rock Island House I got hold of the
"Chicago Tribune," and turning at once to the
column of "Wants," found the following notice:

WANTED, Agents, both ladies and gentlemen to
canvass for "Tried and True, or Love and Loyalty," a new book destined to have an immense sale.
Apply to W. J. Holland, 38 Lombard Block,
Chicago.

The name of the work struck me favorably, and
I determined to apply at once for a situation. But
it was too late to do anything that evening, and
beside, I was a little in hopes that Ford would
keep his promise, and call on me that evening. I
therefore cut out the advertisement, resolving to
call at the place indicated early the next morning.

The next morning at ten o'clock found me at No.
38 Lombard Block. The gentleman in attendance
was very kind and pleasant, and, in answer to my
inquiries, told me the work was just out; that he
was the general agent for Illinois, and he thought
an active, energetic agent could do well with the
work. He gave me the terms upon which the work
would be furnished to agents, and the price at

which they would be allowed to sell it. I was at that time very green in relation to such matters, and thought the margin allowed was enormous, and that a fortune would in a short time crown my efforts. Though I have since learned by experience that the colors in which the business was then presented to my view were more roseate than the facts warranted, still I take occasion to say that the energetic, active book agent, who pursues the business with tact and judgment, need never fear such a thing as a failure. If properly doing their duty, they are certain of fair returns, in a pecuniary point of view, while the avocation presents the ever-recurring charm of novelty and change, and affords facilities for the study of human nature almost unequaled by any other pursuit. But to return to my interview with Mr. Holland.

He asked me where I wished to canvass, and suggested Peoria County, Illinois, as a good place; and having no objections to going there, I finally made arrangements with him to canvass exclusively that county, if I should decide to canvass for him at all. He then told me that my first book would cost two dollars and a half, which must be paid in advance, and that circulars, subscription books, and all other necessary documents would be furnished free of charge. I had not the money to pay him for my first book, but was too proud to tell him so, and therefore left, promising to call on Monday, and acquaint him with my determination.

I at once began to cast about to see where I could raise the money necessary to start in business. It would cost me between fourteen and fifteen dollars to pay my hotel bill, buy my book, pay my fare to Peoria, and meet such other expenses as I must necessarily incur before I could get to work. What could I dispose of to raise it? I had no clothing with me that I could spare, and I could think of nothing but my canary birds. And yet, how could I part with them? They had been my companions since that cold parting with my husband at the Central Depot in Chicago; they were my only pets, and seemed almost as dear to me as though they had been children of my own flesh and blood. Then I thought of my watch. Perhaps something could be raised on that. I went to a pawnbroker, and showing him my watch, asked how much he would loan me on it. He replied eight dollars was all he could afford. This would not meet my necessities, and now no resource was left but to sell my birds.

I took them and went upon Madison street, and was there told by a gentleman that I might leave them with him for a time and let him hear them sing, and if they suited him he would buy them. They were, I think, the sweetest singers I ever heard in my life, and were certainly the most perfect pets I ever saw. One of them in particular, would come out of the cage and lie in my hand as if dead, while I would pretend to cry over it and mourn for it. But this time it was no pretense with me. As I displayed this little trick to the gentleman, I cried in reality as though my heart would break at the thought of parting with them.

When I came back, after an absence of about an hour, I told the gentleman I could not sell my birds, but if he would let me have seven dollars (the amount he proposed to give me for them), I would leave them with him, with the understanding that if at any time I came back and paid him the seven dollars, with interest at the rate of twenty-five per cent., he should return them to me. To this he assented, and then I cried worse than ever. Had they been children it would not have been more painful to me to have parted with them, but it was finally done, and I went back to the hotel, where I took another crying spell. The landlady came in and asked me what was the matter. I told her I had sold my birds—that I was going out canvassing, and, of course, could not take them with me, and hence had sold them. I was too proud to tell her that they had been sold to raise the money to start me in business, and hence put it upon the ground of my inability to care for them. She replied that I need not have sold them, for she would have taken care of them for me, but I answered it was now done and could not be helped.

I was now in possession of fifteen dollars, my sole and entire capital, and was about starting out with that sum (or rather what would be left of it after paying my hotel bill) to seek my fortune. This may seem like rather a slender foundation for such a fortune as I hoped to accumulate in time; but it is one of the beauties of our business that it requires little or no capital to start in it. If, like me, you can raise funds enough to buy your book and an old basket to carry it in, and can then pay you fare to the place where you are going to work, you are all right.

I waited until Monday, then went to Mr. Holland and paid him for a book, thus concluding the contract between us, and made my arrangements to proceed to my field of labor that very afternoon. Before going, however, I must purchase something or other in which to carry my book and papers. Time enough for that yet, however, and, as my business was finally settled and my mind relieved, I went to call upon an old friend for a short time before leaving the city, most likely forever.

This visit was productive of pleasure in more ways than one, aside from a little matter of business, by means of which my outfit was finally completed. In the first place, I had a very pleasant visit with the lady upon whom I called, told her all about my plans and prospects for the future, and received her congratulations and well wishes. Then, just as I was about leaving, another old and valued friend came in—one who had been a friend to me in time of trouble—and my story had to be repeated to her, much to her astonishment. Mrs. Gregg, the last comer, was one of those kind, clever

bodies, whom everybody loves and regards as a
sister, and can keep any article, be it clothing or
anything else, forever and a day after. She had in
her hand an old-fashioned basket, one, perhaps,
that had been used to hold the fragments of fish
we read of in the fifteenth chapter of Matthew, but
which, owing to her wonderful tact in the art of
preservation, was still sound and in good repair. As
I looked at this basket, it suddenly occurred to me
that this was the very thing to answer my purpose.

"Mrs, Gregg," said I, abruptly, "what will you
take for your basket ?"

"My basket," said the good old lady, turning it
over and looking at it on all sides ; "don't make
fun of my basket. It has been my constant companion for a great many years."

"I am not making fun of it, I assure you. I am
in sober earnest. It is just the thing to use in my
canvassing, and I really want to buy it of you."

"Well, Minnie, if you are in earnest, I may,
perhaps, let you have it. But I supposed you
were only making fun of it because it is old-
fashioned."

"Indeed, I was not."

"Well," said the lady, again turning the basket
around, and look at it on all sides, "you may have
it for one dollar."

"I will take it."

I paid her the dollar, she emptied the basket,
and it was transferred to my possession, and has
been my constant companion ever since. I have

carried it wherever I went, and shall always keep it as a souvenir of one of the best friends I ever had ; and she can keep a certain pitcher to remind her of me and a certain moving-day.

I then went to the hotel, paid my bill, went to the depot and bought a ticket to Peoria. This left just ten cents in my possession, and with this small fortune I took my seat on the cars, and was soon whirling out of the city to my new field of labor.

CHAPTER XIX.

As the cars bore me rapidly onward toward the place selected in which I was to begin my career as a "Book Agent," I had abundant time to review the situation and decide upon my course of action when I should finally arrive at the field. And the first point to determine was, how to get along with my ridiculously small fund and pay my way until returns from my labors began to come in, which would most likely be a week or more. Rather a difficult problem, say you, my dear reader? This may be so; and yet I found means to solve it to my entire satisfaction. Upon one thing I was determined—not to betray the low state of my finances to any one, for this could not be otherwise than disastrous to all my future plans. Such is the disposition of the world; let it be supposed that one has money, no matter whether he possesses honesty, merit, or anything else which should commend him to the confidence of the public, and every one is ready to stretch forth the helping hand; men will go out of their way, get down on their knees and crawl in the dirt, for the purpose of doing him a favor, whether they expect to receive any reward for it or not. But no matter what his merits may be, let it be understood (whether correctly or otherwise) that his purse is light, and none are ready to assist him, even though by so doing they were sure to immediately and pecuniarily benefit themselves; no faces are wreathed in smiles at his approach; no hand is stretched forth to relieve his most pressing necessities : but he is regarded with looks and frowns of ill-concealed contempt and aversion, while pockets are sternly buttoned up, and freezing coldness chills his very soul. Yes; if one wishes to cut himself off from all hope of success in this world, let him only cause it to be understood that he is poor. This I was resolved not to do. No one should know that I was without funds, and was dependent upon my daily labor for my support. I would stop at the best hotel in Peoria, leave my baggage (I had sent to Indianapolis and obtained a trunk full of my clothing) in the hands of the landlord as security for my bill, and go to work with energy and vigor, trusting in a kind Providence to crown my efforts with success. And I may add here that the result has more than justified my expectations.

In due time we arrived at Peoria, and then, for the first time, my heart failed me in regard to the task before me. Entirely without experience in the work to which I had addressed myself—alone, in a large city, where there was not a single human being whom I had seen or of whom I knew anything—no one to whom I could apply for advice or assistance in case of emergency—is it strange that my heart should be somewhat cast down, and that

my soul should shrink, somewhat, from the contest
at hand; the bitter struggle with poverty and
want, in which there were, at least, as many
chances against me as there were in my favor?
Add to these reflections the confusion created in
my mind by the din and bustle ever attendant upon the arrival of a train; the hackmen, porters,
omnibus-drivers, and all of that ilk, filling the air
and torturing the ear with cries of all kinds; each
one praising his own line, or his own house, or his
own carriage, as superior to any and all others,
and the reader (who doubtless has experienced, to
his or her satisfaction, all these annoyances of
travel) will not be surprised that, for a short time,
our new-made book agent stood utterly bewilder-
ed, dumfoundered, and at a loss what to do or
where to go.

Notwithstanding the fact that I had so carefully
laid and so fully digested all my plans of action
during the passage of the train from Chicago, I
fancy I was, for a time, as pitiable a spectacle of
indecision and uncertainty as was ever seen upon
this mundane sphere. It now affords me much
amusement to recall the incidents of that first arrival in Peoria; but, then, believe me, dear reader,
it was no laughing matter. I have no doubt the
bystanders all thought that was the first time I
had ever disembarked from a railway train; and,
most certainly, my conduct was such as not to
give the lie to such a supposition. But relief at
last came. As I stood, surrounded by a crowd of

porters, hackmen, and the like, each one of whom was anxious to serve me (they did not know that ten cents was all my fortune), a gentleman and lady, whom I had noticed on the train, but with whom I had had no conversation, approached me, and the gentleman kindly asked me where I wished to go. I told him that I was a stranger in the city, having never been there before, and that I wanted to go to a good hotel. He informed me that he lived in the city; that himself and wife were going up in town, and that if I would accompany them they would show me the way to the Peoria House, the best hotel in the place. I thanked him heartily for his kindness to a perfect stranger, and we at once set out, on foot, for our destination. After walking three or four blocks, we came in sight of a large brick house near the public square.

"There, Miss," said my guide, pointing to a large brick building, "is the Peoria House."

Again I thanked him for his kindness, and, crossing the street, went up a short flight of steps into the house, and passed into the parlor. My heart beat violently as I rung the bell. "What if I should fail, after all," I thought; "what will become of me?"

A boy came in answer to my summons, and stood awaiting my order. I told him I wanted a room. He retired, and in a short time a gentleman came in with a key in his hand, and, bowing poliltely, inquired if I wished a room.

"If you please, sir."

"Have you any baggage, madam?

"My trunk is at the depot," I replied, handing him my check; "will you send for it?"

"Certainly, madam; will you have it sent to your room?"

"Yes, sir. Can I have supper?"

"Yes, I will show you to your room, and will then order supper. What will you have?"

"Nothing but a cup of tea. I am not well and can eat but a mouthful."

He led the way up one flight of stairs into a small room above the parlor, placed the light (for it was now quite dark) on a small table in the room, bowed again and withdrew. I was alone. Yes, in the immense building filled with guests, in the very heart of a populous city, I was alone. There was not a soul among all the many thousands almost within sound of my voice upon whom I could call for assistance of any kind, for comfort, or even sympathy. I had fairly launched my frail bark upon the tempestuous ocean of life, and was about to undertake the voyage with no comrade to cheer me, no chart or compass to guide my wanderings, and no hope save in the kindness of an overruling Providence, and my own courage and energy. Ah! what if they should fail me at some critical moment? I looked around the room. It was furnished as hotel rooms usually are; a single bed, two chairs, a wash-stand and small table, while a hempen carpet covered the floor. There was nothing peculiar in the room, but it seemed to me that I could see the word "failure" written on every article it contained. Doubtless my nervous excitement tended to give the room a more gloomy look than it really possessed, for I afterward found it to be one of the most pleasant rooms in the house. Such is the influence of the mind upon our outward senses.

At length there was a tap at the door, and the messenger boy came in to tell me my tea was ready and show me the way to the dining-room. I went down and found they had prepared a very fine lunch for me, for it was past the usual supper hour, but it was impossible for me to eat. Every morsel I tried to swallow seemed to choke me, and, after drinking part of a cup of tea, I rose from the table and returned to my room. I found the bit of candle with which it was supplied had entirely burned out, and my room was in total darkness. With some difficulty I found the bell handle, and rang the bell, then waited patiently in darkness for the messenger, my heart beating so violently that I could hear its pulsations. I am not cowardly, but on this evening I was so much oppressed with my own feelings, hopes, doubts, and fears for the future, that I felt a degree of timidity entirely foreign to my nature. I was really and truly, in feeling and character, "a cat in a strange garret."

The boy finally came and brought me a lamp, and, as soon as he had gone, I undressed and went to bed, but not to sleep. Fears and apprehensions of failure still ran riot through my brain, and most effectually banished slumber from my eyelids. But as I lay and tossed upon my sleepless couch, I resolved anew that no such word as failure should be found in my vocabulary; by my energy and industry I would deserve success, and if it did not crown my efforts, the fault, at least, should not be mine. No; I would yet show that I could live independent of Frank C. Ford or any one else; that I could carve my own way in the world, in spite of the frowns of fortune, the inconstancy of friends, or the treachery of those from whom I had a right to expect better things. This was my resolve; how it has been carried out let the sequel show.

I rose early in the morning, made my toilet, and went down to the dining-room. Breakfast was just ready; the long hall was filled with guests and boarders, but, though I scanned each one closely, there was not a single face I knew. But my nervousness of the night before was all gone, and the fact that every one in the room was a stranger to me did not annoy or discomfort me in the least. Nay, it was rather a matter of gratification to me that it was so than otherwise, for I had not succeeded in ridding myself entirely of the idea, so sedulously inculcated by sundry newspapers, that there was something discreditable about the business I was about entering upon, and I rejoiced in the belief that my first attempt was to be made entirely among strangers. I have since learned to believe that the avocation of a book agent, though perhaps less elevated in the judgment of the world than some others, is still, if pursued in a proper and becoming manner, just as creditable as any other, and certain it is that it is as useful and beneficial to society as many others which might be named. It is undeniable that a vast deal of useful, interesting and beneficial literature, which might otherwise remain for years, or perhaps forever, in comparative obscurity, is brought prominently before the public by means of the system of canvassing now so much in vogue among publishers and wholesale and retail book houses. And surely no occupation which tends so directly and so powerfully to the dissemination of light and knowledge among the masses, as does book agency, can be called useless, degrading, or disreputable. Through the efforts of the book agent, many a family, who otherwise would not purchase a book of any kind from one year's end to another, is induced to subscribe for some work of interest and benefit. A taste for reading is thereby cultivated, for it is well known " the appetite grows upon what it feeds upon," other books are purchased, periodicals are subscribed for, and in time this family, first reached by the judicious and persevering efforts of that much abused class of individuals of whom the writer is proud to be one, is elevated from the slough of ignorance in which they formerly wallowed, to a position of respectability and credit among the intelligent ones of the land. This is no picture of the imagination.

The writer can point to numerous instances in which a taste for reading and literature has been first developed and called into being by publications of which she was the fortunate seller. But, says the querulous, objecting fault-finder, the business is not followed for the purpose of doing good, but only to put money into the purse of the agent. Very well, my cynical friend, what avocation do you follow? Do you pursue it for the purpose solely of being useful to your fellow-men, or is not the hope of gain a slight—just a very slight—incentive to your exertions? And yet, you would be hardly willing to admit that your chosen pursuit was on that account useless, and ought to be frowned out of existence by community, or that it was degrading to you. And why judge us more harshly than you are willing to be judged? No, all occupations, not in themselves hurtful or immoral, are alike honorable and useful, and all are alike pursued by their respective votaries for the purpose of gain. The accumulation of money is the prime object with all, and no one is disgraced by following any laudable employment with all the energy God has given him, simply because that is the object. Human nature is by the Omniscence of the Almighty so constituted that all occupations and all professions are necessary to each other, and it does not become the follower of one occupation to sneer at another, and to say, " I am more respectable and more use-
20

ful to community than thou art." But let us return
from this digression.

My abstinence of the evening before, together
with my long railroad ride, had given me a keen
appetite ; we had a good breakfast, and the reader
may be assured I did ample justice to it. Then,
armed with the veritable old basket purchased of
my friend Mrs. Gregg, and containing my subscription book and specimen copy of the book, I sallied
forth in quest of subscribers. It must be confessed that my heart palpitated a trifle quicker than
usual, as I approached a gentleman and asked him
to look at my book, and, if it pleased him, to subscribe for it. He was the proprietor of a large dry
goods store, and he looked at the book with so
much apparent interest, that I felt very confident
my first attempt in the line of my new business
was about to prove a success. But not so. After
looking at it for some time, he finally handed it
back to me, declining to subscribe ; but his refusal
was couched in such kind and gentlemanly terms,
that so far from feeling disheartened by this first
failure, I was rather encouraged than otherwise.
Had I met with such an unkind and ill-natured refusal as I have since frequently done, I am by no
means sure but my book agency would have terminated then and there, for my spirits were not
then strong enough to endure a very severe rebuff.

But his kindly disposition encouraged me, and
I turned from that first interview more resolved
than ever that success should finally crown my

efforts. I left the old gentleman and went into
another store where my utmost efforts to obtain a
single subscriber were doomed to disappointment.
There were several clerks there, all of whom looked at the book, but none were willing to invest any
amount in it. And the same result attended my
application at several stores in the same vicinity;
all declined to subscribe. The reasons given for
refusal were as various and as numerous as the
persons to whom application was made. One said:
"I would take the book, but have no place to keep
it;" another, "That is not my style of reading at
all;" another, "I am not able to buy it;" while
still another, belonging to the class who believe
everybody dishonest, perhaps because they judge
others by themselves, perhaps from some other
cause, said: "I never subscribe for anything; if I
want a book, I go and buy it, but no book agents
for me." I have often since heard the same reason
given, and I never heard it without thinking to
myself that the utterer would take the last crust of
bread from a widow and her starving children provided he could do so with safety; that nature designed him for a knave and sharper, and that
nothing but lack of opportunity, want of ability,
or the fear of law prevented him from becoming
one. No man ever charged all his fellow-men with
being dishonest unless he was conscious of some
want of principle himself, or, unless he was de-
ficient in good sound sense, and thought to acquire
a reputation for being sharp by suspecting the

motives and intentions of everybody else. But
those who belong to the latter class can rest assured that, so far from achieving such reputation,
they are certain to be rated at their true value by
those who listen to their silly pretensions.

And thus the time wore away. I visited place
after place, and tried in vain to awaken sufficient
interest in my book to induce somebody to buy it,
until the forenoon was nearly spent; nothing had
been done, and I was almost disheartened. It
seemed almost impossible for me to go back to my
hotel without at least one subscriber, and yet the
prospect that I would be compelled to do so seemed very bright. Coming at length to a flight of
stairs running up from the street, I mechanically
ascended them, though, it must be confessed, with
but little hope of effecting anything. Near the
head of the stairs was a law office, occupied by a
Mr. King, and I hesitated some time whether to
venture in there or not, but finally decided to try
it. Mr. King received me in a very gentlemanly
manner, listened courteously to my request, examined the book, and, better than all, subscribed
for it. Eureka! I have made a beginning at last.
The ice was broken, and, with renewed confidence,
I went in search of further patronage, for I now
had a name to which I could refer those whom I
solicited to subscribe.

The next room was occupied by a lawyer by the
name of Brown. As soon as I showed him my
book, and told him Mr. King had subscribed—

"Well," said he, in an abrupt, but pleasant sort of way, "if King can stand it, I guess I can." And down went his name. Just across the hall was a sign informing the public that H. M. Harris dispensed law (and, I suppose, justice,) to those who were in need of his services, and I went in there. Upon making my business known, Mr. Harris at once put his name down. I went down that flight of stairs with a much lighter heart than when I went up. Three subscribers had been secured, and they were names which would be available to me as references in my future canvassing. And in the very next room I found proof of this opinion. It was a shoe-store, situated at the foot of the staircase I had just decended. The gentleman in attendance received me very politely, and when my book was presented for his inspection, seemed very much pleased with it, and in answer to my remark that I had just commenced canvassing, and had only taken three names, asked to see my list. I handed it to him.

"H. M. Harris; good lawyer and good man. W. P. Brown; I know him: he is a fine fellow. And King, too—Madam, you have three of the best names in Peoria. How much did you say?"

"Two dollars and seventy-five cents."

"I will take one. When will you deliver?"

"I will bring the book in a few days. Good morning, sir."

"Good morning, madam. Success to you."

I went into the next store; but there my good

names availed me nothing. They wanted nothing of the kind—would not even look at my book, or even hardly let me tell them what it was. It is just barely possible, from what I have since learn-ed of the politics of that establishment, that the last word in the title of the book was offensive to the proprietor, and hence his very abrupt refusal to look at it. This did not, however, occur to me at the time. I only thought he was decidedly mean in refusing to look at the work at all. I thought, even if he did not wish to subscribe, he might at least have treated me kindly, and refused in a gentlemanly manner. But, never mind; I had already, in the first half day of my canvassing, sold four copies; and this was anything but dis-couraging.

It was now noon, and time for me to return to my hotel for dinner. But with how much more elation of spirits I entered that hotel than I had quitted it in the morning the reader may well im-agine. My success in the avocation I had chosen seemed to me now assured, and the idea of fail-ure was now forever banished from my cogitations. In proportion as my spirits had been depressed before fairly entering upon my work, they were now elated; and visions of wealth and ease arose before me. My mind was just as much in fault in one instance as in the other, and I had yet much to learn in regard to my new profession. I had yet to learn that, because one half day's labor had been attended with some degree of profit, I was not to regard my success as fully assured; but that in this, as well as in all other avocations, constant, energetic and judicious perseverance was necessary to attain one's object; that reverses of various kinds were to be anticipated, and that the book agent who fancied his calling an easy as well as lucrative one, was doomed to the most certain and painful disappointment. That the business is profitable if well and judiciously pursued is undoubtedly true; but it is equally true that it is profitable only when pursued with the most ceaseless and indefatigable energy.

After dinner was over—and, by the way, I ate much more heartily than at breakfast, from some cause or other—I went up into the parlor. There was a large number of ladies in the room, and the idea occurred to me that it would be a good time to exhibit a pleasing, as well as profitable combination of business and pleasure. Accordingly, I went up and got my book, and asked the ladies to look at it; telling them I had arrived in the city only the night before; had been out that morning, and had sold four copies, and that I hoped to sell a large number in that very room before going out again. The book seemed to please them very well; for five of them put their names down at once, and others said they would subscribe as soon as they could see their husbands. While we were still talking about the book, a young man came in to call on a young lady who was in the room, and she at once besought him to make her a present of the book. Of course he could not very well refuse, and down went the name of Miss Kate Freeman, the gentleman handing me two dollars and seventy-five cents, and telling me to deliver the book to her when it came.

I fancied I had now done a very good day's work, and, as I had some letters to write, decided not to go out that afternoon at all. I accordingly wrote to Mr. Holland to send me twenty copies of the book, the price to be collected on delivery by the express company, and then set about finding some place where my living would be less expensive than at the Peoria House. Although my business appeared to be prosperous, still two dollars a day was a heavy drain on my finances, and one that I was anxious to avoid if possible. I found a very pleasant place with a most estimable lady, and secured a room at six dollars a week, and then went to settle my bill at the hotel and move to my new home. At the Peoria House my bill was two dollars and a half, and a drayman took my trunk to my boarding house for twenty-five cents; so that I arrived there with just the same amount of money I had on arriving in the city, to wit, ten cents. But I did not feel as much disheartened as then; for I now had on the subscription book, which was then a blank, no less than ten names, each of which was worth a dollar to me; that being the profit allowed me on each copy sold. Even if I did not take another name this week, I

would still be able to pay my board and have
some money left; and, of course, it was not to be
expected that I would do nothing in that time. I
liked the business, and certainly my prospects
were all that could be desired.

After a good night's rest in my new place of
abode, I went to work again with vigor, and worked
hard all the next day, excepting only the time absolutely necessary to go to my meals, and, when I
came to count up the proceeds of the labor of the
day, found that my list had been increased by
eleven names. I now had, in all, twenty-one
names, representing, as the net proceeds of two
days' canvassing, no less than twenty-one dollars
in my purse. True the money was not in my
hands yet, but then I felt sure of it all. Surely it
would not be difficult for me to live at that rate.
Twenty-one dollars in two days, was more than in
the wildest dreams of my imagination I had ever
dared to hope. Who would not be a book agent
when such returns as this were received? But, on
the other hand, who would be a book agent when
such scenes as are described in my opening chapter
are presented? But in my experiance the good
has far outweighed the evil since adopting my
present calling.

The next day I canvassed all day, and came
home at night with eight new names, and one of
them, a gentleman boarding at the same house,
had paid me in advance tor his copy, upon condition that he should be allowed to read my copy at

once. To this I agreed upon the further condition that, inasmuch as I had never read the book myself, he should read it aloud to me. I would then be much better prepared to explain the character of the book, and doubted not the effect upon my sales would be very considerable. I found the book to be very interesting, and well worth the price asked for it.

The next day my efforts were rewarded with the addition of six names to my already very respectable list. It is true my sales to-day had not equaled those of either of the other days, but still six dollars was no mean day's work, and could I only be assured of that each day of my labor, it would be very satisfactory. At any rate it would afford me a very comfortable living, and enable me to " lay up something for a rainy day," and for old age. And this is all any one ought to ask in this world, for it is all that is really worth having.

In the evening I went to the express office, and found that my twenty copies had come, but there was no less than thirty-five dollars to be paid on them, and my purse contained, in treasury-note and postage currency, the sum of two dollars and eighty-five cents, all told. I counted it over and over again in the vain hope that more could be made of it, but the result was just the same every time—one two-dollar bill, one fifty-cents piece, one twenty-five cent piece, and one ten cent piece, all current money of the United States, was everything I could find. The agent observed my perplexity and kindly relieved me from my difficulty, after asking some questions, by telling me to take one book and deliver it; then with the proceeds of that sale get another, and so on until the whole were taken.

How gladly I accepted his offer. I paid him one dollar and three quarters for one book, then got the money for that and had enough to get two more; then got three and delivered them, paying in each time what money I received until the whole twenty were delivered, and I had twenty dollars in my purse. Twenty dollars did I say? Let me not forget the faithful ten cents which had stood by me so long. I had twenty dollars and ten cents, less, of course, the amount paid at the hotel, and the amount I paid the drayman for moving me to my present very comfortable quarters.

But why inflict upon my readers the details of each day's work? Why annoy them with the particulars of each refusal I met with, from purse-proud, haughty, self-sufficient individuals, who could see nothing meritorious in a woman struggling against adverse fate to earn an honest livelihood, or in the book which such a woman would sell—why mention the covert sneers, under the cloak of friendly advice, with which my applications were often met by those who claimed to be gentlemen, but whose gentility would never be recognized by the world, but for this claim—why recount the particulars of the kindly words and friendly wishes, which with some noble natures even took away the pain of their refusal, and which were really strengthening to my soul—I say, why burden the pages of this record with all these? Suffice it to say that when my weekly report for the week ending on Saturday was sent to the general agent, I was able to report sales of no less than forty copies.

Forty subscribers in one week! Only think of that! Forty dollars earned fairly and honestly by my own honest toil! Why, Ford only received fifty-five dollars *a month* from the railroad company, and I could earn nearly that amount in a week. Hurrah for the life of a book agent! No more washing for the miserable pittance of a few dollars a day—that was "played out," to use a slang phrase. No, indeed. I was far above that sort of labor. I would soon be rich. I would save all the money I earned, and, in a short time, would be able not only to redeem my watch; but my darling pets, my precious canary birds—they, too, were in pawn, and must be redeemed. Oh! yes, I had use for all the money I could earn, and it could not come too fast.

Such, dear reader, were the reflections caused by my first flush of success in the business of a book agent. How these reflections and these hopes have been realized will appear in the subsequent pages of this book.

CHAPTER XX.

I CLOSED my last chapter with an account of my first week's work as a book agent, and certainly the results of that week were sufficient to justify the most sanguine anticipations for the future. But, like everything else, the business had its ups and downs; its dark as well as its light seasons; its rainy days as well as its sunshine; and, having had a season of the latter, I was now about to take my turn at the former.

On Sunday it began to rain, and continued nearly the entire day: not a fierce, dashing rain, such as, by its very violence, gives the very best possible evidence of speedy cessation; but a dull, drizzling rain, which, while it is sufficiently violent to heep one within doors, not unfrequently lasts a week or more: just the kind of rain to dampen one's ardor in any enterprise, and most effectually depress the spirits. How I hoped it would not rain on Monday! With what eager anxiety, as evening approached, did I scan the horizon in hopes of detecting some indications of an abatement of the storm, which, if it continued, would be very likely to prevent me from doing anything the next day. Vain hope. The sun went down with his face entirely hidden in clouds; and, as the shades of night rapidly gathered around, the storm, instead of giving any indications of abatement, seemed to thicken and gather additional force, and I finally retired to rest with the conviction that the next day would be marked " lost " in my calendar.

And the morning did not give the lie to my anticipations of the evening before. It seemed to me, as I gazed at the dull, leaden sky, and listened to the dreary, monotonous patter of the falling rain, that a more gloomy or dismal day had never dawned upon my vision, and I knew not what to do. At one time I thought that, in spite of the elements and in defiance of the wrath of the storm-king, I would venture out and try to do something. It really seemed to me that the state of my finances would not admit of my losing the day ; that I could not afford to be idle, but must go to work, rain or shine, at any and all hazards. But, then, no one would buy books on such a day as this. My efforts to do anything would be unavailing, and would, perhaps, only result in inducing a fit of sickness, which would not only cause me to lose much more time, but would absorb all my little accumulation of the last week.

Accordingly I decided not to go out, but to put in that day at least in reading my book, make myself acquainted with it, and trust kind fortune for the morrow. But fortune, at least so far as the weather was concerned, refused to smile upon me. The next day the storm still continued and still I staid at home. On Wednesday it was the same and my spirits sank to the lowest possible ebb.

The next day I resolved to wait no longer, but to go to work in spite of the weather, and trust my own determined energy to accomplish something. Accordingly I borrowed an umbrella of one of the lady boarders, went out and bought one for myself; then, with my dress looped up to keep it out of the mud, and my faithful old basket on my arm, I set out upon my doubtful mission.

I went to a large building, the second story of which was filled with offices, for I had found that the men usually termed professional were those who most liberally patronized me, and if anything at all could be done, it would most certainly be among that class. The first place I visited was the office of a celebrated physician of the city. He was sitting with his feet upon a table, his hands clasped behind his head, and gazing moodily out of the window. I accosted him and explained my business to him.

"The day is too dull and gloomy to buy or read books," said he, without changing his position in the least.

"But, Doctor, consider. A gentleman certainly ought to be willing to patronize a lady who has the hardihood to go out on such a day as this."

"Well, why don't you get married, and then you will not have to go out to work on such days as this?"

"Thank you, sir. I am not on the marriage list.

I do not think I would be any better off married than I am unmarried. But will you subscribe for my book?"

"Did I not tell you I would not?"

"No, sir; you said no such thing. But even if you had said it, I am sure you would not allow my industry on such a day as this to go unrewarded."

"What is your industry to me? Why should I care whether you are industrious or not?"

"Because it is natural for every industrious man to like to see others as much so as himself."

"But how do you know that I am industrious?"

"Because, no man without the greatest amount of industry could attain to the eminence you have in your profession. Come, Doctor, give me your name."

"Well, you are certainly persevering, as well as industrious, and you deserve to succeed. It shall not be my fault if you do not."

With that he put his name down on my list. The little bit of flattery in which I indulged, though very barefaced, had evidently found the weak spot in his armor and settled the business for him. I thanked him, and went out from his presence smiling to myself at the ease with which I had penetrated his reserve.

My next stopping place was an insurance office. Sundry brass plates and signs gave information that the occupant was fully prepared to insure against fire, death, sickness, accident, and everything else, while the walls were covered with show cards of every description, setting forth the special merits of each particular company represented there. At the desk sat a gruff, cross-looking old man, and, at the first glance, my heart sank at the prospect of making any impression on him. However, I would not go away without trying, and so I approached him.

"I have called this morning, sir, in hopes to sell you a book. It is just published, and is very interesting. Will you look at it?"

"No; I don't want to buy any books. Go away. Don't bother me. Don't you see I am busy?"

"But, sir, I think if you would look at this, you would subscribe for it."

"I tell you, I don't want it. I never subscribe for books."

"I have come out this dismal, rainy day, to try to earn an honest living. Please, sir, look at my book: I think your daughter would like it."

"Who told you I had a daughter?"

"No one, sir."

"How did you know it, then?"

"I only thought so. You look like the kind, indulgent father of a lovely daughter. Have you a daughter, sir?"

"Yes; I have as lovely a daughter as any parent need wish. Let me look at your book."

"Here it is, sir."

"It is very nicely bound, and appears to be readable. I guess my girl would like it. Let me see your list of names. You have a good many subscribers, but my daughter's name is not here; so I will put it down, and you can deliver the book here."

"Thank you, sir."

"There, you have got me to subscribe after I said I would not: now, take your traps and be off. You touched me in the right place when you spoke of my girl."

"Good day, sir."

And as I went down stairs I almost laughed aloud at the result of my little impromptu stratagem for circumventing old "Crusty," as I have named him. Should he see this book he will recognize the circumstances above related, and may not feel specially honored by the patronymic here given him. But he must learn to be more civil to callers, even if they do not come to have their lives or property insured, and thus put money in his purse.

I called at several other places that forenoon, but with uniform want of success. Not another name could I obtain, either by persuasion, entreaty or stratagem. Well, two names in half a day, and such a day as this, too, is better than nothing, and I will e'en go home to dinner, and hope for better luck next time. But in the afternoon the rain was even worse than in the morning, and go out I could not, though it seemed almost impossible for me to be idle. It had taken all I had made last week to pay my way thus far and redeem my watch and birds (which I had already done), except six dol-

lars and a few cents. I could pay my board that
week, but where was the means to come from to
pay the next? Still, it would not help matters any
to fret over it; and all that could be done was to
wait, and hope, and pray for better weather.

It was well for me that I made hay while the sun
shone, for it was utterly out of the question for me
to do anything more that week. The rain poured
down so unceasingly that it seemed to me it must
stop from sheer exhaustion of the elements long
before it did.

Saturday evening finally came, and my weekly
report had to be sent forward to the general agent.
The weather had not admitted of my doing anything more, and I had but the two names to report
instead of the forty which had crowned my first
week's labors in this place. The contrast was so
great that I was almost tempted not to send any
report, but, upon reflection, concluded that the
matter could be so explained as to leave no unpleasant impressions on the mind of the general
agent. Most certainly the horrid, rainy weather
of the past week was a sufficient excuse for the
small amount of work done. Accordingly, I sent
off the document with such explanation as I could
give, and in due time received a letter from the
general agent to the effect that it was satisfactory,
and wishing me better luck in the future.

Sunday was a clear day, and I thought that the
storm-god had exhausted his forces, and that I
would surely go to work on Monday with some

prospect of success. But when the morning came I found that he had only been accumulating fresh strength for the next day, for it poured down harder than ever, and all hope of doing anything for that day was at an end. I had paid the landlady my board for the week just closed, and had but a few cents left in my pocket; and unless the weather cleared up soon, I should have nothing when the next installment became due. But, be that as it might, it was now very clear that nothing could be done that day, and I therefore made no effort to go out at all.

Tuesday came, and 'it was still no better, and another day was lost, and I was getting almost discouraged. But I tried to do a little something. I went out in the afternoon and went to all the public offices, but all my efforts were in vain. No one would subscribe; and heart-sick and weary I wended my way home again in the evening, almost willing to surrender my agency and resort to some other means of earning a livelihood. Indeed, had I been able at that time to think of something else which promised sufficient returns to support me, it is very likely I should have embraced it; but all around me were strangers, and with no one to recommend or aid me, nothing could be done aside from the path already marked out, and all I could do was to take the bad weather with what patience I could muster; and, by this time, my small stock of that virtue so necessary to every book agent was well-nigh exhausted.

And so the week passed away in rain and mud and idleness. It is true that on Thursday, with a sort of reckless energy, I went out for a while, and tried to redeem a part of the lost past; but, after spending half an hour or more in inducing one man to subscribe, I gave up in despair, and went home again, fully resolved that even the prospect of starvation should not attempt me to go out again until the weather moderated and the storm ceased.

And thus, finally, Saturday came, and I had but one solitary subscriber to report. If I felt ashamed and mortified at sending in my report of the week before, what must have been my feelings now, that the amount of this week's sales was but half as large? But there was no help for it. The report must be sent, and the apparent failure must be explained as best I was able.

But there was a still more serious consideration than the smallness of my report to the general agent. My weekly board-bill was due to-day, and where was the money to come from to pay it? And not only this week, but others would come, and even if my indebtedness on this account were now paid, what provision could be made for the future? Such horrid weather as we had been having for the past two weeks would most effect-ually keep me from earning any money, but it would not prevent my weekly bills from becoming due, nor would it keep my landlady from demanding payment or sending me adrift, if I failed to comply with her very just demands.

This, dear reader, was the gloomy day referred to in my opening chapter. This was the day upon which, for the second time, I pawned my watch— not my watch, but brother's watch—a precious treasure, and which nothing but death, or the demand of him from whom I first received it, shall ever take from me. I hardly knew how to part with it the second time, so soon after redeeming it; but I could not starve, and I am sure, if brother should read these lines, he will not blame me for thus temporarily parting with it to avoid that or a worse fate. Be assured that nothing shall in- duce me to part with it permanently so long as life and reason are spared to me.

But just now my situation was gloomy in the extreme. Six dollars must be paid weekly for my board or I must leave my present place of abode, and then what could be done? I had only made one dollar this week, and even that I had not re- ceived; for I could not order a solitary copy of the work, and must wait until the weather would en- able me to resume my labors again. What could I do but pawn the watch for means to provide me with food and shelter?

I wanted something to do to pass away the time, and keep my mind from dwelling upon the horrors of my situation. I felt like a guilty thing after my return from the pawn-broker's, and something must be done. I went to my room in pursuance of the resolution mentioned in my first chapter, and wrote for some time ; but this only increased the gloom resting upon my spirits, and I finally threw down the pen, and going to my landlady asked for work. Even if it paid me nothing, it would at least keep my mind employed, and pass away the time. She had a quilt on the frames, and told me I might work on that if I liked, and she would pay me whatever it was worth. Accordingly I went to work and worked all the evening for her, for the sole purpose of diverting my mind.

The next day was Sunday, and it cleared off once more. The clouds dispersed, the sun came out beautifully, and all nature appeared in gay and smilling colors once more. My spirits rose; for I felt sure that on the morrow I would be able to resume my labors, and regain all and more than I had lost.

And this time my predictions of fair weather were verified. The sun rose clear and beautiful on Monday morning, and so impatient was I to be at my work, that it was with difficulty I waited for my breakfast. When that very necessary affair was disposed of, I at once set out in search of subscribers. Heretofore I had paid my respects to stores, offices and the like, but to-day my eyes and footsteps were turned in another direction, and private residences were my objective points. And my efforts were crowned with fair success, for when I turned my footsteps homeward, at nightfall, six names had been added to my list. What

mattered it that I was weary and well-nigh worn
out with my incessant labors, or that food had not
passed my lips since the matin meal—I had earned
six dollars, enough to pay my board for a week,
and my heart was light. What matter if brother's
watch was in pawn for fifteen dollars—I had a
month in which to redeem it, and that day had
brought me nearly half enough for that purpose,
and I was happy. I was in a good humor with
myself and all the world, and began to think that
this earth was not such a bad place to inhabit,
after all, and that the people of Peoria were not
really the outcasts of creation. Nay, I even abated
a very considerable amount of my hostility to the
weather-god, and felt very much inclined to forgive him for the unfavorable character of the
last two weeks. In fine, I was very much
mollified.

The next day I went to that part of the city
called "The Bluffs"—I know not why, unless because the people there are more inclined to
"bluff" a stranger than elsewhere—and took, by
the hardest of work, only three names. On my
way home, however, I succeeded in getting a poor
woman, whom I had asked for a drink of water, to
put her name down, subject, however, to the consent of her husband. And I may add, in this
connection, that that consent was given, and the
book taken with a hearty good-will, which was
far more agreeable than that very often displayed
by those who were rich in money, but poor in

spirit, as compared with this loving and hard-working couple.

I had, therefore, obtained four subscribers this day, which gave me ground to hope for better success on the morrow. Ten subscribers this week thus far. Even if unsuccessful, or if the weather should again become bad so as to prevent me from working at all, my report this week would compare very favorably with those of the last two weeks, and my faith in future success was so strong as to induce me that night to write for twenty copies more.

My faith in the future was not disappointed by the result, for on the next day no less than eleven names were added to my list of subscribers. This was something like old times, and made me feel quite rich once more. I even began to consider in what bank it was best for me to deposit my earnings, so as to be sure that they would be safe, and I very seriously contemplated going to my old friend "Crusty," and asking his advice upon this important subject, or at least getting him to insure my fortune against loss by thieves, burglars, fire or flood, but finally concluded to wait until I had paid my debts, or at least received my money for the books I had sold to those eleven persons. The next day I got only one subscriber; but never mind—that was one dollar, and I would not starve if I only made that amount each day.

To illustrate the fact that book agents have all kinds of customers to deal with—a fact that has

already to some extent appeared in these pages—
let me here give the reader an account of my interview, on the next day, with a dentist by the name
of G——, one of the first dentists in the city. I am
sorry that I am unable at this time to give his
name in full, for it is meet and proper that his
name and business should be advertised in full in
these pages without cost to him. And thus was
the interview.

"Dr. G., I have a book to which I would like to
call your attention for a few moments. I would
like to add your name to my list of subscribers,
and think you would be pleased with it."

"I don't care about looking at it. Don't know
as I want to buy any books. They generally cost
more than they are worth."

"I called at your house and showed this to your
wife. She was very anxious to get it, but did not
like to put her name down without your consent,
and referred me to you."

"Oh! yes, of course. My wife wants everything
she sees any other woman have. Get two women
together and they will ruin any man with their
silly notions."

"Will you look at my book, sir?"

"Yes, I can look at it, but can't buy it."

"Can't you spend two dollars and seventy-five
cents to please your wife? She wants the book."

"Of course, she wants it, but she don't need it.
Besides money is very scarce. Don't you want

your teeth fixed? If so, may be we can come to
terms in that way."

"Yes, sir; I have two teeth I want extracted,
and if you will subscribe for my book, I will have
it done. If not, I will go elsewhere."

"Let me take out three teeth—enough to pay for
the book, and I will subscribe."

"No, sir. Two are all I wish to lose."

"Well, sit down."

He took my subscription book, put down his
name, and then proceeded to the extraction of my
teeth, thus combining a fine stroke of business
with the pleasure of making his wife a present of
the value of two dollars and three-quarters! If
that man does not succeed in accumulating a
fortune, it will be only because meanness is not
the surest road to wealth. I wanted the teeth extracted, but the idea of making that a condition of
presenting his wife with a book which she wanted,
and which she would have subscribed for, but for
her wholesome fear of her lord and master! Perhaps the reader will think I would be in a hurry
about delivering a book sold under such circumstances, but really I was not. When I had collected the money to redeem brother's watch, I rested
very easy about it, and it was not until I had finished my canvassing in Peoria, and was ready to
leave, that Mr. Dentist got his book. In taking
leave of this subject, I beg to advise my fellow
book agents to give Mr. G. a wide berth, unless
they are ready to suffer the loss of teeth for the

purpose of selling their publications. After leaving Mr. G. I went to several other places, and, by
dint of hard and constant work, succeeded in getting eight more names that day, and this, too,
without having to submit to any surgical operation
of any kind. Indeed, in all my experience as a
"Book Agent," Mr. G. is the only man whom I
ever met who insisted upon my paying his subscription by eliminating some of the members of
the unfortunate canvasser. There may be others
in the world, but it is extremely doubtful, and he
should be preserved, in a glass case if need be, as
a sort of curiosity for the edification and amusement of the rising generation.   .

The next day a hard and persistent canvass,
from "early morn to dewy eve," only added one
name to my list. I had got into a part of the city
which was inhabited by the poorer classes, many
of them Germans, just from "Faderland," and they
had neither the means nor inclination to purchase
anything in the way of English literature. I was
not really surprised or disappointed at the result
of my labors among that class, for but little could
be anticipated, but still it would not do for me
to pass them by. I was bound by my obligations
and duties as an agent to canvass the city thoroughly, and this I would do whether I obtained
subscribers or not. And if I did this and failed to
make sales, the fault, at least, would not be mine.

On Saturday I made my report to the general
agent of sales of thirty copies that week. I felt

very proud of the favorable contrast between this report and the one that had preceded it, and was still better satisfied when Mr. Holland wrote me saying he was "glad to learn from account of sales that the flood in Peoria had decayed and dried up, and that the waters were failing from off the ground."

The Sunday following was a lonely day, and as I contemplated the work of the past week (don't think me, dear reader, irreverent or wicked for thinking of these matters on the Sabbath day; my mind was so full of the subject, and it was so necessary to my existence that I could not help it) my heart welled up with gratitude to Him by whose overruling providence the storm had been stayed, and I had been enabled to resume my toil with some prospect of success. To-day I attended church for the first time in Peoria. I had heretofore been so down-hearted that I had not felt like going to church or anywhere else, but to-day, I, in part, made amends for lost time heretofore. I went to the Baptist church in the morning; to Sabbath-school in the afternoon, and to church again in the evening; heard good sermons, and passed the day very pleasantly, feeling better at night, both mentally and physically, than I had for some time.

The next week the weather was fair, and I worked all the week, with varying success. On Monday, I took six subscribers; on Tuesday, the utmost number possible to obtain by hard work was five; Wednesday my success was good, and ten

names were added to my list before nightfall compelled me to desist; Thursday, only three names
rewarded my exertions, and Friday I was compelled to content myself with barely one. And
thus it went. I could compare my work to nothing
in the world but fishing. On one day business
would be good, and almost every one I asked
would subscribe; on another day, under precisely
the same circumstances, and, so far as it was possible for me to judge, with just as fair prospects of
success, the utmost that could be done would be
to take one, two, or three names. Every lover of
piscatorial sports will recognize the similarity in
this to his own experience. Nevertheless, my report this week turned out to be very respectable,
being no less than twenty-five subscribers, while I
had delivered thirty copies previously taken.

About this time I had some difficulty with the
agent of the express company relative to a lot of
books shipped to me by Mr. Holland. It was
during the rainy weather which had just closed,
and while the books were in charge of the company they had been exposed to the rain, and some
of them had got wet and were very much damaged.
I found that five of them were so much damaged
' as to be almost entirely unsaleable at any price,
and I thought the company ought to take them
and pay for them. Indeed, I was advised by my
friends that they could be compelled to do so;
but the agent declined to make any compensation,
and the amount involved was so small that it did

not seem to me worth while to make much fuss about it. Still it was a very heavy loss to me in the present condition of my finances; but I finally took them, and let my subscribers have them at cost, thus losing my profit of one dollar on each book, and getting nothing on that day's work. Up to this time the express agent had treated me very kindly and gentlemanly; but in this instance I regarded his conduct as anything else, and did not hesitate to tell him so. He had not scrupled to take advantage of the unfortunate circumstances in which I, a woman, without money and without friends, was placed, to repudiate an obligation which law and justice alike imposed on him, and had thus displayed a want of principle which, though perhaps not unusual with some men, should still be but a poor recommendation for the position he then occupied. It shall not be my fault if the world does not rate him at his true value.

Having by this time about completed my canvass of the city of Peoria, and believing that my difficulty with the express agent would render further transactions with that office unpleasant, I decided to change my locality, and canvass the little town of Elmwood in the same county—leaving, for the present at least, so much of the city as I had not visited.

I must not omit, however, to bear testimony, in this place, to the kindness and generosity which were displayed toward me by a Mr. Tripp, residing in the city, before my departure. He was a

merchant and was one of my subscribers.   I had a
lot of books—thirty in number—to be delivered in
order to supply my customers.   After the difficulty
to which allusion has been made, the agent, contrary to his practice, and to vent his spite on me,
refused to allow me to open the package in the
office, and I had not money enough to pay the
charges on them and take them away.   In this
emergency Mr. Tripp generously came to my assistance, advanced the money to pay the charges
and allowed me to take them away as I was able—
paying him for them as I could raise the money.
Some of my subscribers were not ready to take their
books, and when I went away there were twelve
copies still undelivered, which Mr. Tripp consented
to retain and wait for his pay until the subscribers
were ready to receive them.   How different was his
conduct from that of the express agent!   For this
kindness to a comparative stranger, he has her
heartfelt thanks, and will assuredly some day receive his reward.

CHAPTER XXI.

I ARRIVED at Elmwood about two o'clock in the afternoon, and immediately set about finding a suitable boarding place. In this I was extremely fortunate. The place selected for my headquarters there was the family of a Mr. King, a kind and considerate Christian gentleman, while his wife was one of the most pleasant and agreeable ladies it was ever my fortune to meet. They were kind and consistent followers of the meek and lowly Jesus, and their treatment of me during my stay in their midst partook more of the character of that which might be meted out to a dearly loved sister, than of that which keepers of boarding-houses are wont to display toward their guests. There will ever be a green spot in my memory to record the kindly deeds of this family toward the lonely wanderer, who had come to them with no recommendations save those which appeal to the heart of every true Christian. "I was a stranger, and ye took me in."

Indeed my heart holds grateful recollections of every one in Elmwood, with whom it was my fortune to be brought in contact during my stay in that place. Never has it been my lot to be treated with such uniform courtesy and kindness by every one. Surely if good works and kind

22　　　　(337)　　　　.

deeds toward the lone and unfortunate are a pass-
port to future happiness, the people of that loveliest of rural villages are on the high road to eternal
bliss. The reader must pardon my enthusiasm
upon this subject, for my situation there was so
different from what had been my usual experience,
that it seems almost impossible to express my
satisfaction at the contrast.

I have alluded particularly to the kindness of
Mr. King and his wife. The reader must pardon
me for referring particularly to another instance of
the unparalleled generosity with which the deni-
zens of that place were wont to treat me, a perfect
stranger. Among my earliest acquaintances was
a young man by the name of J. Hopkins. He was
a young man of the purest integrity and uprightness of character, and his heart overflowed with
kindness to all with whom he was brought in contact. He had, too, one of those frank, noble natures
which, suspecting no ill, regard every one as worthy
of the same trust which his fine, manly countenance
inspired in every one who met him. Altogether he
was one of those men in whom, at first sight, you
feel that it is safe to confide, and who never betray
a trust reposed in them. He had been a soldier,
and had lost an arm in the service of his country,
but was now engaged in business which his goodness and universal popularity naturally rendered
profitable.

Situated as I was, it was but natural that I
should confide to him my situation and pecuniary

embarrassments : with a nobleness and generosity
which may sometimes be equaled but never excelled, he came to my relief, and freely tendered me
any assistance I might desire.   And during all the
time that I remained in Elmwood, the same generosity was continued.   Was money needed to take
a package of books from the express office? his
purse was at my command, and without security
of any kind he allowed me to take my books and
pay for them as I chose. Nay, more, any business which I was at a loss how to transact, I had
but to submit to him, and it was done in the most
correct and expeditious manner, and that, too,
without fee or reward beyond my poor thanks and
my most fervent gratitude.   He took my pawn-
ticket, and redeemed my watch from the grasp of
the old skinflint, in Peoria, with whom I had pawned it—I of course furnishing the money to do so—
and when I offered to compensate him for his
trouble, he positively refused to receive anything.
I owed him frequently, during my stay in Elmwood, as high as thirty, forty or fifty dollars at a
time, and he never asked me for a cent of money
at any time, but just left the time of payment to
my own convenience.   A brother could not have
done more for me, and his kindness will never be
forgotten.

It took me but a few days to canvass Elmwood,
when I finally got at work.   There was a weekly
paper published in the place, in which I had advertised the work upon my first arrival, and every-

body was ready to subscribe or refuse as soon as
the work was submitted for their inspection. I
have very often in small places derived great benefit in my canvassing, by advertising my publications in the local papers. The same results do not
follow advertisements in large cities, but in a small
village like Elmwood, destitute of anything which
tends to excite the public pulse, the local journals
are read with an avidity which the residents of
the city never know, and when anything is once
advertised, it attracts the attention of the entire
community; it is canvassed in every possible.
aspect, and people have their minds made up one
way or the other as to its merits. And when the
agent finally appears, every one is ready to give a
decided answer. I did very well in Elmwood,
having succeeded in selling no less than forty
copies of the work in a little town of not more, I
should think, than one thousand inhabitants. And
this, as before stated, was accomplished in but a
very few days.

There are several little country towns, as Southport, Pittsville, etc., lying about equal distances
from Elmwood, and off of any railroad or other
public conveyance. Having finished my work in
the latter place, I decided to go and canvass these
little towns; but the puzzling question was how
to get there, and how to transfer my books and
baggage there. After considerable cogitation upon this subject, I finally concluded not to move my
headquarters from Elmwood; but to retain my

present boarding-place, and, taking a few books, go by some chance conveyance, which might present itself, to one of the little towns before mentioned. A single instance will illustrate my mode of doing this business.

Having, for several days, tried in vain to obtain a conveyance from Elmwood to Southport, I finally, on one bright Monday morning, took a large mar-ket-basket—it would hold just fifteen " Tried and Trues," and was so heavy that it was all I could do to lift it—filled it with books, and going out a little way on the Southport road, sat down under a tree to "wait for the wagon." I sat there for several hours before any conveyance came along going my way, though quite a number passed me going the other way. But, reflecting that the stream would by and by be flowing the other way, I maintained my seat with what patience I could. Noon came, and no team had made its appearance going my way. I took out a lunch I had brought with me, ate it, and still waited, hoping that my patience would finally be rewarded by the sight of an approaching wagon, and at last one made its appearance. As it drew near, I approached the roadside and signaled the driver to stop, which he did.

"I give you good day, sir. Are you going to Southport?"

· "I am, madam. Is there anything I can do for you?"

"I want to get there. Can I ride with you?"

"I have a tolerably good load; but if you do not mind riding on a load of shelled corn, guess I can accommodate you."

"Oh! sir, I can ride anywhere. If you will take me and my basket of butter, I shall be ever so much obliged."

"Very well, madam; I can take you. Just bring your basket here. Why! you can hardly lift it. How many pounds of butter have you there?"

"I don't know just how many pounds I have."

By this time I was in the wagon; he started up his team; and, for some little time, we jogged on in silence. At length he spoke—

"Your butter is for sale, I suppose?"

"Yes, sir."

"How much do you ask for it?"

"It is put up in rolls of the value of two dollars and seventy-five cents each."

"Two dollars and seventy-five cents! Why, they must be very large and heavy rolls."

"No, sir; not very large. Would you like to see one?"

"Why, yes, if you please."

"Here, sir," said I, raising the cover of the basket, and producing a copy of "Tried and True," "is one of my rolls of butter."

"Why, that is a book. Bless my heart, madam, is the basket full of books?"

"It is, sir. You can look for yourself," said I, raising the cover of the basket as I spoke, so that he could have a good view of its contents. "How do you like the looks of them?"

"But you said you had butter in the basket."

"Well, I sell these books, and, when I want any butter, I buy it with the proceeds of the books. It is the only way I have to get any butter, or bread either, for that matter; and, hence, there is nothing wrong in my saying that they are my butter. They are; and my bread and clothing, too."

"Well," said he, laughing, "you make out a very good case."

"I think so, sir. Won't you help me to make out a still better one by buying one of my rolls of butter?"

"I can't see what it is."

"Well, let me take the lines and drive the team a little way while you examine it. I think you will buy one if you only look at it."

He laid down his whip, took the book and handed the lines to me. He was soon absorbed in the book, and I drove on, while he took no note of anything at all. I could have driven the team to Chicago, and he would never have known the difference, so interested was he in the story he held in his hand. I finally grew impatient lest he should finish the book before we reached our destination, and, touching him on the shoulder with the whip, said:

"Had you not better buy the book and read it when you get home? We shall soon be at South-port."

He started, looked a little ashamed of having so forgotten himself, but paid me for the book without a word. I thanked him and resigned the lines to him, and in a short time we arrived at Southport, where I bid him "good day," while he passed on through the town. He lived at Princeville, a few miles farther on, and was then on his way home.

This, dear reader, was the manner in which I reached the village of Southport, and this may serve as a sample of the way in which I went about to canvass the several other little towns which are scattered throughout Peoria county. Of course, the reader will not understand that I always rode on a load of corn, or that I was always so fortunate as to sell a copy of my book to my impromptu coachman. But I visited all these little towns simply by watching by the roadside for a chance to ride. And I say to the credit of the farmers of that county, that I never found one, no matter what the circumstances, who was unwilling to transport me and my "basket of butter," or who treated me in any but the most respectful and courteous manner.

It was about five o'clock in the evening when I dismissed my carriage in the streets of Southport. I had never been there before, but had by this time become pretty well accustomed to being among strangers, and it gave me no uneasiness. There was no hotel in the place, and I went to a private house, made known my name and business to them, and engaged lodgings for the night. I succeeded in interesting them in the merits of "Tried and True," and sold them a copy of the work.

The next morning I went to work with a will, and canvassed the entire town, selling all the books I had with me but five copies. With these I started on foot for Elmwood, intending to sell them out at the farm-houses along the road. I was several days in getting back, for I stopped at every house along the road, staying each night just where nightfall overtook me, and finding but few persons who were able or willing to buy. However, when I finally reached Elmwood, about two o'clock on Saturday afternoon, I had not a single book left, and had beside, taken orders for three more, to be left in Mr. Hopkins' hands. He again displayed his generosity by advancing me the money upon them, and taking his chances of getting it back from my subscribers—and I am very happy to say they all paid him in a very short time. Had they not done so, I should most certainly have refunded him the money before leaving that section of the country.

In this way I worked until I had canvassed the entire county, and the time came for me to leave Elmwood and its vicinity, perhaps forever. How I hated to leave! I had been so happy there, and had so many good friends, that I almost dreaded to leave them and go among entire strangers again. I had seen more real happiness there than I had at any time or place since the sad discovery in Cincinnati which led to the separation of Mason and myself. Would I ever see as much happiness again?

In one particular I had deceived my Elmwood friends; but, under the circumstances in which I was placed, I can not think they will blame me very sorely. I had not imparted to any one any portion of my past history, and had held myself out to them as a widow. It was not altogether right, but no one was injured thereby, and it seemed to me to be almost necessary to my self-preservation that my past life should not be known to them. If any of them should by chance read this story, they will understand my reason for the deception; and, while once more thanking them, one and all, for their uniform kindness to me, I most humbly beg their pardon for the trifling deception I practiced upon them. Had I known them as well when I went among them as I do now, I should not have hesitated to tell them just how I was situated; but I did not, and when I came to know them well, it was then too late to correct the error; at least I feared that it was, and dreaded the loss of position which I feared would follow an exposition of my real situation. Once more I beg the pardon of each and every one for the deception.

During this time I had not heard one word from or of my truant husband. I knew not whether he was living or dead, or, if living, what he was doing, and it is not to be supposed that he was any

better informed as to my movements. At times
this gave me very little trouble, for though I had
loved him with all the power of affection, and
regarded him as almost more than mortal, and had
in my fancy clothed him with attributes of nobleness which belong to none but the most perfect of
God's creatures, still it was impossible for me to
forget that he had insulted and abuse me; had
put upon me the foulest wrong which can be
offered to a faithful and trusting wife ; had violated
every vow which he assumed in the presence of
God and man; had betrayed the confidence and
trust I had reposed in him, and to crown his infamy, had driven me from the home and protection he had sworn to give me, to support myself
or perish among strangers, while he gave no care
or thought to the fate of her whom he had en-
dowed with the sacred name of wife. When I
reflected upon these things; when faithful memory
presented the picture of the wrongs I had endured
at his hands—oh! then was my once ardent love
for him turned to hate, and while praying heaven's
choicest vengeance upon him, I had wished that
his hated name might never again be sounded in
my ears. But there were other times when the
memory of my former love for that base and unworthy man would sweep like a torrent over my
soul; my heart would soften toward him, and I
would willingly have forgiven all my wrongs for
the poor boon of one kindly word of remembrance
from him; one single token to show that he

cherished a pleasing memory of the past, now gone forever. But it never came.

Oh ! there is no anguish like that endured by a faithful, true-hearted woman who has loved with her whole soul ; who has reveled in all the bright dreams of mutual and sanctified affection, and has been rudely and suddenly awakened from her bright dream of happiness, only to learn that she has been betrayed, deceived, and imposed upon ; that all the priceless treasures of her soul have been given to an unworthy object, and have been remorselessly thrown aside, and trampled into the dust of the earth by him whom she believed to be true and faithful as the needle to the pole. Happy then the heart that can break, and thus avoid the storm, the fierce conflict of passion, which, unless tempered by the kindness and mercy of Him whose handiwork we all are, will shatter to atoms the frail fabric upon which its violence is spent, and leave it, at the last, a shapeless and unsightly wreck ! Happy the spirit which has power to transform its former love into hate, and avoid the dread conflict by thus filling the soul with an inhabitant which, though unpleasant and detestable, is still able to expel forever the love which there formerly reigned supreme.

Upon bidding adieu to my kind friends in Elmwood, I shipped all my baggage to Chillicothe, accompanying it myself as far as Rockhill, where I stopped off to canvass for a few days. I only did tolerably well there, selling not more than a dozen

or fifteen in all, and not liking the place, and feeling but little encouraged by the prospect there, I
shook off the dust from my feet against that town
and returned to Peoria, where several little matters
of business claimed my attention. The reader must
know that, up to this time, I had not delivered any
book to the man who pulls teeth to pay his subscription—my old friend, Mr. Dr. Dentist G.— and
this must be done ; beside, I was still a little in
debt to Mr. Tripp, and wanted to discharge the pecuniary obligation to him under which I was laboring, for my other obligations it was impossible that
I ever should discharge.

Accordingly, I arranged these little matters in
Peoria, and then took the cars for Chillicothe, where
I arrived in due time, and, for a short season, worked with very fair success. I sold quite a number
of books there, and business finally becoming dull,
went in a wagon to Princeville. But my experience
there was such as to induce me to warn all my
fellow book agents, if any of them should, perchance, attempt to canvass that section of country,
to avoid Princeville as they would the deserts of
Arabia. The people there seem to have a most
holy horror of all kinds of literature, and to regard
traveling book agents as, in some sort, enemies of
the country, aliens and outlaws. I labored three
days, assiduously, to break through the crust of
exclusiveness which surrounded them, but with
such poor success that I only sold one book, and
that through the aid of my old friend, the wagoner,

upon whose load of corn I rode from Elmwood to
Southport. It is barely possible that the seed thus
sown may have fallen upon good ground, and that
some other agent could do better there than I did, but
it is extremely doubtful, and I think the language of
Holy Writ might, with safety, be applied to Princeville, changing only the names to suit the case,
"Princeville is joined to her idols, let her alone."

'From Princeville I started in a wagon for Lawn
Ridge. Observing that the road was good, and the
country well settled by what appeared to be a
class of well-to-do farmers, I took five copies, and
directing the wagoner what disposition to make of
the balance of my books upon his arrival at Lawn
Ridge, walked down a lane to a comfortable-looking farm-house, which stood but a short distance
off the main road. An old woman was sitting on
the porch knitting, while a large and fierce-looking
dog came growling toward me, as I opened the
gate. The old woman made no effort to check him,
and I was really afraid of him.

"Good morning, madam. Will your dog bite
me?"

"Oh! no. He never bites nobody. He does a
mighty sight of growlin', but he haint never bit
anybody yit. Come in."

"Madam, I have some books to sell, and am very
much in need of money. Won't you take pity on
me, and buy one?"

"Where you goin', miss?"

"I am going to Lawn Ridge."

" Why, you don't say ! Are you goin' to walk to Lawn Ridge, and carry all them there books ? "

" I am, indeed, unless I sell them before I get there."

" Well, really! Why, where did you come from ?"

" I came from Princeville."

" Du tell ! Well, now, mebby my boy Tom will buy one on 'em, jest to help you along. Tom ; come here. Here's a book would jest suit you— come and buy one of this 'ere woman. She's come from Princeville, and is goin' to walk all the way to Lawn Ridge and carry 'em, if she don't sell 'em."

Her " boy Tom," a great, awkward lout, of twenty-five or six, who was working in a garden hard by, came up, and expressed almost as much sympathy for my hard lot as his mother, and, out of pure charity, bought a book. I thanked them for their kindness, but have very grave doubts whether that book has ever been read to this day. However, I had accomplished my mission, and, with a light heart, and my load lightened by one copy of " Tried and True," I returned to the road, and again bent my foot-steps in the direction of Lawn Ridge. After walking a mile, I came to another house, where I called, and, exposing my wares, tried to make a sale, but here the same appeals to their charity were in vain. They expressed sympathy for my hard lot, but were unable to raise the money. Thanking them for their sympathy and good will, although I derived no pecuniary benefit from its expression, I rested a short time, and then pursued my journey.

The next house was half a mile distant, and it was now almost noon. When I arrived there I was weary and hungry, and asked the lady of the house for something to eat. She gave me a bowl of milk and some fresh bread and butter, saying they had been to dinner, and that was all she had at hand. I sat down to my frugal meal, and, while appeasing the cravings of my appetite, asked them to look at my books. The entire family gathered around, and were much pleased with the appearance of the work.

"What is the price of your book?" said the lady at last.

"I am selling them at two dollars and seventy-five cents. I think the book is really worth three dollars; but I only ask two and three-quarters. Will you take one?"

"I think we will," said she, producing a purse and counting out the exact sum.

"Thank you, madam," said I, rising as I spoke; "and now what shall I pay you for my dinner; for it is time for me to go."

"Nothing at all. I charge nothing for such a dinner as that."

"But, madam, it is worth a good deal to me."

"Well, if it is worth anything to you, you are entirely welcome to it. It is worth nothing to me."

I thanked her heartily for her kindness, and re-sumed my journey. There are bright spots in this

gloomy world of ours; and this kind lady, thus
bestowing her simple refreshment, without reward,
upon an entire stranger, whom she never expected
to see again, demonstrated that she inhabited one
of those bright spots, and that the true religion of
Jesus Christ abode with her there.

At the next house I met one of those over-zeal-
ous people who attach all importance to the name,
while they entirely lose sight of the substance. An
account of my interview with the lady of the house
will illustrate this fact.

"How do you do, madam? Can I rest a short
time? I am walking to Lawn Ridge, and am very
tired."

"Certainly; come in."

"Madam, I am a book agent, and would like to
sell you a book. Will you look at them?"

"We have plenty of books; but I will look at
yours."

"This is a new work, madam—has been published but a few weeks, and is one of the most
interesting I ever read. I charge nothing for looking at them."

"Oh! this is a novel. I never read novels. I
do not think it is right to waste one's time in that
way."

"You don't! Madam, what papers are those
lying on the table?"

"That? Why, that is the New York Ledger."

"Do you take it?"

23

" Yes, ma'am ; and have for a good many years."

" Who reads it—you or your family ? "

"Oh ! we all read it.   We could not get along without that."

. " And, yet, you never read novels ! "

" Never."

" The New York Ledger, I suppose, is not a series of novels from one year's end to another. It is only a newspaper.   But is it any better to read a long tale of fiction in the Ledger than it would be to read the same story done up in book form.   But, as you never read novels, it is not worth while to waste time in trying to sell you one. Good morning, madam."

And, gathering my shawl majestically about my person, I stalked from her presence, indignant at her hypocrisy, or pitying her ignorance.   I was not certain which feeling predominated.

After passing and calling at one or two other houses, without effecting any sales, I arrived at a comfortable-looking place ; and, as it was nearly night, and I was very weary, I decided to stay all night, if they would keep me.   To my application for lodgings, the answer was :

" We never turn anybody out of doors, and you can stay."

I rested very well that night, and the next morning prevailed upon my landlady to take a book, and pay me two dollars in money, allowing my bill for supper, bed and breakfast, to settle the balance of the price.   I finally reached Lawn

Ridge, about four o'clock in the afternoon; having sold all the books with which I started. My long walk had made me very weary and footsore, but still I had done very well, and felt content.

Upon arriving at Lawn Ridge, my first care was to secure a good stopping-place for the night, after which I went to the store of Mr. Parsons, where my wagoner had informed me he would leave my package of books. I found them all right, and Mr. Parsons very much of a gentleman. He gave me the books, and before I left the store I succeeded in selling him one. This favorable beginning, I thought, augured well for my success in Lawn Ridge, and I was not disappointed, for, though the place contained only about twenty or twenty-five houses, I sold some five or six copies there, and was ready by the middle of the afternoon to take my seat in a wagon which I fortunately found going to Chillicothe. It was now absolutely necessary for me to return there to order more books, my present stock having become almost exhausted.

There was some delay about getting my books, and I had to wait several days for them. I very much hated to lose the time, for it was pleasant weather, and it was very uncertain what it would be when I was ready to go to work again, and, beside, I could not afford to remain idle. Finally, however, my books came to hand, and, without the delay of a single day, I set out for the country, having decided to try and introduce a little light among the benighted farmers of that region.

Candor, however, compels me to admit that the dissemination of knowledge was not the only, nor, indeed, the principal, motive which induced me to take a basket of heavy books on my arm, and start on a pedestrian excursion for the rural districts. No; anxious as I am to do all the good I can in this world, it is very doubtful if this alone would have induced me to adopt the character of a missionary among that people. Nay, more: I will confess that the desire to replenish my purse had more to do with my resolution than the desire of being serviceable to my fellow men. But so long as the motive was not in itself evil, I am confident my readers will not withhold from me the credit of the good which my itinerancy in that region may have done.

One good effect resulting from my present trip was the discovery of some cases of destitution, at which humanity must shudder, and Christianity weep; and which demand the immediate attention of the overseers of the poor for the county of Peoria—cases, too, which would never have been known but for my journey, because from outward indications, no one would have supposed them to exist. Allow me to illustrate this by recounting a single incident.

On my first day out I called at the house of a Mr. ——, but, no, I will not publish his name to the world, but will furnish it to the overseers of the poor upon their addressing me at Indianapolis, Indiana, and sending a stamp for return postage—

so let the name pass for the present. Suffice it to say that the poor wretch lived in a large two-story frame house, while the yards, filled with stock, and barns apparently bursting with plenty, seemed to indicate the possession of many of the comforts of life, and even some of the luxuries, by the proprietor—so deceptive are appearances often found to be in this vain world of ours.

As soon as my soul fell upon this supposed abode of plenty, I chuckled with glee, and my heart was glad. "Now," said I to myself, "here will I sell large numbers, to-wit: one copy of 'Tried and True,' and my purse shall groan with the additional burden of two dollars and seventy-five cents, current money of the United States, while the load upon my arm shall be proportionately lightened. Alas! how vain are all human calculations—how deceptive all merely mortal appearances. I would not for a moment have supposed that the place before me was the abode of poverty and misery, sufficient to have drawn tears from the eyes of a potato. But I was soon undeceived.

As I opened the gate, a large and fierce-looking dog came forward, with much noise and many demonstrations of anger at my intrusion. Now, if I have any pet horror, it is big dogs, especially when they act as this one did; and for a short time I stood trembling, and actually fearing I should be rent limb from limb, after the very unpleasant manner in which the rulers of the world were wont to treat the early Christians. At length, however, the master of the canine brute before me made his appearance.

"Good morning, sir."

"Good morning, madam."

"I am afraid of your dog. Will he hurt me?"

"O no, he won't hurt you. Go away, Beaver. Come in, madam. Go away, Beaver—do you hear me?"

"I am so much afraid of dogs, especially such large, savage ones as this, that I hardly know what to do."

"He is not savage. He makes a great deal of noise, but never bites, except at night."

By this time we had entered the house where sat a lady sewing. The house was furnished in a very comfortable style, and even yet I had no idea of the wretched poverty which existed among its inmates, and which was soon to be revealed to my astonished vision. I resumed the conversation:

"I am a book agent, and have here, 'Tried and True,' a new work, just published, and would like to sell you a copy. Madam, I think you will like the book. It is so very interesting that I sat up all one night to read it. Will you look at it?" and I handed her a copy.

She hesitated, but finally took the book, looking, in a sort of scared, startled way, at her husband. He spoke:

"Well, really, madam, I should like to buy the

book, but really times are too hard, and I am too poor to buy books now."

"What! with all that stock in the yard; with this fine house, furnished in the best of style; those barns, doubtless filled with grain—you are too poor to buy a book, the price of which is only two dollars and seventy-five cents!"

"Yes, madam, I am really too poor. Two dollars and seventy-five cents, did you say? It is a large sum, and can not be picked up every day."

"Do you own this farm?"

"Yes, ma'am."

"And is it paid for? and this stock, those cattle and horses—are they yours, and paid for?"

"Yes, ma'am; I own it all, and do not owe any man a cent in the world."

"And yet you are not able to pay two dollars and seventy-five cents for a most interesting book?"

"Indeed, I am not."

"Have you any children?"

"Yes; we have four—two sons and two daughters; and I tell you, it costs a heap of money to feed and clothe them."

"Well, sir, if you have four children dependent upon you for support, and, owning all the property I see around me, you are still unable to invest two dollars and three-quarters in food for their minds, I pity them and you. I would not be as mean and miserly as that for the wealth of Crœsus. Had you given any other reason than poverty for your refusal to subscribe, I should have accepted it, and gone my way without a word; but the idea of lack of ability, on your part, is too ridiculous. Rather say you are too miserly to afford your children that which they need to fit them to discharge their duties in life with due propriety and credit to themselves. Good day, sir."

With this exposition of my feelings upon this subject, I took my book from the lady and left the house. I earnestly commend those four children to the attention of the commissioners of Peoria county; for, if allowed to grow up under the kind and fostering care (?) of their unnatural and miserly father, they are sure to become fit candidates for the gallows or the State prison, and it may cost the county more to care for them in that way than to see that they are properly cared for and educated in their youth. "An ounce of preventive is worth a pound of cure."

But such instances of meanness, I am happy to state, are, so far as my experience as a book agent goes, rare in the United States. I have canvassed in nearly all of the north-western States, and have generally found the people more ready to part with their money for the purpose of procuring the aliment necessary to the culture and development of their mental faculties, than for any other object. And it is this peculiarity of the American people which gives them their high standing as an intelligent and enlightened nation among the powers of the earth, and renders the overthrow of liberty among us a moral impossibility. It is no unusual thing to find the house of a poor man, who toils from day to day for his daily bread, furnished with a well-selected little library, in which works of history and the sciences are familiarly intermingled with those lighter works, which, while they serve to amuse and occupy a passing hour, are still not without their lessons of wisdom and instruction to the inquiring mind. What, though such a man wear patched clothes, or be even clad in tatters; what, though his wife's best dress be but a "calico," or a simple muslin; what, though his furniture be plain, and his table be furnished with no silverware or costly viands : still can I respect and admire such a man, for I know that in him goodness and honor abound, and that the liberty bequeathed to us by our forefathers has there a sturdy and uncompromising defense. But, once more to my labors.

I canvassed all this week (or rather what was left of it, for I did not start out until Wednesday), sold out all my books, and finally found myself, on Saturday night, the inmate of a farm-house, about eight miles from Chillicothe, which place, the reader will please to remember, was now my headquarters. I had now canvassed, pretty thoroughly, all my county, except one little town, by the name of Loudon, and its vicinity; and I was so anxious to finish my work that I decided to go to Chillicothe the next day. Sunday morning came. It was a bright, pleasant day, and there being no conveyance at hand, and learning that the roads were good all the way, I set out, in the early morning, to walk there. It was quite an undertaking for me, considering that it was not my intention to stop by the way; but it must be remembered that I had been practicing pedestrianism considerably of late, and I boldly essayed the march. I reached my boarding-house a little after noon, pretty thoroughly worn out, and entirely willing to rest the next day; thus gaining nothing whatever by my Sunday's tramp.

On Tuesday, however, feeling sufficiently refreshed, I set out for Loudon, and, going vigorously to work, canvassed the place in a short time, selling ten copies of the work there. Loudon I found to be a very pleasant little place; and the result of my labors there will demonstrate to the satisfaction of every one that it was inhabited by a class of people very different from those I had found at Princeville and one or two other places in the county. But it mattered very little to me now. I had finished my work among them, and was about to leave their midst, while it was extremely uncertain whether I would ever meet any of them again.

At that time I had but little idea of ever publishing this sketch of my life—much less that I should, in person, canvass Peoria county for subscribers, which I shall, in all probability do, if Heaven spares my life, and nothing occurs to prevent my doing so.

Upon leaving Loudon I returned at once to Chilli-

cothe, from which place I intended to take my
final departure to Chicago, there to perfect arrangements for more extensive work in my new line of
duty; for I had no idea of giving up the business
of selling books by subscription. It was reasonably profitable, and would afford me a comfortable
living; I liked the sort of excitement and change
attending it; and, beside, it kept my mind constantly employed, to the almost utter exclusion of
contemplation of the hideous past.   For these reasons it was my intention to still pursue it; and, in
order to render that pursuit even more successful,
it was necessary that I should repair to Chicago to
make some new and more extended arrangements.

CHAPTER XXII.

It had become absolutely necessary for me to visit Chicago in order to provide means for my future support. I was now out of work—had finished the task assigned me— and without work it was impossible for me to live. And work I could not get except by going there. There was one consideration which rendered my contemplated visit somewhat distasteful to me. Frank C. Ford still lived there, and I did not wish to meet him under any circumstances. Of course it was not absolutely certain that we would meet—my stay there would be brief—but still we might, and a meeting would be in the last degree unpleasant to me. But I could not sit still and starve, and go I must.

Before going, however, I must get myself a few things which were necessary to render me presentable in the city. I needed a new bonnet to replace the one I had worn last winter; my gloves were worn out; my shoes, though very suitable for canvassing on foot throughout the county of Peoria, were hardly the things to wear upon the streets of Chicago; in fact, I needed a full supply of those little articles which ladies buy when they go "shopping." But, dear me, I would rather canvass half a day on foot in the country than to go out

"shopping" for a single half hour. How ladies
can admire these shopping expeditions is more
than I can conceive. There is nothing in life that
seems more annoying to me than to start out and
go from place to place, looking for this article or
that, and finally going home after having bought
perhaps a dollar's worth of goods. But there are
women who really enjoy this sort of thing; who
will go from place to place for an entire day, for
the sole purpose of looking at goods, and with no
intention of buying anything, and who finally return home, after having annoyed, as much as was
in their power, every shop-keeper and clerk on
their route without having bought a single thing.
I said they were women—pardon me, they are not
—they are mere puppets of fashion, the extent of
whose ambition is only to appear in the latest fashion, and to serve as a sort of walking advertisement
for certain fashionable milliners and dress-makers.
But for them the latter class would starve.

But however distasteful it might be, my shopping had to be done, and so I set about it energetically. I was now out of debt, and had fifty-five
dollars in money, honestly and fairly earned by
my own toil, and there was no reason why I should
go to Chicago looking as shabbily as I now did. I
therefore went out and bought what I needed, including a black bonnet; for, as I was passing for
a widow, it was but proper for me to assume, to
some extent, the appearance of one. Besides, if
black is a symbol of sorrow, surely my past life

had been such as to entitle me to wear black as long as I should live, even though I should attain to the age of Methuselah.

When I had completed my purchases and fitted myself out to my entire satisfaction, I took the cars for Chicago, arriving there without any incidents worthy of note. I went at once to the Sherman House, and registered myself as Mrs. Ford, of Chicago. I knew they published daily lists of their arrivals, and thought Frank would thus learn that I was in the city; for though I should take no pains to find him, still I was weak enough to indulge a little hope, in spite of my resolution not to see him, or have any communication with him, that when he found that I was in Chicago, he would come to see me. What might have been the result if he had done so, is more than can now be told, for at times I still loved him, in spite of myself, but he never came, although I heard of him before leaving the city, as will presently appear. I now rejoice that he did not come.

After getting settled at the Sherman House, I went to call on Mr. Holland, at 38 Lombard Block. He was very glad to see me, and complimented me very highly on my success, saying my sales had exceeded those of any other of his agents during the same time, and that he hoped that I would take another county. I told him I wished to go to Indiana, and would like to have two points there, Indianapolis and Michigan City. The reader is well aware of the reasons which induced me to seek the former place ; and I had good, and, to my-self, satisfactory reasons for wanting to go to the latter, though it is not necessary to tell what they were.

Mr. Holland replied that he could give me Mich-igan City, but that Indianapolis was not in his district, it was under control of the Columbus, Ohio, general agency, but he thought he could get it for me, and would try and do so. I thanked him for his kindness, and having no further business to transact with him, went at once to make arrange-ments for my departure to my new field of labor.

I went back to the Sherman House, eat my din-ner and paid for it, and then went to call on Mr. Kennedy, the publisher of " The Home Circle," and largely interested in the sale of " The Memorial of President Lincoln," and applied to him for the agency of both those publications. Mr. Holland had given me some very flattering testimonials, and I had no difficulty in forming an engagement with Mr. Kennedy, not only to canvass Michigan City, but also Indianapolis. I then went back to the Sherman House, ordered my baggage to the depot, and checked my trunks to Indianapolis, intending to stop but a short time in Michigan City. It was still some hours until the train would start, and I again went down town and bought a dozen photo-graphs of distinguished Generals, for which I paid the sum of one dollar. I had to purchase copies of " The Home Circle," and of " The Memorial," and I now had but two dollars and some few cents left in my purse.

As I was walking down State street, on my way to the depot, a gentleman bowed to me from a street car which was passing, and stopping the car got out and came toward me. At first I did not recognize him, but when he came up and offered me his hand I knew him. It was Robert Ford, a brother of my husband. He told me Frank was somewhere in the city, and was doing much better than he had formerly done. I told him he might tell him when he saw him that I was living in Indiana, and was now on my way home; that I was doing well and asked no help from him, and that I had called on him the last time for assistance. He asked me when I was going to leave the city; and I told him I should go on the first train over the Michigan Central Road. Would he come to the depot? I would like to have a talk with him. He asked me what time the cars left. I told him about seven o'clock; and he said he would be there before that time.

We then parted, and I began to reflect upon the probable results of the proposed interview, and decided that it had better not take place. I was afraid he would bring Frank with him, and that they would suspect my motive in removing to Indiana, and would take steps to prevent the accomplishment of my purpose. And, to tell the truth, I was afraid to meet my husband. In spite of all his wrongs I still loved him, and I was afraid my treacherous heart, in case he made any overtures to me, would betray me into living with him again, which I had fully made up my mind never to do. Accordingly I changed my plans, and instead of waiting until seven o'clock, went away on a freight train which left at five. If Robert Ford reads these lines, he will understand why he did not find me when he came to the depot that evening, if he came at all.

I arrived in Michigan City with but fifteen or twenty cents in my purse, but this gave me very little trouble. I had been in just as bad a situation as this before, and by putting a bold face on the matter, and going to work with reasonable energy, had succeeded in getting through with my troubles; and there was no reason why I should not do so again.

I went to the hotel and freely told the landlord my situation—how I had come there to canvass the place for subscribers for "Tried and True," and "The Life of Mr. Lincoln;" that I also had some photographs for sale, and that I had neither money nor baggage, having sent my baggage to Indianapolis, whether I was going as soon as I had canvassed that place. He heard me through, then asked to see my photographs. I showed them to him, and told him the price at which I sold them—twenty-five cents each. He took four in payment of my bill for supper, bed and breakfast, and I started out to sell the balance, which I did in a very few minutes and could have sold three times

24

as many more if I had had them. The people of
Michigan City are very patriotic, and the photographs of successful leaders of the Union army are
good stock to sell among them. I had further
evidence of this patriotism the next day.

The next day I went to work, and by vigorous
exertions succeeded in obtaining four subscribers,
three of them being to the life of our late murdered
President, and only one to " Tried and True." I
returned to supper at night almost tired out and
went to bed very early. It was plain to me that
something must be done by which I could realize
more money among these " sand hillers." They
all admired Mr. Lincoln and would buy his life if
they had time to read it, but the excitement about
the construction of their harbor was just beginning
to assume the form of an epidemic, and no one
seemed able or willing to spend any time in reading, or even talking about anything but perches of
stone, Government piers, dredge-boats, water lots,
and eligible corners. One man, a prominent lawyer of the place, upon my asking him to buy ." The
Life of Lincoln," somewhat startled me by reply-
ing, " If the title is all right I will give you one
hundred and twenty dollars a foot. Did you say
it fronted on the creek ? " I explained to him that
it was a book and not a water lot, or sand-hill, I
was trying to sell, whereat he became disgusted
and refused to hold any further communication
with me. But, with all their hurry, they would
take time to buy and look at photographs, for these

took neither time or mental labor to comprehend, and left them free to pursue their favorite speculations. It was plain, then, that this was my best line of investment. Accordingly I ordered another lot of these from Chicago, and while waiting for them to come, made one more effort to break through the crust of speculation which seemed to enclose the entire people. My success was but limited, for a hard day's work only added two names to my list of subscribers for the life of the President, and one to the list of " Tried and True." But when my photographs came business revived again, and I soon disposed of all I had and ordered more.

But my day of usefulness in this place was evidently on the wane, and I decided to go to La Porte and try my fortune there for a short time. I could not canvass there for " Tried and True," but I could sell photographs and take names for " The Memorial; " for, although Mr. Kennedy had only appointed me agent for Indianapolis and Michigan City, he had told me verbally that the entire State was open, and that I might sell anywhere I could. But at La Porte I fared even worse than at Michigan City, though from causes altogether different. The people there were not so madly engaged in absurd speculations upon the value of inaccessible sand mountains; but their superior intelligence and devotion to the memory of our martyred President had already induced them to invest very liberally in remembrances of his greatness; and in nearly

every house I visited I found a copy of some one of
the numerous "Lives" which had already found
their way into print. At another time and with
another work I found La Porte to be a most excellent place for book agents who pursue their labors
legitimately and honestly ; but the community was
already supplied with what I had now to sell, and
of course my labors were in vain. But, notwithstanding my poor success, I liked the place so much that
I almost decided to settle there permanently if I
ever should get money enough ahead to buy me a
home anywhere. Some of my warmest friends reside in La Porte ; and whether I ever settle there or
not I shall always retain a most lively recollection
of that most beautiful city of northern Indiana.

Returning to Michigan City after an absence of
three days I was fortunate enough to strike a vein
which, by being vigorously worked, yielded some
very substantial returns. The first thing I did after
my return was to procure and sell two dozen photographs, which I did in one day. The next day I
spent in canvassing and with a degree of success
which astonished even myself—taking no less than
eight subscribers for "The Life of Lincoln," three
for "Tried and True," and five for "The Home Circle." Such success in view of my former experience there was truly surprising, and inclined me to
think more kindly of Michigan City and its inhabitants than had been my wont. Nay ; I even for-
gave the lawyer before-mentioned for his absent-
mindedness, and nearly resolved not to put him in

my book; but I finally compromised the matter by
deciding to publish the incident, but to keep his
name to myself; hence none of my friends need ask
me for it. I hope Mr. —— will thank me for even
this degree of forbearance.

Having about finished my work in Michigan
City, I ordered books for all my subscribers, for-
warded Mr. Kennedy the names of subscribers to
"The Home Circle," and, when my books came,
proceeded to deliver them without delay, having
done which I took an account of funds on hand,
and found I had enough to pay my fare to Indianapolis and to pay a week's board after I got there.
This was eminently satisfactory; for I felt sure
that before the week would expire I could do
enough to again replenish my purse.

Accordingly, I settled up all my bills in Michigan City, and, embarking upon the cars of that
horror of all travelers, the Louisville, New Albany
and Chicago Railroad, in due time arrived at the
capital city of the Hoosier State. Upon inquiry,
and presenting my checks at the baggage-room of
the Union Depot, I found them all right, they
having been there, the baggage-man said, with an
air as if he were relating some wonderful circumstance, a full week, if not more. I beg to remind
the reader that my trunks had been sent direct
from Chicago, and that it had not taken me a week
or more to come from Michigan City to this place.

I make this explanation in order that no injustice may be done to the rapidity with which

the Louisville, New Albany and Chicago Railroad transports its passengers; and I take great pleasure in saying, that a person might, even at that time, go by this route, from Michigan City to Indianapolis, in less than a week; and, since then, the management and speed of the cars upon that road have been materially improved.

My first care was to look for a suitable boarding-place—the man with whom I had left my trunk, when there before, having gone away; leaving my baggage, however, at the house of a neighbor until I should call for it. I found a good room at the house of a Mr. Joseph Aston, No 44 South Tennessee Street; paid him six dollars for a week's board, in advance, and moved my things there, designing to make it my home, at least until I had accomplished one of the objects which first induced me to remove my residence to Indiana.

CHAPTER XXIII.

BEHOLD me, then, dear reader, fairly domiciled in the State which was to be my future residence.

'Tis true, my home had been here for some time, but I had been so much away on business, that, up to this time, I hardly ventured to call myself a Hoosier, even by adoption; but now I felt that the title really belonged to me, and I could say, without any mental reservation, that I was an Indianian.

I did nothing more than to establish my quarters, upon the day of my arrival in the city, it being near nightfall, and I very much wearied when I arrived there; but the next day I went to work with a will, and, by hard and steady effort, succeeded in getting ten subscribers to the "Life of Lincoln," and two for "Tried and True." I ordered a lot of books, of both kinds, and went on with my canvassing, thinking the prospects were very favorable for my doing a good business there. But, alas! how deceptive are all human appearances. I soon found that the flattering prospects, under which I had started out, were but for a day; that they were even more ephemeral than the butterfly, and that, with the works I had, it was impossible to succeed there. The citizens of Indianapolis were too well supplied with literature of the

(375)

class I was selling, and it was necessary for me to have something else—something which had not been already sold there; and at the same time I was sufficiently aware of the state of the public mind to know that something connected with the late rebellion would sell better than anything else.

Accordingly, after having labored over a week, and taken about twenty-one names for all my publications together, I wrote to a Mr. Lillie, of Chicago, for the agency of "The Lost Cause," a Southern history of the war, by Mr. Pollard, late editor of the "Richmond Examiner." Mr. Lillie referred me to Mr. George B. Fessenden, of Cincinnati, and I at once addressed him on the subject, receiving by express, in return, the agency of the work, accompanied with a prospectus, subscription book, and some instructions. As for the last, however, I fancied that I knew about as much about the business of a book agent as Mr. Fessenden did.

I immediately went to work with my new book, and found that, if I only knew what parties to approach, a very good business could be done; but I was too much of a stranger in the city, and knew not where to apply. I thought if I could get an agent who was well acquainted in the city, and have that agent take orders, while I would deliver the books, we could make the arrangement mutually profitable. Accordingly I inserted, in the "Herald," the following notice:

WANTED—A person, well acquainted in the city, to canvass for the "Southern History of the War, by E. A. Pollard." Call at No. 44 South Tennessee Street. No one need apply unless they are well acquainted in the city, and can bring good references.

In a few hours after this notice made its appearance, I had several callers, and soon succeeded in making an arrangement with a gentleman to canvass on my own terms. It is not necessary to give these terms to the reader, suffice it to say that it worked well, and I soon found I could pay my agent all that I had agreed to, and still make more money than when I was alone. While he canvassed, I delivered the books, and also continued my trade in photographs, of which I sold a great many; and the profits upon them being enormous, I was doing a very fine business. In about two weeks we had sold no less than fifty copies of "The Lost Cause," and my profits from that source alone were about fifty dollars. Add to this the fact that I made about as much more from the sale of photographs, and the reader will have no difficulty in comprehending the fact that my business was in a flourishing condition.

About this time I learned that the property left by my brother Frank, when he went into the rebel army, had been confiscated by order of the authorities at Washington, and made application for its restitution; alleging my own loyalty as the ground of my claim. I received a favorable reply to my application, and was fully satisfied that if I had the money to go South and hunt up the proofs and submit them to the consideration of the proper officers, there would be no difficulty in my succeeding; but there was the rub. The one hundred dollars in my possession would go but a little way in the prosecution of a claim of so much magnitude as this, and whatever was to be done must be done quickly, and the only thing I could do was to work the harder, and raise all that I possibly could for this purpose.

The holidays were close at hand, and it occurred to me that if I had a book suitable for a Christmas or New Year's gift, I might do well with that for the next two or three weeks, and having noticed in the Journal the advertisement of such a book, published by a Mr. Newell, in Vinton's Block, I called upon him and secured the agency for the sale of it. It was called "The Republican Court," and was a most beautifully gotten-up book—just the thing for a young man to use in softening the obdurate heart of his lady love. Armed with this document, in addition to those I had on hand already, I went to work with a vigor which produced the most happy results, and, in a short time, felt myself able, pecuniarily, to undertake my contemplated journey to the South.

Before starting, however, I shipped, by express, to a dear friend in San Francisco, California, a copy of The Republican Court, The Lost Cause, and a finely-bound copy of Robinson Crusoe, as a holiday gift. I trust he received them in due time, and that they served to assure him that there was

one in the world who will never, never forget his
kindness to her in her hour of trouble.

I then arranged my affairs so as to leave all my
business in the city in the hands of the agent before referred to, and started out, intending to go to
the South before I came back to Indianapolis
again, which must be by the first of April next ensuing. I had commenced proceedings for a divorce
from my husband, and as the case would be tried
in April, I felt that it was necessary for me to be
in the city at that time.

I went as far as Shelbyville, in company with
another lady; stopped off there, and staid a few
days, selling several books, and then went on to
Cincinnati, where I wished to have an interview
with Mr. Fessenden, relative to affairs in Indianapolis, and some other business matters. In due
time I arrived in Cincinnati and at once called on
Mr. Fessenden, who was not a little surprised to
see me, and earnestly asked me why I left Indianapolis. I replied by giving him the address of my
agent there, and telling him that I had left everything in his hands, and that I thought he would
find no cause of complaint against him.

"But, Mrs. Ford," said he, "we cannot give you
up as an agent. You are altogether too valuable
to us."

"But I have worked a long time for you," said
I, "and now I must work for myself a little."

"Have you not been working for yourself at the
same time you were working for me? Has not the

sale of my publications been profitable to you as well as to me?"

"Yes; but there are other matters which claim my attention."

"What are these other matters? Are you going to marry and give up selling books?"

"No," I replied laughing; "I am not going to marry. I am going to return to my old home in the South."

And then I told him about my application for the restitution of the confiscated property of my brother, and that I was going South to find the evidence relative to it.

"Just the thing," said he. "Take some of my publications along with you to sell, and thus help to defray your expenses. I have no agents in the South, and you can sell wherever you see proper."

"But times are so hard down there, that I am afraid nothing can be done."

"I do not suppose you can sell as many books there as you can in the North, but still I believe you can do something, and every little helps, you know."

"What have you that I can sell there?"

"Take 'The Lost Cause.'"

"I would prefer something else."

"Well, I have a new book, just out, with which I am sure you can do well there. I will appoint you a roving agent anywhere in the Southern States."

"What is it?"

"The General History of Freemasonry in Eu
rope ; translated from the French of Emanuel Re-
bold, by J. F. Brennan, Esq."

The title of the book struck me favorably. I
had long been an ardent admirer of Freemasonry;
my father and brother Frank had both been
Masons, as also my stepfather, Captain Lake ; and
I felt that these facts gave me some claims upon
the fraternity, and that, aside from the intrinsic
merits of the work, they would aid me in effecting
sales of it among the craft. I knew, too, that Freemasonry had very many followers in the South,
and that they were generally very ardently attached to the order, and would be more likely to
buy a book upon that subject than any other. I
had my father's diploma in my possession, and the
exhibition of this would help to prove my claims
upon the Masonic brotherhood; and, even if I failed in the attempt to sell, it would involve but very
little expense—only the cost of the outfit—while,
if I succeeded, the result could not be otherwise
than good, in more senses than one. These reflections decided me in favor of taking the appoint-
ment he offered me ; and I told him I would accept
his proposition, paid him for a book, bid him good-
bye, and returned to my hotel.

Upon examining the book, I found the names of
some of my ancestors honorably mentioned in its
pages, and was more than ever satisfied that I had
accepted Mr. Fessenden's proposition. I now felt
that I had a direct personal interest in the work ;

for, while I was carrying on my accustomed avocation, I was also spreading a knowledge of the virtues and usefulness of my revered grandfather;
and this afforded me no small satisfaction. And
this is one reason, among others, why I have continued in the sale of this work until the present
time, and why I regard it with more affection than
any work I have ever sold.

The same evening I left Mr. Fessenden I took
passage on board a river packet for Memphis; and
about five o'clock in the evening she cast off her
moorings, and quietly dropped down the stream.
It was dark and there was nothing to be seen, and
nothing to detain me on deck; so I went to my
state-room, and at an early hour retired to rest.

In due time and without incident worthy of note
I arrived at Memphis. My trip down the river had
been very pleasant, and I had enjoyed it very much;
but a period was now put to my enjoyment; for
when we rounded to the landing at Memphis it was
raining with violence, and the mud lay in the streets
apparently of an interminable depth. In view of this
state of facts, I decided to make my stay in Memphis of very brief duration. I had intended trying
to sell some books there; but the weather was
such as evidently to render hopeless any attempt at
canvassing, and of course I must forego it for the
present, and hope for better weather on my return.

There were two or three men in Memphis whom
it was necessary for me to see in connection with
the business which had originally brought me to

the South, and the labor of wading through the
mud and rain to hunt them up was all I cared about
attempting ; but from that it would not do to shrink.
Besides I had encountered these adversaries before
and had learned the very important fact that I was
neither sugar nor salt, and that there was not the
least danger of my melting away. . Accordingly,
armed with a formidable cotton umbrella, and a
pair of stout brogans, I plunged into the apparently
endless and bottomless sea of mud before me, and
bravely breasting its waves in due time found the
parties of whom I was in search. My interviews
with every one of them were in the highest degree
satisfactory ; and it was with no little elation of
spirits that I announced to myself that my business
was completed, and took the cars for Atlanta, the
next step in my journey, and where I hoped to
complete the evidence which was to put me in possession of my deceased brother's estates.

As we rolled onward toward Atlanta, through a
region of country every foot of which had been the
scene of the desolating operations of hostile armies,
how did my heart throb with anguish as I gazed
upon the almost entire destruction of that once
lovely land ! For miles upon miles the country
was destitute of fences, and, in many instances, of
houses, while the very humblest forms of vegeta-
tion seemed trodden out of existence, and even out
of sight, under the hoofs of animals and the feet of
thousands of armed men ; acres upon acres of ground
which had once borne magnificent crops of corn, and

cotton, and tobacco, and wheat, now wearied and
pained the eye by their broad stretch of lifeless
brown, unrelieved by the least display of green;
the long lines of trenches and rifle-pits told eloquent
stories of hours of toil expended for the sole purpose of more effectually destroying our fellow-men;
the little mounds of earth, which here and there
marked the landscape in every direction, spoke
eloquently of some brave soul who, clad either in
the blue or the gray, had offered up his life upon
the altar of a cause which, to him, was holy and
just; while occasionally a thicker and more numerous collection of these tell-tale heaps of earth would
speak of the mortal and breathless struggle in
which those who now rested there so quietly, had
once manfully and bravely borne their part. What
mattered it to me, as I gazed upon these speaking
monuments of brave men's prowess, whether they
held the corses of our own brave soldier boys, or
whether those lonely resting-places were filled with
the remains of the misguided, but no less brave,
soldiers of the Confederacy? They were alike the
resting-places of brave and true men, each one of
whom had some friends in some far-off land, perchance, to mourn their loss, and shed the silent tear
of sorrow o'er their untimely decease; and though
I had no sympathy with the cause which had called
these brave men to arms, still I could respect their
manhood, their devotion to their convictions of
right, and could drop the sympathetic tear over
their violent and bloody decease. I could not but

think that somewhere in the broad, sunny lands of which those around us were a part, I had an only and dearly loved brother, whose head was pillowed until the last great day upon just such a lowly bed as these; who had fallen in the same cause, which I believed to be unjust and unholy; who had fallen as the brave men around us had fallen in the discharge of what he deemed to be his duty; and my heart was incapable of entertaining any feeling of bitterness toward any of the fallen braves amid whose tombs our train was wending its way.

From these reflections my mind naturally wandered away to the fate of the unfortunate people who had inhabited this country before the breaking out of the rebellion. Although a long time had elapsed since the close of hostilities, the country, in this particular, as well as in all others, still bore traces of the fearful struggle through which it had passed, and in the plainest manner indicated the fearful character of the punishment which their folly and madness had brought upon this miserable people. It was true, it was the fruit of their own crime and folly, and for which they ought to suffer; but surely their punishment had been equal to the magnitude of their offense, and ought to fully satisfy the most clamorous demands of vengeance. Surely their ruined, desolated farms; their property destroyed, or taken for military purposes, without the possibility of their receiving any compensation; their once happy homes, from which they had been compelled to flee to avoid the dead-

25

ly hail-storm of bullets which swept over them,
and which were too often mere masses of black-
ened and shapeless ruins; the accumulations of
years of toil and privation swept away forever;
and, above all, the sable weeds of mourning,
which enveloped every Southern face, were most
powerful evidences of the severity of the punishment meted out to them, and ought, as far as
human vengeance can go, to fully compensate for
the wrong they had done. It is true that the suffering caused by the war had not fallen upon this
section alone; it is true that by the firesides of the
North, places had been made vacant, and many a
brave son, noble brother, and kind, indulgent husband and father had gone forth from loving friends
never to return; that woe and misery had there,
too, as well as in the South, been sown broadcast
to gratify the most gigantic and criminal ambition
of the age; but all the other sad results of the
conflict had been visited upon the South alone. I
am no apologist for the crime which the leaders of
the rebellion inaugurated against the most beneficent and freest government upon which the sun
ever shone, and upon them I would willingly see
visited the most direful punishment which the
human imagination could devise; but for their
poor, deluded, misguided followers, the evidences
of suffering which I saw on all sides awakened in
my breast naught but feelings of the most intense
pity.

There was another reflection which occurred to

my mind, in connection with this subject, and which seems to me to have no little bearing on the determination of the policy with which the two sections ought to be regarded in contemplating the results of the contest. While both sections alike mourn the loss of thousands of fallen braves, the sorrow of the loyalists is tempered with their well-earned and well-merited thought of glorious victory won, and they can exult in the proud consciousness that the friends whom they mourn fell in defense of a holy and noble cause, and by their deaths aided in the achievement of the grand triumph of right and justice. But to the South none of the consolations flowing from this reflection are vouchsafed. Their cup of sorrow is unmixed by any pleasing thoughts, save the recollection of the personal bravery of the fallen, while its bitterness is enhanced by the deep humiliation of utter defeat, and the fact that the valuable lives so lost were sacrificed in an unjust and iniquitous cause. If anything can add poignancy to the sorrows they must endure, it must be this very reflection.

But while my mind was thus dwelling upon the results of the war, the cars were bearing me onward to Atlanta, and at last the Gate City of the South burst upon our view; but, alas! it was no longer the lovely, flourishing city it was when I last beheld it. Then long rows of magnificent structures lined all its principal streets, while its suburbs were filled with magnificent private residences, adorned with all that wealth could pur-

chase, or that taste of man could devise to gratify
the senses, or enhance the peace and happiness
which there reigned supreme. Now, the entire
business part of the city was a mass of shapeless
and unsighty ruins. Whole blocks, which had
once stood erect, tall and stately, and were the
pride, not only of their owners, but of every deni-
zen of the city, were now mere heaps of rubbish,
bricks and mortar; while, in many instances, the
palatial residences and magnificent grounds of the
suburbs had, by their occupancy as quarters for
troops, been shorn of all their original beauty, and
reduced to a state of chaos and confusion, from
which it would take years to resuscitate them,
even if they could be restored to anything like
their former condition. I had read in the public
journals the accounts of the hard fate which befell
the city of Atlanta when, at the end of a campaign
almost unparalleled in history, she fell into the
hands of Sherman and his victorious legions; but
I was utterly unprepared for the sad scene of desolation which was presented to my view. Although
I knew that such was the fate of war, and that the
curse had been brought upon the city by her own
people and friends, still I could not but feel saddened in my inmost heart when I came to fully
realize the ruin that had been wrought; and I
covered my eyes to shut out the hateful sight, while
the hot, scalding tears of agony bedewed my cheeks.

CHAPTER XXIV.

Such was my return to Atlanta, after an absence of nearly five years. What a blight had fallen upon the place during that time! And yet it was no worse than the blight which had fallen upon my own life during the same time. The contrast between Atlanta, as it was then, and as I now beheld it, was no greater than the contrast between my situation then and what it now was. Then I fondly believed myself the wife of a noble and honorable man, and with every prospect of a long and happy life before me, in the enjoyment of which I should cease to remember the sorrows of my childhood. Since then I had learned that I was not his wife; had separated from him, and united my fortunes with those of a man who had proved to be only less base than he—had finally parted with him forever, and was now alone in the world, with no one upon whom I could lean for support under any circumstances. Then I had a dearly loved brother, on whom, in times of sorest distress, I could rely for relief and assistance—now my brother was gone, and I stood alone, the last of my family, and comparatively helpless. Is it strange that, as this terrible view of my situation rushed across my mind, my heart sunk within me, and I again almost wished that I might lie down, too, and die, and be at rest forever? But why indulge these gloomy reflections? I had work to do, and would strive in the midst of my labors to forget all my sorrows. But this was easier ˜said than done, for'at every step I took there was something to remind me of the past, and of my bitter loneliness.

I went out to the Lake mansion. It was like all the rest, in ruins. Some portions of the walls were standing, but that was all—the grounds, the shrubbery, the fences, the grove which had once been the pride and admiration of the surrounding country—all were gone, and only sufficient traces remained to indicate what had once been there and remind me of their former beauty. At the negro-quarters I found some of the old servants of the plantation, who were living there and cultivating some of the ground, under the protection of the Freedman's Bureau. Tom an.l Silvie were both dead, they told me, while Caroline had married, and was living at some distance from there, with a little family of children growing up around her.

Sick at heart, I turned away, and went in search of the graves of my loved ones. There they lay, side by side, but so neglected and overgrown with weeds that it was with difficulty I could find them. There were the graves of mother, Henry, Kate, baby May, and my own little darling, and another had been added since I was there last. A plain board stood at its head, with simply the words General Frank Hamilton on it. This, then, was the last resting-place of the last survivor of my family. As I stood thus alone by the graves of my departed friends, my mind wandered back to the time when I stood thus by the side of my father's tomb, in the far off city of Philadelphia, and a sense of my utter loneliness so overcame me that I burst into tears, and, offering up a prayer to my Heavenly Father for protection, I turned and left the ground. As I wandered back to the city, I thought how much pleasure I had anticipated in the early days of my marriage with Frank Ford, in paying the visit I had just made. I had then contemplated this visit with him at my side, while his tears would mingle with mine in silent respect to the memory of my departed kinsmen. There, too, by the side of those graves, I would put him in possession of all the facts in my past history, of which he had hitherto been kept in ignorance, and would implore his pardon for the partial deception I had practiced upon him; but, like all my other castles of air, this had now fallen about my ears, and was lying in ruins at my feet. Such had ever been my life—one constant scene of disappointments and sorrows.

I returned to the city and put up at the only hotel there was in the place, where I passed the night almost in tears, for sleep I could not. My mind was too much occupied with gloomy reminiscences of the past, and dark forebodings of the future, to allow me to rest, and with the first flush of the dawn I arose from my uneasy couch to attempt the work which had brought me there, in-

tending to transact it as speedily as possible, and
bid adieu forever to a place so fraught with sorrowful memories as was now the city of Atlanta.
How I fretted until the arrival of business hours
would enable me to visit the public offices, and
attend to the matter which I hoped would put me
in possession of wealth, and enable me to give up
the life of a book agent forever. I may now whisper in the ear of my reader, however, that were I
in possession of the most boundless wealth, I do
not think I would give up the avocation of buying
and selling books as an agent. I would still follow the business, not as a means of making money
simply, though, as has already appeared in these
pages, it is very profitable, but from pure love of
it. This is in confidence, and is the result of my
present views—then everything was distasteful to
me, and my only thought was to get the means
which my brother had provided for my support;
get my divorce from Ford, then finish this history
of my life ; and, after placing a copy of it in his
hands, retire from the public gaze forever. Yes, I
would recover my property ; would get Carrie, and
adopt some little orphan boy for a playmate for
her ; would let Frank Ford know what he had lost
by his cruelty and treachery to me ; and would
then, in seclusion, and in the society alone of my
dear children, find consolation for all the sorrows
I had endured. These were, then, my plans ; but
I am bound to confess that, to a great extent, they
have thus far failed of being realized.

The mystic hour of nine—standard hour with men who are elected to serve the will of the people —having at length arrived, I sallied forth to see what could be done toward the fulfillment of my mission. My first call was at the office of the Register of Deeds, which I found occupied by a very polite and accommodating gentleman. The records had, fortunately, escaped the storm of general destruction which had swept over the devoted ' city ; and we were soon immersed in a profound examination of their pages. We soon found where Frank had made over all his property to me, in the event of his decease. This was the first step gained in the investigation ; but now the question arose, what was the present condition of the property thus conveyed? Was it in such a condition that it could be identified, and a tangible claim for its restitution be presented to the General Government? Further investigation revealed the fact that much of it had been sold for taxes, under the authority of the Confederate Government—all had been confiscated, upon the suppression of the rebellion, and there seemed little prospect of recovering anything, except at the end of a long course of expensive litigation, which I was but illy prepared to undertake. My heart was not a little dismayed at the prospect before me; but, nevertheless, I had already gone too far, and expended too much money, to think of shrinking from the contest at the present stage. Accordingly I procured from the recorder duly certified copies of

all the deeds in any way bearing upon my property (or that which I claimed), and went to the office
of an attorney, whom he recommended as the best
in the city, designing to place all the papers in his
hands, and leave him to pursue his own judgment
as to the best course of proceeding, while I returned to my home in Indiana, obtained my divorce,
and supported myself at my business, until the
final issue of my application at Washington.

I was fortunate in securing the services of an attorney of the highest degree of talent, and whose
eminence in his profession was a sure guarantee
that my affairs would receive the most prompt and
careful attention at his hands—none other than the
Hon. F. M. Goodman. He at once undertook my
case, and assured me that no pains or trouble
should be spared to bring it to an early successful
issue. Satisfied that I had done all that could be
done to insure success, I decided not to remain any
longer in Atlanta, but to return, at once, to Indiana.
I hated to leave the place without making any efforts whatever for the sale of my book; but, the
truth was, that everything was in such a depressed
condition there that I felt sure any effort of mine
would be vain. There was no money in the country,
and without that "root of all evil," it was but little
use for me to take any names for the book, even if
the people would, under such circumstances, be
likely to look with favor upon a proposition to
subscribe. Beside, there were too many unpleasant
memories clustering around that section of country

for me to remain there any longer than stern necessity demanded.

Accordingly, as soon as my arrangements with Mr. Goodman were completed to my satisfaction, I settled my bill at the hotel and took the first train for Chattanooga, having been in Atlanta just four days, instead of four weeks, at least, as I had intended when leaving Cincinnati.

I omitted to say, in its proper place, that I had written from Memphis, on my way down, to a son of my husband in Chicago; to which letter, however, I never received any answer; thus proving that I was not only cast off by my husband, but also by the whole family; no doubt through the influence of him from whom I had a right to expect different treatment. But the only effect of this neglect was to strengthen and confirm me in the resolution to sever my connection with them forever, by means of the decree of divorce for which I was about applying.

From Chattanooga I pursued my way through Nashville to Louisville, whence I went by mail-packet to Cincinnati, only stopping at each place so long as was necessary on account of the delay in connection of trains and the like. I reached Cincinnati in four days from the time of leaving Atlanta—having only been absent about three weeks.

I called at once upon Mr. Fessenden, who expressed no little astonishment at seeing me back so soon, and still more when I informed him that I

had not sold a single copy of the History of Freemasonry.   I did not tell him that the book had
not been once offered for sale, but told him that
times were so hard there that nothing could be
done, and that I had, therefore, decided to return
to a more promising field. He asked me something about the business which had taken me
there, but I evaded any direct information relative
to it, and only told him that in the present confused state of affairs there it was impossible to
accomplish any thing in any line of business.

I then returned to the subject of "The General
History of Freemasonry," and told him that, as I
had done so poorly in my trip to the South, I
thought he ought to give me a chance to make myself whole by giving me an opportunity to sell
the book where there could be something made of
it. He asked me where I would like to work. I
told him I would like the entire State of Indiana,
and the counties of Southern Michigan along the
line of the Michigan Southern & Northern Indiana Railroad. He replied, with a smile, that my
desires were very moderate, and that he thought
he could gratify them, adding, with a slight dash
of flattery, that he knew of no one to whom he
would rather entrust this district than to myself.
I also made arrangements with him to canvass the
same territory for "The History of Morgan's Cavalry," which last, however, I kept but a short time.

My business in Cincinnati being ended, I left
that city the next morning, for Indianapolis, to

devote myself once more to my chosen avocation,
and, at the same time, attend to getting my divorce, after which I would be free to change my
location, or do anything else, at my own pleasure.
I had not said anything to any one about the motive which induced my visit to the South, nor, indeed, did anybody in Indianapolis know that my
journey had been extended beyond Memphis;
and I decided not to enlighten anybody at the
present, either as to where I had been, or as to my
prospects in the South. Certainly, it was nobody's
business, and I would only leave them to suppose
that my absence had been caused by some matter in connection with my agency.

In due time I arrived in Indianapolis, and went
at once to my old boarding-house, at No. 44 South
Tennessee street, where I was gladly welcomed by
all the family. In pursuance of my resolution,
I said nothing about my Southern journey, merely
going about my business as usual, and occasionally dropping a remark about the condition of affairs in Memphis, in order to convey the impression that that city had been my stopping-place
during my absence from home.

In the meantime, my attorneys had commenced
proceedings for my divorce, and, Mr. Ford being a
non-resident of the State, it was necessary to advertise the pendency of the suit in some newspaper
published in the city. This was rather unpleasant,
as giving too much publicity to a matter about
which I, very naturally, desired as much secrecy

as possible ; but there was no help for it, and accordingly, the necessary affidavit was filed, and
the cause duly published in the Weekly Indiana
State Journal. After this expose of one of my objects in locating at Indianapolis, it was with fear
and trembling that I attempted to do anything in
the way of canvassing. It seemed to me that
every one must have read it, that they would know
who I was, and would make unpleasant comments
about it whenever I applied for a subscriber.
Doubtless my fears were entirely unfounded, and
that not one persons in every thousand of the inhabitants of Indianapolis had ever seen the notice,
or would know to whom it referred ; but still they
existed, and they finally made so much impression
on my mind as to induce me to withdraw almost
entirely from active canvassing myself.

But as I had not yet succeeded in getting an
agent to my satisfaction, I had to keep on at work
myself, and with my Masonic work I was doing
very well. In three days' time I took no less than
twenty-five subscribers for this work, the mayor of
the city being the first one ; and to his kindness I
am indebted for much of my success there. I was
but little acquainted with the Masonic fraternity
there, but, having been informed that Mayor Cavin
was one, I had asked him to give me the names of
men whom he thought would be likely to take the
book. He very kindly gave me a long list of
names, and in no one instance did I fail to sell a
copy of the work to one whose name he had given

me. I sold, in all, about one hundred copies of this work in Indianapolis; many of them to members of the Legislature, which happened to be in session at the time I was canvassing there.

During the same time I had sold only five or six copies of the "History of Morgan's Cavalry," and feeling that I could not devote sufficient time to this work, without interfering with the other, I gave it up entirely, and returned to Mr. Fessenden several copies already ordered. In fact, I was so much interested in the sale of the Masonic history, and was succeeding so well with it, that I really felt but little inclination to work for anything else.

Having, however, learned by accident that all the subscribers to "The Lost Cause" had not been supplied, and that there was some dissatisfaction among them in consequence, I called upon Mr. Barbour, the gentleman in whose hands I had left the agency for that work upon my starting South, took from him his list of subscribers, revoked his agency, and took charge of the sales of the work in person. I delivered books to all whose names he had taken, and two or three new subscribers; then, finding it an up-hill business, I declined to work for it any more, and finally gave up canvassing for everything except the Masonic history, devoting all my time and attention to that.

With this work I was doing very well, indeed. I had now been at work for it only about a month, and as the reader is already informed, had sold about one hundred copies; but Indianapolis had been pretty thoroughly canvassed, and sales were getting very dull. I, therefore, decided to leave there for a time, and try my fortune a little farther north—at Lafayette, and some of the other towns alone the line of the Wabash Valley Railroad. I also decided that I would not try to get subscribers for anything but the Masonic history, believing that it would only be a waste of time to do so. My experience had taught me that the agent who attempted to canvass, at the same time, for five or six different works, was not likely to do well with any of them. The best way, in my judgment, is to select some good work, and give all one's efforts to that, to the utter exclusion of everything else. Of course, a reasonable degree of sagacity must be exercised in the selection of a suitable work with which to travel; but if one attempts to work for several publications at the same time, he is likely, by a division of his exertions, to succeed in making a failure with all.

Having decided to visit Lafayette, I called upon a prominent Mason of Indianapolis, and asked him to give me a letter of introduction to somebody in that place, who would be likely to extend to me some aid in introducing the work. He very readily and cheerfully complied with my request, and gave me letters to several parties there. Perhaps there is no more suitable opportunity than this, to acknowledge the obligations I am under to the Masonic fraternity, as a body, for the kindness and assistance they have invariably rendered me in selling this work. It has been my usual custom, upon visiting any place for the first time, to call upon some prominent member, or members of the fraternity, for lists of names to guide me in my canvassing; and again, upon leaving for another place, to ask for letters of introduction to some leading member of the Order in the place whither I was going; and in no solitary instance has compliance with these requests been refused; and the assistance thus rendered has been invaluable to me, and will be ever most gratefully remembered; and I desire here to return my heartfelt thanks, not only to each and every one of the members of that ancient and honorable Order, for the uniform kindness and courtesy with which they have treated me, but especially to those who have assisted me in the manner above indicated. May their kindness be returned to them a thousand fold.

In due time I arrived in Lafayette, and at once called upon one of the gentlemen to whom I had received a letter of introduction. He treated me with the kindness which has always marked the conduct of the fraternity toward me, bought a book, and introduced me to several other gentlemen, all of whom purchased books. I sold five or six copies there, and having thus sown seed which I hoped would, in time, bear abundant fruit, I decided to leave Lafayette, a short time, go up to Delphi and Logansport, see what could be done there, and return to Lafayette again on my way to Indianapolis. This trip was the poorest which ever oc-

26

curred in all my experience as a book agent. I was absent some three days from Lafayette, and did not sell a single copy of the work during the whole time. The Masons, in all the places visited by me, seemed more dead than alive—more intent on making money than acquainting themselves with the history and origin of their order—more devoted to the worship of Mammon than to the cultivation of a knowledge of the science of which this fraternity claims to be one of the principal exponents. There was among them a state of coldness and indifference to the good of the Order which I have very rarely found. May they arouse from their lethargy in time to prevent their everlasting dissolution as an order.

The same feeling prevailed to a considerable extent, though in not quite so great a degree, at Lafayette; and I became convinced that, for the present, at least, I could not do enough there to pay expenses. My trip had already cost me much more than the profits realized from it, and, under such circumstances, it was worse than folly to extend my stay in the place. I therefore packed up my "traps" and returned home, fully resolved never to canvass along the line of the Wabash Valley Railroad, or, at least, until there was some evidence of more vitality among the Masons there.

CHAPTER XXV

UPON my return to Indianapolis, I decided to change my plan of operations, for a time. I had been traveling constantly since entering upon the duties of a book agent, was weary and somewhat worn down, and needed some rest. The plan adopted, for a time, was this—to advertise for agents to canvass in my field, while I would supply them with the work, as a sort of general agent, and would take a class in my old occupation—that of teaching painting. Accordingly, I resumed the agency of two or three works which I had discarded; obtained one or two others, so as to be able to supply my agents with any thing they might desire; obtained a suitable room in which to receive my pupils, and advertised in several of the leading papers, throughout the State, for agents. I also inserted advertisements for pupils in all the papers of the city, and commenced reviewing and furbishing up my artistic qualities.

Applications for employment, as agents, were soon very numerous, and in a few weeks I had no less than a dozen agents at work for me, in different parts of the State. The works with which they were furnished were all that I had ever canvassed for, with the addition of a most beautiful little book for the juvenile portion of the community,

. entitled " The Children's Album." I do not think
I have ever known a work more interesting, or
more beneficial, to be put in the hands of the rising
generation. I charge the publishers nothing for
this notice of their work, for it merits all and more
than can be said in its favor by so poor a pen as
mine.

While making and perfecting these arrangements, the other branch of business marked out for
myself had not been neglected. Applications for
admission to my school of painting had poured in
upon me, and my class was soon as large as my
rooms would allow me to accommodate, and several applicants had been refused admission for want
of room. And so assiduously had I practiced my
art that I found myself qualified to impart instruction, not only to their entire satisfaction, but, what
was much better, to my own. And thus matters
went on swimmingly, and, for a time, I succeeded
better, pecuniarily, than I had at any time since
starting as a book agent. But my expenses were
very heavy, and I did not lay up money very fast.
Aside from my ordinary expenses of every-day
life, the extensive litigation I was conducting, both
at Indianapolis and Atlanta, was a constant drain
on my finances, and kept·me at rather a low ebb.
There were constant applications from my counsel
for money for some purpose or other—now, five
dollars to pay for a certified copy of some old deed
or other; then ten or fifteen dollars to pay for
taking depositions; again ten dollars would be

wanted for searching some record at Washington, and so it went on. I was making money fast, and, had it not been for these constant demands upon my purse, could have accumulated some property, but it would take a princely income to stand these prodigious drains upon it. But I looked forward with hope to the time when it would all be at an end, and the money I was now forced to expend for these objects would be saved to me, when better times must certainly ensue.

About this time I had an operation performed on my left eye, which had been affected from my birth. It turned outwardly, and, aside from its disfiguring effect upon my countenance, it was, at times, a source of considerable annoyance to me, and not a little interfered with my sight. There was a professional oculist in the city, by the name of Dr. Charles Wall, who sustained a very high name in his profession, and who had published some certificates of very remarkable cures performed under his treatment; and I had myself known of several very bad cases of "cross eyes" which he had treated with the utmost success. I made up my mind to apply to him for relief from my affliction, and, accordingly, called at his office and asked him if he could straighten my eye. He examined it, asked me some questions about it, and said he could cure it by performing a surgical operation upon it. I told him, if it was to be operated upon, I would like to have some friend present at the time, and he replied that he would like to have some medical gentleman witness the operation, and that, if it suited me, he would perform it at ten o'clock the next day. I told him that Dr. Athon and Dr. Barnes were friends of mine, and that, if he had no objections, I would bring them with me at that time; to which he very readily assented, saying it was just what he would have desired.

At the appointed time the next morning, Dr. Athon, Dr. Barnes and myself, went to Dr. Wall's office, No. 21 West Maryland street, and I took my seat in the operating chair. The doctors wanted me to take chloroform, or some other anæsthetic agent; but this I refused to do, feeling assured that my courage and nerve were sufficient to endure the operation, and wishing to see all that was done, especially as I was myself to be the victim. Well, I had my own way, and the operation was performed while I was in my natural state; nor would I even suffer any one to hold my hands or head. The operation was short, and much less painful than I had anticipated, but still very unpleasant.

I immediately returned to my boarding-house, and, for half an hour or so, experienced no uneasiness from the cutting of my eye: then suddenly began a sharp pain in the eye-ball, which continued all day and all night, and gave me no little alarm, lest it should involve the loss of sight in that eye. When I arose the next morning and looked in the glass, I found that quite a large lump had grown upon my eye where he had cut it; and, still more alarmed than ever, I hastened as early as I could to Dr. Wall's office. He smiled at my fears, and told me the lump would all disappear in a short time; that it was but the natural result of the operation, and need give me no uneasiness. He gave me some eye-water, and a small brush to apply it with, and I went away, feeling very much relieved; for I had the utmost confidence in his skill and ability.

As I shall not recur to this subject again, I may remark here that my expectations of benefit from this operation have been but partially realized, and that, though I paid Dr. Wall a very liberal fee for performing the operation, my eye has really received but very little benefit from it. It is better than when I went to him, but still far from perfect, as will be apparent to any one who will examine the portrait which forms the frontispiece of this work. Still, I do not condemn the doctor, for I doubt not, he is well-skilled in diseases of the eye; though in my own case his success was not so decided as I hoped, and had been led by him to expect.

Finding that the condition of my eye interfered somewhat with my convenience and success as a teacher of painting, I concluded to give up my class for a time, and resume my travels, at least until my eye should be fully recovered from the effects of the recent operation. Before setting out, however, I wanted to learn the art of cutting

dresses by a new method, and connect that with
my book agency, believing it would be a source of
considerable profit to me. I accordingly went to a
Mrs. S. C. Ewing, and applied for instruction in
the coveted art. She charged twelve dollars for
giving lessons, which was more money than I
really knew how to spare; but I had a painting,
worth fifteen dollars, which I proposed to give her
for my course of instruction, and she accepted my
offer. The art was very easy to acquire, and in
one day I could cut and fit dresses by this mode
as well as Mrs. Ewing herself.

With my books and some charts, I then started
out, not doubting I should do well ; but, as I soon
found, and as the reader will soon see, the result
did not equal my anticipations ; and I found upon
this trip another illustration of the truth of the
proposition I advanced some time since : that the
book agent whose exertions are divided among
several things, is not likely to succeed well with
anything.

Upon leaving Indianapolis I went at once to
Lebanon, the county seat of Boone county. It was
just about dark when I arrived there, and, of
course, nothing could be done that night. I went
to the Andrews House for the night, wading
through mud nearly a foot deep to get there, for it
had been raining several days, and the streets were
almost impassable. The next morning I went to a
printing office and engaged one hundred small circulars to be printed and distributed, setting forth

the value of my new system of cutting dresses, and
went out to canvass for "The History of Freemasonry" while they were being circulated, for I had
brought ten copies of the work with me. I visited
all the business places in Lebanon, during the forenoon, and succeeded in selling three copies of the
book, which, I think, was doing very well, considering the size of the town.

By this time my advertisements had been distributed, and, after eating a hearty dinner, I set
out to see what could be done with my charts. Of
course, my calls were now made upon the ladies,
at their houses, instead of at the business places.
At the first house at which I called, the following
conversation ensued :

"Good morning, madam. I am selling charts
for a new mode of cutting· dresses—the most perfect thing of the kind I ever saw—and teaching
the use of them. Would you like to learn?"

"Well, I don't know whether it would be of
much benefit to me or not. I generally have my
dresses cut by a dressmaker."

"But, by the use of this, you can cut and fit
your own dresses, and thus save trouble and
expense."

"There are so many humbugs, now-a-days, that
one hardly knows what or whom to trust; and I
believe I will not have anything to do with it."

"But, madam, you can see for yourself that this
is no humbug. It is so simple and plain that any
one can understand it, and so certain in its results

that it is almost impossible to make a mistake, or have an ill-fitting dress. I am sure you would like it."

"Well," said she, after examining it some time; "I do like its appearance, and would like to learn, but, to tell the truth, I have not got the money."

"Well, madam, I shall be in town for several days—it may be for a week—and if you will board me while I stay here, I will teach you the art, and furnish you with a chart."

"How long will you be here?"

"I can not tell exactly. Until I have canvassed the whole of the town. It may be two or three days, or it may be a week; though probably not so long."

"Upon those terms I will take lessons. You can come here at any time you choose."

I at once sat down, gave her a lesson, and explained the use of the chart to her; then sent to the Andrews House for my baggage, and again set out upon my canvassing. I felt very well, for I had made a beginning; the lady whose name I had obtained, was one of the leaders in the little social circle of the place, and I felt no doubt her influence would aid me in the prosecution of my work; and the result showed that I was not mistaken.

At the next house the lady was very cold and distant; did not care about looking at my charts, or hearing my explanations; but as soon as I told her that Mrs. Dr. M'Cloud (the lady with whom I was stopping) was learning as was also Mrs. Andrews at the hotel, her whole manner changed, and she at once manifested the utmost interest in it. She finally concluded she very much wanted to learn, but would not subscribe until she consulted her husband, who would not be at home until tea-time. Could I call again in the evening, or the next morning? Certainly; I would call the next morning, and hoped to be honored with her patronage. With this assurance I left her, receiving from her a parting injunction to call the next day; and I may remark here, that this injunction was cheerfully and faithfully obeyed, and that I added her name to my list of subscribers. Such is the result and power of rank and fashion! Had not Mrs. Dr. M'Cloud become a subscriber, this lady would not; and, doubtless, the same remark will apply to every lady whose name I procured in Lebanon. Fashionable society in Lebanon, as elsewhere, is very much like a flock of sheep; they will stand huddled together, uncertain what to do, until some one, with more decision than the others, makes a break in some particular direction, when, pell-mell, away go the whole herd following closely in the tracks of their leader, without the least regard for consequences. This gregarious disposition of the human race has been of immense service to me in many instances beside the one above mentioned.

I canvassed the remainder of the day, and at night had four ladies engaged to learn dress-cut-

ting, beside several others who, like my friend
above mentioned, wanted to consult their husbands about the matter before incurring any expense; and I found that, in every instance of the
kind, the promise to consult "husband" was
equivalent to a promise to subscribe; thus proving
to my mind either that the ladies in Lebanon have
very kind and indulgent husbands, or that they
have the art of governing their liege lords more
skillfully and successfully than their sisters in
some other parts of the world of which I have
some knowledge.

I remained in Lebanon about a week, and finding that my work there was practically done, and
that no more money was to be made there, I went
to Thorntown, in the same county. I had done
very well in Lebanon, but was destined to fare
still better in the place to which I had now come,
owing, in part, to the spirit of rivalry existing be-
tweeen the two towns, in which the ladies of each
bore their full share; for no sooner did I exhibit
to the ladies of Thorntown the list of names I had
obtained at Lebanon, than they at once said Lebanon should not go ahead of them in anything
pertaining to the world of fashion, and I soon had
all I could do. This rivalry seemed very foolish
to me, but as long as I was reaping the benefits of
it, I was not disposed to utter any complaints, or
attempt to quell it.

I remained in Thorntown three days, sold five
copies of Masonic history, disposed of a large

number of charts, and instructed several ladies in
the art of cutting their own dresses, when I left
there and went to Attica. Here I fared the poorest,
for some time, that I had anywhere on my present
trip. For two days I labored faithfully; but could
not get any one either to buy a book or to patronize the new mode of cutting dresses. Meantime
my bill at the Revere House, where I stopped, was
accumulating, at the rate of three dollars a day,
while I was earning nothing at all; and I was fast
becoming disheartened. The people all seemed as
poor as Job's turkey, or as stingy as a miser, I
could not tell which, and I was almost tempted to
give up in despair and leave the place, though it
was very much against both inclination and principle to give up without doing anything. After
reflecting some time upon the matter, I concluded
to stay one day longer, visit some of the places I
had visited already, and make one more effort to
penetrate the crust in which they had intrenched
themselves. There was a Mrs. Rodgers, who lived
in a fine stone house, and seemed to be a sort of
leader among the *ton*, and, though I had already
called upon her once, I determined to go there
again, and try to make the same arrangement with
her that I had with Mrs. M'Cloud, upon going to
Lebanon. I could not afford to stay there any
longer, and pay three dollars a day for my board,
while doing nothing; but if I could get to stay a
week with Mrs. Rodgers, and pay my way by
giving her instruction and selling her a chart, I

could afford that.   Beside, I would then be able to say I had made one sale in the great city of Attica.

Accordingly, the next day I called, for the second time, upon Mrs. Rodgers, at the stone mansion. She received me quite coolly, and seemed, for a time, very much disinclined to even talk about receiving instruction; but I persevered, and finally made her the same proposition which had succeeded so well with Mrs. M'Cloud. At this she seemed to relent a little, and we finally made the same arrangement—I was to board with her during my stay there, be it longer or shorter, and, in return, was to teach her the art, and furnish her with a chart.   In pursuance of this arrangement, my baggage was removed to her house that very morning; and I went to work, with renewed zeal, feeling that the crust was now penetrated, and that I might hope for some degree of success.

And I was not disappointed.   The gregarious nature of fashionable society, as at Lebanon, was my very good friend.   I told every lady upon whom I called that Mrs. Rodgers was learning of me—a *furore* was created upon the subject, and in two days I had all the applicants for instruction that could possibly be attended to by working early and late.   I was more than gratified—I was delighted at the result of my tactics—and had learned that, to succeed anywhere, it was only necessary to get some leader of fashion interested in my work.   Such is the influence and importance which attaches to a single name; and I determined that, hereafter, wherever I might go to work, I would adopt the same plan, which had succeeded so well here. If by its use I could make sales in the town of Attica, surely I need have no misgivings about trying it anywhere else. Anything which would break through the crust there, would penetrate any shell, however old or firmly formed.

I remained in Attica a little over a week, and, upon leaving the place, found that I had made more money than at Lebanon and Thorntown both, notwithstanding the discouraging prospects of the first two days. So much for society being like a flock of sheep.

From Attica I went to Danville, Illinois, and at once entered upon a very good course of business, having had much less trouble in effecting a start there than at any other place visited on my present journey—the people there seeming much more inclined to patronize a traveling agent than in Indiana. They seemed less inclined to suspect the honesty and motives of a stranger than the Hoosiers, and to realize more readily the value of the articles I was offering for sale.

But my stay there was destined to be of short duration. Just in the midst of my career of prosperity, a letter arrived from my attorneys, informing me that my presence was very urgently and imperatively necessary in Indianapolis, in connection with my suit for a divorce. Of course it was very unpleasant to leave my present location while business was so flourishing; but the affair at Indianapolis was of paramount importance, and such a summons must not be neglected; and, accordingly, I packed up my things, left my business there in the hands of an agent who had been appointed and fully instructed by me, and hastened homeward by the most direct and expeditious route. Upon reaching Indianapolis, I found, however, that my presence might just as well have been dispensed with as not, had it only been known in time; for, owing to an unexpected decision of the Court, we would be compelled to postpone the case until another term. My counsel were not to blame for this delay, for it was a matter which they could not foresee, but it was none the less a most bitter disappointment to me, for I had counted upon closing up that affair at the present time, and then I would be free to return to the South, and attend closely to the prosecution of my claim for the restitution of my brother's property. This I did not wish to do so long as affairs were in such a shape that Frank Ford could claim any part of the property which I might recover; and hence the delay was very annoying to me, beside involving considerable expense, which I was but illy able to afford. But there was no help for it, and nothing for me to do save to go to work again to raise the funds necessary to meet these demands upon my purse.

And these demands had recently been increased by my own action. The reader will remember that Carrie was with a relative of Captain Lake's, in

New Orleans, whither he had sent her to be raised and educated. I had not seen her for a long time, and my heart yearned to clasp the little darling to my bosom once more. She was all I had to live for, or to love; and my business had prospered so as to enable me to support her by my own exertions, and, accordingly, I sent for her. The friends with whom she was staying were very much opposed to her coming, but my claim upon her was stronger than theirs. She wanted to come to "mamma," and they finally yielded, and sent her to me. She arrived in safety, and the fond mother who has been for a long time separated from a dearly-loved child can imagine the pleasure with which I once more held in my arms the darling little one who, though no relative to me, had still become so dear to me as though of my own flesh and blood.

Besides Carrie, I had another little, helpless being depending upon me for support. I have already mentioned my intention to adopt a little boy as a playmate for Carrie. Some time had elapsed since that resolution was formed, and I had met with no opportunity to obtain a child whose appearance pleased me. But, visiting one day the county asylum for the poor, I saw just the boy I wanted. He was an orphan, with no friends to care for him; his father had been a brave soldier in defense of his country, in the hour of peril, and had died in the battle of Five Forks, just as final victory was perching upon the National Banner; his mother, a

27

frail, delicate woman, had survived the shock of
her husband's violent death but a few weeks, and
he was left alone in this cold, wide, unfriendly
world. He was just about Carrie's age, about five
years; while his light, curly hair, deep, earnest,
blue eyes, and finely molded features, sufficiently
resembled hers to warrant me in calling them
brother and sister. I accordingly took him from
the asylum, and by order of the Court of Common
Pleas of Marion County, formally adopted him as
my own child, and presented him to Carrie as her
little brother. She had still some recollection of
the brothers she had lost, and her little heart was
delighted beyond measure at the restoration of one
of them to her. They are as happy together as
it is possible for children to be, and my heart
throbs with all a mother's pride as I gaze upon my
beauties ; for though they are no earthly relation
to me, they are as dear to me as they could possibly be, were they of my own flesh and blood.

But, of course, I could not support them in idleness, and I must at once go to work to provide the
means for their sustenance and education. My
first care was to find a good boarding-school for
children, at which I could be certain they would
be properly cared for, and receive such attention
and education as was necessary and suitable for
children of that age. After some trouble I found
a location which I thought possessed all the requirements which my jealous care of their mental
and moral necessities demanded, and arrangements

were soon made for their reception by the matron of the establishment. And it affords me pleasure to say here that it would have been simply impossible that a selection of a location for my darlings could have been more fortunate; for the lady, in whose charge they still remain, combines within herself all the elements necessary to render their stay with her both pleasant and profitable to them. Of large and extended experience in the management of children; tender and kind, but firm and prudent in her government; she brings to the discharge of the important duties of her position a Christian consciousness of the weighty responsibilities devolving upon her, and a devout, prayerful determination to discharge those responsibilities in the wisest and most beneficial manner for the interest of the little ones under her care. Under these circumstances, how could they be otherwise than happy and properly cared for, or how could they be better situated, so long as it is necessary for them to be deprived of a mother's care? And, indeed, I am not sure but they are better off with Mrs. —— than they would be with me.

Having concluded this arrangement to my satisfaction, I decided to visit northern Indiana, and, perhaps, some parts of Illinois, and canvass for my Masonic history. I had had sufficient experience in trying to work for two or three publications, or other articles, at one time, and my mind was fully made up never to be guilty of that folly

again. So long as I continued to travel and canvass as an agent, my attention should not be
divided between a half dozen different objects, and
be thus prevented from doing justice to any of
them or to myself. I could canvass for a set of
books by any author if published by one firm and
they would not conflict with each other. But to
take books by different authors and work for more
than one firm at once, I will not do so again, for I
cannot do justice to either by so doing.

CHAPTER XXVI.

My present destination was La Porte, Indiana, where I had been informed the Masonic fraternity were quite numerous, and very active, and where I hoped to sell a large number of books. Before starting, however, I called upon William Hacker, Esq., Secretary of the Grand Lodge of the State, and he very kindly gave me a letter recommending the work in very flattering terms, and also gave me letters of introduction to several prominent members of the fraternity there. Armed with these documents, and provided with a policy of insurance against the accidents of travel, I once more committed myself to the tender mercies of the Louisville, New Albany & Chicago Railroad Company, and in due time, without any incidents worthy of special note, reached the very pleasant town for which I had set out.

Upon reaching La Porte, my first care was to secure a good and suitable boarding-place, during my stay there. I was fortunate enough to find a good room, and the best of accommodations in a house kept by Mr. C. D. Church (lately a lieutenant in the Union army), at the corner of Jackson and Prairie streets, but a short distance from the main business part of the city, and at once made arrangements with the gentlemanly proprietor for remaining there so long as I was in La Porte.

I next called upon Mr. E. G. Hamilton, to whom I had a letter of introduction, and had a long conversation with him about the Masonic fraternity, and the prospects of success there. I found Mr. Hamilton a fine, portly gentleman, rather below the medium height, somewhat bald, very affable and polite, but with a peculiar nasal twang or whine in his voice, to listen to which tried my risibilities sorely, and tempted me several times to overstep the bounds of the politeness which he was so continually exemplifying before me—not from any want of respect for him, but because his manner was simply amusing to me. No one could be kinder to me than he was, and, from the bottom of my heart I thank him therefor. Indeed, the fraternity in and about La Porte are all entitled to and receive my heartiest thanks for favors received at their hands.

Mr. Hamilton informed me that there were two lodges in the city, with an aggregate membership of about one hundred and forty; that both lodges were in a flourishing condition, and rapidly increasing in numbers; and that the interest in the welfare of the Order had never before been as high, in La Porte, as at the present time. Through his instrumentality I formed the acquaintance of several Masons of great prominence, and whose virtues and devotion to the craft have already given them high positions in the Masonic world; among whom

may be mentioned P. D. G. M. John B. Fravel; Dr.
G. M. Dakin, W. M., of Excelsior Lodge; P. G.
Winn, W. M., of La Porte Lodge; E. G. McCollum,
Esq., R. A. Hews, Esq., and many others whose
names it were useless to enumerate. Mr. Hamilton
himself is one of the most ardent disciples of Masonry I have ever met, and, though of but little
more than two years standing in the Order, has already penetrated deeper into its arena than many
a man who has spent a long life in connection
with the mystic brotherhood.

He gave me quite a list of names of men whom he
thought would be likely to subscribe for the work,
and I set out upon my labors, meeting, in almost
every instance, with the most gratifying success.
Very few, indeed, were the Masons in La Porte,
whom I asked in vain to purchase a work which
so well portrayed the origin and principles of their
order. They are live Masons there, and everything which tends to elucidate the benefits of their
institution, and its claim to the confidence of the
world, they gladly welcome.

Of course, here, as elsewhere, there are excep-
tions to this general rule, one of which I must be
permitted to mention. In the office of a friend,
who was furnishing me a more extended list of
names than Mr. Hamilton had done, I one day
met and was introduced to a Mr. Walker—"Elder
Walker," I think my friend called him. This pre-
fix, at any rate, he was entitled to, having been,
at one time engaged in the work of the ministry,

though now, I believe, not laboring in that field.
He was a stout, wiry old man, with white hair, and
a complexion of such floridity that, but for his
well-known character of sterling morality, and his
intense hatred of drunkenness in all its forms, he
might be almost suspected of having, at some time
or other, tampered too much with " the worm of
the still." His portly, rotund person, indicative of
good living, terminated in a pair of pedal extremi-
ties of extraordinary size, which were inclosed in
most hideously-squeaking cowhide boots ; while a
massive, square head was connected to the upper
extremity of the trunk by a short, thick neck,
which looked as though it might safely bid defiance to the hangman's rope, even if the Elder
should ever be brought to test its qualities—an
event which seems exceedingly improbable. His
form was very erect, his movements quick and
nervous, and an air of the most supreme satisfaction with himself and the rest of the world pervaded every feature. He was one of those men
who constantly annoy you by assenting, in the
most gracious manner, to everything you say, and,
at the same time, remove all pretext for anger by
their ready compliance, and against whom the
shafts of argument or sarcasm are as harmless, and
glide off as easily as water poured from a tin dip-
per upon the well-mailed back of a duck ; and, to
crown all, he enjoys among his large circle of acquaintances, by whom he is sincerely respected.

the reputation of being just the least bit of a
" bore."

" There," said my friend, after tne ceremony of
introduction had been performed, and the requisite
bows had been made, "is a subject for your art."

" Y-e-e-s," chimed in *the Elder*, "I am a very
proper subject for the machinatioﬂs of your art.
What is it?"

"I am canvassing for ' The, General History of
Freemasonry in Europe,' and would like to sell
you a copy."

"'The General History of Freemasonry!' Well,
really, that must be a very fine thing, and a work
which ought to be in the hands of every Mason in
the country, especially of those who are just beginning to tread the thorny road which leads to the
flowery repose of Masonic peace and happiness."

I was quite startled by this somewhat extraordinary poetical display, but my friend seemed to
take it as a matter of course, and I returned to the
charge.

" The work is highly recommended by prominent
Masons in all parts of the country, and, among
others, by William Hacker, Grand Secretaﬂy of
the Grand Lodge of the State."

"It is? Why, it must be a spiendid work!
Brother Hacker is a good man, and would recommend none but a work of sterling merit to the confidence of the brotherhood, to whose service he has
earnestly and consistently devoted the best portion

of a long and well-spent life. And he really recommends the book, does he?"

"Yes, sir, I have a letter in his own hand-writing, recommending it in the highest terms."

"I want to know! So you know Brother Hacker? He is a splendid man."

"Yes, sir, I am acquainted with him."

"You are? And he has recommended this work in a letter composed by his own mighty mind, and indited by his own hand?"

"I have said so sir."

"Yes, yes; I know you have. Have you the letter with you?"

"It is in my trunk, at my boarding-house. I can show it if necessary."

"Yes. Hum. Where do you board?"

"At Mr. Church's."

"What! Lieutenant Church."

"Yes, sir."

"Why! he is a good man. I guess he keeps a good boarding-house, and ministers to the necessities of the weary, hungry, and way-worn traveler in the most approved manner. I never stopped at his house; but have always heard that character ascribed to him by his patrons and admirers, whose name is legion."

"Yes, he keeps a very good house. But let us talk about the book."

"Certainly. Such a work as that; from the pen, doubtless, of one of the most eminent authors and philologists the world has ever produced, and recommended by a man of such gigantic intellect, such sterling integrity, and such unquestioned devotion to the good of Freemasonry, as Brother William Hacker, Grand Secretary of the Grand Lodge of the State of Indiana, is worthy of being the theme of conversation wherever civilized language prevails, as long as the sun shall roll his ceaseless rounds. Why Brother——," turning to my friend, "you ought to purchase a copy of this most invaluable work, and place it among the most cherished volumes of your family library, there to remain, and be read and admired by your children and your children's children, down to the seventieth generation."

"But," said I, laughing in spite of myself, at this rhapsody, "he has already bought a copy, and now I want to sell you one."

"He has! Well, he has done just right. No man, in his situation, can afford to be without it."

"Then, sir, I hope you will take one."

"I must take time to consider the subject, madam. Men very often get themselves into almost inextricable difficulties by acting from impulse and without proper reflection. But, in the first place, I must premise that my situation and that of my friend here is vastly different. It is unnecessary that I should enlarge upon the points of difference between our respective positions— they are apparent at a glance. But I will consider of the subject, and advise you of my conclusions."

I saw that it was useless to urge the subject further, and made him no answer, and he soon after withdrew. I was not a little amused, as well as somewhat disgusted, at the result of this interview; but my friend laughed heartily at my discomfiture, saying it was no more than he anticipated; that he was very sure "the Elder" could not be induced to subscribe; and that he had introduced him merely for the purpose of getting a good joke on me. I thanked him for his kindness (?), and promised him I would be even with him some day; and thus the matter ended.

I canvassed in La Porte about a week, and sold some sixty copies of the work there, being the best week's work I had yet done since I became a book agent. I also visited several little towns throughout the county, and sold quite a number of works there. My trip, thus far, had been very profitable, and I was, in consequence, very much elated in spirits. Surely, at the rate at which I was making money, I should have no difficulty in providing for my two little ones; and they were all I had to care for in the world. If God would mercifully spare my life, and protect me in health and strength, I had no fears but I could raise them comfortably, and in a manner that would render them a credit, not only to me, but to themselves.

But my work in La Porte was done, and it was necessary for me to seek other fields. I very much hated to leave this place, for I had made some warm friends there—friends who will dwell in my memory, and whose kindness will not be forgotten, so long as my life is spared and reason remains an inmate of my soul—but necessity demanded it, and it is an old adage that "necessity knows no law." Accordingly, I procured from my friends letters of introduction to several of the prominent Masons of South Bend, and started for that point, where I arrived about seven o'clock in the evening, and retired to rest for the night, without learning much about the town.

The next morning I arose early, and took a walk before breakfast, in order "to spy out the land," and decide upon my chances for success there. At first sight I did not like the appearance of the place much, and was almost tempted to go on without trying to do anything there. There were scarcely any sidewalks in the town, and what there were were in a sad state of dilapidation; the weather had been rainy for some time, and the streets were in anything but a pleasant condition for pedestrian feats; many of the business houses had an old, tumble-down appearance, and altogether the place was not, at first view, calculated to inspire any great love in the mind of a stranger. But I remembered that I had done very well in places of no more promising appearance than this, and I decided to try to do something; but, at the same time made up my mind to recommend to the Mayor and Council that they do something to improve the condition of their streets and sidewalks, and to suggest at the same time, that their place would appear much more attractive in the eyes of strangers if this recommendation were complied with.

Having decided to remain and try my fortune here for a short time, I called upon several of the parties to whom I had letters of introduction, delivered my letters and introduced my work. All seemed much pleased with it, and my success was such as not to cause the least regret that I had decided to remain there. The Order seemed to be in a very healthy, flourishing condition there, and to be composed of men who had its real good at heart, and were more interested in perfecting themselves in a knowledge of its mysteries than in merely increasing its membership. Among such men my success could not be other than most gratifying, and I am happy to record the fact that, in the four days which I spent there, I sold no less than thirty-one copies of my favorite work. Surely, a most auspicious result in a town of such unpromising appearance as, at first view, to almost discourage even me, in spite of my extensive experience.

From South Bend I went to Mishawaka, only four miles further east, and found it a very pleasant place—indeed, to my notion, a more pleasant place than South Bend, though the latter is the larger town, and is the county seat of the county. There seemed to me to be much more life and animation in Mishawaka, and more business done than in South Bend, considering the size of the two

places; but it might be that it was owing in part
to the more favorably auspices under which I saw
Mishawaka.   The weather was magnificent while
I was there, and the whole town was clad in its
holiday attire, while South Bend was in mud and
sorrow when I saw her last.

I canvassed Mishawaka in three days, selling
something over a score of books, but, although
they had been ordered sometime before, they had
not yet come, and, of course until they arrived,
they could not be delivered; so there was nothing
for it but to wait with what patience I could command under the circumstances.   For a week I
remained there idle, and my anxiety to be at work
mounted to almost fever heat.   But there was no
good in fretting.   The books would not come any
sooner for it, and the only thing in my power was
to amuse myself in the best manner possible, and
thus pass away the time while waiting.   I was
boarding in the family of a Mr. Taylor, a very
nice, pleasant place, and both Mr. Taylor and his
wife were very fond of fishing.   They had often
invited me to join them in their piscatorial expeditions along the banks of the silvery St. Joseph, but
I had as often declined.

But at length time grew so heavy on my hands
that one "bright day in the morning," I decided
to accept their oft-repeated invitation and accompany them.   Armed with proper tackle, rods,
lines, hooks, bait, etc., and an immense basket in
which to deposit the finny spoils of the deep (river),

we wended our way to a pleasant nook, where Mr. Taylor assured us we would find plenty of fish. I could not bait my hook myself, but Mr. Taylor affixed the tempting morsel, while Mrs. Taylor performed the same feat for herself, and we cast in our lines, nothing doubting (at least I did not) that we should soon be blest with as great an abundance of fish as were the Apostles when, at the command of our Saviour, they cast their net upon the right side of the ship. Soon after casting in her line Mrs. Taylor drew it out again to the surface, and with a flourish and a "whish," landed a fine large sunfish upon the bank just back of where we sat. Again she put in her hook, and again drew it forth, and this time a noble perch was dangling at the end of her line. Again and again was this scene repeated—now sunfish, now perch, now something else—until she had caguht five or six fine fellows, and her husband nearly as many more; but I had not had a solitary nibble. I was getting out of all manner of patience when, suddenly, I felt the short, quick jerk which indicated that a fish was after my bait. Trembling with eager anxiety, I drew it to the surface, when, low! a gigantic water-dog made his appearance, securely hooked to my line; but how to get him off was the question. It is no trouble for me to eat fish when they are nicely prepared for the table, but the idea of taking hold of a live one— ugh! it makes me shudder even to this day. Several times I tried to muster sufficient courage to accomplish this feat, but each time his flopping and floundering drove me away demoralized, until at last I was fain to give it up. Mr. Taylor then came to my assistance, and removed the monster, baited my hook again, and again I committed my line to the pearly deep. Another season of anxious waiting and watching, another nibble at my line, another sharp pull, and this time I brought out a large catfish. I tried to take him off, but he looked so much worse than the other, with his huge gogle eyes, immense mouth, and wicked-looking horns, that he frightened me more than the other; and again Mr. Taylor was compelled to come to my assistance. Once more I tried my luck, and this time another water-dog was the result of some half hour's patient watching.

By this time the sun was getting high in the heavens and it was time for us to retnrn home; so we proceeded to enumerate the results of the morning's sport, or rather labor, for such it was to me. Mr. and Mrs. Taylor had caught some twenty-three fish, every one of which was fit for use; while I had succeeded in landing three, not one of which was of the least possible value for any purpose. I was not a little disgusted at my luck, or rather at my want of it, and made up my mind that nature never designed me for a fisherman, and that I could succeed much better as a book agent. As I said before, I can do something in the way of eating fish when they are

28

properly prepared and on the table, but this is the only part of a fisherman's life I am fit for.

But I had already wasted too much time in this place, and decided to stay here no longer, but would go and canvass Elkhart and Goshen, and then return here and deliver my books. I had ordered books to be sent to Goshen at the same time that I had ordered those at Mishawaka, and, doubtless they would be there by the time I had finished canvassing, and I could then deliver all at once, and thus close up my business in this part of the country. I therefore packed up my " traps," bade adieu to the kind friends who had tried so hard to initiate me into the mysteries of the sport of fishing, but with such poor success, and took the cars for Elkhart, where I arrived in due time without incident.

Upon reaching this place, I went to work with a vigor which was intended to make up for all the time lost by the neglect of my publisher, with whom I was already quite out of patience for his dilatoriness; but my patience was yet to be more sorely tried from this source.

My efforts here were very successful, and in a week no less than forty names of subscribers had been added to my already magnificent list of sub-scribers for the Masonic history. I felt proud of my week's work, and thought that what had been done was deserving of compliment. Surely the sale of forty copies of a single work, in a little town like Elkhart, was something to be proud of,

and I venture the assertion, that not five canvassing agents in the United States can show a better
report for the same time and under the same circumstances; but it shows what energy and determination, when properly applied, can accomplish,
even under unfavorable circumstances.

From Elkhart I went to Goshen, nothing doubting that I should find my books there, as more
than two weeks had now elapsed since they had
been ordered; but again I was doomed to disappointment, for, to my inquiry for books, the express agent politely replied, "There is nothing
here for Mrs. M. Ford." What could it mean?
Surely my orders had been received by the publishers, and why there should be so much want of
promptness in filling them was entirely beyond my
comprehension. I would write to Mr. Fessenden,
give him a piece of my mind, and learn what he
meant by thus keeping me idle through his neglect, and, in the meantime, would canvass Goshen
and the surrounding country, and by that time my
answer, as well as the books, would most likely
arrive. Accordingly I indited a letter, "short,
sharp and decisive" in its terms, mailed it, and
went to work.

For about a week I labored faithfully, and with
very fair success, having sold twenty-eight or
twenty-nine copies to the citizens of Goshen. I
had called almost daily, during the time, at the
express office, and each day, "Still not arrived,"
had been the answer of the agent to my look of

inquiry. I was becoming disheartened, and, to add to my annoyance, was still without any reply to my letter of inquiry, written one week ago. But what could I do? Manifestly nothing more than to wait, with what patience I could command, until such time as his majesty, Mr. George B. Fessenden, should see fit to honor me with his notice once more.

I wrote him another letter, and then went to canvass in the country, for a few days, until he should have time to answer this. I worked energetically among the farmers of that region, and succeeded in selling books enough to pay my expenses and something more, at the end of which time I returned to Goshen, and again presented myself at the Express office. "Nothing has come for you, Miss," said the agent.

I turned away without any reply, almost sick at heart, and bent my steps to the Postoffice.

"What name?" said the delivery clerk.

"Mrs. M. Ford."

"Yes, here is one," and he handed me a letter.

It bore the Cincinnati post-mark, and I broke the seal with eager anxiety. It ran thus:

"Mrs. M. Ford—I am sorry to say we are out of the General History of Freemasonry, and will not be able to fill your orders for some time to come. In about two weeks we hope to be able to supply all your calls. Regretting the delay, but hoping it may prove no serious inconvenience to you, I remain, etc., GEO. B. FESSENDEN."

Out of books, indeed! No serious inconvenience, forsooth! This letter capped the climax—this was the last feather that broke the camel's back. What business had he to get out of books? He knew I was selling a great many—he knew that I was at work all the time, and that, in the last three months, I had sold over three hundred copies. I reported my sales to him weekly, and he knew, or ought to have known, about how many I would require; and why did he allow his stock to become exhausted? It was easy for him to say he hoped it would put me to no serious inconvenience; and it was a small matter to him that I had to lie idle, or almost so, for weeks at a time, on account of his neglect; but to me it was not a small matter. It was my meat and drink: upon the sales of the book he was "out of" depended my support and that of my two little babes, at Indianapolis; and to me it was a very "serious inconvenience." But I would see that the same thing did not happen again while I worked for him. I would order books for a month or more before I expected to visit a place, and would report that place canvassed, and thus I might possibly get them when I wanted them.

Such were my reflections as I read this letter, but, for the present, I could do nothing. I would have to wait the two weeks any how, and what should I do during that time? I had heard that there was a very superior school for little children at Springfield Illinois, and I decided, while waiting Mr. Fessenden's "inconvenience," to go there and see if it was desirable to send my children there, inasmuch as the lady in whose charge they now were, had intimated to me that she might possibly break up her establishment and remove from the city. By the time I could make that journey, his two weeks would likely be up, and then I might hope to have my order filled, and be able to supply my subscribers in this part of the country. So it was determined.

CHAPTER XXVII.

In pursuance of the determination mentioned at the close of the last chapter, I settled up my affairs at Goshen, so far as it was possible for me to do; called upon the express agent and informed him of my intended absence for about two weeks, and requested him to retain in his office any packages coming for me until my return, which he promised to do; took leave of my friends there, and embarked on the cars for La Porte; for it was my intention to stop there a short time, and visit some of my many friends in that city. Arriving there in due time, I found my friends all well, and passed a day or two as pleasantly as I ever did anywhere in my life. I had taken the degrees of the Eastern Star during my stay in Goshen, and as the friend who had introduced me to Elder Walker was very proficient in these degrees, I availed myself of his kindness to become more acquainted with them than I had hitherto been.

And just here I desire to bear my testimony to the value of these degrees, and to express my surprise that they are not more generally worked and understood among the Masonic fraternity and their wives and daughters. Nothing within my knowledge will secure that protection and assistance which every wife and daughter of a Mason has a

right to demand at the hands of the entire fraternity so readily and certainly as a knowledge of
these degrees ; and certainly there is nothing
which brings us, who are debarred by the rules of
the Order from full admission to its secrets, into
such close fellowship and affiliation, so to speak,
with this ancient and honorable Order, as a
thorough acquaintance therewith. The only difficulty in the way is the fact that Master Masons,
who are thoroughly posted in the secret work and
ritual of the Order, do not, as a general thing,
take the pains to acquire a thorough knowledge of
these degrees, and that ladies upon whom they
have been conferred, do not take sufficient interest
in them, from the very fact just cited, to retain
enough of them to make them useful. To remedy
this evil, I would have every Master Mason as
much required to perfect himself in these degrees
as he is in the three symbolical degrees of the
blue lodge, and would have ladies upon whom they
have been conferred organize lodges, schools of
instruction, etc., as do our husbands and brothers,
and render themselves as perfect in their mysteries
as do Master Masons in the rituals of their institution. In this way the Order of the Eastern Star
can be made really and permanently useful, and
the beneficent design of its founder be carried out
to a full and practical realization.

That the "Eastern Star" lodges here alluded to
can be made really useful and beneficial, as well
as permanent, is proven by the fact that they are

already in successful operation in some parts of the United States, though by no means generally organized throughout the land. There is one at Goshen, one at New Albany, and probably in other parts of the State, and also in the State of Michigan, and probably other States of the Union. Let the number of these organizations be extended until they become as universally known and recognized as are Masonic Lodges, and then woman will really derive some benefit from that which was invented by an eminent and worthy brother for her sole good. But to return to myself and my visit.

Among other things, I had a good hearty laugh with my friend about my attempt to " canvass " Elder Walker. I was still a little sore over the matter, and could hardly believe the assertion of my friend, that the " Elder " had not put on a little extra style for the occasion, and that this was his natural style of conversation whenever he wanted to be very impressive ; but he insisted so strongly that this was the case that I was forced to yield my own opinions, though insisting that it was certainly a very extraordinary style, and the " Elder " a very remarkable man. Doubtless he got into this high-flown style while laboring in the pulpit, and has seen no particular reason for dropping it. I remained in La Porte some two or three days, visited all my friends, and then pursued my journey to the capital of Illinois.

I did not visit Springfield for the purpose of canvassing for the Masonic history, it being beyond my jurisdiction, but I was still nominally agent for one or two other works which I had a right to sell in that field, and I took them along, thinking I might perhaps, sell enough to pay my expenses there and back. I also took my specimen copy of the Masonic history, merely because it was in my trunk, and I did not care to leave it, lest it should be lost.

Upon arriving in Springfield, I learned that there was no agent in that territory for the Masonic history, and concluded that as I had a sort of " roving commission," authorizing me to sell anywhere except in territory occupied by other agents, I would try that awhile, and, accordingly went to work for it. I also offered for sale at the same time, the other publications brought with me, and for nearly a week I did a very good business, taking something over fifty names for the various works. I then made arrangements with a gentleman there, to deliver the books when they should be sent to him, and collect the pay for them, allowing him to retain a certain per cent. for his trouble. I ordered the books sent to me at La Porte, and intended shipping them from there to him myself. I had an object in this which the reader will not fail to perceive.

While pursuing my labors, I had not neglected the object which originally induced me to come to Springfield, and my inquiries had almost satisfied me that, although the school there was a very good one, still nothing would be gained by sending my children there, especially so long as the present arrangement could be maintained at Indianapolis. The reader will bear in mind that there was no positive certainty that the school there would be discontinued at the present, and even should it be, I thought I knew of places where, without intending any disparagement to the institution at Springfield, my little ones could be sent with much more satisfaction to me than there. Still, I had come to investigate the merits of the institution, and would not do it injustice, or depart without making that investigation as thorough as my abilities and circumstances would admit.

I therefore visited the establishment, and had a long interview with the lady who officiates as principal. She was a very lady-like and matronly personage, somewhat past the middle age, and evidently desirous of doing justice to the mental, moral, and physical qualities of the little ones intrusted to her care. The school was well and pleasantly located, the children seemed to enjoy themselves very well, and my impressions of the school from this examination were just the same as those formed from my inquiries—that there was no doubt of its genuine merit, still there were places where my little ones could be established more to my satisfaction than there. Others might differ with me, might be better qualified to judge than myself—it is the right and duty of every one having the care of children to decide these matters for themselves—but I could not see this school in a light which would induce me to give it the preference over several others within my knowledge.

My work in Springfield was done, and still I was not ready to leave. In and about Springfield are several places which the events of the last six years have rendered of historic value to every American whose heart thrills with true devotion to his country, and reveres all that is great and good in her history, and I could not leave the place without visiting the tomb and the former home of Abraham Lincoln. Securing the companionship of a friend, who was well acquainted with the locality, we set out the next day, while the morning was yet in its infancy, and the air was cool and fresh, for the cemetery where lie the mortal remains of a man who occupies a place in the great American heart second. to none of the elevated and noble characters who have adorned the pages of her history.

The cemetery at Springfield is, I thing, the finest, in its arrangement and ornamentation, I ever saw. Other cities and other communities have taken pains to ornament and render attractive the last resting-places of their loved and honored dead, but to Springfield must be awarded the palm of having more nearly attained perfection, in this respect, than any other place within my knowledge. The smooth, green, and closely-shaven lawn, cut hither and tither with finely graveled walks; the regular and beautiful arrangement of lots and burial places; the pleasant arbors, scattered here and there, throughout the grounds, give the place more the appearance of a finely-arranged garden than of a charnel-house; while the splendid firs and other evergreens, which rise on every hand, and through which are peeping forth, in every direction, tall and stately obelisks, more simple monuments and plain white marble slabs, are suggestive of a sense of coolness and peace, which at once brings to the mind, in all their loveliness and sweetness and power, those beautiful lines in which Montgomery has described the calm rest of the grave. And as we passed within the gate, and I stood enchanted with the beauties of the scene before me, I found myself almost unconsciously repeating:

> " There is a calm for those who weep,
> A rest for weary pilgrims found,
> They softly lie and sweetly sleep
> Low in the ground."

I was completely lost in admiration, and, for a time, could do nothing but stand and gaze upon the beauties of the scene; but we passed onward, and at last stood by the tomb of the noble man, who, with a singular unselfishness, and the most noble devotion to the good of his country, had stood unmoved at the helm of the ship of state, and by his own mighty genius had guided her safely through the storm which threatened to ingulf her, and had finally, when she was just entering the harbor of peace and everlasting security, and when he could see the approaching end of all his toils and labors, fallen by the hand of an assassin, whose name and memory will be execrated by every lover of liberty and free government down to the latest fragment of recorded time.

Ah! what emotions thrilled my soul, as I stood by the tomb of this man, who, born in the humblest walks of life, and in his youth devoted to the most menial avocations, had, by the force of his own unaided genius, and the native goodness of his character, risen to the highest position in the gift of a proud and powerful people, and had achieved for himself a crown of glory, by the side of which the brighest and most costly diadem of a European monarch sinks into the most utter insignificance.   The mighty struggle through which the nation had just passed, and the burdens of which she was still bearing, from the firing of the first hostile gun at the unarmed steamer Star of the West, to the last closing drama in the wilderness of Georgia, passed in review before my mind's eye, as I stood, with bowed head and reverent demeanor, beside the tomb of him who, under Heaven, had directed the armies of the Union to final victory.   In fancy's eye I beheld the marshaling of squadrons, and the setting in array of hostile forces; I heard the clang of arms, the trampling of armed hosts, the roar of cannon, and the crash of musketry; I witnessed the ever-varying and shifting scenes of the battlefield, as victory now hung in the balance, now inclined to this side, now to that; I beheld the gory aspect of the field of

conflict when the strife was ended, and heard the
low moans of the wounded and the dying, as the
thirsty earth eagerly drank up the life-blood which
was fast oozing from their contracting veins; I saw
a mighty procession of mangled, armless, legless
men closely filing by, and exhibiting their wounds
as claims to the memory and gratitude of the
country which their valor and their sacrifices had
helped to preserve; I looked upon a long line of
gaunt, haggard forms, clad in tatters, and with
reason half dethroned by the horrors of Anderson-
ville, and Salisbury, and Belle Isle, while closely
following in their train, came half a million of
spectral phantom figures, who had bidden adieu
to home and friends, and gone forth to lay down
their lives in this unnatural, unholy, and needless
war; and among this last procession I recognized
the tall and stately form of an only and dearly-
loved brother; and, as I reflected that he had
fallen, not in defense of his country, but in the
mistaken and misguided effort to destroy it, my
heart throbbed with anguish, and I turned away
my head, and wept in the bitterness of sorrow.

But I looked yet again, and, lo! the brighter
side of the picture appeared. I beheld the nations
of the earth in mighty conclave assembled, and
among them towered one tall and stately, upon
whose escutcheon no blot was to be seen, whose
banner gleamed in all parts of the habitable globe,
whose government, founded upon the rock of eternal truth and justice, bade defiance to the assaults

of the mad waves of passion and prejudice; I listened to the glad songs of four millions of beings elevated by this struggle from the condition of mere chattels to the glad estate of men and women; I saw the shackles stricken from their limbs, and cast into the sea which is bottomless, and whence they shall never be resurrected; I witnessed the eyes of the struggling poor among every kindred, nation, tongue, and people under the whole heaven turned toward our own beloved land, as the beacon of all their hopes, and the aim of all their desires, and I said within myself, "Surely this result is well worth all it cost to obtain it."

I looked yet again, and the future was unfolded, as a scroll, to my view; and I saw the starry banner—emblem of our nation's sovereignty—waving, in calm and peaceful triumph over the whole of the habitable globe. I beheld liberty, free government, law and order everywhere prevailing, and dispensing their richest blessings to the entire human race; I heard the rejoicings of countless millions, because of their release from bondage and oppression which had so long bowed them to the very dust; I witnessed the sword beaten into the plowshare, and the spear into the pruning hook, the nations of the earth refusing to learn war any more, and the whole human family devoting themselves to the arts of peace; I saw love and fellowship and good will prevailing among all ranks and classes of mankind, and every man seeking his neighbor's welfare before his own; and I

said, "Surely this man was an instrument in the
hand of God, and this Rebellion one of His appointed means to work out the high and noble
destiny which he has appointed for the children of
men "—and the vision was gone.

I bowed my head in reverent devotion beside
this shrine of the pilgrimage of a nation, plucked
a rose from a vine planted there by the hand of
affection, turned away with my friend, and, casting one last, long, lingering glance at the magnificent beauties of this silent house of the dead, we
left the cemetery, and returned to the city, where
we had still another pilgrimage to make — another
visit to pay.

Our destination was now the house which had
been the home of Mr. Lincoln before he had been
called by the voice of the nation to assume the
mighty responsibilities which had eventuated in
his death; and thither, without delay, we bent our
steps. It is a large, old-fashioned, two-story
structure of wood; and its situation bears testimony to the true and correct taste of him who had
formerly occupied it.

We found the house in charge of a kind, elderly
lady, by the name of Mrs. ——, who, as soon as
we expressed our desire to visit the house and
grounds, kindly offered to accompany us on our
tour of exploration. She first took us to the
family sitting-room, where Mr. Lincoln used to
unbend from the cares of the world, and, in the
bosom of his family, showed himself the kind

29

husband and father, the tender-hearted man of
affectionate feeling, the faithful monitor and profound instructor which he really was. It is in the
bosom of his family alone, in the quiet of the home
circle, whence all deception is banished, and
where trust and confidence alone abound, that
man can throw off, entirely, the mask which contact with the world compels him to wear, and appear, in truth, himself; and Mr. Lincoln is said
never to have appeared to more advantage than in
those moments of ease and happy confidence.
And the affectionate veneration, amounting almost
to idolatry, in which his memory is held by all
who ever had an opportunity of enjoying these
seasons with him, prove how fully he was qualified to act his part there.

We next visited the large old-fashioned parlor,
and stood in the room where Mr. Lincoln had received his friends in the pleasant moments of con-
viviality; where he had entertained and amused
his guests with his quaint humor, solid sense, and
inexhaustible fund of anecdote, and where it was
said to be impossible for any one to spend an
hour in his society without going away sensibly
improved and made happier. In the social circle
he was conspicuous. His fine conversational
powers, his genial humor—which had not the
least tinge of unkindness or sarcasm, except when
called forth by some covert or direct attack upon
himself or upon some of his ideas of right, when
he could make it act like a two-edged sword, and

invariably turned the laugh against his antagonist —and his well-known goodness of heart, made him a universal favorite in society, and the center of every circle, and gave him a power and an influence in community which is seldom equaled, and which was always exercised for good.

From the parlor we went to the room which had been used by Mr. Lincoln as his library, and where, by constant study and patient reflection, he had trained his naturally great mind to habits of discernment and patient steadiness under trial, which so admirably fitted him for the high and mighty destiny which he was to fulfill—that of being the chosen leader of a mighty nation in a dreadful struggle, involving its very life, and the issue of which was, for a time at least, doubtful, but which, under the direction of Divine Providence, had at last reached such a glorious termination.

But why particularize further. Suffice it to say that we visited every room in the house, and that each recalled some pleasing recollection of the great and good man who had once inhabited it, but who now, by the instrumentality of a murderer, slept the sleep which shall know no waking until the last great day, when the dead of all nations shall be gathered together, and the murderer and his victim shall meet before the Eternal Throne, to receive the reward of their deeds in this life.

We then went to the garden and our kind hostess

gathered me a bouquet of flowers which had been planted and cultivated by the hands of Mrs. Lincoln, and which were, from this association, more precious to me than any gift of jewels could possibly be. They have long since faded and withered, but still I keep them, and shall until they moulder into their original dust.

With heartfelt thanks for her kindness, for she steadily refused any other compensation, we bade our kind entertainer farewell, and I returned with my friend to her home, musing upon the end of all human greatness, which I had seen exemplified by so striking an illustration. Abraham Lincoln had occupied the most exalted station which any man can attain in this world; he had achieved for himself a reputation second to none of the illustrious personages who have adorned and illuminated the pages of the world's history; a nation loved and revered his name; an entire race hailed him as their deliverer and benefactor; but all this could not shield him from the assassin's hand, and he now slept in the silent tomb—honored, it is true, by all mankind, but alike unmindful of a nation's reverence and honor, the tears of mourning friends, the blessing of those whom he had delivered from bondage, or the regrets of the world.

THE NOBLE BRAVE.

Great men have died and passed away,
Our nation mourns for them to-day,
And are rearing monuments on high,
Towering away toward the sky,
Telling of deeds that have been done,
And the victory they have won.

How many soldiers just as brave
Fill to-day an unknown grave!
And with intellect just as bright,
Died in battle for their country's rights,
With no one even to mark the spot!
And oh, how soon they are forgot.

Sad eyes have shed many a tear
For the lost one, to them so dear,
Had they means, how glad would they
Rear a monument to his memory to-day.
Not to tell of his good, grand, noble deeds,
But to show loved ones he leads.

There is many a veteran in this nation to-day
Without a home or a place to stay,
Who left father, mother and perhaps a wife,
And for his country risked his life,
Who pleads in vain with outstretched hand,
For a pension from dear old Uncle Sam.

Did they not nobly win the cause?
Are there no just and honest laws?
There should be a law of just regard,
That would give to each his just reward.
May our next congress this law pass,
A pension give old soldiers of every class.

The next day I left Springfield and returned to
La Porte, where I found awaiting me the books
ordered there for my subscribers in the place just
left. Of course, they were at once shipped to my

agent there, and, it may be remarked here, that they reached him in safety, were promptly delivered, and the proceeds as promptly and faithfully accounted for; for which he is hereby tendered my warmest thanks. I remained a day or two in La Porte, visiting my friends and transacting some business relative to matters aside from my agency; then went to Mishawaka, where my books had already arrived, and supplied all my subscribers; did the same at Elkhart and Goshen and the surrounding country, and my work in northern Indiana was ended, for the present, at least. In all probability, however, I shall revisit that locality at some future period; for my heart holds a sincere affection for it, and some of my most cherished friends reside there.

But I had been a long time absent from my little adopted darlings, and was naturally getting impatient to clasp them once more to my bosom, gaze upon their beautiful features, all beaming with affection and love for me, and to witness the improvement and development which they had made since my departure. Accordingly, my course was turned thitherward, and in due time I arrived at my home in the capital city of Indiana. I found my darlings well and happy, under the care of their kind instructress, and was proud and happy to note the manifest improvement in each, which had resulted from her judicious and faithful labors. They, on their part, were as glad to see me as I was to see them, and though it is possible

the world contained at that time three happier beings than we were, I must be allowed to say that
I regarded it exceedingly improbable.

CONCLUSION.

LET the reader imagine that some time has
elapsed since the close of the last chapter, and has
brought with it corresponding changes in our
heroine's situation. She no longer resides in Indianapolis, nor does she pursue the avocation of a
book agent. She has abandoned it, not from
choice, for she still, at times, longs for the pleasant
scenes and incidents which marked the days of
her canvassing, and which, in spite of some unpleasant events, invested it with a charm which
can never fade from her memory ; but because it
was no longer necessary for her to pursue it, and
she felt that duty to her adopted children demanded that she should cease from her wanderings, and devote her time and attention to their
care and education ; and if the reader will call at a
pleasant mansion in the midst of a beautiful grove,
two and a half miles from the city of Lexington,
Kentucky, he will there find Annie Ford, happy in
the society of her two children, Carrie and Willie,
both of whom have steadily improved in beauty
and intelligence.

We will ask Mrs. Ford, Why do you select this
place for your home ? and her answer is, Simply

because it more nearly resembles the home of my childhood than any other place within my knowledge. The house stands upon the same gentle elevation, and is surrounded by the same lovely grove ; while in the rear a lovely spring bubbles up from the ground, and lends the same air of delicious coolness to the appearance of the whole. My old servant, Caroline, together with her husband and family, occupy a house on the farm, and, under his careful and thrifty tillage, mine is the model farm of the surrounding country.

But whence came the means necessary to purchase this beautiful home ? A portion of it I earned at my chosen avocation, and the balance I realized from the sale of some of my property in Georgia, my application for the restitution of which was, after some delay, granted by the general government, and my independence and comfort for life was thus secured.

That I am happy in my present situation, it is needless to say. My life has abounded in sorrow and misery ; it has been a stormy and tempestuous sea ; of almost every species of wretchedness I have endured my full share, but through the goodness and mercy of Him who overruleth all things, my lot of bitterness and woe has been turned into joy and gladness. Through His care and protecting kindness I have surmounted all my troubles, and have at last gained the haven of peace and earthly happiness, and my heart daily and hourly goes out in praise and thanksgiving toward Him for all his care and watchfulness over me.

A word or two in relation to certain characters who have appeared in the history, and I take my leave of you.

Long after my final separation from Eugene Giles Mason, I learned that the child who is so dear to my heart, and whom I have taught to call me by the name of "mother"—my own little Carrie—was the child of him whom I then supposed to be my husband, by the only daughter of a wealthy Georgia planter. Her mother died in giving her birth, and was thus spared the long life of shame and sorrow which would otherwise have been her portion. It was Mason himself who brought her to the door in the basket on that night of lonely watching. He had resorted to this means to conceal from me the knowledge of his crime, as well against morality as against myself, and, after ringing the door-bell, had concealed himself in the shrubbery until Silvie took the basket within the door, when he sneaked away until it was time for him to come home. It matters not how I learned these facts—their authenticity is entirely unquestionable. And this was my Carrie's birth.

As for Mason himself, his life was wicked and his death was sudden and violent. He was descending the Mississippi river in a steamboat, and having engaged in a violent altercation with a fellow passenger, he was suddenly struck overboard, and, in spite of the utmost efforts to save him, he was finally drowned, and his lifeless body was not recovered for some days. In the confusion attending his disappearance, his murderer leaped overboard, swam ashore, and finally made his escape. And so died Eugene Giles Mason, a man whose talents and business qualifications, if properly directed and controlled by virtuous and upright sentiments, would have rendered him an ornament to any society, but who, by his moral deformity, had rendered himself only a curse to the world and to humanity. And thus he was hurried into the presence of his Maker, unwarned and unannounced, with all of his sins upon his head unexpiated and unrepented of. May we indulge the hope that He who is all goodness and kindness, and who wills that none of His creatures shall perish, judged his soul, not in anger, but in mercy and tenderness. His body lies buried in a lonely, neglected and unknown grave, on the bank of the Mississippi river, but a short distance from the city of Memphis.

Frank C. Ford is dead and buried. His children are all living in Illinois. Some are married.

Dear reader, we will now bid you an affectionate farewell, hoping soon to meet you again, in Happy at Last, a sequel to The Life of a Book Agent.

THE END.

www.ingramcontent.com/pod-product-compliance
Lightning Source LLC
Chambersburg PA
CBHW022022110726
47901CB00006B/1631